IFWG AUSTRALIA DARK PHASES TITLES

CAPED FEAR

SUPERHUMAN HORROR STORIES

EDITED BY

STEVE PROPOSCH, CHRISTOPHER SEQUEIRA,
AND BRYCE STEVENS

INTRODUCTION BY
MARK WAID

A DARK PHASES TITLE

Caped Fear

ISBN-13: 978-1-922556-47-9

IFWG Publishing International
Gold Coast

www.ifwgpublishing.com

DEDICATIONS

For my father, Robert Alan Proposch. *Steve Proposch.*

For Cloud Sequeira: One father's absolute superhero, flying into the future to genuinely make the world a better place, thank you for being you. *Christopher Sequeira.*

For my sister, Gail. *Bryce Stevens.*

And from all three of us, to the late William F. Nolan, a giant not just in the field of speculative fiction, but equally a master in genres like western or crime fiction. You were a dazzling adept of many forms, including the screenplay and the verse, and we were truly honoured to have worked with you, sir.

ACKNOWLEDGEMENTS

The editors have many people to be grateful for at the completion of a journey of this type, so please indulge us a paragraph or three to highlight some particularly outstanding people.

Sincere appreciation goes to the owners of the *Dr Weird* material, Gary Carlson and Ed DeGeorge, who allowed its use herein, as well as to George R. R. Martin and Jim Starlin who also kindly OK'ed the reprinting of this rarely seen early work of masters showing they had the necessary chops at the beginnings of their careers. Thanks, too, to Spencer Beck who put us in touch with Mr Starlin in that regard. And any mention of *Dr Weird* should prompt gratitude to the late Howard Keltner who beautifully collaborated with Messrs Martin and Starlin on the piece, but who must also be seen as a visionary in publishing these talented people's early efforts some years ago.

Thanks to the good folk at Writers House: Chad Buffington, Rebecca Eskildsen, Merrilee Heifetz, and Erica McGrath, and Neil Gaiman's assistant, Sarah-Kate Fenelon, for expediting the Neil Gaiman and Roz Kaveney piece. Similar appreciation goes to Rich Henshaw at the Richard Henshaw Group and to Robert Bloch's daughter, Sally Francy for the piece by the late Mr Bloch. For the Brian Lumley story we are thankful for Silky Lumley's handling of all matters. For the William F. Nolan story—one of the final pieces the great man wrote before his unfortunate passing mere months ago—we are thankful to Jason Brock for managing all our communications as the story was developed by Mr Nolan.

Lastly, very special chorus of appreciation must be raised by us in honour of literary agent, Cherry Weiner, who very kindly facilitated contact for us with a number of the people whose work appears within this tome, for no other reason than she wanted to help. A generous, wise and hard-working professional is Ms Weiner; thank you so much, Cherry.

TABLE OF CONTENTS

INTRODUCTION
MARK WAID

Generally, when you think about superheroes, you think about capes and toothy grins and bright, primary colors and spandex, all of which is pretty much the antithesis of this book's remit: horror. And that, to my mind, is what makes this collection of stories so enticing. Anybody can imagine Superman saving a kitten from a tree. It's kind of his thing. It takes a special kind of writer with a special kind of mind to twist a feat like that into a moment of abject dread.

And, honestly, despite the mental imagery they immediately evoke, superheroes haven't always been totally synonymous with Truth and Justice. The earliest adventures of Superman characterized him as a no-nonsense maverick social activist who was plenty scary if you were a negligent mine owner or a cruel orphanage mistress or a crooked banker. Absolutely true anecdote: in Superman's first story in the Sunday funnies, these exact words came out of his mouth as he was holding a safe over his head: "Nice bank you've got here. It would be a pity if anything happened to it." That man knew the value of fear.

The early days of superheroes were also flush with any number of macabre, unsettling figures: the Spectre, a ghost whose cold gaze could flay skin and turn a crook into a skeleton; The Face, who spooked criminals with his ghastly green mask; even the original Black Widow (not that one), who viciously slaughtered evildoers in her role as Satan's ambassador to Earth (more fodder for the hellpits). I can think of two kids who were unquestionably scarred by creepster heroes such as those. Just look around the central pages of this book for a rarity from 1970—an original comic book story starring the macabre Dr. Weird, as written and drawn by two young tyros determined to make something of themselves someday—George R.R. Martin and Jim Starlin. (Achievement unlocked.)

But there's more to horror than turning crooks into skeletons. In these pages, by and large, the authors recognize that wanton violence and gore isn't as fearful as suspense, paranoia, and good old existential fright for fright's sake. Check out Colleen Doran's tale for a subtly wicked turn on not only the concept of superheroes but of the traditional superhero team. Let her introduce you to the dark side to a group of ostensible do-gooders not-strangely-similar to another one for which she and I share a longtime mutual affinity.

Jim Krueger, one of comics' most inventive minds, creates a weapon of ultimate fear, at least if you're a caped crusader. Jim's story is less in-your-face horror and more of an eerie melancholy, weighing in on the literal and figurative ghosts of superheroes and what extremes one might have to go to in order to finally end a never-ending battle.

The legendary Robert Bloch, himself a longtime friend to DC Comics editor Julie Schwartz, brushes up against the wish-fulfillment aspect of superhumanity, with a reminder that your dreams are sometimes someone else's nightmares.

There isn't any leaping of tall buildings in Robert Silverberg's disquieting story. Instead, taking his cue from the old saw that superheroes are "modern myth," Silverberg reaches back to the "original" superheroes, if you will—the Greek gods, who were not terribly kind and whose own quiet anxiety is the discovery that they are merely fictions today.

Jonathan Maberry has his own take on superheroes—as seen through the eyes of ordinary law enforcement officers. Would they be wondrous of superpowered vigilantes? Jealous? Terrified? Or, perhaps, all three...?

William F. Nolan is clearly no stranger to superhero convention, refusing to settle for simply namechecking a famous comic book right off the bat. Instead, he twists the familiar trope (germane to dozens of masked manhunters from Blue Bolt to Captain America to Deadpool) of the we're-not-going-to-come-right-out-and-say-he's-a-reformed-Nazi scientist who uses medical science to transform an ordinary guy into a being with powers and abilities far beyond those of mortal men. Nolan's tale answers the disturbing question, "In order to be made a superhero...what has to be taken out of you?"

In the eyes of Brian Lumley, the alarming side effect of super-heroic power is that there's always a want for more, and the junction of want and ethics is almost never a safe place to stand.

Joe R. Lansdale is historian enough to know that superheroes existed in pop culture before the Big Red "S" outraced his first locomotive. The precursors to comic books, the American pulp magazines of the 1920s and 1930s (so named because of the cheap, rough-textured paper on which they were printed), were the laboratories from which science fiction as we know it today was birthed, just as their mechanical men, bronze-skinned dynamos, and vengeful champions were direct ancestors of today's caped crimefighters. Lansdale closes us out pitch-perfectly with a yarn—there's really no better word for it—paying homage to the evil-busters of that era.

Barry N. Malzberg, Jack Dann, Karen Haber, Neil Gaiman and Roz Kaveney, Heather Graham, Ramsey Campbell, Janeen Webb...they're all here with their own unique glimpses of super-heroes and fables as viewed through a dark, warped lens. The tales in this book are weird, quirky, and downright scary, as superheroes very much can be. In fact, the next time you hear someone shout, "Look! Up in the sky!", pray that it's an exclamation of celebration and not a scream of terror.

PROLOGUE:
A POST-MOON-AGE NIGHTMARE

CHRISTOPHER SEQUEIRA

You open your eyes and discover you are seated on a lichen-covered tree stump in an odd clearing with a floor of natural stone, surrounded on all sides by irregular rock formations. The vast daytime sky glows azure above you, down through a canopy of branches and leaves. It's a cave, you realize; a vast cave. But this portion has no ceiling, the rocky walls open to the air via a natural skylight, so trees and grasses have developed here. Several tunnels snake out from this natural amphitheatre into the darkness of true, enclosed caves and tunnels. You have no idea how you got here. The last you recall you were sitting in a subway car heading home after an unusually easy day at the office.

You have so many questions: about the abrupt gap in your memory, about how you came to be here. You can think of no geographical location within a minimum of many hours of travel from where you were that might resemble a place like this. And yet a terrible fear of certainty grips your insides. You are here because They brought you here. Because, somehow, even though you have not breathed a word to anyone, They know you have figured them out. They: the beings that are haunting your dreams.

And suddenly, your eyes no longer see what surrounds you in the cave, but as in a dream when the scene shifts in a compressed blur, you've suddenly been transported and all you see now is a featureless, white infinitude, a blank-walled chamber of unknown size. And into this canvas of the mind human figures begin to materialise; to form from the atoms in the air. THEY are now here.

Standing, or floating above you, forming a startling, living panorama in the white-room of your mind; in many ways they are like a come-to-life version of such deities as were once carved into the walls of Egyptian temples. And this seems an eternal truth. In our image-obsessed, over-armed, modern world, *these* are our era's immortal superiors; our latest iteration of gods. They represent the fusion of celebrity to militarisation, might-makes-right exemplars wielding an array of weaponized physical attributes, festooned with perfect abs and perfect teeth. The superheroes who walk among us with identities obscured, their true names and faces shrouded in darkness and mystery, the ones who, of course, act only for our collective and individual good. Of course…

But with the quickening of a pulse-throb in your temple, the dream changes, like flowing water, and you see what you could not see before but was surely always there. Reason begins to wrestle with instinctual revulsion in your dream-mind: *What if, just as a serial killer wears the mask of a benign, pedestrian occupation, the primary-coloured personae of superheroes—living gods—were used as cover for horrifying crimes and vile manipulations? What if the narrative of public saviour was mere camouflage, hiding the fact that these hyper-mortals wield their power primarily for outcomes of fear, and grotesquerie?* The voice that is your higher self in a dream yells at you like a parent: "No! The shine and the spandex hide terrible, awful truths!"

It is a chilling insight, but more than that, it is a *dangerous* knowing, that, until now, you thought was safe and secure as any of your most private thoughts. Clearly no longer private.

And so you find yourself re-awakened with awareness, and back in that odd, natural cave, surrounded by rock under a clear sky. Alone. But one is never alone for long in a Meeting Place.

You hear a soft step to your left and turn to see little glints of light emerging from the tunnels that empty into the clearing; glimmers of reflective, body-hugging costumes and sleek, metal weapons. Then, bathed in a mist as if they had indeed stepped from the clouds of a deep fever-dream, a troop of magnificent beings—of incredible stature, developed musculature, and radiant beauty bedecked in swirling capes of vivid hues—enter the cave to surround you, and block every exit. You glance above, and there are more there, falling like feather-light meteors, raining from the blue expanse, slipping into being from gossamer streams in the heavens.

And you know They know; They know that you have pierced the paradigm, uncovered their cabalistic secrets, and arrived at previously unthinkable conclusions...about them.

Not all of their stories are tales of the hero's journey. Some are...horror tales.

So, you aren't dreaming anymore. You have entered a nightmare. Worst of all, you now know it's only one of many that inhabit the darkness.

THE TOWERS OF EDEN

BARRY N. MALZBERG AND JACK DANN

7216 Anno Domini: Rusticating in the Desert,
Driving on the Wine Red Sea

And here, with extraordinary punctuality: here the millennium comes to die.

Michael Evreux Brevard driving along the hardpan packed channels of his ever-receding desert, driving at what once would have been considered to be a hundred and ninety-two kilometres an hour (top speed), driving what once would have been known as a 1963 Cadillac De Ville Series 6300 Convertible: a plum-coloured streamlined megalith, a small-finned shark that inhaled petroleum and exhaled the most sensual and poisonous hydrocarbons and particulate matter. Brevard inhaled, luxuriated in the irradiated wind soughing over the windscreen, tasted the acrid fumes, the desiccated dryness of the ever-mobile desert, which rushed past him as if he, the president, king, owner, and ruler of sky and sand were sitting still in this leather and chrome accoutred living room. Ahead, twisting like sand devils in the dying sun were the desert's fairy chimneys, enormous amorphous extrusions of stone, as mobile—and as stationary— as Brevard in his Cadillac. As the tuff cones and heady spires danced for Brevard's pleasure, so they also changed colour and texture: the kaleidoscope desert.

"Are we there yet?" asked Zahia Falaise, his ghost-creation who had the guileless face of a child made perversely sensual— an ultimatum of sensuality—by her poise and presence. She sat next to Brevard, her long bare legs squelching on white leather as she crossed and uncrossed them annoyingly. She wore an iridescent blue Bali gown with a sheer black top. Her breasts were too large for such couture, but she was Brevard's creation. Although he was father and lover, she was her own. He could not inhibit, nor channel her behaviour.

As a creator he was a merciful, if broken god.

Brevard didn't answer her, and the two startlingly beautiful women in the bolstered back seats laughed, asked the same irritating question, and then continued their intense discussion of the topology of six-dimensional manifolds.

Thus for minutes hours perhaps days of concentrated pleasure, for time itself, for the soft subtle thrill of anticipation did Brevard drive. He drove until their chimed question was answered in the darkness of a moonless night, answered by the constellations of city lights in the great distance, a haloed phosphorescent cloud, which imitated the coruscating stars above. There…there were his towers, his mechanical city, which, should he will it, would move like fog or settle like dust; and as he drove on, the sun rose purple and red, blinding the enormous glass city of sky-tipped towers.

"Are we there yet…?"

"No," he said, seeing a sudden flare in the distance, "No we are not, and we had better hope that we never will be."

Naked Lunch Redux

Having reached the desert, his penultimate goal, Brevard decided to prepare a picnic for his ghosts. Zahia was to his right: his archangel, his muse perched like a flamingo on an extrusion of silica. To his left, reclining on the soft blanket of ferrite sand were his back-seat angels: Leandra Cassiel and Denise de la Calle. The two sylphs had Brevard's complexion and features. They were his adolescent fantasies of self transformed: his sisters, his lovers, himself. Their long blonde hair was braided and piled atop their heads, their skin—his skin—was faultless. Brevard was indeed his own Botticelli. He removed his clothes to allow his body to burn in the sun; and Leandra and Denise, his differentiated selves, repeated his every movement. Only Zahia remained as she was; and as a result, Brevard's desire could not be shared: it was forcibly focused entirely on her; and as the promised platters of food materialised around them, she stared him down.

Leandra and Denise continued to argue topology, Denise insisting that she was unique, that the mathematical paradigm of the many in the one did not—could not—hold true here; and when they all finished eating, when they finished sunning themselves and comparing blisters, they made love.

Later, as Brevard perceived the undetermined flow of time, he stared at the women, unblushing in his own nakedness. He had long ago, eternities ago, moved past lust to a kind of safe, sterile place in which desire and departure commingled: the radiation suntan, burns, and attendant crepuscular sickness had no context in this consciously generated, post-apocalyptic place.

"Wake up, Michael," Zahia said forcefully. "You are not dreaming this. This *is* happening…this is how the ruins of the millennium speak."

Leandra and Denise giggled. They had since agreed that each was indeed singular. Brevard felt the itch of radiation as a warm wash of light. "Ruins of the millennium?" he said. "There *is* no millennium."

Zahia laughed at him. "What an utter fool you are, Michael."

Once, perhaps, her laughter would have disconcerted him, but not now, not in this known landscape, not in this endless desert where moments trudged past like little messengers.

Zahia: Redacted Time and Unintended Consequence

In the last hours (that is how he described it to himself) Zahia had been all insistence, all strategy as she argued him toward what she took to be the only possible protocol. "We cannot do this alone," she said. "We must not do this alone. We need help, lest we repeat what was and will be."

Brevard continued to quote Genesis to her—the first gospel of events that followed the Towers of Eden—but she was dismissive. "We need to expand the perimeters of possibility," she insisted. *You* need to expand the perimeters of possibility."

"I already have, darling," Brevard said, laughing ruefully, "which is probably the reason why we are back here once again." Later again, when they were in the car driving west, ever west, he said to her, "Oh, by the way, we are utterly and absolutely alone."

On the Matter of Being Absolutely Alone

Hands on the clock of his destiny, Kennedy preens before a large crowd of reporters, nosy parkers, and fans on the tarmac at Love Field in Dallas. "Perhaps you will remember me," he says to Bob Walker of WFAA-TV 8, "or perhaps this is how I will be remembered: as the man who accompanied Jacqueline Kennedy to Paris." He flushes with satisfaction, nods to the thin applause. It is going well. Everything is going well. Soon he will be eating a good Texan steak and delivering a speech to the local government, business, religious and civic leaders at the Business and Trade Mart downtown and his triumph will be complete. Someone hands him a hat, one of those enormous, grotesque constructions which the Texans seem to equate with being a really great fucker. Kennedy knows better. Being a really great fucker has more to do with prestige and positioning than a silly hat. He feels a twinge in his back and is suddenly reminded of old perils. "We are joined together in a great task," he says to nobody in particular and everyone in general. The Mayor gestures: he wants Kennedy to don the hat. Screw that, he thinks. "I'll take it home, wear it in Washington," he says. Perhaps he is imagining this, perhaps it has not happened; or, then again, perhaps it has already happened so drastically that he was/is/will be impelled by its ragged consequence. Is he standing on the tarmac or has he just given his Chamber of Commerce breakfast speech at the Hotel Texas? Is he enjoying his steak at the Dallas Business and Trade Mart luncheon, or is he sitting with Jackie and John and Nellie Connally in the Presidential limousine approaching Dealey Plaza? Complex and twisted, all of it.

Whether here, there, or everywhere, someone invisible as clean air whispers into his left ear: *Destroy time and chaos may be ordered.*

A Twentieth Century Literary Reference
With Attendant Footnote

"**D**estroy time and chaos may be ordered," whispered Norman Mailer's ghost, the aforementioned Sergius O'Shaughnessy, to the hapless Svoboda in an infinitely distant century. That had seemed like good advice in the penumbra of Nagasaki, only a dozen years earlier; but this was a new gleaming era, an era in which technology had become interchangeable with both death and life. Didn't matter! Brevard knew that Mailer's strange and megalomaniacal ghost had had it right for this century as for every century: "Destroy time and chaos may be ordered" is was and will be inevitable truth. But Brevard had a powerful intention. He could and would destroy chaos by re-enacting a new sequentiality, a glittering new sequentiality for an ever-new eighth millennium. Thus, for example, sacrifice John Fitzgerald Kennedy again and again (and again) until you get it right, until the act through repetition is rendered numb to any past, present, or future emotive significance. Until it is remembered by no one but perhaps a first citizen/president/god/creator/king such as Brevard. Then (now? before? after? ah, sequence, where is thy sting?) kill the king and kill him and kill him until he is no longer the king and in fact no longer dead but merely a character or a scrap of dialogue in the story. But Kennedy *was* the century...*was* the story, the life the death, the character, the scrap of dialogue. Born in one wartime, came near death in another, a projectile then to the boundary of what could have been the third and last war but was instead talked off that peak, screwed the sister deities who spun the threads of fate and destiny with single-minded abandon if with no *real* emotion (like a grounded V-2 rocket he could only be a simulation of flight and flame) and then, as a kind of gift to the hundreds of millions of future observers, left with a flourish. The mission was always to leave with a flourish, then exit left and leave 'em laughing; and if Sergius O'Shaughnessy had uttered the utter truth, the 'golden rule', then the 'mission' was its corollary: destroy the weavers of chaos and (the threads) of time may be ordered.

Dimensions of Memory in a Standard 4/4 Time Signature

Breakfast in that huge, closed hotel restaurant space, then the empty air itself, everything heated like stones in a fire, and then, and then the great limousine prowling to the edges of consciousness. Most of the time now he had to fuck passively because of his goddamned wrecked back, but he comforted himself: this was an age of fundamental passivity, of submission, of diminished resistance to the waves lifting into a tsunami of implacable force. On the ocean, clinging to a raft, he had learned of dimensions of passivity so cruel that inert fucking by comparison was a goddamned pleasure.

The 1812 Trackless Steam Powered Symphony

Of course Mailer's ghost, the doomed O'Shaughnessy, might have been dead wrong. Nothing could be certain in Heisenberg's world, a world refracted by the sprawl of the Grassy Knoll.

So much, more than enough, for Brevard being all knowing… so much for the frailties of omniscience, the vicissitudes of the godhead, the mediated difficulties of the local imperator creator. Perhaps Zahia was right: perhaps he was not creator-in-chief, the isometric dreamer of realities; and perhaps he might be existentially rather than absolutely alone. But alone or multitudinous it was (or would soon be) a crowded solitude containing all manner of ghostly constructions, all or some or perhaps none of his own making; and what a troupe-band-bevy-collection it would be: geologists, paleontologists, physicists, astronomers, et al.; a diverse collection of expertise from the applied, earth, life, and natural sciences; and, too, all manner of philosophers, religious quacks, and humanitarians. All these ghostly constructions willingly contained in the twelve caboose-red first-class carriages of a steam train powered by a Salamanca locomotive that is being driven by none other than its inventor Matthew Murray of Holbeck, Nottinghamshire, Great Britain, England, Europe, the great globe itself, the solar system, the galaxy, the universe, the mind of God. Address a letter to him in this way and await its return: ADDRESSEE UNKNOWN.

As yet unseen by Brevard or his angels, Murray is chasing Brevard, the coupled drive wheels of his locomotive and the free wheels of the carriages following in the fused indentation trails of the atomic Cadillac. Matthew Murray of Holbeck has enormous plans of his own. He follows Brevard not as a supplicant approaching his god, but as a spider running along its web after its prey.

However, it might also be noted that Murray is no less grotesque or dangerous than the atomic catalogue driving them all to a disaster so encompassing, so final, that it will render irresistible its fetching answer to this iterated century of flame.

A Short Pause Before the Recrudescent Crash

It should be noted that (if O'Shaughnessy is right and Zahia wrong) all which occurs previously and prospectively has been planned, researched, extrapolated, simulated, and engineered by Brevard. Of course the crux is whether this depiction is a (fictional) reconstructed simulation or an authentic iteration of the great work of time and possibility. Either way Brevard is trapped. Whether he is a god controlling or simply one of his created angels cannot be answered and probably should not be answered. Better to be god from Brevard's perspective, even if a recurring string of 'facts' mitigate against desire.

But for our selective purposes, it is probably sufficient to know that Brevard's obsession with time and events thousands of years in his putative past, his need to model events irrelevant to his time without end, cannot be really understood out of his time. We can only create and substitute a metaphor—in our case, no less than that of the about-to-be-foreclosed JFK, we chose a sexual metaphor—for his driving needs and frustration, needs and frustration which he vents into a fractured reflection of a time when ending is commonplace and death is itself something of a metaphor. A difficult take-down, to be sure: a puerile minimisation rather than a deconstruction of the profound.

You may, of course, substitute a metaphor of your own. For our part, we like the (sexual) metaphors of the ancient incidents of the assassination of JFK and 9/11, for they are time tangible and contain a seductiveness which Brevard himself had hoped would mimic the desire which had shaped the creation of his experiment. And we should not forget the still puissant metaphor of sex: the plunge of objects into the unassailable, the assailable, the impermeable, the damned.

The Near and Distant Experience of Event

It's time. Pasts, presents, and futures are all right now, all here at exactly 8:19 on this cobalt blue morning. Reflecting the sunlight like a black mirror, the plum coloured Cadillac is now parked just beyond the glass suburbs of the towered city. The city sparkles and flashes and gleams in geodetical splendour. The desert shimmers as night chill meets morning warmth, and the sand swirls into newly shaped dune concretions as if shivering in anticipation (if, indeed, anticipation can even be considered as a state of mind in this interleaved time).

The convertible top is down. Brevard and Zahia Falaise are in the front seat. Leandra Cassiel and Denise de la Calle are holding hands in the back seat.

"Well?" asks one or the other. Leandra and Denise are twins, after all. Their voices, if not their thoughts, identical.

"Shut up and wait for it," Zahia says.

A voice crackles in the sky, loud as a god: "The cockpit is not answering. Somebody's stabbed in business class. And I think there's mace. That we can't breathe. I don't know. I think we're getting hijacked."

"That would be Betty Ong, a flight attendant on American Airlines Flight 11," Zahia continues.

"Ah," says Leandra and Denise in chorus.

But Brevard doesn't move, doesn't say a word. It's as if he's dreaming time, experiencing the events unfolding forward and backwards simultaneously, seeing from the perspective point of himself sitting in the car and from inside the cabin of the Boeing 747 airliner. He sees the airliner arcing out of the blue, another mirror reflecting the blue day, a mirror arcing toward another mirror, or, rather, toward *two* other mirrors: the tallest glass towers in this crystal city, which Brevard has named Eden. (His

prerogative, for—according to his lights and purposes, at least—
he is god.) "Now we shall return to memory," Brevard said
to himself, his reconstructed heart beating like a metronome.
"*Now* we shall finally and conclusively acquire sequence and
significance."

But Zahia overheard him. She always overheard him. She
laughed and said, "Oh, so you think, my dearest darling." She
straightened herself, a lascivious look on her face as she touched
Brevard, who was already excited. "Wait for it...one...two...
three..."

And right on time (?) another voice of the gods crackles across
the sky, echoing through all the circles of time. "Something is
wrong. We are in rapid descent. We are all over the place. I see
buildings. We are flying very low. We are flying way too low.
Oh, my God, we are way too low."

"That's not Betty," says Leandra.

"That's must be Betty," says Denise.

"No, that's Amy Sweeney," says Zahia. "I caressed her just
before..." Her tone has shifted from the seductive to the satisfied.
Meanwhile—

The 747 crashes silently into a glass tower, or, rather, from the
vantage of the Cadillac, it looks like the glass tower has swallowed
the forward part of the plane; and Brevard and Zahia are now
in the aircraft (it's all simply a matter of perspective, after all);
they can smell fear, can hear the screaming; and they can't help
but cling to life, cling to these very last seconds before oblivion,
oblivion, oblivion receding, oblivion turning backwards; and
Brevard and Zahia are transported instantly back into the car.
There, Zahia naked and glowing in the morning. Zahia touching
him as he responds against his will, as he realises she is right and
he is wrong, that the dreadful is happening even as he breathes
in ecstasy and exhales misery, for before the second aircraft can
strike the second tower, before the first tower can collapse like a
million breezeblock dominoes, time reverses.

The 747 is ejected/rejected from the tower and flies backwards
into the blue.

Zahia removes her hand from his lap as all their clothes press once again upon their bodies like winding sheets wrapped around corpses. The twins giggle and then descend into a fierce argument about the types of infinities that actually exist. It is when Leandra says something about the impossibility of infinite discrepancies that Brevard glimpses something rising on a dune then disappearing, then rising again: Matthew Murray's train of scientists. Matthew Murray, the other. The antagonist. The usurper. The proof that Brevard isn't god, isn't sleeping, isn't alone. If this is his creation, it has been compromised by those (i.e. Murray) who would reverse everything back to chaos; and there was nothing that Brevard could do but race toward the city and make sure that he reached the Kennedy motorcade in downtown Eden before Murray and company. If he could protect past time and event, if he could prevent Murray from interference, then he might yet—and if Eden is indeed Brevard's creation, if Zahia is wrong and O'Shaughnessy right, then he might yet strengthen memory and sequence enough to encompass chaos and isolate time. If not, then all this would indeed be nothing more than a constructed dream. And so this never would have happened. The World Trade Center would reassemble itself back into its known form, the speeding planes would speed backward to be summarily erased from the sky by the ass-end of an ubiquitous No.2 pencil, otherwise known as the arrow of time. All we (might) know is that somewhere in this abyss between occurrence and possibility Brevard and his companions must work to shape and mould the millennium.

Of course, if Brevard is right—and if he can succeed—then he will have to accept Murray and his scientists as his own creations. His driving will to failure and reversal.

And so he drives. What else is left to him?

After some measure of infinity, Leandra and Denise ask, "Are we there yet?"

"Wait for it..." Zahia answers.

The Butterfly Effect

But although caught in simultaneity, caught in the constantly expanding waves of the singularity itself, he does *not* wait for it. He drives, drives toward the collapsing towers, drives toward what he cannot help but consider as his destiny—and what an odd and antique analogy that is! Drive on, driving over the imagery of cobalt blue sand, driving along and upon and within this degenerating simulacrum of simulation.

In the back seats, Leandra and Denise giggle and laugh with childlike delight. They stand up, balancing like marionettes on the floorboards, and shout, "Look, the butterflies, can you see them?" And one or the other identicals calls to them, calling them away, calling them to their advancing car, as if insects could be and had been trained like dogs.

Nonplussed, Zahia shouts over the screaming wind-draft of the speeding Cadillac: "They are certainly *not* butterflies."

"They are! They are!" shout the twins, trembling with joy; and whether Brevard has injected his wishes into the tangible reality, or whether butterflies large as pterodactyls are simply part of this time lapsed landscape, you can see for yourself that there are indeed butterflies emerging from the towers.

Brevard presses the accelerator, and the Cadillac spins into overdrive.

He is impatient to reach—and pass through—the emptiness that was the towers, although he can clearly see them (now as after-images or present images or future images) falling slowly toward their majestic crashing slumber. And as he drives across this past present future landscape, ever more butterflies emerge, each one a tiny refraction of light describing wide or smaller arcs from the square footage that was and is and will be the towers, each giant butterfly flirting with some micro-destiny, each one moving with the solemnity of gravity toward some secret ending which must fall away from Brevard's plane of sight. And Brevard, for his part, feels exhilarating duration, feels that he is towering over circumstance; and perhaps he is…perhaps he *is* circumstance. Or perhaps, as we have argued and questioned and surmised, he is just another radioactive bit of the flotsam caught in its tidal force.

Another flirting butterfly.

Summary Intimations

Passing through the city, driving along streets of constructed metaphor and history, driving through an overlaid, reconstructed map of every city, any city, future city, past city, present city, its specificity dawning like the radioactive blotch of sun pouring its life-and-death giving rays upon Brevard and company...and upon his nemesis Matthew Murray and his clackity-clacking train of scientists, who are out of Brevard's sight, but not out of mind. Brevard can *feel* their imposition.

And a Word About the Model

When Brevard had established this world, this universe, this investigation, it was ostensibly to produce *the* most accurate reality: an ever-shifting floor of forms, ideas, and constructions human and otherwise. A grand reality, the last link of the great chain of being. This then would be the final situation, the final solution that would take the very ethos and pain out of desire. Desire in brackets. Desire as metaphor for mind and causality and progress, the truth of which we readers and writers can never know from our bounded twenty-first century perspective. That was Brevard's goal: a final, summary disaster...a disaster so large, so finally encompassing that Brevard, Murray, Zahia, Leandra, Denise, the assassins, all of them could give up any responsibility for their lives. In the century of flame, all consequence would be equal. But this construction had been compromised by the unprompted arrival of Murray.

Brevard—who had not created Murray, at least not to his knowledge—experienced the selfsame dumb embarrassment that Frankenstein must have felt when his creation began to complain about the laboratory; and a new insight came to Brevard, or perhaps it had always been with him masked as old knowledge but now revealed in its terrific force that he could not through creation control: God must have felt the same way when he released Abraham. Ah, well, so much for omniscience, even in this carefully created and contained speck of a universe.

Assignation+Assassination=Topography

He could see the glistening towers superimposed upon their ruins in the rear-view mirror of the Cadillac de Ville Convertible. In that glancing instant, he could also see Leandra and Denise huddled together as if they'd just been attacked. Their eyes were wide, their thick blond hair whipped around their perfectly symmetrical faces like the snakes of agitated Medusas. Brevard redirected his concentration forward. Zahia sat beside him, as still as a statue, a beautifully cold, patient, life-like statue. But whether statue or breathtakingly alive and mortal, she was a reflection or rather a refraction of mindfulness itself and understood that the next few seconds would be either/or: she would in the fullness and compression of time have the sour proof that she was in the right and that Brevard and his ghost O'Shaughnessy were, had been, and would be infinitely, iteratively, and forever wrong.

It was baking hot. Not a cloud in the sky. On either side of the road which we shall call Main Street were crowds of people and behind them rows of buildings, some high some low; but these were not the buildings associated with Brevard's City of God, the Eden of crystal towers perfumed with perfect memory. No, these buildings were brick and mortar, and it is 12:27 pm, November the twenty-second, 1963.

Brevard did not turn right on Houston Street along Dealey Plaza and then left onto Elm Street in front of the Texas School Book Depository, but double-parked on Main Street, parallel to Elm. He looked around: if the sun had not turned the windows of the Book Depository into mirrors, he would be able to see directly into them.

"There," he said to Zahia, as a white Ford followed by a 1961 Lincoln Continental convertible turned onto Elm Street, "there's the motorcade, and I"—he scanned the surrounding area—"I can't see or feel or sense Murray's presence."

"Perhaps you're not looking hard enough," Zahia said. "Or were you expecting his train to come crashing through these buildings?" A slight smile played on the corners of her mouth. "Or perhaps it is chug-a-chugging down Elm Street as we speak. The railroad bridge isn't far from here, you know."

Brevard allowed himself to appreciate a sensation akin to happiness; and it was as if that momentary lapse into hope heightened his sensitivity…or, more likely, it was a slight shift of sunlight, a passing cloud, which revealed who was really perched behind the sixth-floor window of the Texas School Book Depository.

Need we tell you? Do you *really* need clarification? Everything to this point has been historic, long frozen in academic replication, devoid of the speculative. Credulity will get you everywhere. The political forces of that ancient century (and all the others) have proven that.

Time's Boomerang, Superposition and Decoherence… Or, You're Dead!

Matthew Murray of Holbeck, Nottinghamshire (and, as previously acknowledged, England, Europe, the planet, the solar system, the mind of God, Matthew himself, et. al.), unappeased and centred, fired the first shot at the President of the United States from that sixth-floor window, and that bullet struck Michael Evreux Brevard like the prick of a sewing needle. It then moved through his body and exited just below his throat, finally ending its jagged journey in Texas Governor John B. Connally's left leg.

And Murray is now about to fire his eight pound Carcano 6.5 millimetre rifle again. The plan is working. He feels little instantaneous flares of satisfaction moving rapidly inside him, moving toward some kind of culmination. He knows full well that this second shot will tear away the President's skull, huge flaps dangling as pendants of the twentieth century. Murray's face—unnoticed of course—bears a rictus of satisfaction as he squints into the sight of the rifle's four-power scope and begins to squeeze the trigger. But he is interrupted, gazumped, swindled, done over. Kennedy is indeed shot a second time, but not by Murray. Who is that shooter, that carrion born interloper on the Grassy Knoll? Murray is stunned, unmanned by this sudden intrusion. What other force, what gangling demon has intervened? Astonished, cheated, Murray hurls his rifle aside and prepares to bolt. Leave it for the keepers. Leave it to larger forces. He always knew, always *should* have known that this would happen. The President's shattered skull is surrounded by a halo of blood. Figures are furiously running away from the Grassy Knoll.

Murray departs. It is easier than he ever would have surmised. Easier for Murray, but too late for Brevard.

Last Thoughts Before and After Death's Cruel Curtain

As John F. Kennedy explodes, his wife Jackie Kennedy screams beside him, screams at Special Agent Roy Kellerman who is in the right front seat, screams at the Connally's, at the broken doll beside her that was Jack, at the street, the buildings, the sun, the shrouded, invisible moon: "I have his brains in my hand!" And a few seconds later, as if encouraged by an invisible prompter, she shouts again, "Jack! Jack! They've killed my husband!" But who were "they?" Who are "they?" If we knew this we might in fact know everything: the great conundrum sealed. Unfortunately we will never know. This will remain the greatest mystery of that ancient ceremony, never to be solved within the myriad conjunctions of real time.

Beside her, holistic fragments of Brevard/Kennedy's shrapnelled brain think distant, numbed thoughts as he, or rather as they realise that time and this very act of passage existed only in his broken head. It was time's own remorseless gunshot that struck him/strikes him dead. It is time's own remorseless gunshot that struck him/strikes him dead. "You win, Zahia," he murmurs, his breath and words corresponding to the extension and contraction of phantom limbs. "You lose, O'Shaughnessy." And not only does Brevard experience phantom thoughts after death, but phantom hopes as well. He hopes that Zahia has been distracted. It also occurs to him as he stares through the halo's surrounding, narrowing circle that for her too this will be a last chance. He hopes, ah hope!, that his calculation was not wrong. He hopes that in her distraction and fear she will find some rudiment of clarity. But it would seem that poor Zahia is only distracted. *Momentarily*—a word we have arbitrarily fixed with meaning—her defenestration is arrested. A frieze of impossibility. A single, singular *demoiselle d'Avignon*.

Momentarily...

Ah, moment and sequence: perhaps O'Shaughnessy the superpositional ghost is having a last laugh after all!

And a Final Entomological Epiphany...

Zahia—*demoiselle d'Avignon*, time's custodian, time's catamite—watches the great butterflies rising from the ruins of Brevard's construction, the city, desert, sun, and sky their manifold chrysalis. Behind her, the twins rustle in ecstasy and extend their newly-formed wings. Then they, too, rise to join the others. They rise to form the sky. Although Zahia might have been at one time more purposeful than the twins, she accedes to this last iteration. She follows them. But even in this eye-melting sunlight, her irradiated wings glow as if in pure thought. She rises magnificently; and Brevard, ah, Brevard! He lies somewhere below, a desiccated pupa to their imago, an absent god to their absent Abraham now lost to view from the killing floor. What did Abraham know and when did he know it?

What did *any* of them know?

THE OMNIVORE

COLLEEN DORAN

"**W**e have too many bodies."

"Pardon?"

"Bodies."

"I heard you the first time. I'm not sure I understand you."

The forensitech spread her arms helplessly and shrugged.

"We're a body farm. A research facility," she said, "for the study of decomposition, specifically the decomposition of the remains of sentients who are or were exposed to Supers."

She tapped the console. The screen displayed a holo-array of Supervillains and beneath each image, codified data spreads, with names in bright green letters accompanied by registered trademarks: The Raptor, The Array, Mutable Man.

And Mucus.

I'd had a sticky encounter with him a couple of years ago. Took forever to get the slime off my uniform.

The forensitech must have noticed my pause. She flicked her finger and the array spun settling on the image of a golden skinned man half buried in a pit, his blue hair long, filthy, trailing over brown, wet muck, red eyes milky-rimmed and staring. I vaguely remembered something on the news about a Super who died while trying to rob a shuttle.

Mucus's mouth was half open. He looked as if he were trying to speak.

I leaned closer as if to hear what his dead lips were trying to tell me. And then the dead lips moved.

I yelped and jumped back, which pleased the forensitech

immensely. "Watch," she said.

I watched.

Mucus's lips trembled. His red eyes rolled. Then his chest pitched.

"He's alive!" I squeaked. This pleased the forensitech even more.

Mucus vomited a swell of small, glowing pale green worms in a shiny slimy trail. They undulated from him in a scattering rush, their tiny red mouth pincers opening and closing in eerie choreography.

"Now that they've eaten, they're calling for mates," the forens-itech, explained.

She waited for further response from me. Getting none, she continued.

"We keep meticulous records of what goes in and what goes out of the facility. Mucus and other deceased Supers, they went unclaimed at death. Donated to science."

"Of course."

"But we have other bodies we can't account for." The forens-itech leaned forward, intent.

"Someone's dumping dead people here." That part had been made obvious to me already, and I didn't understand why she was dancing around the issue. The tech had a pinched expression under her spikey green hair. I couldn't tell if the color was real or if she was from Trall.

"What I do not understand," I said carefully, pulling at the bright green sleeve of my uniform, "is why you've called us." I hoped the next bit wouldn't come out sounding patronizing, but from the expression on her face, I could tell it did. "It's really not the Sol Squad's sort of thing."

She lifted her chin. "I think it is." She waved me toward another computer array, her hands flying over buttons and pads. I got a closer look at her hair as I leaned over to observe. Green to the root, with a tiny line of pale yellow toward the scalp. Trallian.

"As you know, many Supers have powers with a unique energy signature. We can tell who was killed, or exposed, at least, to a particular Super by searching our database and comparing radiation from the body."

I was vaguely aware of this phenomenon. Like all natives of Bismuth, I can eat virtually all forms of matter, except I do it better and faster than anyone else on my planet. As the Omnivore, however, I don't emit a power trail.

I wondered if a forensitech could identify where I'd been by my bite marks. I looked closer at the holo-array, at images of bones and flesh wounds, gnawed, raw, pustulant and withered. Animals and insects making a meal of the dead. Devouring Mucus from the inside out.

We of Bismuth don't eat flesh, but nature is the ultimate omnivore. Dinner spread out and served up daily.

My own eating talent landed me a spot on the Sol Squad. It's also why I ended up with this unsavory assignment: investigating a complaint at the Paranormal and Exceptional Super Research Body Farm.

It's not the cool sort of gig Sol Boy or Lunula gets. Even though I am the son of a Senator, which comes with privileges, eating as a superpower doesn't rank as glamorous. If I didn't look good on the Squad posters, I wouldn't be on the Squad at all.

"It's amazing how ambient radiations from different Supers can affect body decomposition. Or even preserve a body. This guy," she waved at an image on the screen which showed a naked humanoid form partially covered with red and gold autumn leaves which clashed with his bluish, glistening skin, "has been dead for over a month." She tapped the projection and smiled.

"You don't say."

"That makes our job tricky, you see. Determining time of death, circumstances. The normal effects of environment, insects on a body. All that goes out the window when we're dealing with Supers."

I whistled, light dawning. "And you think a Supervillain is dumping bodies here." A serial killer. Well, it wouldn't be our first, though the Sol Squad tends to deal with galactic issues, and this seemed like something the Terrene Gendarme should handle.

I frowned. "Excuse me, I didn't catch your name…"

"Kahmi."

"Nice to meet you, Kahmi."

She smiled again, then suddenly her lips parted, and her bright green tongue flicked out. It snagged a wandering fly. She gulped. Then she looked at me, her smile broadening. "I really shouldn't indulge. You never know when a fly's guts are carrying evidence."

There was a jar of the insects on the desk. One of them escaped and buzzed its way around the room before Kahmi terminated its flight. I don't eat meat, common knowledge anyone could read about me in the Super Tween tabloids. I wondered if her tongue action constituted flirting on Trall. When I didn't react, she continued.

"What we've found on these bodies is why this is of special interest to Sol Squad." She paused theatrically while I waited for the denouement.

"Time travel radiation signature," she said.

"Shit," I said.

My conversation with Kahmi had been streamed back at HQ. I got a demerit for saying "Shit!" while in uniform. They'd take it out of next month's pay.

Someone leaked the news. It was in the tabloids before I reached Sol Squad tower.

"Omnivore Needs To Eat Some Soap!" was splashed across Times Square in green and gold neon letters 80 feet high.

Great Bismuth.

Fortunately, the Pottymouth Scandal was quickly replaced by the broadcast of Squad rescue action off Jupiter where I'd have been useless, hence my assignment at the Body Farm. Mento strategized the effort, but for optics, Sol Boy took point. Sol Boy's gorgeous smile dominated the holoscreens, red hair flaming, energy warming the cruise passengers as they scrambled onto the rescue ship.

In the monitor room, I looked away into the distance toward the setting sun, my finger tracing a line on the glass over the horizon.

Bright. Clean. A world away from rotting bodies and flies.

While the story about my demerit was everywhere, the other details of The Time Travel Murder Mystery remained sealed. I asked Lunula to read the team to find the leak. As always, she cited ethical issues about scanning Squad members. She shrugged when I pressed her, said the forensitech probably sold the info.

"Could be anybody!" said MagniBoy. For a moment, I thought he meant the tabloid tattletale. Then I realized he was talking about the murderer.

"Stalin, Starko the Conqueror, Marie Antoinette..." Stellar Boy sneered. MagniBoy was many things, but smart wasn't one of them. But he was kind-hearted, and I hated the way Stellar took shots at him. I was also certain Stellar was the leak who turned Omnivore's Pottymouth Shame into letters 80 feet high.

Asshole.

I turned and glared out the window again. The city was an endless stream of golden spires and flying cars, draped in decorations for the Elan Vital Festival which took over the city for days. Government offices shuttered. Traffic clogged with revelers.

The Sol Squad, always on duty, ran through a list of possible suspects. The Manipulator. The Paricknoid. The Corruptor.

Now that the matter proved interesting, the others were quick to try to take the case off my hands. Stellar Boy was probably already working out his poses for the photo op. I annoyed him because I was taller, slimmer and could eat whatever I wanted.

More like I had no choice but to eat whatever came my way: a metabolism that could digest all kinds of matter from rocks to steel required constant energy. I had a huge tray of veg MagniBurgers delivered and was downing them while I admired the sunset. I could see Stellar Boy's reflection in the window regarding me with envy while he fingered his lucky charm, a fragment of magnetite on a chain.

Stellar Boy absorbed the energy of the stars making him the Squad's battling powerhouse, but instead of that energy rendering him dense and lean like a black hole, he blew up like a gas giant. In battle, he expended the power and became slender again. He scheduled publicity events for the aftermath of epic fights.

MagniBoy was the spokesperson for the MagniBurger restaurant chain, and his big broad grin was seared into the bun of each sandwich. I reached for another thick burger of vegbeef.

"The Time Travel Murder Mystery," Chem Lad said solemnly. He'd come up with the name and seemed very happy the Squad approved of it.

Chem had the good looks Sol Boy liked to see on recruiting posters but he always lost the vote for team leader because despite the fact that he was good at almost everything, he was also a prig. That the team actually seemed to like one of his suggestions would quadjump his starship for a month.

"Any ID on the victims?" asked Lunula.

I turned to the Squad. "All unknowns."

"Two of them," continued Lunula, "are decrepit. Age-related illnesses. Wrinkles."

"What causes that?" asked Magniboy.

I smiled. "Being from the past causes that," I said. "They had no cure for age diseases then. They got old. They died." Like most of the Sol Squad, I was a tween, between 20 and 100. Yet at 47, I would have been near the end of life had I lived a thousand years ago.

MagniBoy frowned. "How did they get here?"

"That's what we're trying to figure out, you dope!" Stellar was really making my day.

"One body," said Lunula, ignoring them, "is not decaying. Look."

HQ's computer screens flared. Humanoid corpses, a man and a woman, bloated, wrinkled, flanked a prone young man with a large wound on his breast.

I had the feeling I'd seen him before, but the face didn't seem like an image from memory, more like the echo of a memory. He looked peaceful. Asleep.

"He's dead all right," said Lunula. She read my stray thought but refused to find out who leaked my swear word to the tabloids. Typical.

"No heartbeat," she continued. "No brain activity." She pointed to the wound and dark blue discoloration on his clothes. "Others have necks crushed. But he's been shot with some sort of projectile."

Stellar blinked. "A projectile?" He looked a little MagniBoy stupid at that moment. Only primitives use projectile weapons, though if Dead Guy had been transported from the past, it followed that he wouldn't be dead from a pulse gun.

"Yes," I said, picking up from Lunula. "But the forensitech can't get under his skin to figure out what it is. He's harder than rock."

"Also," said Lunula, "the body has a radiation signature we can't identify emanating from the entry point of the wound."

She turned to Chem Lad. "That's why I had the body brought back here. For you."

MagniBoy's voice hit a register I hadn't heard coming from him since Ultrino hit him in the balls during that bank heist caper on Sarina 4. "EW!"

"I suggested it," I said.

Chem Lad's eyes narrowed in annoyance, but he knew why I'd made the call. Chem was the sole survivor of a planetary genocide. Initially, I'd objected to his being on the Squad, not sure Chem could handle the pressures we face after the horrific loss of his world and everyone on it. I didn't want him around a Body Farm.

His power over chemistry and elemental change meant he had to control his every thought. The reality of that never left him. And the reality that he was the last there would ever be of his world never left him either.

"I should be able to identify the elements in the projectile," said Chem. "Maybe even remove it."

"That's what we're hoping for," said Lunula. "Will you need a moment alone?" Chem looked like he could use a bit of quiet time now.

I felt like a jerk for not voting for him in the last team leader election.

His wrist com beeped: a message from Sol Boy affirmed that

the mission to rescue the cruise ship passengers was successful. The team would be back shortly. Chem curtly cut the relay.

"I want to get this over with now," he said.

We gathered in the lab and looked at the dead man with his black hair in a thick thatch over his forehead.

"The clothes are early 20th century," said Lunula.

"A thousand years ago!" exclaimed MagniBoy. Stellar was on the verge of making a crack about Mag's being able to do the math. I shut him up with a preemptive glare.

Chem stepped toward the slab, his face drawn. He extended his hand.

"Wow," he said. "That's...wow."

"What's wow?" Like carrion eaters we bent over the carcass.

"I've never encountered this before. It's some sort of...well, an anhedral crystallite. Sodium...boron...fluorine and talunanite, pumping radiation and flourescence. I've got its structure down." He lowered his hand. "I can get the projectile out, but I'll need to covert it to gas and back again to do it."

Lunula nodded.

Chem extended his hand once more. A stream of smoke rose from the body, coalescing into a ball. I smelled eucalyptus. Just like Chem to take a moment for a bit of aromatherapy. Then he turned his hand over, cupping it. The ball of gas became solid, dropped itself into his palm.

It was bluish white, and glowed faintly. Lunula held a small lead box out and he dropped the ball into it. She snapped the box shut.

"The radiation shouldn't be dangerous to us," said Chem.

"I'll be convinced of that when Mento has examined it in a secure environment," said Lunula.

"I thought you said he was hard as a rock," muttered MagniBoy.

"That's disgusting!" Stellar sputtered. "Stop poking the body!"

Chem looked like he was going to vomit.

"He's not hard at all," MagniBoy pressed on. "Check it out." He pushed his finger into the flesh. "Soft," he said.

Lunula gaped. She stretched out her hand, prodded the dead

man's chest. "Warm," she mused.

Then he sat up.

I'm not ashamed to say I squealed.

The man looked around with bright violet eyes, pale face greyish, mouthing incoherent noises.

"Old English, I think," said Lunula. "Let me set the translator."

"I said, where am I?" Ancient history sitting before us, and a language that hadn't been spoken in a thousand years echoed by the interpreter program.

Lunula stepped forward, smiling. "You're going to be all right."

He blinked at her. He was handsome and appeared charmed by Lunula as well. "Your hair is purple," he said.

Then the door opened. Sol Boy, radiant in the aftermath of another successful mission, stepped in then came to a halt with a screech. Dead-Guy-who-was-not-dead-anymore, violet eyes piercing as lasers, looked at Sol.

"Fuck," said Sol Boy.

"Demerits," said Stellar.

Sol began to shudder. Then he glowed.

"Enviro-suits engage!" shouted Lunula. My suit enveloped me the second before Sol went hot.

"Get a suit for Dead Guy!" shouted MagniBoy.

Dead-Guy-who-wasn't-dead didn't need our help.

He leaned forward, sucking the radiant energy pouring from Sol Boy in roiling golden-red rays. Sol shuddered violently, lifted off his feet. Not Dead Guy rose above him into the air. The gaping wound in his chest shimmered, oozed bluish fluid that reached to the edges of the frayed flesh, peeling it back into place, leaving no trace of the gash that had been there moments before.

The red-gold light grew blinding, my lux filters engaged, monitor screens flickered uncontrollably. I heard something sizzle.

"What do we do?" Stellar screamed.

The exchange took seconds. The light blinked out. Sol fell to the floor. Not Dead Guy hovered.

"Hey," Not Dead Guy said. "I feel great."

Sol Boy was still in a coma when his mom Solanis arrived. She was gorgeous, and despite being over 200 years old, she didn't look much older than the Squad tweens did. Her fortune had been made in life extension, and the monthly doses cost dearly.

Everyone paid.

Solanis created the Sol Squad, bankrolled it, and turned her kid into a superhero by throwing him into the path of an experimental power array which, instead of frying him to a fritter, gave Sol powers.

This act didn't make Solanis great mother material. She wasn't shedding tears for her son now, even as he was laid out in medlab. Solanis was focused on Not Dead Guy sitting at the edge of the next bed while Mento examined him.

Solanis explained Not Dead Guy had come from the past to learn how to be a great superhero.

"Gosh!" enthused Not Dead Guy who, we discovered, was named Ken, alter-ego of Ultimate, the superhero whose ancient exploits inspired Solanis to create the Sol Squad.

The Squad, upon hearing Ultimate was our forefather, looked at one another blankly.

"The timeline has changed," explained Mento.

"I've spent years studying Ultimate," Solanis explained. "Data I collected survived the time disruption." She held up a chip, which she handed to Lunula. "But someone attempted to murder Ultimate, probably thinking to thwart the formation of the Squad."

"Solanis was directly involved in incidents leading to the time shift. She remembers the past that we cannot," said Mento. He fired directly at Ultimate with a pulse gun. We jumped.

The ray bounced off Ultimate's chest, leaving no mark, but it did richochet off a computer array. Sure demerits for damaging equipment.

"Interesting," said Mento.

Ultimate looked at Mento and smiled.

"Ultimate has one weakness: an element from his destroyed home planet Tarlon." Solanis, enthused. "In the past, Ultimate tracked down every sample in the universe and destroyed it.

The Ken we see here hasn't become Ultimate yet so that didn't happen in this timeline.

"Ultimate can fly, he can shoot lasers from his eyes. He is invulnerable: except to Tarlonite, of course. And he has super-speed. Such great speed he can go forward and backward in time."

"Gosh!" enthused Ken.

"Swell," muttered Stellar.

"Ultimate stores the power of the sun," Solanis went on. "When Chem removed the Tarlonite from Ultimate's body and Sol arrived, Ultimate absorbed Sol's solar powers, restoring his life. Sol will be fine after a recharge."

Solanis was positively fawning over Ultimate and blasé about her own comatose kid.

I never thought I'd feel sorry for Sol with his perfect face, glamorous power, and huge credit account. But suddenly I did.

Lunula looked intently at Ultimate. She seemed puzzled for a moment. Then she radiated empathy. He melted toward her. "Ultimate...Ken...can you remember who shot you?"

"Yes," Ultimate nodded. "Yes, I do."

"He shot me." He pointed to Sol Boy, splayed out in the bed next to him.

"Shit." said Stellar.

I didn't call him out for demerits.

The drama was cut short by another emergency in space.

An explosion caused by a rogue asteroid hit Pluto, and Great Bismuth, were we going to get bad publicity for not spotting it before it hit.

Sol was put in a powermetric cell. Solanis threatened everyone with reprisals if word of the murder accusation leaked. Then she flew off in her private shuttle to strategize damage control.

I got monitor duty.

"You stay, Chem," ordered Lunula. "If anything happens... well, you are the only one of us who can stop Sol."

Chem nodded.

"Might as well study this while we're gone," she said, handing him the data chip.

"I can help, too," offered Ultimate.

"No," said Lunula. Her voice was hard. She glanced at Ultimate, then at me. "I can't read him," she said in my mind. To Chem she said aloud, tapping the chip, "Give it a look."

"Is she angry with me?" asked Ultimate as he watched her stalk away with the rest of the team.

"No," I said. "She's just...Sol's our friend. You understand."

Ultimate sighed. I offered him a MagniBurger. He accepted meekly, then took a seat on the far side of the room and stared out the window while Chem uploaded the data chip. No sandwiches left, so I ate the tray.

"What do you think?" I asked Chem, quietly.

Chem shook his head. "Sol doesn't like to be outshown. You saw how Max doted on Ultimate."

"Sol would never violate Squad code," I said. The Squad doesn't kill. It's a solemn vow we all take. Sol was a showboater, but I couldn't see him pining jealously for his mom's attention. And I couldn't imagine he'd time travel to do it, risking all our futures in the process, too.

Mento was right. Some Supervillain had attacked Ultimate in the past and tried to change history. But who?

The signal array buzzed, an incoming call from Kahmi at the Body Farm. I left Chem to his history lesson and toggled the monitor.

"I need that body back," Kahmi said. "I discovered a new energy signature. Didn't catch it at first because I wasn't looking for it, but it radiated over a 1000 square meter area and has affected the cadavers exposed to it."

I paused trying to figure out how I was going to explain Dead Guy wasn't dead and his name was Ken, but opted for, "What's it doing?"

"Some sort of animation." She bit her lip then added, "I've got the affected corpses locked in a powermetric chamber."

Chem now stood beside me leaning over the comm. "The point of origin of the radiation could be the pellet that was used to shoot Ultimate," he said. Damn. Lunula locked the sample away as evidence before she left. I didn't have her keycode.

"I think I'd better get down there," I said. "Chem, you can spot that element again, or remake it, can't you?"

"Yes. I'll go with you."

"Someone has to stay on monitor duty," I interrupted.

"You think I can't handle it," he said, his face tight. "Being in that place."

"You need to keep an eye on Sol."

"Sol's in a coma in a cell. The monitor's on auto. If there's an emergency we'll be back in minutes. And we'll bring him along." He nodded toward the window where Ultimate was gazing out at the city. "We can compare the radiation sig at the Body Farm with—"

I turned and jumped. Ultimate was gone. Chem tapped my shoulder, pointed.

Tears streaming down his face, Ken leaned over the console where the data chip replayed the story of his life. Images flashed across the screen at such high speed I could barely see them. "My parents," he said softly. "This was my life. The life I was supposed to have."

"You can't look at that," Chem said sternly. Ultimate was not only seeing his past, he was seeing his future.

"You don't understand!"

I glanced at Chem who bowed his head. Then I put my hand on Ultimate's shoulder, patting it ineffectually.

"I understand," said Chem, softly. "We're going to find out who hurt you." Awkwardly, he patted Ultimate's shoulder, too.

We traded Ultimate's tattered 20th century garb for a Squad trainee uniform, then we were off. I flew lead, Chem behind me, Ultimate trailing.

The Body Farm was 240 acres of wilderness and rot. The lab was empty but for an excited Kahmi who rushed forward then came to a halt at the sight of Ultimate, alive and wearing Squad branded gear. I explained the events of the day and Kahmi responded with demerit-earning utterances.

"Golly," said Ultimate. "She's salty."

Quickly, Kahmi shuffled us toward the powermetric chamber eyeing Ultimate with fascination. "I need to examine you, but first you've all got to see this," she said. "I'd call the rest of my techs in, but you know, it's Elan Vital. But I thought the Sol Squad would want to know immediately."

Powermetric chambers were employed to contain Supers: its matrix fluctuates to disable whatever power is thrown at it. We gathered around the window on the door.

Inside the bright chamber, dead bodies in varying states of decomposition were strapped onto gurneys, lined up in neat rows.

"What are we looking for?"

"Wait," said Kahmi. She looked nervously at Ultimate, then gripped my forearm. Chem was next to us, stiff, silent.

Soon there was movement. In the middle of the line of bodies, a blue man, his skin sunken, stringy and covered with what looked like small bite marks, began to shudder.

Then his hand moved.

At first I expected him to vomit a stream of bugs as Mucus had when I'd first arrived. But he lurched upward against the straps groaning, then emitted an awful wail. He writhed against his bonds, bits of flesh slaking off as he did so, black bile spewing from his mouth. He tried to reach the straps holding him down with his teeth, gnashing at them and wailing but he succeeded only in biting off what was left of his tongue. The blackened lump flopped onto his chest.

Chem screamed. I think I did too, but I was concentrating on not pissing myself, so I'm not sure.

I looked again. The dead man, still crying out in rasping sobs bent over as much as he was able and chomped his teeth onto the severed tongue. He devoured it.

Then he cried again in a dry, choking bark and vomited up his gruesome meal.

Suddenly, he fell backward, silent and still again.

"What the hell was that?!?"

Chem spewed sick into a waste receptacle.

"The dead reanimated," said Kahmi, glancing at Ultimate and back to me.

"I'm not like that," said Ultimate.

"No," said Kahmi. "You're not." She looked at her wrist com. "I see your life signs. I don't know how, but those things…" her voice trailed off.

"And they're hungry," I said quietly, handing Chem a napkin. "You think the radiation that preserved Ultimate reanimated these bodies?"

"Reanimated or alive? Don't know. But I'd appreciate it if you could get me that element sample you discovered so I can-"

"Oh my God! My parents!" Ultimate cried. His nose was pressed against the glass, his face white. "Dad! Dad!"

"Shit," I said.

"You've got to get them out of there!"

"Where? Which ones?" I cried.

"In the corner. Oh, my God, MOM!" Ultimate clawed at the door. "Open it or I'll break it down!"

"Don't do that! We don't know what those things will do if they get out!" Kahmi gasped.

"Those are my parents, please!"

Kahmi placed her hand on the lock. It responded to her touch with a shushing sound.

Chem leapt toward her and cried out, "No! Those aren't his parents! Stop!"

The next moment went so quickly I can't recall if I witnessed it or pieced it together from memories of the aftermath.

Kahmi screamed, her severed hand dropped to the floor along with her wristcom, sheared by Ultimate's laser gaze. As another beam shot from Ultimate's eyes, my com exploded into searing hot shards.

Chem raised his hands to form the Talonite he'd pulled from Ultimate hours before, but his com exploded too, throwing him off his feet. Before he could recover, a casual smack from Ultimate's hand sent Chem smashing into the wall. He slid down leaving a bloody trail on the tile. Then Ultimate's eyes shot another laser ray into the center of Chem's forehead. Chem shuddered and went limp.

I stood there, frozen, stupidly relieved I still had my hand.

In the next second, I was swept off my feet. In another second, I found myself on my back inside the pyrometric chamber with a screaming Kahmi, an unconscious, bleeding Chem, and a pile of the rotting bodies. My head whirled from superspeed sickness. The door slammed behind us.

"Gosh, I really hated to do that," said Ultimate.

"What the fuck!" I struggled for balance.

Kahmi gripped her wrist where her hand had been, weeping. I groped inside my belt for another napkin which I smeared with Plastilene to seal Kahmi's wound.

"What the hell is this?" I screamed.

"I wanted to be friends." He said. "I want to be a great hero. And I will be. With the Sol Squad! Just you wait!"

"You are piling up a lot of demerits," I muttered. "Fucking asshole."

"That's nasty. We don't talk like that in Oklahoma."

I earned a lot of demerits with my response.

"Boy, did you earn that Pottymouth nickname."

"I'd really like to know," I said, "what this is about." Maybe if I kept him monologuing, someone would find Kahmi's message and find us.

"I saw what I was supposed to be," said Ultimate. "I saw what I could have had."

"What? You mean on the data chip you read at HQ?" I asked.

"Yeah. That was...that was the life I had before Solanis changed me."

Kahmi stopped weeping. She stared at Ultimate's sad face in the window.

"I was supposed to have that life. That simple life. Those parents."

I turned toward the elderly dead people in the corner. Their eyes were open. The last thing they must have seen was their adopted son reaching for their necks.

"No," said Ultimate. "Not them. I mean, Chem is right, in a way." I glanced toward Chem's body. His eyelids fluttered, the wound on his brow cauterized when Ultimate's laser burned a hole in it. But the back of his head...

"Those aren't the parents Chem saw on my data chip. But they're the parents I had in my time stream. Solanis chose them for me. They had all the things the other parents didn't have. Money. Status. That stuff.

"Solanis thought with the right upbringing, Ultimate would grow beyond superhero, and into a world leader who would turn the last thousand years into a time of unmatched Sol-centered advancement."

"Solanis fucked up the timestream..." I groaned.

"She didn't mean to," said Ultimate.

"Well, hell," I said sarcastically. "No one ever does."

"I knew I'd be a great crime fighter. And I did fight criminals. There's two of them over there!"

The freshly dead, found on the Body Farm with Ultimate and his parents, were also in the chamber. "That guy is an embezzler and the other one stole a television."

"You killed people for that?" I had a vague memory of what a television was from history class, but I was pretty sure that stealing one wasn't a capital offense.

"I don't want to be kicked out of the Sol Squad for killing bad people!" he cried.

"Great Bismuth!"

"I know you're trying to delay me with all these questions. But with my super speed, I was able to read all about you on the computer at HQ. I also figured out how to delete records of Kahmi's call bringing you here. No one knows you came to this place.

"I also know you are an alien from Bismuth and you need to eat almost constantly. So, you're stuck in there for a week with your friends and the dead. Dead bodies which eat the dead. So, it's up to you who eats who first."

"You're insane."

"I'm Ultimate. I'm superior."

I began to cry.

"I don't want to kill you," said Ultimate with something that sounded like sympathy. "It's not the Sol Squad way. I'm learning to be a better person, just like the Ultimate in the history vids.

I'll forget about all this and…it's not like you're valuable to the team. No one will miss you."

In a ridiculous place in the corner of my ego, that stung. "Well, fuck you very much, but Chem is valuable. And you just punched a hole in his head."

"He's the last of his kind, just like me," said Ultimate, sadly. "I only wanted to make sure he couldn't use his power against me." He hesitated than added, "He seemed nice."

"That projectile," Kahmi gasped, gripping the stump where her hand had been. "It's the source of this reanimation?"

"Tarlonite," said Ultimate. "The most valuable element in the universe." Ultimate's face went hard. "Solanis found the records from my world. She taught me who I am. Tarlonite can disable my people, put us into a suspended state, but Tarlonite can also resurrect. Thousands of years ago, the galaxy went to war over it. They destroyed my people to get it, thinking it could grant all eternal life. I escaped in a pod. Took me thirty lightyears to reach Earth."

"Great Bismuth," I breathed. "That's what the Solanis financial empire is based on: life extension."

"Tarlonite wasn't destroyed. She had me harvest it in the past and she synthesized it into a new form. It's the medicine that keeps people alive for a really long time."

"But in its pure form, it causes…"

"Reanimation," said Ultimate. "Like zombies. Never really liked those kinds of movies much."

"What happened to your parents, Ken?"

"They're not my parents," Ultimate said coldly. "They were the people Solanis chose to raise me until it was time for me to be who I was meant to be: Ultimate; the ultimate superhero!"

"And you killed them, because…"

"They weren't very nice."

"Is that kind of like killing someone who stole a television?"

Ultimate frowned. Odd watching him struggle through this conversation, his wholesome face and chirpy, friendly tone at war with the horror of his actions. "My parents disapproved of what I was becoming. I had a couple of bodies in the garage, it's not like

I was going to keep them there. I do good in this world and give thieves and liars the punishment they deserve. What do I get?"

"What indeed?"

"I don't like people who shout. Anyway, that's when Sol Boy showed up. It's in the history books. Or it was. In the original timeline, Sol Boy came to the past to bring me to the future where I trained with the Sol Squad. In this timeline, he found me with—"

"Bodies."

"Then I got shot and his time travel emergency trigger pulled us through the portal. The other bodies came along by accident. The portal grabs whoever is in field range."

I groaned and closed my eyes. Sol must have struggled with how to tell his mom he'd brought her superhero crush back to the 30th century, only he was dead, and oh, by the way, he was a psychopathic shithead. Sol dumped Ultimate and his victims at the Body Farm, then rushed off on another mission. He had issues with procrastination.

With the timeline changed, the memory of Ultimate was wiped from all of us except Sol and Max Solanis.

I looked up again. "Sol Boy didn't shoot you, did he?" I said.

"Oh, heck no."

"Who did?"

Ultimate bit his lip then said. "Everyone will think Sol was jealous of me and my relationship with Solanis. She's really pretty, and she loves me. I'll join the Sol Squad and history will go back to normal."

"This is the part where I say you'll never get away with this."

Ultimate smiled icily. "This is the part where I say I can move so quickly that even if someone does manage to find you, my super hearing will pick it up and I'll fly back here and fry every damn one of you before you get out of this building.

"Oh," he added. "And by the way, they're aroused by blood." He pointed and tapped the glass. "Your friend there...he's bleeding." He smiled and was gone in a flash.

Chem's life ran away from him in a gory smear across the floor.

And then I heard the growling.

Kahmi screamed.

The creatures moved.

The gurneys rattled, the straps holding the bodies down creaked under the strain of an awakening army of the hungry dead.

I pulled Chem toward the door, fumbling in my belt for the emergency med kit and shot Chem with a dose of Stasis to throw him into a dormant state. Nanomeds worked to seal the wound.

The gurneys jumped under the thrashing of the screaming corpses.

"Isn't there an emergency release in here?" I asked Kahmi.

"Already tried. He disabled it."

I put my mouth against the door handle, bit down and was rewarded with a brutal shock. "Powermetric, remember?" said Kahmi. "Force returned by force."

Her severed hand was on the floor in the middle of the rattling gurneys. Impulsively, I moved to retrieve it. "Don't go over there," she said.

"Ultimate gets his energy from the sun," I wondered. "He was restored to life and health when the Talonite was taken away.

"Do they get their energy from the sun too? Will they be healed if they do? Do they…are the…alive?"

"Academic at this point, I think," said Kahmi.

Something tore. The ripping was louder even than the growling and snarling cadavers. One of the corpses had torn his arms free of its bonds. And then it rose, roaring, and came for us rotting arms and claws and mouth agape, blackened teeth and mouth open in a howl.

Great Bismuth, it was GouramiMan. I'd arrested him for illegal smuggling of aquatic life forms. My fist went through his head, and stuck in the muck of his skull. His gills flapped uselessly. I yelled, pulling my arm back and forth to release it from the smelly grime. I brought my other hand up to balance against what was left of his skull. My arm broke free with a squelching sound, taking what was left of GouramiMan's brain with it.

GouramiMan's remains shuddered and heaved. He went quiet.

But the other corpses continued to howl.

stared at my hand covered in brain and bone and slime, then flicked the slop to the ground. The force of the action made me fall on my ass. I scooted backward toward Kahmi, Chem, and the door.

In a moment, even with half his head gone GouramiMan moved again. He turned from me and crawled toward Kahmi's severed hand. His shrunken claws grabbed the meat and he devoured it, crunching loudly on gristle, knuckle and bone.

Then GouramiMan sat up, his great gaping head wound pulling its pieces together in an awful semblance of healing. He turned to us and he smiled. Then he fell to the floor and made way to Chem's blood trail, lapping at it like an animal.

The wound stitched itself together. Fresh skin grew and molded itself across his skull.

Kahmi stifled a wail.

Another terrible sound of ripping and clawing and another corpse rose from its gurney. And another.

"It's healing them," she said with a cry, "They don't need the sun...they need...they need flesh and blood!"

"The Squad doesn't kill," I murmured. "The people of Bismuth don't eat meat."

I turned to Kahmi. She put her hand on Chem's shoulder. In the corner of the room, a corpse so rotted its liquified guts spilled from it as it slid from the gurney fell onto the floor and crawled toward us.

"We can't eat meat," I pleaded. "We don't dare."

"Us or them," she said.

"Turn around," I told her. "Don't watch."

The body in the corner pulled itself to its knees. So did I.

"Dinner time, motherfucker," I snarled.

GouramiMan energized by its small meal, came at me, mouth open, drooling black foul-smelling liquid, flesh dripping from its limbs. I slammed it with a savate kick. Ribs shattered under my blow. He swirled, teeth gnashing, closed its mouth on my arm. My suit didn't tear, but I felt my skin rip under the assault, I felt the blood flow, but he tasted nothing. My suit, made for the rigors of space and battle, refused to yield.

I yowled as he ravaged me, then leaned forward and clamped my mouth on the Gourami's face, ripping it apart, devouring the putrid skin in two bites. He howled, outmatched, my next bite shattering its skull pushing into the brain, destroying what had just been restored. I sucked the contents down with loud, hungry slurps.

It was absolutely delicious.

I gorged. I crushed bone and sinew and ligament and rotting putrid flesh, devouring with ravenous glee.

"Look out!" Kahmi screamed.

Kahmi launched herself as another creature rose behind me, pummeling it with her remaining fist. I pushed her aside, and threw myself at the shambling dead hulk. I tore its throat, severed its head, then shoved my fist into the cavity of its neck, scooping out the sticky contents and shoving the dripping mass into my greedy maw.

Kahmi scrambled backward to the door again. I feasted.

The alluring scent of my fresh blood inflamed them. They crawled, shambled, lunged toward me, but they were starving and none had my power, my desire. I scooped out brains, pushing my fist through eyes, ripping out mouths, teeth and rotting craniums. I yanked out yards of intestine, slurping it, twirling it around my tongue.

They bit me again and again, but their rotting teeth could not breach my suit. I was bruised, torn and felt bones crack, but I pressed on, tireless, and all-consuming, and feeling nothing but pure satiation, pure joy.

I heard Kahmi quietly crying behind me.

I held the bowels of a woman in my hands. I think it was... yes, Ultimate's foster mother. "Don't look," I said.

"I'm not afraid," said Kahmi.

Covered in muck, and dead blood, torn flesh and matted hair, I turned to her.

"My people don't eat meat," I explained. "Now you know why."

"It's OK. Finish it."

I returned to the corpses. I feasted, shoving my fists deep into the gory, fleshy spread. Already I was developing a preference: too fresh was too soon for me. A bit of rot made the meat piquant, pungent. The thick thighs and buttocks were absolutely glorious, big and beefy and not at all like a vegburger imitation which would never satisfy again. I pulled the long shank off GouramiMan and tore at it with my teeth in juicy hunks .

The bodies were no longer moving, no longer fighting. No longer predators. They were my meal. Meat.

Suddenly, there was a sound at the door, and I saw...holy shit, it was Stellar.

"What the flaming fuck are you doing in there?"

"Get us out!" cried Kahmi.

I heard Stellar through the speaker fumbling with the lock and we were free a second later. Stellar froze at the open door and looked at me in horror.

"What have you been doing?" His voice was quiet.

"He saved our lives," Kahmi barked. "Help him!" she waved at Chem, as I quickly attempted to explain the madness of the day.

"No fucking way," said Steller as he scooped up Chem's limp body and placed it on an examination table.

"Ultimate will be back any minute, you have to bring the Squad!" she cried.

"Hell, Stellar, I thought you were on the way to Pluto!"

"I was," he said, running his com over Chem's body grimly reading the med data. "I forgot my lucky charm. Went back to HQ...". He dangled the magnetite on its chain, then shook his head. "No one on monitor duty and Sol is gone."

I closed my eyes.

"Nanomeds did its best with this wound but," Stellar shook his head. "Chem is really bad. I'm calling a medtech."

"We have to leave now!" pleaded Kahmi.

"We can't move him, or he'll die," Stellar said firmly.

"How the hell did you know where we were?" I cried.

"Your girlfriend left a message. And when I got here, there's blood everywhere, not hard to follow that trail, genius."

"Girlfriend…" I looked at Kahmi.

"Oh, yeah." Kahmi looked at me under her lashes. "I guess… when Ultimate wiped out the message about how I called you for help at the Body Farm…well, you guys must have already been on your way here when I called the second time." I raised my brow. "To ask you out. On a date."

"Oh."

"Yeah. Oh." We all jumped.

Floating in the doorway was Ultimate in his shiny Sol Squad gear, his kindly face fixed in a smile.

Then he took his shot.

We dove for cover as Ultimate's lasers swept the room, equipment exploding under his gaze, alarms clanging. The lab was in flames and we were trapped between fire and the power of Ultimate.

Stellar reached out with his big, weighty arm, and wrenched a girder from the wall. With his starborn strength, he flew toward Ultimate, feinting with one arm, the massive girder balanced in it as Ultimate smiled cockily, ready to block the blow. Then Stellar quickly switched the girder to the other hand, whipping it in a lightning fast motion, which wrapped the metal around Ultimate's head.

Raging, Ultimate struggled with the girder, his laser vision stifled, giving Kahmi and me enough time to gather Chem and run for the door. Moments later, Stellar and the blinded Ultimate burst through the roof of the building, rising into the night sky as they grappled, whipping back and forth against one another's might.

"Ultimate's too strong for him," Kahmi wailed. I knew she was right.

Then it hit me.

"The sun!" I shouted "Stellar, he's full of solar power!"

Ultimate wrestled the girder away from his head, lasers shooting in all directions as Stellar pressed against his back.

Stellar smiled. I knew he'd heard me. He closed his eyes.

Slowly, the men began to glow and I saw fear on Ultimate's face. He had time to speak one word: "No."

Now it was Stellar's turn to feed.

Even as Ultimate had drained Sol Boy, Stellar, who fed on stars, drained Ultimate.

His light grew brighter and brighter, he swelled. Ultimate wiggled feebly in his arms shrinking, becoming thinner, wraithlike. Stellar bloated, sucking Ultimate dry until there was nothing left of him but a husk. Stellar opened his arms and Ultimate dropped to the ground, making an arid, empty sound as he hit the grass.

Kahmi rushed forward. "Give me your cape!" she shouted at Stellar. "We have to get him away from solar rays before he can recharge!"

"That won't be necessary."

Through the flames of the burning lab, Sol Boy flew toward us accompanied by a young man with glossy black hair in a red uniform with a big U centered on the chest. He trailed a flowing blue cape.

Ultimate.

He hovered over his time twin, gazing sadly at his other self. Then his feet touched the ground. He removed the cape in a graceful motion, then wrapped the withered body in cloth shutting it away from light.

"I'm sorry you had to go through all that," Ultimate said.

"Sol," I breathed. "You're OK."

"We're all going to be OK," he said. "Except for my mom, I think." In the distance I could hear emergency teams approaching us.

"I have to go back," said Ultimate. "I have to repair the time stream. When Solanis violated it, she created this alternate reality, a temporal paradox. And the reality is…" he looked down at his corrupted body, "some things can send you down the wrong path."

"You killed him, didn't you?" I said.

He looked up, smiling. "It's not murder if you kill yourself, is it, old friend?" A friend I didn't remember, who would be a good friend someday. I didn't know what the Sol Squad code would say about this, because if the time stream repaired itself, none of it would happen. Had happened.

"When I leave you," said Ultimate, "much will be undone. Much will be restored. You'll remember and no one else will. But remember this too, no matter what anyone says about me, no matter what I do...I'm just a man like you."

In the next second, he was gone, the boom as he broke the sound and time barrier reverberating through the wood.

In minutes the medtechs arrived for Chem. Time flickered. Reality changed. Patches on Gendarme uniforms which had once sported the Solanis "S" now mimicked Ultimate's insignia. As we flew back to HQ, Elan Vital floats dedicated to Ultimate dominated the parades. An enormous statue of Ultimate graced the park in front of our tower.

"I'm just a man like you," he'd said.

He left his cape behind, and the body of his other self. The cape went into a museum display case in HQ's lobby.

Stellar never spoke of what he'd seen me do. Our days of picking at one another were over.

Sol's rift with his mother was irreparable. His blackmail about what she had done kept the squad financed.

Chem didn't make it.

Kahmi and I spend a lot of time together.

My tastes have changed, as you may have guessed. Nothing but a big meaty meal will satisfy me now.

The body farm gets an endless supply.

The corpse of Ultimate's time twin was disposed of in a manner that would ensure he'd never rise again.

His withered carcass tasted like jerky.

I walked into the newly reconstructed Farm lab. Kahmi invited me over to examine some new samples and to enjoy a late-night dinner.

She smiled at me as I arrived, her new hand sweeping across a spread of meaty corpses prepared just for me, their tasty flesh lightly mottled, cured just the way I like it best, a week of exposure under a hot sun.

She spoils me.

She held a small jar toward me. It buzzed.
"Would you like flies with that?"

PROOF OF BULLETS

JIM KRUEGER

Let me begin by thanking you. I know my requests were strange. Recording studios are not usually lead-lined. And the way I asked you to fold the paper to be able to read the words, while looking in a mirror, almost like an origami jigsaw puzzle, I know that that was odd as well. I got the idea, ironically, from a being that existed in another dimension and tried repeatedly to get to ours. Certain words, mixed like an anagram and spoken in reverse, condemned it to return to the realm from which it came.

If only our world could return to what it was like before…in the same way.

I didn't want Him to be able to hear us. By Him, I speak of the man I have been incarcerated for killing. Not the thing from another world. Well, he's from a different world too, I know that. So not the thing from the other dimension, that's what I mean. I suppose I will need to be careful with my references.

To be clear, lead-lined or not lead-lined, I fear that to say his name, to utter it, even once, will result in his attention. He will hear me. He will turn, no matter how far away he may be, and he will see me.

You're confused. Please forgive me my cryptic ramblings. I'm here because I am being blamed for killing, and I have confessed to as much. So why then should I be afraid of Him hearing me speak his name?

It was already a risk when I wrote down what my requests were; but he's not omniscient. He needs to look for something… to look at something…to be able to see through to what is on the other side of a wall, or a building, or a city. He needs to focus his hearing to be able to really hear what he desires to. Otherwise, he'd go mad.

And I hoped, that here in prison, maybe, he wouldn't be looking or listening too hard. After all, we're here. And there is so much for Him "to do" out there. He has very little interest in me, I imagine, at least now that I'm here.

As I said, I didn't want Him to be able to hear us… or see us… because I wanted to be able to tell you the story without being stopped. After all, you were his friend, his pal. And you wrote so many of his stories up until the end. I wanted to offer you the last one. It's only right.

Yes to your first question, he's dead. The hero that you, and everyone else like you, worshipped and cheered and looked up to, he's dead. I made the gun that killed Him. I pulled the trigger as well. I murdered Him. The superhero of superheroes. The one who makes people think that it's a bird above them. Or an aircraft. And now it is, of course.

This isn't a ghost story. And I don't believe in devils or hells, but this is more like that kind of story. This is a story of possession from beyond the grave.

He died almost a year ago. That was when he supposedly left you all. But it's only been a few months since he "left" me. Only been months since my trial.

He may call what happened to me, what he's done to me, as some form of justice. But really, it's just revenge.

I suppose I should begin with the days before I shot Him. And then talk about the death. And then what happened after that.

Let me begin with the gun.

You might think of it as a kind of Frankenstein gun, a device built out of parts of things that normally would not fit together. Maybe what made me a criminal in the first place was my desire to say "no" to the things that nature tells us can't happen. Why can't I mix oil with water? Why do I have to be affected by gravity? After all, it never stopped Him before. Or so many of his friends. Their presence alone is a reminder to me how far I fall. And a challenge, therefore, of how high I pushed myself to rise.

I'm a collector of sorts, not only of ideas and philosophies, but of trophies and discarded weaponry. The bullet that killed a billionaire that marked the once proud Chicago's fall into ruin and decay and led to the rise of vigilante justice years later; I have that bullet. I also have a couple of pearls from the necklace the dead man's wife wore that fateful night. Their child couldn't find them all, I hear.

I have a piece of an airplane that can't be seen. There was a crash at some point; I think that what I have is part of the wing that couldn't be repaired, only replaced. I have a ring that they say is made of an alloy that won't exist for hundreds of years, but supposedly once gave the wearer the ability to fly. It has an L-shaped symbol on it. I cannot tell you how tempted I have been to wear it.

I have a slide that contains a droplet of blood from a man who it is said is comprised of every element known to man…and also the unknown elements--the secret foundations of mystery and superstition, all the things hidden from the brightest minds of this and centuries to come.

I have these things because things get lost in this world. Things that come from other worlds. I find them, the things that disrupt the status quo of accepted knowledge.

And because I find them, I also found pieces of a weapon you-know-who once used to kill others from his world. There were three of them.

He says he didn't kill them, but of course he did, the great hypocrite. He has to. Everyone with power kills, even if in secret. And I got my hands on pieces of the weapon that killed his fellow beings and proved that he wasn't such a good guy. One's reputation can be a disguise even more than a mask.

And if it could kill those beings that were like Him, of course it could kill others. Other superheroes, I mean.

There are people who specialize in the guess-work behind

technologies that have dubious origins. Ex-Government scientists. The blacklisted architects of broken dreams. Former enemies that would face death were their backgrounds known, for example.

All have been disenfranchised and betrayed at one point or another. And they all want to be paid for their worth.

Using everything I could beg and borrow and steal, with an emphasis on steal, I set to work to build the Frankenstein gun I mentioned before. Like using DNA to clone extinct beings of another age; these beings set to work on the gun. I called it a Frankenstein gun so you would understand, but it's really an Achilles gun. So from here on out, that is what I will be referring to.

It is a weapon that once fired, reconfigures its bullet to strike at the weakness of its target. This reconfiguration happens in a flash. In a moment. I don't know how the trials worked. It took more than a year to construct. And those who built this have since disappeared. I made certain of this.

Like I said, it cost me everything I owned. Everything I could get my hands on.

But I knew it would make me a star. A bigger star than even he, for all his travels through space, would ever reach.

Think about it. If I had a weapon that could kill Him, it could kill all of them. It could kill every living, breathing, dead and undead, automated and organic self-called superhero in the business. Any who opposed crime would leave their costumes in the garbage cans to be collected.

Some cannot be exposed to elements of their own worlds. Others can't bare even the appearance of fire due to a childhood trauma. Still others cannot abide certain mythological superstitions that can render them once again as things of clay. Like I said, it's an Achilles gun indeed.

Now, there are a lot of heroes out there. Thousands. And I had a gun that could kill them. Kill them all.

I had considered going after a lesser hero. Like the one who was in that group that the vigilante led in the 90s. The one with the earth powers. But who cared about Him? Eventually, he was going to die anyway. The same was true of so many of them. It didn't matter if the gun killed them. They were all but obsolete.

I also considered the team made up of various alloys. They were jokes as it was. But killing a Misfit hardly mattered. Nor did going after the sidekicks. Kill a sidekick and then there's a vendetta against me. As well as the rantings of various upset mother groups from around the world. I am a businessman, you know.

No. Kill Him. Kill "Him" good and proper and anyone would pay for the death of any other superhero on the face of the planet. It would be easy street. And not the teleporting street that that that faculty-head and his freak friends discovered.

No, Easy Street. There would be no limit to what would be available to me. Also, kill Him and they would all know that their number was up…that there was no one to run to. No one to avenge them. The greatest of them would be dead, and they would all seek the shadows to protect themselves.

And those that were already in the shadows? In their caves and their mansions with the rooms that lead to other worlds and times, and their cigarettes and secret bars…these places would no longer be secrets. Their back doors would have to have back doors.

And they would all know I was gunning for them. Yes, gunning.

Let me pause for a moment. I can see from the look on your face that you are not surprised. Of course, anyone who would ever claim to be bulletproof would have to be killed by a bullet. It's irony. It's the very tyranny of story structure itself.

So, despite my thinking, I wanted to try the gun out on someone lesser first. Someone no one would remember. And so I went after that kid with the weird skin color. He was one of the sidekicks and could become any animal imagined. But, to me, no animal form he would take was safe. Every goddamned one of them was endangered by me and my gun. He was once a part of another team, but he should have known he was doomed from the start. The freak. The little beastling.

Animals, it is not surprising, have an instinct. They recognize death when it comes in a way that humans do not. The thing that was many things looked at me, like a deer in a target. It was nothing for me to pull the trigger. Nothing to let the ever-changing bullet fly. I filmed my killing of course, and only know what I am telling you because of a meticulous slowing down of what I had recorded.

My prey became many different things in the heartbeat of the space between a trigger pulled and a target struck. Many things. And not all of them were of this earth. I think even he was surprised by the myriad forms he took as death came for him. If life passes before our eyes before we die, he might have become every form he ever took and then some in the wink that happened before he bit the bullet, so to speak. Struck by a bullet that was every bullet for every conceivable form he could take.

He was dead. And no one cared. In fact, no one even knew. There was nothing left of the body. It wasn't until the trial that it was even revealed that it was gone.

But the gun worked.

Now to go after my target.

He'd be dead. As dead as all his people.

Of course, it's important to know all there is to know about a target. So because I knew all the catch phrases about Him, I went to Manhattan's train station. Grand Central. The place where speeding trains come to rest. And I began to speak. I even whispered my call to Him, testing his hearing.

He hears everything, if you didn't know, but I know you do. You're a bigger fan than I am. Anyhow, I began to speak and of course he heard me.

I confessed to the murder of the funny-colored shapeshifter. Not the green one from another planet, the one from this one. I told Him that I did it.

And I even warned Mr Bulletproof that I had a gun.

I had a gun that kills superheroes. And if he didn't come to me immediately, I would begin killing them randomly, wherever I could find them.

I told Him that I knew he was a killer. And I had the weapon he used to kill the only other survivors of his planet.

I held the gun close, waiting for Him. Counting moments instead of minutes. Knowing that seconds were hours to Him. This wasn't New York. Not really. It was Troy and I was Paris.

I counted the minutes and wondered about all the times a bullet bounced off of Him. Did he care if the bullet hit someone else? Of course he did. He had to. It was an important detail. How many "innocent" bystanders did he "save" without them ever knowing it? How many ricochets did he bypass over the years without anyone noticing? If he had let even one witness get struck, he would have been liable. His entire "career" would have put under the shadow of suspicion. No, he knew the media. He knew the news service. He knew how a story can grow through the printed headlines because so few actually read the entire article.

And so he saved them all. In secret.

But this moment was not a secret. This moment was the moment. When trains converged, when paths came together. And he had no idea. I once heard that a certain lawman in the old west, maybe the first masked hero, ironically, believed that he was fighting werewolves. That's why he used silver bullets. He didn't know whether, when he faced an opponent, he was actually facing a cursed beast dressed in human form, and so he used blessed bullets.

I was that lawman the day I faced the foreigner. I was that hero using blessed bullets.

It didn't take long for Him to arrive. He could fly, after all.

He landed. He was obviously upset. Maybe it was because the shape-changer was a side-kick...or maybe because the shape-changer was a boy. Maybe he was a friend, or some forgotten colleague from some stupid team-up.

He let me know that he heard me, which I knew he had.

I aimed. And I fired.

I'm not sure if it mattered if I aimed. I knew the bullet would find Him, no matter if he flew away or not, which he didn't. As it flew towards Him, it "read" Him like some sort of expository upside-down box at the bottom of a comic book.

It read his genetic code. His social-being. His superstitions.

The bullet saw Him and knew Him better than a god could. It loved Him and it killed Him and damned Him and sent Him to whatever hell was right for Him. Not that I believe in that sort of thing.

Bulletproof my ass.

There was now a hole in Him.

It wasn't the gun that was smoking, though, it was the hole.

And then the hole was sucking. Sucking Him into it. Like a black hole swallowing a world. A world filled with a billion people begging to be saved who wouldn't be.

He looked down at the smoke from his chest. And then he looked at me. He wasn't sad. I wanted Him to be sad, but he wasn't.

He was more understanding. And I hated it. I hated that look of wisdom on his face. He looked at me like he knew it wasn't over.

He took a step closer and confessed…that he had never killed anyone.

I told Him to give up the ghost.

He smiled and spoke his last words. And then he winked that insufferable wink of his.

And then, that was it. He was gone. Gone, gone.

There wasn't a body, I wish there had been, but there wasn't. He, and all traces of Him, had disappeared.

At least there were witnesses. They ran in all directions once there was no hero to save them. I left the train station, got in my car, and was unmolested by police. I just drove home.

I woke the next day expecting an outcry of sadness. And there was. But not for Him, not initially.

I watched as tragedies that once would have been averted by Him, now were not. More died in earthquakes. More died in fires. There were less who escaped gunshots.

Did he really stop so many people from dying in a single night? Did he really avert so many moments? Did he ever stop to rest?

This was just the morning news. The next day's morning news. What about tomorrow?

You were the reporter who asked the world what had happened to Him? Where had he gone? Was he in space? How could he let this happen? You even asked if he was okay?

I went into my bathroom, waiting for my coffee to finish its brewing. Waiting for one of the witnesses to come forward and tell the world what they had seen.

I looked into the mirror and did not like what I saw.

I wouldn't need coffee this morning. I'd need whisky. And more than one.

It was Him. In the mirror. He looked back at me. And he looked pretty alive to me.

I looked at my hands. Still my hands. I felt my face. There was still stubble on my chin. Still no hair on the top of my head. That little bump on my nose was still there. But...the reflection that looked back at me was not my face, it was that of my enemy looking back at me in the same way there would be no reflection of me at all if I were something out of the Bram Stoker library. My face was the same. It's was only what I saw that had changed.

We began to speak, but I had already begun piecing together what had happened, exactly like I put together that damnable gun.

I suppose this is a good time to mention his last words, the ones he said to me before he died. I had just told Him to give up the ghost.

He looked at me and said that this wasn't a ghost story, that it was actually a...No, wait.

I need to keep his last words to myself. I'm not telling any reporter that, especially you. I need to keep some things to myself at least. He said what he wanted me to hear, and then he was gone...the hole in his chest became so large that there was nothing left of Him. Nothing...until I looked in the mirror. And he began to explain himself.

'I never killed those three murderers from my home-world. The device you recovered was a way to banish them to an existence where they could do no harm. It was a compassionate way of allowing the guilty to live while at the same time taking away their ability to cause more harm in the world.'

The reflection continued to speak and explained that his father invented this weapon that banished them to another realm as an act of compassion, and that he knew all its secrets.

He possessed me.

He had become my demon.

To be possessed is different than any experience I have ever had. It is like being a passenger in my own body. And I had a demon who had not experienced the novelty of limitation.

Let me explain. I am not a well man. Have I eaten too much? Yes, and I drink as well. I don't exercise. My right arm is stronger than my left because that's the arm that I shoot with. And I come from a family prone to both cancer and heart disease. As a result, I have learned to be careful. And it's fair to say that if I have any fear in this life, it is pain. And largely because I know it is coming for me one day.

He, inside of me, was excruciating. He was like a child at first. Clearly, he had never experienced pain before. He stopped when he realized the harm that I too was experiencing. But initially, rather than recoiling like any normal human, he instead would, for example, hold his hand close to the flame a little longer than one should, and gaze amazed at the blisters. An hour later, we went for a run. And he pushed me to just shy of what I fear would have been, or could have been, a stroke. I won't even go into how many times, from greater to greater heights, he would jump off of things.

I will never walk without a limp again. The doctors here at the prison joke that if I had had such flat feet, I should have been a street cop.

There was conversation between us. He would ask me things. This would not be out loud. It would an inner monologue that was no longer a monologue.

When I refused to answer Him…when I remained silent…an empty thought balloon, we would begin to search the echoes of my origins. He was clumsy as he did, uncovering the memories of the first dead body I had ever seen. Of the brother that was the reason that body was dead. And of the blood that was on my hands, by being silent, or by not turning Him in, or by lying on his behalf and delivering packages I knew were criminal in their intention. My hands were bloody red before I even took my first shot, and he brought back to the forefront the brilliance of their hue.

This, this was a different type of vision he had, the ability to rifle through my emotions, through my mind. I even began to see my motivations and narrative, like dominos, a series of memories that stacked their way through me and marked me a criminal.

But I didn't commit crime because of an adolescence of circumstance. I committed crime because I wanted power. It was not truth or justice or our nation's way of doing things for he and I not to be equal.

He should have understood something about having power. And he was taking mine away just as I thought I had taken his. His voice in me, as time went on, became softer, more understanding and I hated it for that reason. Again, I am not an example of a poor upbringing. I didn't need his voice inside me to show me compassion.

What he really wanted to know is where the syndicate would operate again. What they would do now that he was gone. He wanted to know who they were. How they operated. How to turn them against each other.

My gun had turned Him into something else, something even more powerful than he had been before. And that something else was staring back at me. He then began to tell me what he was going to do. How once, there were walls he could see through or have to leap over or break through. But now, because of me, there were no walls.

Once he could listen to a heartbeat and know based on its rhythm whether the owner was afraid, or lying, or sick. But now, thanks to me, he could step into that person and know their innermost thoughts.

I hadn't killed Him at all. I had killed the syndicate. I had killed organized crime. The Mafia. The Kingpins of the world. The Dons. The Cartels. They would all be brought down because of this body-jumper.

He wasn't just going to use my body and my knowledge to bring justice to the world, he was going to use anyone's knowledge and every "body" necessary. And thanks to me, there was now an end in sight for what he had always assumed was a never-ending battle.

And so he began to work his way through the system, work through our ways, through our fear and our superstitious nature. He even told me that this is what characterized our lot. He said he learned it from a friend. And now that he saw me from the inside, he knew it was true.

Long alliances that dealt in human misery suddenly broke because of the knowledge I gave Him. Families with oaths that had been written in the blood of fathers long dead found themselves betraying each other.

And so I watched Him pit us against each other. I watched Him fuel our mistrust, our lack of cooperation. Our inability to hope that the other would be anything but selfish.

That thing inside of me, that dead man still living, took us apart. He moved from me to others, sometimes. And then came back to me. Always with his presence, like a ghost reminding me that it was my fault, condemning me with my actions.

Soon, drop offs became known to the police. Drug busts that weren't meant to be known by the police were known. Identities that had been set up for years were unmasked. Crooked politicians who had been bought off were suddenly being forced to pay the proper, public price for actually doing just that. We were coming apart. Around the world, we were coming apart.

There were moments, of course, that he wasn't inside me. Moments when I could see Him inside the others in the syndicate. Working and reworking our aims. But those others he possessed, he also reworked their memories, never letting them know he had been there. I was the only witness.

He winked at me more than once from their eyes. That wink. That damnable wink. Like this was all a joke to Him, a moment of mirth.

He was daring me to say something, to confess what was happening. But I couldn't. I had become his mask. And he knew what I knew about myself. I wasn't bulletproof. And they would kill me before they even let me explain that I was a disposable mask at best. They would kill me before I had the chance to explain this, that he had walked in any number of their shoes already. Killing me would not stop Him. Not at all.

I had truly made Him bulletproof.

This was supposed to be my greatest success.

With more clarity, when he wasn't inside me, I began to think this through. What was it like with that hearing of his? What was it like to hear so many people cry out at any given time for help?

He could only save a couple at a time. But he would hear those he couldn't save, still crying out, still hoping for a salvation that wouldn't come. He'd have to live with the deaths of the nine out of ten he couldn't save while he saved the one.

But now, he could save so many more than ever before. And I helped Him. I helped Him.

Oh, and I should mention that those people that die of earthquakes and fires and so-called Acts of God. They were being saved now. I think that when he wasn't in me, he also went to the other super heroes, all those that should have been dead because of my gun by this point. And spoke to them and told them how he saved people, motivating them and helping them organize in a way that took their league and grew it into a legion.

There was a battle he fought all those years he was alive. A battle he never thought would end. But it was ending with me.

And so here, I sit. And I am a dead man. Because there are criminals still out there. And they are now gunning for me.

They know it was me who set them up, me who talked in the trials. But I didn't talk. I didn't open my mouth. Didn't say a word against them. It was Him all the time. I only hope that they...that he...I was being haunted by a ghost.

...What did you just say? "This isn't a ghost story? It has more to do with *phantoms?*"

Did you really say that? But I didn't tell you those were his last words. I didn't...you asked...I didn't tell you. Oh my God. It's you, isn't it? You're inside the boy reporter? Right now. All this time you've been here.

There should be a law against this. You can't step from person to person. You can't get rid of people like me.

What?

You can…You've done to me what your father did to other killers from your planet. You've let me live while making certain I cannot harm anyone else? This is compassion?

I don't want you to protect me. Let them kill me. I don't want to live this way. It's my right to be killed and die as the criminal I am. It's my right to ignore your words. My right.

What? You're trying to prove to me that I'm wrong? You have hope for me because of the way you were raised? Because of your father?

I don't want you to have hope for me. I don't want to hear about the future world you are trying to grow.

Or about the humankind of tomorrow.

I want this over, and right now. Listening to you, knowing what you are trying to do, it's a never-ending torment.

Why can't you just leave me alone? It's not fair.

Not everyone wants someone who protects the innocent and guilty alike.

STUPORMAN

ROBERT BLOCH

If it hadn't been that I was dying of hunger, I never would have stuck my nose into Jack's Shack. It really isn't safe to stick your nose into that restaurant, because you are liable to smell some of the food.

But there was another reason why I hesitated.

Down at one of the tables, I saw the tall, angular figure of Mr Lefty Feep. He was leaning against the back of a chair with a great air of business about him—other people's business, as usual.

I was afraid he might see me and come over, and for certain reasons I wished to avoid meeting him. Because when you meet Lefty Feep he talks to you, and when he talks to you, you listen, and if you listen, you'll hear something that will distress you for days.

However, I was pleased to see that Feep was already attached to a victim—a little thin man with eyeglasses and a nervous expression. He was talking to the small, bespectacled stranger quite earnestly, and the stranger was listening. I didn't recognise the fellow, but I felt sorry for him. It grieved me to see that he had a bandage around his head, but it grieved me more to see the way Feep was talking to him. I knew what suffering he was going through.

I tiptoed over to a table. Feep didn't look up. I called the waiter. Feep was still talking. I gave my order. Feep gabbled on. My food came, and I ate. Feep was rattling away.

I grinned. This was one time I'd get away scot-free. I laid a tip on the tablecloth and rose to go.

"Do not scurry in such a hurry."

The voice of Lefty Feep cut through my complacency. I looked up. The one-man crime wave against the English language was standing at my table. He sat down.

I sat down, too, when he pushed me into a chair.

"You must please believe that I grieve when l do not perceive you until you are about to leave," announced Feep, picking up a toothpick and signalling the waiter for a glass of water.

"I'm sorry, Lefty," I answered. "But I must be off."

"Never mind your mental condition," he smiled. "I want to talk to you."

"But I must go now."

"Kindly do not bring up biological problems," Feep insisted. "I see you are wearing your golf socks today."

I glanced down at my feet.

"Golf socks?' I echoed.

"Yes," said Feep. "The ones with the eighteen holes."

l rose again. "Listen, Lefty, I have no time to waste listening to your insults. Why don' t you go over and bore that fellow you were talking to before?"

Feep caught my coat-tails and pulled me down again.

"You notice that personality?" he asked. "The little skinny guy with the goggles?"

"Of course I noticed him. Who is he?"

"Who, is he?" gasped Feep. "You mean to inform me you do not recognise him?"

"No."

"Why, that is none other Joe Blow."

"Joe Blow?"

"The famous Stuporman."

"Who in the world is Stuporman?" I asked.

"Why, I always figure everybody knows who Stuporman is," Feep sighed.

I shook my head

"Well," said Feep, "I will tell his story, if you insist."

"I don't insist."

"You are just being polite," said Lefty Feep. "It is such a yarn as is not unravelled every day. Kindly lend me your ears and I will bend them for you."

He did.

With a lightning flick of his tongue, Lefty Feep began his tale.

When I first hear of this personality, Joe Blow, he is a reporter on *The Daily Bulb*, a news-bladder. I see him hanging around Gorilla Gabface's pool palace oncely or twicely, and when I examine this specimen of manhood I am more depressed than impressed.

Joe Blow is a little insignificant jerk who is too weak to lick his own lips.

I hear from some of the downtown boys that he is not a very good reporter, and he is always having trouble. It seems Joe is very much in a fatted condition over a beautiful girl reporter by the name of Effie Fink.

But Effie Fink does not yearn and burn for Joseph Blow. She thinks he is a sissy. First his draft board turns him down and then his girlfriend turns him down. In fact, he gets turned down oftener than the lamp in the parlour of a sailor's girlfriend.

Joe Blow is also turned down around the mouth when I meet him on the street one day. He recognises me from the pool hall and ambles over with a sad, un-glad smile.

"Hello Joe," I greet him. "What's heating for eating? What, I inquire, is on the fire? In a word, what's cooking?"

"My goose," answers Joe Blow, very mournful.

"You have troubles?"

"Like Mussolini," sighs Joe. "I will live in a hotel for five years, and the manager rents my nice room to somebody else and gives me a bum room instead."

"Bum room? That's bad."

"I have worse," sighs Joe Blow. "My editor also gives me the bum's rush. On top of that, the other fellows at the paper are always picking on me. And to finish it all off, my girlfriend, Effie Fink, is running around with a racketeer."

I sympathise with this little runt. "You must assert yourself," I tell him. "You must be impressive and aggressive."

"Just look at me," sobs Joe Blow. "I could not be more run-down if I would get hit by a truck."

"Why not take some vitamins?" I suggest.

Joe Blow shakes his head. "I am too weak to swallow them," he tells me. "Besides, they take too long to do any good. I must work fast to regain my girlfriend, also my self-respect."

"How about a muscle course?" I inquire.

He shakes his head again.

"I send in for one, but they do not mail me my muscles yet."

I try to console him. "We should be able to think of something. With my brains and your troubles—wait a minute! Brains—troubles—I know just the thing for you to do!"

"Commit suicide?" asks Joe hopefully.

"Not at all," I cackle. "We will go to see the psychologist, Subconscious Sigmund. Any time you need your wits sharpened, he is the guy to grind your mind."

"How can he help me?"

"He can psycho-analyse your condition. He can explain the pain in your brain."

"Let's go," says Joe Blow.

So we do. I steer him up to Subconscious Sigmund's office in the quickest kind of a hurry.

We walk inside and see Subconscious Sigmund talking on the telephone, but he nods for us to sit down and wait.

I gather that Sigmund is phoning a barber shop because his kid needs a haircut.

"Let me know when two barbers are free," he says, hanging up.

"Why does your kid need two barbers for a haircut?" I ask.

"The kid has two heads," says Subconscious Sigmund. "And now, what can I do for you?"

I point to Joe Blow and introduce him. "I wish you to tell me what is numb with his skull," I request.

So Sigmund takes Joe Blow into his private office and gives him the third degree. He pumps him for his life history. He grills him like a weenie.

Joe Blow is soon pouring out all his troubles.

Subconscious Sigmund listens very carefully. "Do you ever dream?" he asks.

"Of course I do."

"What about?"

"Oh, I don't know," says Joe Blow, kind of embarrassed. "I have very peculiar dreams. I dream that I am strong, powerful, dynamic. I can lift great weights and have remarkable endurance. I have the ability to see through walls, and hear any sound. And in some dreams I can even fly."

"Aha!" says Subconscious Sigmund.

"Also," says Joe Blow, blushing, "in some dreams I am always having dates with movie queens."

"Really," says Subconscious Sigmund. "You are strong, powerful, forceful, eh? And you have dates with movie queens."

"That's right," says Joe Blow. "Can you do anything to help me?"

"Sure," snaps ,Subconscious Sigmund. He fumbles around and hands Blow a little white box.

"What's this?" asks Blow.

"A box of sleeping tablets," grunts Subconscious Sigmund. "With dreams like that, what do you want to stay awake for?"

Joe Blow sighs, puts the box in his pocket, and plods downstairs. I follow him.

"Do not be discouraged," I remark, when we hit the street. "I have another idea that might help you."

"Nothing can help me."

"Rome wasn't burned in a day," I tell him. "We will try again. I think we ought to go over and see Skeetch and Meetch."

"Who?"

Sylvester Skeetch and Mordecai Meetch," I answer. "The famous scientific Americans. They run the *Horsecracker Institute*, and they are always inventing stuff in their laboratory, such as new ways to avoid paying the rent."

"Can they help me?"

"If anybody can, they are the personalities," I brag. "They are scientific, but terrific."

So Joe Blow trims his limbs over towards the *Horsecracker Institute.*

We climb the stairs to the big private laboratory where Skeetch and Meetch hang out, mostly around the elbows.

Little fat Skeetch and his chubby partner glare over their goggles in the outer office when we come in.

"Lefty Feep!" yells Skeetch. It's a pleasure to see you! Sit down! Have a cigar? Good—then give it to me!"

"I want to read you my latest monograph,' Meetch interrupts. "It is entitled 'AN APPREHENSION OF AN INTENTION FOR THE PREVENTION OF INVENTION' and it just won an Honourable Mention at the Convention."

"I haven't time," I tell them. "I only come here because I bring you a case."

"Open it up and I will get the glasses," says Skeetch.

"Not it—him," I correct, pointing at Joe Blow.

"What do you want us to do—bury him?" inquires Skeetch.

"No, I want you to listen to his story and help him."

So Joe Blow gives out with a pout about his fate. He tells about his bum room, his overbearing editor, his reporter friends that pick on him, and his girlfriend who runs around with a racketeer. He mentions that he is weak and meek and the future looks bleak.

Skeetch and Meetch sigh and shake their heads.

I can see they don't know what to suggest.

But Joe Blow goes on. He tells about seeing Subconscious Sigmund, and answering questions about his dreams. He mentions dreaming of flying and being strong and dynamic.

Suddenly both Skeetch and Meetch jump up and yell.

"We have it!" yells Meetch. "Eureka!"

"So do you," I snap.

"You come at the right moment," Skeetch babbles. "We are just looking for a subject to experiment on with our new machine."

"Machine? What do you mean?"

"The most keen machine you've ever seen!" raves Meetch. "We call it the *Morpheus Arm*."

"Why?"

"Because it works while you sleep. It is a mechanical hypnotic device which translates the subconscious images of dreams into waking realities, utilising subliminal concepts and energising the psychic trauma until a visualisation occurs which impinges imaginative free-fantasies upon a framework of actuality, thus setting up a basis of positive activity actuated by the psyche."

"The hell you tell," I exclaim.

"What does he mean?" asks Joe Blow.

"Why it is simple," I inform him. "He means he invents a machine that turns your sleeping thoughts into waking realities. Whatever you imagine you can do while you dream, you actually can do."

"Right," says Meetch. "I couldn't explain it better myself. In fact, I couldn't explain it.

"But how does this machine operate?" persists Blow.

"Very simple arrangement," says Skeetch. "The subject goes to sleep. As he sleeps, electro-magnetic impulses, due to photo-electronic control are set up. The subject's heart action is synchronised to the movement of the machine. At the same time, a hypnotic force draws bodily magnetism from the sleeper as he dreams. The dreams, in a word, become part of the machine—and the energy of the machine operating in ratio with the dream image, flows into the body of the sleeper.

"When the sleeper wakes up, he has the ability and strength to carry out his dream activities. Simple?"

"You are simple," I tell him. "It sounds screwy to me."

"The machine is in our laboratory now," protests Meetch.

"I'd like to look at it, anyway," sighs Joe Blow. So we drag into the big laboratory.

Sure enough there is this huge arm, attached to a big black cluster of wheels and wires, mounted on a heavy metal base set above an operating table.

"Looks like they've got something here," says Joe Blow.

"Yeah—something for the scrap drive," I sneer.

"I believe these gentlemen," says Joe Blow. "I think I would like to make the experiment. After all, what have I got to lose? I am down and out. But if I could be the way I am in my dreams— oh boy!"

"All you need to do is go to sleep," says Skeetch.

I shrug. If that is what Joe Blow wants, he will have it. But I cannot wait around for him to go to sleep.

Still, I am always glad to do a friend a favour.

So I walk behind Joe Blow and tap him over the head with a hammer.

He falls asleep at once

Skeetch and Meetch lift him up on the table. He lies there under the laboratory lights, looking weaker and skinnier and littler than ever.

Skeech and Meech go into their act. They indulge in a lot of wire-connecting, strap buckling, switch-fiddling, button pressing, and assorted dial-turning.

All at once the machinery begins to hum in various keys, like the Four Ink Spots. Then it gains a little power and begins to sing, off-key, like the Andrews Sisters.

Sylvester Skeetch and Mordecai Meetch swing the big arm of the machine over until it hangs just above Joe Blow's head. The arm jiggles up and down. A little screen in back of the machine base lights up and long streaks of electricity crackle across it.

The pinball operators will pay real money for stuff like this, I figure.

But Skeetch and Meetch are more of the screwball operator type.

All at once Meetch utters a mutter.

"It isn't working right," he says. "We can't synchronise the heart action because the patient's pulse is too weak."

"Adrenalin," suggests Skeetch. He runs over to a glass cabinet and comes back with a hypodermic needle.

"Let's go," yells Meetch. "Shoot the harpoon to me, goon."

They give Joe Blow the needle.

The machine begins to groan and shake. So does Joe Blow. But in rhythm with the machine!

Now I notice the electric streaks on the screen also move in rhythm with Joe Blow's breathing. Everything is synchronised. And the arm above Joe Blow's head seems to be conducting energy from the machine into his body.

I sit there watching, and eating a banana, with rapt scientific curiosity. What will happen next? A short-circuit, I suspect.

But there is no explosion.

All at once the two geniuses rush over to Joe Blow and unstrap him. Meetch goes over to a wash stand and comes back with a glass of water which he throws in Joe Blow's face.

Joe Blow wakes up, sits up, gets up.

He is awake, and that is no fake.

I stare at him. He doesn't look any different as he climbs off the table.

In back of him the machine grinds away, but that is the only evidence that anything happened during the last ten minutes. Except for that, it might all be a dream.

But if you ever see a dream walking, it is Joe Blow—as I soon discover.

"How do you feel?" I yell, above the machine's humming noise.

He smiles.

"Wonderful! Marvellous! Superb! Not so bad!" he announces.

Skeetch rushes up to him.

"It's a success," he gasps. "The machine works! Congratulations for helping our experiment."

He shakes hands with Joe Blow. Suddenly he starts to scowl and howl.

"Ouch!" yells Skeetch. "Leggo—you're breaking my fingers!"

Joe Blow lets go. He takes off his glasses and throws them away.

"Don't need these any more," he announces.

We look at him, wondering if it is true.

"My friend," says Meetch, "if you benefit from this machine, we are very happy. As long as it continues to operate you will be living your dreams. We will not shut it off. So if you are indeed stronger and more capable due to our efforts we are very pleased. We urge you to take full advantage of the machine's powers, so we can study the effects. In a word, make your dreams come true."

Joe Blow stands there. He is still a little, scrawny-looking guy, but he has a new smile on his face.

"Very well, gentlemen," he says. "Thank you for all your trouble. But if you will pardon me," he murmurs, "I must go now."

"Goodbye, Joe," I tell him.

"Goodbye," says Joe Blow, stepping over to the open window and flying away into the night.

Yes that is exactly what he does! He marches to the open window and hurls himself through the air like a rocket.

"For sobbing out loud!" I yell. "Look at that!"

Skeetch blinks, but Meetch winks.

"That's what he dreams about," he tells me. "With the aid of the machine he should be able to do that. He is almost walking—or rather, flying—in his sleep now. His brain is awake, but his soul is in a sort of a stupor."

"Stuporman," says Skeetch.

"Exactly," Meetch answers. "Joe Blow is now a Stuporman. As long as we keep our machine running, he can do whatever his imagination will allow."

Skeetch rubs his hands. "Well, that's that," he says. "We will let the machine run awhile and see what happens to our subject in this little experiment. But now we must go back to work. What is next on our programme, Meetch?"

Meetch looks at his list.

"We are supposed to build a rocket-ship," he announces.

"All right," says Skeetch. "I suppose it will take us several days, at least. You had better go now, Lefty."

So I take my leave of Skeetch and Meetch, wondering all the

while what Joe Blow does after he flies off into the night.

I do not find out until a long time afterwards. But this is the way it works out.

Joe Blow is very delighted to find he can fly. He glides along over the rooftops, hoping an Army patrol doesn't spot him, and practises gliding and swooping and dipping, and maybe a little peeking into second storey windows.

But after a while the novelty wears off and Joe Blow realises he has a job to do.

So he heads over to his hotel. He lights down in the alley in back and walks in very normally. He prances up to the desk, where the manager is sitting—a fat, tough-looking number.

"Pardon me," he coughs, looking meek.

"Why should I?" growls the manager, looking up. He is the fellow who imposes on Joe Blow by kicking him out of his good room and putting him in a cubbyhole a few days before.

"I should like to have my old room back," Blow remarks.

The manager glares. "I already tell you it is quite impossible. That room is rented to somebody else now."

"But it has a nice southern exposure," argues Joe Blow. "I lived in it for five years and like it. Now you transfer me to a little closet with no windows at all. What can I do for air?"

"You can get the hell out of here," suggests the manager. "I have no time to waste arguing with an insignificant little pip-squeak like you.

Joe Blow shrugs. "No southern exposure?" he mumbles. "All right. Suit yourself."

He walks out of the hotel. The manager laughs.

But a minute later, the manager is not laughing. He is shaking. In fact, the whole building is shaking.

The shaking turns into a terrific shudder. Then there is a rumble, a totter, the building seems to lift in the air, and everything whirls around.

When the manger opens his eyes again, everything is quiet. And normal.

He rushes to the door and looks outside to see about the earthquake.

He looks around and almost collapses.

"I'm on the wrong street!" he whispers.

The explanation, of course, is simple. Joe Blow wants a room with southern exposure. So he merely goes outside and lifts up the building and turns it around until his room faces south.

Then he puts it back down, punches a hole through the wall of his room for a window, and flies away.

"This Stuporman business is all right," he thinks to himself, lighting on the pavement across from his newspaper office.

He starts to cross the street.

A car whizzes around the corner, almost clipping him. A tough but gruff voice sings out, "Whyn'cha look where youse is going, huh? Wanna hold up traffic?"

Ordinarily, Joe Blow cringes when somebody yells at him. But now he yells right back.

"Yes I do want to hold up traffic," he says.

And he scoops up the car in his arms and holds it up. He puts it down out of his way, and crosses the street.

The tough but gruff guy is now sick but quick.

Joe Blow ignores him and marches into the newspaper office. He heads straight for the back where the editor hangs out.

Usually he does not dare to invade his privacy, but today he walks right into the inner office and sits down.

The editor looks up.

"So here you are, eh, Blow? What the hell's been keeping you?" he snarls.

"It's my day off."

"Day off? Day off? You just have a day off last week when your appendix busts."

"I know, but—"

"Listen, Blow," snarls the editor. "While you are taking your day off, stories are breaking all over town. I get a report about some nut who is flying over the city. Do you phone me in the yarn? No!"

"I can explain—"

"Shuddup! Then the manager of the hotel down the street phones in about an earthquake. It picks up his hotel and turns it around on its foundations. Do you cover this story? No!"

"But listen, sir—"

"You know what I'm gonna do, Blow?" yells the editor, getting up and grabbing Blow by the scruff of his neck. "I'm gonna kick you out."

And he aims a very hearty kick indeed at Joe Blow's stomach while his back is turned.

"Ouch!" moans the editor, hopping around and grabbing his foot. "What you got—lead in your pants?"

Joe Blow pushes the editor back into a chair and smiles.

"Now *you* listen to *me*," he says.

The editor sits back very quiet. He is so quiet you can hear his eyes popping when Joe Blow exhibits his new personality as Stuporman.

"I am sick and tired of your bossing," says Blow. "For ten years I work here on *The Daily Bulb* without a raise. I think it is about time you double my salary."

"What the—"

"Sit down!" snaps Blow. "I am not afraid of you any more, you big yard of lard. You are not as tough as you look. For a while I think you are all muscle, but now I know your secret. Do I get a raise, or do I tell all the reporters you wear a corset?"

"Corset?" screams the editor. "How do you know—are you the devil?"

"No," says Joe Blow. "But my super-vision tells me that beneath your vest is a corset."

The editor blushes. He shakes his head violently.

"Don't be upset," Blow adds. "Your wig will slide off."

The editor gulps.

"We all know you wear a wig," Blow tells him. "Matter of fact, my super-hearing tells me that some of the reporters in the outer office are talking about it right now. They are wondering if you ever find any eggs in that bird-nest you have on your head."

The editor, after screaming, blushing, and gulping, is too tired to do anything. He just sits there.

"Where do you get your wonderful hearing and vision?" he inquires. "To say nothing of whatever you have when I try to kick you?"

"Never mind," Joe Blow cracks. "From now on I will not be taking kicks any more, I will be giving them out. And you are always at the top of my list."

Blow grins. "Yes, sir," he says. "I have a deep-seated affection for you and—"

Just then the door opens and Blow's super-vision and super-hearing get a real workout. For into the room steps his girlfriend, Effie Fink. This damsel is really quite an eyeful and quite high-spirited. In fact she is all curves and nerves.

Joe Blow's mouth hangs open and he forgets all about his abilities as Stuporman.

Effie Fink ignores him and prances up to the editor.

"I think I'm on the trail of that subway graft," she announces. "*The Daily Bulb* will have a scoop tomorrow if your little girl reporter knows anything about it."

"Fine," says the editor. "We ought to uncover this affair. We must find out what's holding up the subway construction."

"I'm following a hot lead," says Effie. "Hope I don't get my nose burned."

Joe Blow sits there gulping and hoping Effie Fink will notice him, but she doesn't.

"Ah—uh—hello, Effie," he yammers.

Effie turns and gives him a look straight from the Deep-Freeze.

"Oh, it's you," she remarks.

"Sure," says Joe. "Don't you notice me when you come in?"

"No," answers the girl reporter. "And I still don't."

"Uh—how about going out with me this evening?"

Effie laughs.

"I'm sorry, but I already have an engagement, thank heaven! I am the guest of Mr Cutter."

"You mean 'Throats' Cutter, the racketeer?" gasps Joe.

"Never mind the vulgar nicknames. Mr Cutter is a gentleman, as far as I know, and I will thank you not to cast any aspersions on him."

"I would like to cast something more than aspersions on that big baboon!" mutters Blow.

The damsel laughs. "You? Why you haven't the strength enough to cast a vote," she titters. "But I cannot waste time. I'm on my way."

Effie Fink breezes, banging the door shut behind her.

The editor looks at Joe Blow sitting there and trying to pick his face up from the floor when it starts falling.

"Huh!" grunts the editor. "You and your super-vision and super-hearing and super-strength! Why don't you assert yourself with her, you super-chump?"

Joe Blow shakes his head. "You don't understand," he says. "When I see Effie I don't think about myself anymore. I forget everything. 1 worship the ground her open-toed shoes toddle on! Besides, I don't want her to know about my power. I want her to love me for myself."

The editor has a slight change of heart. "Don't feel so bad, Joe." he advises. "I happen to know she really doesn't like this 'Throats' Cutter she hangs around with lately. It is merely that she suspects him of being mixed up in this graft to halt construction on the subway. She goes out with him to pump him, try to uncover the deal, and get a story for the paper."

Joe Blow perks up a little when he hears this. "I see," he exclaims. "It's strictly business."

"Exactly. And this subway scandal is important."

"Right," says Joe Blow. "Today I happen to be visiting my scientific friends, Skeetch and Meetch," he observes proudly. "I notice that when the subway is completed it will end very close to their *Horsecracker Institute*."

The editor makes a suggestion. "Why don't you get on this story too?" he asks. "The sooner we find out about the subway, the sooner Effie Fink is through with 'Throats'' Cutter."

Joe Blow is so excited he forgets about his super-strength. He springs to his feet and bumps his head against the ceiling. He comes down gracefully, along with a shower of plaster.

"I'll do it," he shouts. "I'll follow her."

"Probably she is at his apartment," suggests the editor.

"In that racketeer's apartment? I must be off," yells Blow.

He runs to the open window.

Blow blows.

The editor watches him dive out.

"Yes, he must be off," he sighs.

But Joe Blow, flying through the night, is very much on. He swoops down at a corner drugstore and rockets into a phone booth. Every ounce of his new super-energy is quivering with excitement. He calls the Horsecracker Institute, meanwhile tearing the telephone book in half just for practice.

"Hello," he yells, when Skeetch answers the phone. "This is Joe Blow. Have you still got the Morpheus Arm working? Good! Be sure to keep it on. I'll need everything I've got tonight."

He hangs up, whirls through the drugstore, and takes off from the kerb.

A cop sees him flying into the night.

"Hey, you!" he hollers. "Why don't you wait until the lights change?"

But Joe Blow is already a mile up, zooming for the big apartment where 'Throats' Cutter hangs his coat and gat.

In a moment he is perched on the window ledge outside the 19th floor, using his super-vision to squint through into the rooms beyond.

There is Effie Fink, sitting on the sofa with 'Throats' Cutter. Joe Blow looks at the celebrated racketeer and shudders.

'Throats' Cutter is only about five feet six and weighs about 150 pounds, but he is every inch a thoroughbred. A thoroughbred rat. Even if his height and weight are only average, he looks very strong. His arms bulge with muscles and his hip pockets bulge with hardware. He is sitting with his legs crossed, and Joe Blow can see a stiletto parked in his left stocking. He has his coat off and is relaxing in a bullet-proof vest, but hls tie is neatly knotted to hide the blackjack hanging underneath it. 'Throats' Cutter is smoothing back his coal-black hair with his left hand, because his right hand is covered with brass knuckles.

Effie Fink doesn't seem to notice this one-man arsenal's appearance. She is giving him the old oil.

"It must be marvellous to be so important," she sighs. "And have so many people interested in you."

"I get shot at every day," says Cutter, proudly.

"You must be very busy," whispers the damsel. "I hear you are interested in the new subway."

"Who tells you that?" snaps Cutter, his eyes glittering like the teeth on a hungry shark.

"Oh, a little birdie."

"A little dead birdie, if I ever catch him," mutters Cutter.

"But isn't it true?" needles the girl reporter.

"Don't bother your head about such things and you'll keep it longer," says Cutter. "Wait a minute. I'll mix us up a drink and we'll get sociable."

He gets up and walks out very slow, because of all the hardware weighing him down.

Effie Fink doesn't waste any time. The minute he leaves the room she runs to the desk, trying the drawers. They are locked. Then she runs over to the wall safe and fiddles with it. It doesn't open.

Finally she sees a closet door and opens it.

In the closet hangs three overcoats, two suits, and a large man with a bandage in his mouth.

"Eeeeek!" remarks Effie Fink.

She turns around. 'Throats' Cutter stands in the doorway of the parlour, watching her.

"Do not be alarmed," he says, smiling. "He is doing all right hanging there in the closet. I have insect spray in there so the moths won't get him."

"But I know him," the girl reporter blurts. "That's Ambrose Reed, the contractor who is building the subway."

"Not any more," grins Cutter. "From now on I am building the subway."

"You kidnap him?" whispers the girl.

Cutter doesn't grin any more.

"It is too bad you open that door," he says. "Because I do not like for people to discover the skeletons in my closet. Even big fat skeletons like this Ambrose Reed."

"What are you going to do?" asks Effie Fink.

"I am going to tell you everything," Cutter answers. "Yes, I kidnap Ambrose Reed last week. I take over the contracting job and stir up trouble with the men so the work slows down. Because the longer it takes to build the subway, the more it costs. And the more it costs, the more I will make. Understand?"

"Yes." Effie frowns. "But why do you admit all this to me?"

Cutter laughs. "So you will have a good story to put in the paper tomorrow, of course," he answers.

"You mean I can print it?"

Cutter shrugs. "Well—maybe not. I think I've got a better story figured out. With a little female interest in it, see? How does this sound? 'BEAUTIFUL GIRL REPORTER FOUND DEAD IN SUBWAY. IDENTITY UNKNOWN, BUT SEARCHERS ARE CONFIDENT OF FINDING MORE BITS SHORTLY AND PUTTING THEM TOGETHER.' There's a real story, eh?"

It is a trifle difficult for Effie to answer this question, because she is now hanging upside down over Cutter's shoulder as he grabs her up and smothers her mouth with his hand.

He heads for the door and dashes out of the apartment by a rear elevator.

Joe Blow, meanwhile, is very busy on his own hook. Naturally, he wants to save Effie Fink from death.

But once a reporter, always a reporter. There is a big news story here, and he must get a scoop.

So as soon as Cutter and the damsel leave the room, he springs through the window and unties Mr Ambrose Reed.

In a flash he whips out a pencil and notebook and gets the story of his untimely snatching from the kidnapped contractor.

Then Stuporman's strength comes into play. He rips open the

desk drawers and tears the safe door from the wall. He scoops out all the documents about the subway contracts.

In a twinkling he calls the editor of *The Daily Bulb* and delivers his lead story.

"Reed says this delay will hold up the subway six months," he says. "Yes, Reed's safe, with me. Effie Fink? Oh, Effie Fink is with Cutter at the subway. He's going to blow her to bits or something. What? I should save her? Not a bad idea."

Joe Blow, the Stuporman, hangs up, waves goodbye to Ambrose Reed, and jumps out of the window.

"Dammit!" he yells, outside. "I should have enough sense to open the window before I jump."

But there is no time for quibbling. Joe Blow, therefore, does not quibble. He flies. He heads for the dark, yawning mouth of the unfinished subway tunnel.

He swoops down into the black pit and skims along through darkness.

Far ahead a light gleams along the tracks.

In the glow, Joe Blow can see a sight that has not been his privilege to witness since the days of the silent movies.

Effie Fink is lying on the subway rails in the tunnel way beyond. She is tied hand and foot, and looks very uncomfortable.

Coming towards her is a big electric hand-car, whizzing along the rails. On the hand-car is a large keg of TNT, with the fuse sputtering away and burning down.

When it hits Effie Fink in a second or two, there will be a difficult time finding enough left of her to please a jigsaw fan.

This situation alarms Effie quite a bit, and she is uttering loud cries of displeasure.

Way down the tracks stands 'Throats' Cutter, and he does not agree with Effie Fink's complaints. He is laughing in a jolly fashion—a jolly fashion for a hyena, that is.

Now Blow, *alias* Stuporman, takes in this situation with a single super-vision.

In one second the TNT and the hand-car will strike Effie Fink.

He hurls himself forward.

Fast as he is, he is still a hundred feet away.

Too late!

Mustering every ounce of his strength, Stuporman opens his mouth, takes careful aim at the dynamite keg a hundred feet away—and spits the fuse out!

It sputters and dies, but the hand-car rolls.

Stuporman waits until it actually touches Effie Fink—so that the wheels cut the ropes tying her, and that saves him the trouble.

Then he zooms down and pushes the car back up the track. He gives it a powerful shove and it begins to rocket back towards 'Throats' Cutter. Cutter can't run away. He fumbles in the darkness of the tunnel and whirls around as the hand-car approaches with Stuporman sitting on it.

Joe Blow sees what Cutter has in his hands.

A big, black-barrelled sub-machine gun.

And it is aimed at him.

Stuporman or no Stuporman, he doesn't think he can stop bullets.

So as soon as Cutter shoots, Stuporman Blow leaps up, comes down on the barrel of the gun, and bends it backwards while Cutter is firing it.

The bullets enter Mr Cutter very rapidly, and he becomes very dead.

Effie Fink comes running up, after taking all this time to pull up her stockings and put on fresh makeup.

"Oh, Joe, you're wonderful!" she whispers. "You will be a hero for saving the subway."

Joe Blow, the Stuporman, frowns.

"The subway!" he mutters. "That's right. I know I forget something."

"What is it, darling?" asks Effie Fink.

"Get out of here," orders the new Joe Blow. "I've got work to do."

Meekly, Effie Fink walks up the tunnel and out of the unfinished subway at the nearest exit.

Joe Blow turns to the wall of earth beyond.

He glances at his wristwatch and sighs.

"Gosh! It's almost midnight. Well, that leaves me a couple of hours anyway."

So taking off his coat, Stuporman gets to work and finishes building the new subway before morning!

Yes, all night long he tunnels and digs, and hauls and props and scoops and cements and pushes through under the streets.

By six a.m. he is dizzier than a cross-eyed octopus in a Hall of Mirrors.

Even Stuporman gets tired.

And that, of course, must be why he gets so confused and makes a mistake. His super-vision is reading blueprints while his super-strength is burrowing through the cement to build the terminal station.

Right then and there he goes wrong.

He digs a little too far and a little off-side.

As a matter of fact, he comes up in the basement of a building. The building above him is shaking and he hears familiar voices cursing away.

"What's the matter?" he croaks hoarsely. "What's happening? Why do I feel so weak?"

After starting this quiz programme with himself, Joe Blow takes one look around him, gulps, and falls flat on his face.

When he wakes up he stares into the goggled eyes of Sylvester Skeetch and Mordecai Meetch.

"Why do you do it?" moans Meetch.

"Do what?" Joe Blow moans back at him.

"Dig up under our cellar and shake the building," Skeetch answers. "When you do that you cause the *Morpheus Arm* to jiggle. It stops cold. Something goes wrong and it will not work any more!"

"You mean I wreck the machinery that controls my dreams come true?" sighs Joe Blow. "I am not Stuporman any more?"

"No more," says Skeetch.

"But you are a hero in today's papers," Meetch consoles him. Joe Blow gets up weakly.

"It's all over, I guess. Now I am just Joe Blow the reporter again. Effie Fink will not go for me now that I lose my superstrength."

"Wait a minute," Meetch suggested. "Nobody needs to know you aren't Stuporman any more. Don't tell her. She will never catch on. Go to her now. I bet she will be your slave for life."

Joe Blow takes this suggestion, nods and beams. He walks out in the early morning sunshine with a smile on his face.

And sure enough, when he gets back to the office, Effie Fink falls all over him. The editor is proud, the subway contractor is overjoyed, and Joe Blow — the famous Stuporman — is a hero.

L efty Feep finished wagging his tale and sat back. I nodded.

"So that's how subways are built," I said, a little sarcastically.

"Joe Blow tells me all about it himself just now," Feep answered. "You do not think he is a prevaricator, do you? And certainly you know that I am 100% truthful."

"You're better than that," I told Feep. "Sometimes you're 200% at least."

He smiled at the compliment.

I turned to stare at skinny little bespectacled Joe Blow.

"Seems hard to believe that such a runt could do so many wonderful things," I sighed.

"You can see the subway for yourself. Doesn't that prove it?" Feel told me.

"I suppose so," I admitted. "But by the way, I forgot to ask you a question."

"Let's have it," said Lefty Feep.

"Why is your Stuporman friend wearing a bandage around his head?"

"Oh, that?"

Feel smiled as he replied.

"It seems he marries this girl, Effie Fink, and she beats the hell out of him."

JUST ANOTHER DAY BY THE POTOMAC

KAREN HABER

It was a dark and stormy morning in Washington D.C. Lightning cracked over the White House and thunder shook the eaves of the East Wing.

The President of the United States was in her bedroom on the second floor. She was wearing gold silk presidential pajamas. Each time the thunder rumbled she hunkered down deeper under her golden bedcovers and told herself that the thunder couldn't hurt her, she was safe, very safe.

Liz Carmichael told herself once more that the thunder couldn't hurt her, and swung herself up out of bed. It was months past the inauguration, and she needed to take advantage of the tail-end of the congressional honeymoon.

She shrugged into her golden presidential robe and slippers and headed to the bathroom. She hadn't reached this pinnacle of power by showing fear, not in the House, never in the Senate, not as Secretary of State, and not now. She was strong, a Valkyrie!

After she had showered and washed her hair, she plugged in the hairdryer. It shorted out with a crackling shock."Aaghh!!" screamed the President of the United States. Her expensive, complicated hair weave was a total wreck. She had to spend an extra half hour to get it under control.

After that she quickly dressed and applied Bronze For Winners to the smooth planes of her cheeks. She frowned in the mirror. Almost time for another Botox treatment.

She was neat, so neat and meticulous, like a cat. She bathed twice a day, and had the bedsheets changed every morning.

Now that she and Steve had separate bedrooms and valets it was much easier to stay tidy.

In her charcoal silk Armani suit, ivory blouse, gold earrings and pearl necklace, she marched down to the dining room, her high-heels clacking against the wooden floor.

She had big plans for the day:

1) Set up Operation Pay Back: a program to arrest and detain any citizens who had not paid off their federal college loans. Those deadbeats owed the country. They could be housed in abandoned schools and shopping malls for retraining as work crews. Somebody had to repair the country's roads and bridges.

2) Next, Operation Pay Up: Establish federal tolls at all state and federal boundaries, all airports and points of entry, to fund her new programs and black ops facilities offshore.

3) Her favorite idea was Operation Push/Shove: Requisition and rebuild Puerto Rico as a holding facility/black ops center. She envisioned a vast network of hurricane-proof tunnels and underground barracks. Those so-called citizens could work for the government or she would have them thrown into prison with the debtors for retraining.

The President sighed happily: she had so much to do. Thank God for ranked voting: she never would have gotten into the White House without it. She shook off that thought, quickly.

Liz Carmichael's oatmeal came with the usual pitcher of nonfat milk. Beside it, a golden bowl with the presidential seal contained blueberries and bananas.

"No raspberries?" she said.

Her waiter nodded sadly. "The kitchen ran out of them, Ma'am."

She stared at him in disbelief. "How can the kitchen run out of raspberries? This is the White House!" She was going to have to give the kitchen manager a warning...again. She was the President of the United States, dammit, and she wanted raspberries with her goddamn oatmeal. And if that meant sending out a government plane to Chili or South Africa to get her raspberries--global warming, if it even existed, be damned-- just do it!

Across the table, her husband Steve was silent and sulking, giving her the occasional side eye. Was he hungover again? Stubble on his cheeks, shirt unbuttoned, and look at the way he was gobbling his food; eating with his hands, for godssake. Was that a belch? When was the last time he'd combed his hair?

"Steve," she said. "You look like shit. Go take a shower. You can talk to me about your trade mission later."

He mumbled something she didn't understand, then got up and stomped out of the room.

She shook her head sadly. Ever since they'd moved into the White House he'd been complaining, nonstop, that she had no time for him, that she'd promised him a cabinet position.

Well, *tough*. This wasn't the only campaign promise she had no intention of keeping. Hadn't she just sent him to Moscow on a trade junket? He probably hadn't remembered a single thing she'd told him to say.

She grabbed her phone and checked her Twitter account. Now she was *really* irritated. Where were all her followers? This couldn't be right. She needed to find a new intern who was better at faking her Tweets. She'd get the press secretary on it right away. Her poll numbers were in the toilet as well, but that didn't bother her. As one of her predecessors had said, it was all fake news. She put down her napkin and headed for the Oval Office.

The morning briefing was the usual recital. Okay, so the Super Harpies had taken control of San Francisco, and were throwing people off the Golden Gate Bridge. What did they expect her to do about it, get out there with a net? Besides, her poll numbers in San Francisco were a joke. That city was filled with lunatics who deserved their fires, earthquakes, super villains, whatever.

The Badass Beasts had turned Lake Michigan into a swamp where they kept anyone in Chicago who was late paying them tribute. If it went on much longer she 'd have to look into unloading her investments there.

Overseas, the news was bad as well. London was being terrorized by the Berserker Beefeaters, Paris was under attack from Les Philosophes Tres Mauvais, and Berlin in the grip of the OCD Drei.

She was tired of cleaning up after the whole world. Let them get out their own mops and buckets for a change.

Now Australia, that was different. *There* was a leader who understood the issues and had the right approach. Okay, he was kind of a religious fanatic, and he really needed to do something about all those wildfires but otherwise he seemed to take care of business.

One of her secretaries—the less hunky one, whose name she always forgot—poked his head around the door of the Oval Office. "Esther Abrams wants to see you, Ma'am. It's about the new Asian Trade Deal."

Again, the President felt a surge of irritation. Why wasn't he cuter?

"Abrams," she said. "That loser? No way."

But even as she protested there was Abrams mincing into the room in her Republican red skirt suit, fake pearls, and sensible shoes. Positively dowdy.

"Esther, tell me something good."

Abrams gave her a sickly smile. "It's stopped raining, Madam President."

"I mean about Congress!"

Abrams winced. "I wish I could, Ma'am. We've got a sticky issue with the special trade deal you're after. I was hoping you might reconsider all those tariffs you've imposed."

At least Abrams didn't waste time with small talk. The woman should be ashamed of putting that melted face in front of the TV cameras. She was too far gone for Botox. Maybe not even plastic surgery. "Reconsider? Let the Senate reconsider!"

"Legally speaking, Madame President, we may need congressional approval for any new trade deals, anywhere."

"Legally speaking?!" The President pounded her desk, knocking over her golden presidential coffee mug. "Am I the President of the United States or not? Why should I care about those crybabies in Congress? They'll approve whatever I want, anyway. The Republicans are a bunch of sissies and the Democrats don't have the numbers. You go back there and tell them I said to shape up and get with my program."

"Ma'am, if I may say so, the Senate has sent a strong signal that they are pushing back on these latest trade deals."

The President kicked her desk, stubbing her toe, and biting her lip to cover the pain. "*I* am in charge. *I* make the decisions. You go back and tell the Senate to do as I say or I won't support any of their pathetic reelection campaigns."

Abrams looked at her smartwatch. "I'm sorry you feel that way, Ma'am. If you'll excuse me, I'm due on the Senate floor for the vote to add the National Rifle Association to the Department of Homeland Security."

Liz nodded her approval. "Make it happen, Esther. Those are all good people in the NRA and we need them in the government."

"I'll do my best, Ma'am." The door closed quietly behind her.

Wasn't it lunchtime yet? Liz checked but it was half an hour away. She drummed her fingers on her desk.

For a minute she thought about summoning Team Terrific to put on a show of force above the White House and remind everybody who was President but then she remembered what stiffs those super-powered do-gooders were and decided against it. On the other hand, Sky Boss, well, he was definitely hot in that glittery thong he wore. But he might not come if called. And to be honest, she was kind of afraid of him, anyway.

Her African-American PA, Paul, walked in wearing a sharp dark suit that really showed off his althletic build. Now *that's* the way she wanted her staff to look. Striped shirt, french cuffs. Yummy.

"Madame President, you have an 11 o'clock with Rick Feney."

"That has-been, Feney?" Liz glared at him." Isn't he dead yet?"

"Greg put it on your calendar."

The President pouted. "Just because he was Vice President a decade ago, he thinks he's still important."

"I'll send him in." Paul walked out, poetry in motion.

Liz felt slightly miffed. Why the hell should she see Feney? But there he was, slithering through the doorway. He collapsed into a chair. His skin was kind of yellow and his eyes didn't seem to focus well.

"Hello, Lizzy." His voice wobbled. "Put on some weight?"

"Rick, how long has it been? Had any heart attacks lately?" The President felt a sudden, strange sensation. Fear? An odd voice in her head told her to get up and leave the room.

Feney droned on. "Now, Liz, I'd like to discuss the proposal mentioned in my letter."

"A letter, Rick? Really? Who reads letters these days?" Liz rolled her eyes.

"Do I have your full attention, Lizzy? I'm here to discuss a new invasion strategy."

The President sat up straight. She didn't care for Feney's attitude. "Still dreaming of invasions, Rick? That must be because the one you managed in the Middle East went *so* well."

"Exactly my thinking. We have to move on Saudi Arabia now, before their nuclear program goes any further."

Feney was *so* clueless. Sad. "Saudi Arabia? Excuse me, but last time I looked, they were our allies."

"Don't argue with me, Liz."

The President stood up. "I don't like your tone, Rick. Just remember who's the President. And frankly, you have no business coming in here discussing government policy. I don't know who you think you are..."

Pounding at the door interrupted her. She heard Paul, shouting,

"Sir, you can't go in there--"

"I'm her husband. I'll see her whenever I damn well want to!" Steve burst into the room, breathing hard. His hair was a mess and he had blueberry jam on his cheek. "Liz, I have to talk to you. *Now*."

The President waved him away. "Steve, you know I'm busy. Make an appointment."

He growled and reached for her phone.

"What's wrong with you today?"

Feney stared in mild surprise. "This *is* a private meeting."

"No. " Steve shook his fist. "Get out."

Feney gargled like a plug being loosened in a bathtub. Slumping in his chair, he deflated, a balloon losing air, as his head fell back, eyes closed, mouth open. Something began to flow out of him. It was dark, coiling, and looked like fog. The snaky fog thing grew arms, legs. Soon it had a face and bright red eyes. The horrible fog thing looked at the President, threw back its head, and laughed with a sound like tin cans being torn apart. Behind it, Feney slid to the floor, obviously dead.

Liz reached for the panic button under her desk but she was suddenly unable to move. Or speak, much less scream.

Steve got between her and the thing that had been in Feney.

"Nyet! You will not do this!" His voice sounded...different. Why did he suddenly have a weird accent?

The damp fog thing glared at Steve. "Get the hell out of my way, lapdog." Its voice sounded female.

Steve seemed to be blurring. Now there were two of him, one more solid than the other. The more solid one fell down and didn't get up. Left standing was a strange hairy figure with terrifying claws, a thick brow ridge, and a mouth full of sharp, jagged teeth. "*Ukhodi. Eto moye mesto!*" the brute growled.

"What?" said the fog thing." Is that Polish?"

"*Nyet! Russian, you bitch!*"

"Who are you?"

"*Chort is name. This my place. You get hell out.*"

"Borscht?"

"*Not borscht! Chort! Am super-telepath. Was in Putin but then Moshchnost Dybbuk come so I must leave Vladmirovich. I take this man, come to America, land of opportunity. Go back to your Feney, pissmacher!*"

"*No way. I'm done with that dead jerk. Finally, I, The Proprietress, will have world power again! I'll force you out of here, Borscht, Chort, or whatever your name is. Back to Moscow.*"

"*Nyet! I live here now. This woman weak. I am strong. I am Chort.*"

"*I never heard of you.*"

"*Destroyer of will, slayer of good. I wipe out you. This woman, marionetka, mine.*"

"*No way. I've waited too long for this.*"

"*Trakhni tebya!*"

"*Up yours!*"

Together they converged on the President.

Liz's body began to tremble and jerk. She flailed, fell, and rolled on the floor. She kicked the walls, tore the golden drapes. Strange noises came out of her mouth.

Her Secret Service agents put down their phones, conferred, and agreed that it was probably "that time of the month" and they should be understanding.

Her desk caught fire. She tried calling for help but her mouth didn't work. Her body was moving in strange violent shudders. She bounced against the doorway and a framed photo of her fell to the floor, the glass in pieces. She jumped up violently and fell down on the coffee table, smashing it to the ground. Now she was flying across the room. She had no control of herself, none at all. She was spinning around in midair, faster and faster. Then it all went dark.

The demons continued fighting. Plaster rained down from the ceiling, and the windows lining the back wall cracked with musical pings.

Steve sat up. "What the hell? Lizzy, what's going on?"

The demons grabbed his arms, his legs.

"Hey!" He struggled.

They threw him sideways through the nearest window, removing the frame in the process.

Once more they attacked each other. The ceiling came down in pieces, leaving behind a pale wooden framework dating back to the McKinley Administration. Part of the far wall collapsed.

Finally the Secret Service decided the situation went beyond lady issues and put out a call for help.

And almost as soon as the call went forth, there, in the sky above the White House--was it a hawk, a jet?--no, it was Sky Boss! He hung in the air, thong glinting, muscles gleaming. Hovering over the wreckage, he made a soft, careful landing into the Oval Office.

"You rang?" he said. "Looks like you've had a little excitement around here."

The President of the United States waved. "S'up, Boss? Come a little closer." She beckoned, reaching for him. "Lemme snap your thong."

Sky Boss squinted. The squint deepened into a frown.

"Oh, I get it. No way. I'm not messing with you, bitch." With a quick flick of his middle fingers he flung himself back into the air, out of reach, and in a moment he was gone, as quickly as he had arrived.

Chort cackled in delight. He had won! He was the President of the United States!

He looked around, admiring his domain.

But what had happened to the White House? Why was his desk covered with carved flowers? Why was a huge framed map of the state of Missouri hanging on the wall? This wasn't the Oval Office. Where was he?

The door opened and a short-haired young woman entered wearing a tweed business suit and glasses. "Sir, City Council is ready to meet on the new transportation policy. They're waiting for you."

"City Council?"

"Yessir." A doubtful note entered the assistant's voice. "You're voting to approve the new trolley line down Main Street, remember?"

Chort slowly got to his feet. He noticed that he was now possessed of a tall African American male body. He was wearing a light grey suit and blue tie. Turning for a moment, he saw the nameplate on the desk: Kevin Foster, Mayor, Kansas City. With a sinking feeling, he realized that The Proprietress had tossed him all the way from Washington D.C. to Missouri. She had won.

He was tempted to force this body to Washington and reengage with his rival. But he knew it would be a long trip. And once he got there, what if he couldn't gain access to the President? It seemed like all the best, most important American humans were already possessed.

Nu chto zh, he thought, and shrugged. Better to rule in Missouri than serve in Hell. "I come."

Liz Carmichael looked around. Where was she? What was this? She wasn't in the Oval Office any longer. She was in a small pink room. The walls were mirrored. There was no door.

"Help! Get me out of here!"

No one answered.

She would send a text. She reached into her pocket, but her phone didn't seem to be there.

"This is the President of the United States speaking!" she yelled. "If you don't help me I'll fire all of you!"

Silence.

She really needed a cappuccino. And some moisturizer. But most of all, she needed a nap. Her eyes closed.

The Proprietress looked out through Liz Carmichael's eyes with a feeling of triumph. She had sent Chort back to Siberia or someplace like it. She had walled off Liz Carmichael's consciousness. She was in total control here.

She flexed her left arm and admired the bicep. This body was much better than her last host. Feney had essentially been dead for years. She could make this one even stronger, eliminate this stupid hair. Maybe get some tattoos and piercings, and have her teeth filed down to points.

A scraping noise behind her drew her attention to the side. Steve Carmichael, bloody and bruised, was halfway through the broken window frame, climbing back into the office.

"Lizzy, you owe me an explanation!" He put his hands on his hips. "Just because you're President now don't think you can ignore me!"

What a pest. The Proprietress sighed, opened a desk drawer, pulled out a gun. Turning quickly, she shot Steve Carmichael in the head. With a grunt of surprise, he shut his mouth, fell to the golden carpet, and proceeded to bleed all over it.

"Oh dear," said the Proprietress. "What a tragic accident. The President's husband has committed suicide." Chuckling, she wiped off the handle and placed the gun in Steve's hand. "He must have cracked under the strain."

She settled into the remnants of the desk chair and took in the wreckage of the Oval Office. Everything had to go. She would redo it in black leather and chrome. Maybe add a few skulls as light fixtures. But it was time to get down to business.

As soon as possible she wanted to start bombing international cities. In the ensuing chaos, she would announce a state of emergency, establish martial law, and dispense with the Constitution. From there she could take over the world. Europe would be easy. As for England, well, once she had the Royal Family eliminated, she might arrange for a sub-demon to inhabit the Prime Minister...oh, wait, wasn't he already possessed? Well, no matter, once she had a proper world war going, it wouldn't matter who possessed the British Prime Minister. The good times were just starting to roll.

She buzzed her secretary. "Get my barber in here. I want my head shaved, stat. Then schedule a meeting with the Joint Chiefs of Staff. I want to talk about strategic targets like Beijing, Moscow, and Berlin."

"Ma'am, the Russian Prime Minister is on the phone..."

"Take a message."

Greg, her chief of staff, stuck his head around the door. "President Carmichael, about Hellmouth opening beneath the Rose Garden? We need a statement on that right away."

The president nodded, sat up tall and took a deep breath. "Just say I know there are some very fine demons in Hell."

CALL ME TITAN

ROBERT SILVERBERG

"**H**ow did *you* get loose?" the woman who was Aphrodite asked me.

"It happened. Here I am."

"Yes," she said. "You. Of all of them, you. In this lovely place." She waved at the shining sun-bright sea, the glittering white stripe of the beach, the whitewashed houses, the bare brown hills. A lovely place, yes, this isle of Mykonos. "And what are you going to do now?"

"What I was created to do," I told her. "*You* know."

She considered that. We were drinking ouzo on the rocks, on the hotel patio, beneath a hanging array of fishermen's nets. After a moment she laughed, that irresistible tinkling laugh of hers, and clinked her glass against mine.

"Lots of luck," she said.

That was Greece. Before that was Sicily, and the mountain, and the eruption...

The mountain had trembled and shaken and belched, and the red streams of molten fire began to flow downward from the ashen top, and in the first ten minutes of the eruption six little towns around the slopes were wiped out. It happened just that fast. They shouldn't have been there, but they were, and then they weren't. Too bad for them. But it's always a mistake to buy real estate on Mount Etna.

The lava was really rolling. It would reach the city of Catania in a couple of hours and take out its whole northeastern quarter, and all of Sicily would be in mourning the next day. Some eruption. The biggest of all time, on this island where big eruptions have been making the news since the dinosaur days.

As for me, I couldn't be sure what was happening up there at the summit, not yet. I was still down deep, way down, three miles from sunlight.

But in my jail cell down there beneath the roots of the giant volcano that is called Mount Etna I could tell from the shaking and the noise and the heat that this one was something special. That the prophesied Hour of Liberation had come round at last for me, after five hundred centuries as the prisoner of Zeus.

I stretched and turned and rolled over, and sat up for the first time in fifty thousand years.

Nothing was pressing down on me.

Ugly limping Hephaestus, my jailer, had set up his forge right on top of me long ago, his heavy anvils on my back. And had merrily hammered bronze and iron all day and all night for all he was worth, that clomp-legged old master craftsman. Where was Hephaestus now? Where were his anvils?

Not on me. Not any longer.

That was *good*, that feeling of nothing pressing down.

I wriggled my shoulders. That took time. You have a lot of shoulders to wriggle, when you have a hundred heads, give or take three or four.

"Hephaestus?" I yelled, yelling it out of a hundred mouths at once. I felt the mountain shivering and convulsing above me, and I knew that my voice alone was enough to make great slabs of it fall off and go tumbling down, down, down.

No answer from Hephaestus. No clangour of his forge, either. He just wasn't there anymore.

I tried again, a different, greater name.

"Zeus?"

Silence.

"You hear me, Zeus?"

No reply.

"Where the hell are you? Where is everybody?"

All was silence, except for the hellish roaring of the volcano.

Well, okay, *don't* answer me. Slowly I got to my feet, extending myself to my full considerable height. The fabric of the mountain gave way for me. I have that little trick.

Another good feeling, that was, rising to an upright position. Do you know what it's like, not being allowed to stand, not even once, for fifty thousand years? But of course you don't, little ones. How could you?

One more try. *"ZEUS?"*

All my hundred voices crying his name at once, fortissimo fortissimo. A chorus of booming echoes. Every one of my heads had grown back, over the years. I was healed of all that Zeus had done to me. That was especially good, knowing that I was healed. Things had looked really bad, for a while.

Well, no sense just standing there and caterwauling, if nobody was going to answer me back. This was the Hour of Liberation, after all. I was free—my chains fallen magically away, my heads all sprouted again. Time to get out of here. I started to move.

Upward. Outward.

I moved up through the mountain's bulk as though it was so much air. The rock was nothing to me. Unimpeded I rose past the coiling internal chambers through which the lava was racing up toward the summit vent, and came out into the sunlight, and clambered up the snow-kissed slopes of the mountain to the ash-choked summit itself, and stood there right in the very center of the eruption as the volcano puked its blazing guts out. I grinned a hundred big grins on my hundred faces, with hot fierce winds swirling like swords around my head and torrents of lava flowing down all around me.

The view from up there was terrific. And what a fine feeling that was, just looking around at the world again after all that time underground.

There below me off to the east was the fish-swarming sea. Over there behind me, the serried tree-thickened hills. Above me, the fire-hearted sun.

What beautiful sights they all were!

"Hoo-*ha!*" I cried.

My jubilant roar went forth from that lofty mountaintop in Sicily like a hundred hurricanes at once. The noise of it broke windows in Rome and flattened farmhouses in Sardinia and knocked over ten mosques deep in the Tunisian Sahara. But the real blast was aimed eastward across the water, over toward Greece, and it went across that peninsula like a scythe, taking out half the treetops from Agios Nikolaus on the Ionian side to Athens over on the Aegean, and kept on going clear into Turkey.

It was a little signal, so to speak. I was heading that way myself, with some very ancient scores to settle.

I started down the mountainside, fast. The lava surging all around my thudding feet meant nothing to me.

Call me Typhoeus. Call me Titan.

I suppose I might have attracted a bit of attention as I made my way down those fiery slopes and past all the elegant seaside resorts that now were going crazy with hysteria over the eruption, and went striding into the sea midway between Fiumefreddo and Taormina. I am, after all, something of a monster, by your standards: four hundred feet high, let us say, with all those heads, dragon heads at that, and eyes that spurt flame, and thick black bristles everywhere on my body and swarms of coiling vipers sprouting from my thighs. The gods themselves have been known to turn and run at the mere sight of me. Some of them, once upon a time, fled all the way to Egypt when I yelled "Boo!"

But perhaps the eruption and the associated earthquakes kept the people of eastern Sicily so very preoccupied just then that they didn't take time to notice what sort of being it was that was walking down the side of Mount Etna and perambulating off toward the sea. Or maybe they didn't believe their eyes. Or it could be that they simply nodded and said, "Sure. Why not?"

I hit the water running and put my heads down and swam swiftly Greeceward across the cool blue sea without even bothering to come up for breath. What would have been the point? The air behind me smelled of fire and brimstone. And I was in a hurry.

Zeus, I thought. *I'm coming to get you, you bastard!*

As I said, I'm a Titan. It's the family name, not a description. We Titans were the race of Elder Gods—the first drafts, so to speak, for the deities that you people would eventually worship—the ones that Zeus walloped into oblivion long before Bill Gates came down from Mount Sinai with MS-DOS. Long before Homer sang. Long before the Flood. Long before, as a matter of fact, anything that might mean anything to you.

Gaea was our mother. The Earth, in other words. The mother of us all, really.

In the early days of the world broad-bosomed Gaea brought forth all sorts of gods and giants and monsters. Out of her came far-seeing Uranus, the sky, and then he and Gaea created the first dozen Titans, Oceanus and Cronus and Rhea and that bunch.

The original twelve Titans spawned a lot of others: Atlas, who now holds up the world, and tricky Prometheus, who taught humans how to use fire and got himself the world's worst case of cirrhosis for his trouble, and silly scatterbrained Epimetheus, who had that thing with Pandora, and so on. There were snake-limbed giants like Porphyrion and Alcyoneus, and hundred-armed fifteen-headed beauties like Briareus and Cottus and Gyes, and other oversized folk like the three one-eyed Cyclopes, Arges of the storms and Brontes of the thunder and Steropes of the lightning, and so on. Oh, what a crowd we were!

The universe was our oyster, so I'm told. It must have been good times for all and sundry. I hadn't been born yet, in that era when Uranus was king.

But very early on there was that nasty business between Uranus and his son Cronus, which ended very badly for Uranus, the bloody little deal with the sharp sickle, and Cronus became the top god for a while, until he made the mistake of letting Zeus get born. That was it, for Cronus. In this business you have to watch out for overambitious sons. Cronus tried—he swallowed each of his children as they were born, to keep them from doing to him what he had done to Uranus—but Zeus, the last-born, eluded him. Very unfortunate for Cronus.

Family history. Dirty linen.

As for Zeus, who as you can see showed up on the scene quite late but eventually came to be in charge of things, he's my half-sister Rhea's son, so I suppose you'd call him my nephew. I call him my nemesis.

After Zeus had finished off Cronus he mopped up the rest of the Titans in a series of wild wars, thunderbolts ricocheting all over the place, the seas boiling, whole continents going up in flame. Some of us stayed neutral and some of us, I understand, actually allied themselves with him, but none of that made any difference. When all the shouting was over the whole pack of Titans were all prisoners in various disagreeable places, such as, for example, deep down underneath Mount Etna with the forge of Hephaestus sitting on your back; and Zeus and his outfit, Hades and Poseidon and Apollo and Aphrodite and the rest, ruled the roost.

I was Gaea's final experiment in maternity, the youngest of the Titans, born very late in the war with Zeus. Her final monster, some would say, because of my unusual looks and size. Tartarus was my father: the Underworld, he is. I was born restless. Dangerous, too. My job was to avenge the family against the outrages Zeus had perpetrated on the rest of us. I came pretty close, too.

And now I was looking for my second chance.

Greece had changed a lot since I last had seen it. Something called civilization had happened in the meanwhile. Highways, gas stations, telephone poles, billboards, high-rise hotels, all those nice things.

Still and all, it didn't look so very bad. That killer blue sky with the golden blink in it, the bright sparkle of the low rolling surf, the white-walled cubes of houses climbing up the brown knifeblade hillsides: a handsome land, all things considered.

I came ashore at the island of Zakynthos on the Peloponnesian coast. There was a pleasant waterfront town there with an old fortress on a hilltop and groves of olives and cypresses all around. The geological disturbances connected with my escape from my prison cell beneath Mount Etna did not appear to have done much damage here.

I decided that it was probably not a great idea to let myself be seen in my actual form, considering how monstrous I would look to mortal eyes and the complications that that would create for me. And so, as I approached the land, I acquired a human body that I found swimming a short way off shore at one of the beachfront hotels.

It was a serviceable, athletic he-body, a lean, trim one, not young but full of energy, craggy-faced, a long jaw and a long sharp nose and a high forehead. I checked out his mind. Bright, sharp, observant. And packed with data, both standard and quirkily esoteric. All that stuff about Bill Gates and Homer and high-rises and telephone poles: I got that from him. And how to behave like a human being. And a whole lot more, all of which I suspected would be useful to acquire.

A questing, creative mind. A good person. I liked him. I decided to use him.

In half a wink I transformed myself into a simulacrum of him and went on up the beach into town, leaving him behind just as he had been, all unknowing. The duplication wouldn't matter. Nobody was likely to care that there were two of him wandering around Greece at the same time, unless they saw both of us at the same moment, which wasn't going to happen.

I did a little further prowling behind his forehead and learned that he was a foreigner in Greece, a tourist. Married, three children, a house on a hillside in a dry country that looked a little like Greece, but was far away. Spoke a language called English, knew a smattering of other tongues. Not much Greek. That would be okay: I have my ways of communicating.

To get around the countryside properly, I discovered, I was going to need land-clothing, money, and a passport. I took care of these matters. Details like those don't pose problems for such as we.

Then I went rummaging in his mind to see whether he had

any information in there about the present whereabouts of Zeus.

It was a very orderly mind. He had Zeus filed under "Greek Mythology."

Mythology?

Yes. Yes! He knew about Gaea, and Uranus, and the overthrow of Uranus by Cronus. He knew about the other Titans, at any rate some of them—Prometheus, Rhea, Hyperion, Iapetus. He knew some details about a few of the giants and miscellaneous hundred-armed monsters, and about the war between Zeus and the Titans and the Titans' total downfall, and the takeover by the big guy and his associates, Poseidon and Apollo and Ares & Company. But these were all stories to him. Fables. *Mythology.*

I confess I looked in his well-stocked mental archives for myself, Typhoeus—even a Titan has some vanity, you know— but all I found was a reference that said, "Typhon, child of Hera, is often confused with the earlier Titan Typhoeus, son of Gaea and Tartarus."

Well, yes. The names are similar; but Typhon was the bloated she-dragon that Apollo slew at Delphi, and what does that have to do with me?

That was bad, very bad, to show up in this copiously furnished mind only as a correction of an erroneous reference to someone else. Humiliating, you might actually say. I am not as important as Cronus or Uranus in the scheme of things, I suppose, but I did have my hour of glory, that time I went up against Zeus single-handed and came very close to defeating him. But what was even worse than such neglect, far worse, was to have the whole splendid swaggering tribe of us, from the great mother Gaea and her heavenly consort down to the merest satyr and wood-nymph, tucked away in there as so much mythology.

What had happened to the world, and to its gods, while I lay writhing under Etna?

Mount Olympus seemed a reasonable first place for me to go to look for some answers.

I was at the absolute wrong end of Greece for that: down in the southwestern corner, whereas Olympus is far up in the northeast. All decked out in my new human body and its new human clothes, I caught a hydrofoil ferry to Patra, on the mainland, and another ferry across the Gulf of Corinth to Nafpaktos, and then, by train and bus, made my way up toward Thessaly, where Olympus is. None of these places except Olympus itself had been there last time I was in Greece, nor were there such things as trains or ferries or buses then. But I'm adaptable. I am, after all, an immortal god. A sort of a god, anyway.

It was interesting, sitting among you mortals in those buses and trains. I had never paid much attention to you in the old days, any more than I would give close attention to ants or bumblebees or cockroaches. Back there in the early ages of the world, humans were few and far between, inconsequential experimental wildlife. Prometheus made you, you know, for some obscure reason of his own: made you out of assorted dirt and slime, and breathed life into you, and turned you loose to decorate the landscape. You certainly did a job of decorating it, didn't you?

Sitting there among you in those crowded garlicky trains, breathing your exhalations and smelling your sweat, I couldn't help admiring the persistence and zeal with which you people had covered so much of the world with your houses, your highways, your shopping malls, your amusement parks, your stadiums, your power-transmission lines, and your garbage. Especially your garbage. Very few of these things could be considered any sort of an improvement over the basic virgin terrain, but I had to give you credit for effort, anyway. Prometheus, wherever he might be now, would surely be proud of you.

But where *was* Prometheus? Still chained up on that mountaintop, with Zeus's eagle gnawing away on his liver?

I roamed the minds of my traveling companions, but they weren't educated people like the one I had chanced upon at that beach, and they knew zero about Prometheus. Or anybody else of my own era, for that matter, with the exception of Zeus and Apollo and Athena and a few of the other latecomer gods. Who also were mere mythology to them. Greece had different gods these days, it seemed. Someone called Christos had taken over here. Along with his father and his mother, and assorted lesser deities whose relation to the top ones was hard to figure out.

Who were these new gods? Where had they come from? I was pleased by the thought that Zeus had been pushed aside by this Christos the way he had nudged old Cronus off the throne, but how had it happened? When?

Would I find Christos living on top of Mount Olympus in Zeus's old palace?

Well, no. I very shortly discovered that nobody was living on top of Olympus at all.

The place had lost none of its beauty, infested though modern-day Greece is by you and your kind. The enormous plateau on which the mountain stands is still unspoiled; and Olympus itself rises as ever in that great soaring sweep above the wild, desolate valley, the various summits forming a spectacular natural amphitheater and the upper tiers of rock splendidly shrouded by veils of cloud.

There are some roads going up, now. In the foothills I hired a car and a driver to take me through the forests of chestnut and fir to a refuge hut two thirds of the way up that is used by climbers, and there I left my driver, telling him I would go the rest of the way myself. He gave me a peculiar look, I suppose because I was wearing the wrong kind of clothing for climbing, and had no mountaineering equipment with me.

When he was gone, I shed my borrowed human form and rose up once again taller than the tallest tree in the world, and gave myself a set of gorgeous black-feathered wings as well, and went wafting up into that region of clean, pure air where Zeus had once had his throne.

No throne. No Zeus.

My cousins the giants Otus and Ephialtes had piled Mount Pelion on top of Mount Ossa to get up here during the war of the gods, and were flung right back down again. But I had the place to myself, unchallenged. I hovered over the jagged fleece-kissed peaks of the ultimate summit, spiraling down through the puffs of white cloud, ready for battle, but no battle was offered me.

"Zeus? Zeus?"

Once I had stood against him hissing terror from my grim jaws, and my eyes flaring gorgon lightning that had sent his fellow gods packing in piss-pants terror. But Zeus had withstood me, then. He blasted me with sizzling thunderbolts and seared me to an ash, and hurled me to rack and ruin; and jammed what was left of me down under Mount Etna amid rivers of fire, with the craftsman god Hephaestus piling the tools of his workshop all over me to hold me down, and there I lay for those fifty thousand years, muttering to myself, until I had healed enough to come forth.

I was forth now, all right, and looking for a rematch. Etna had vomited rivers of fire all over the fair plains of Sicily, and I was loose upon the world; but where was my adversary?

"Zeus!" I cried, into the emptiness.

I tried the name of Christos, too, just to see if the new god would answer. No go. He wasn't there either. Olympus was as stunning as ever, but nobody godly seemed to have any use for it these days.

I flew back down to the Alpine Club shelter and turned myself back into the lean-shanked American tourist with the high forehead and the long nose. I think three hikers may have seen me make the transformation, for as I started down the slope I came upon them standing slackjawed and goggle-eyed, as motionless as though Medusa had smitten them into stone.

"Hi, there, fellas," I called to them. "Have a nice day!"

They just gaped. I descended the fir-darkened mountainside to the deep-breasted valley, and just like any hungry mortal I ate dolmades and keftedes and moussaka in a little taverna I found down there, washing it down with a few kilos of retsina. And then, not so much like any mortal, I walked halfway across the country to Athens. It took me a goodly number of days, resting only a few hours every night. The body I had copied was a fundamentally sturdy one, and of course I had bolstered it a little.

A long walk, yes. But I was beginning to comprehend that there was no need for me to hurry, and I wanted to see the sights.

Athens was a horror. It was the kingdom of Hades risen up to the surface of the world. Noise, congestion, all-around general grittiness, indescribable ugliness, everything in a miserable state of disrepair, and the air so thick with foul vapor that you could scratch your initials in it with your fingernails, if you had initials, if you had fingernails.

I knew right away I wasn't going to find any members of the old pantheon in this town. No deity in his right mind would want to spend ten minutes here. But Athens is the city of Athena, and Athena is the goddess of knowledge, and I thought there might be a possibility that somewhere here in her city that I would be able to learn how and why and when the assorted divinities of Greece had made the transition from omnipotence to mythology, and where I might find them (or at least the one I was looking for) now.

I prowled the nightmare streets. Dust and sand and random blocks of concrete everywhere, rusting metal girders standing piled for no particular reason by the side of the road, crumbling buildings. Traffic, frantic and fierce: what a mistake giving up the ox-cart had been! Cheap, tacky shops. Skinny long-legged cats hissed at me. They knew what I was. I hissed right back. We understood each other, at least.

Up on a hilltop in the middle of everything, a bunch of ruined marble temples. The Acropolis, that hilltop is, the highest and holiest place in town. The temples aren't bad, as mortal buildings go, but in terrible shape, fallen columns scattered hither and yon, caryatids eroded to blurs by the air pollution. Why are you people such dreadful custodians of your own best works?

I went up there to look around, thinking I might find some lurking god or demigod in town on a visit. I stood by the best of the tumbledown temples, the one called the Parthenon, and listened to a little man with big eyeglasses who was telling a group of people who looked exactly like him how the building had looked when it was new and Athena was still in town. He spoke a language that my host body didn't understand at all, but I made a few adjustments and comprehended. So many languages, you mortals! We all spoke the same language, and that was good enough for us; but we were only gods, I suppose.

When he was through lecturing them about the Parthenon, the tour guide said, "Now we will visit the Sanctuary of Zeus. This way, please."

The Sanctuary of Zeus was just back of the Parthenon, but there really wasn't very much left of it. The tour guide did a little routine about Zeus as father of the gods, getting six facts out of every five wrong.

"Let me tell you a few things about Zeus," I wanted to say, but I didn't. "How he used to cheat at cards, for instance. And the way he couldn't keep his hands off young girls. Or, maybe, the way he bellowed and moaned the first time he and I fought, when I tangled him in the coils of my snakes and laid him low, and cut the tendons of his hands and feet to keep him from getting rambunctious, and locked him up in that cave in Cilicia."

I kept all that to myself. These people didn't look like they'd care to hear any commentary from a stranger. Anyway, if I told that story I'd feel honour bound to go on and explain how that miserable sneak Hermes crept into the cave when I wasn't looking and patched Zeus up—and then how, once Zeus was on his feet again, he came after me and let me have it with such a blast of lightning-bolts that I was fried halfway to a crisp and wound up spending the next few epochs as a prisoner down there under Etna.

A dispiriting place, the Acropolis.

I went slinking down and over to the Plaka, which is the neighbourhood in back of it, for some lunch. Human bodies need to be fed again and again, all day long. Swordfish grilled on skewers with onions and tomatoes; more retsina; fruit and cheese. All right. Not bad. Then to the National Museum, a two-hour walk, sweat-sticky and dusty. Where I looked at broken statues and bought a guidebook that told me about the gods whose statues these were. Not even close to the actualities, any of them. Did they seriously think that brawny guy with the beard was Poseidon? And the woman with the tin hat, Athena? And that blowhard—Zeus? Don't make me laugh. Please. My laughter destroys whole cities.

Nowhere in the whole museum were there any representations of Titans. Just Zeus, Apollo, Aphrodite, Poseidon, and the rest of them, the junior varsity, the whole mob of supplanters, over and over and over. It was as if we didn't count at all in the historical record.

That hurt. I was in one hell of a sour mood when I left the museum.

There was a Temple of Olympian Zeus in town, the guide-book said, somewhere back in the vicinity of the Acropolis. I kept hoping that I would find some clue to Zeus's present place of residence at one of the sites that once had been sacred to him. A vestige, a lingering whiff of divinity.

But the Temple of Olympian Zeus was nothing but an incomplete set of ruined columns, and the only whiff I picked up there was the whiff of mortality and decay. And now it was getting dark and the body I was inhabiting was hungry again. Back to the Plaka; grilled meat, wine, a sweet pudding.

Afterwards, as I roamed the winding streets leading down to the newer part of the city with no special purpose in mind, a feeble voice out of a narrow alley said, in the native language of my host body, "Help! Oh, please, help!"

I was not put into this world for the purpose of helping anyone. But the body that I had duplicated in order to get around in modern Greece was evidently the body of a kindly and responsible person, because his reflexes took over instantly, and I found myself heading into that alleyway to see what aid I could render the person who was so piteously crying out.

Deep in the shadows I saw someone—a woman, I realised— lying on the ground in what looked like a pool of blood. I went to her side and knelt by her, and she began to mutter something in a bleary way about being attacked and robbed.

"Can you sit up?" I said, slipping my arm around her back. "It'll be easier for me to carry you if—"

Then I felt a pair of hands grasping me by the shoulders, not gently, and something hard and sharp pressing against the middle of my back, and the supposedly bloodied and battered woman I was trying to help rolled deftly out of my grasp and stepped back without any trouble at all, and a disagreeable rasping voice at my left ear said quietly, "Just give us your wristwatch and your wallet and you won't get hurt at all."

I was puzzled for a moment. I was still far from accustomed to human ways, and it was often necessary to peer into my host-mind to find out what was going on.

Quickly, though, I came to understand that there was such a thing as crime in your world, and that some of it was being tried on me at this very moment. The woman in the alley was bait; I was the prey; two accomplices had been lurking in the shadows.

I suppose I could have given them my wristwatch and wallet without protest, and let them make their escape. What did a wristwatch mean to me? And I could create a thousand new wallets just like the one I had, which I had created also, after all. As for harm, they could do me none with their little knife. I had survived even the lightnings of Zeus. Perhaps I should have reacted with godlike indifference to their little attempt at mugging me.

But it had been a long dreary discouraging day, and a hot one, too. The air was close and vile-smelling. Maybe I had allowed my host body to drink a little too much retsina with dinner. In any event, godlike indifference was not what I displayed just then. Mortal petulance was more like the appropriate term.

"Behold me, fools," I said.

I let them see my true form.

There I was before them, sky-high, mountainous, a horrendous gigantic figure of many heads and fiery eyes and thick black bristles and writhing viperish excrescences, a sight to make even gods quail.

Of course, inasmuch as I'm taller than the tallest tree and appropriately wide, manifesting myself in such a narrow alleyway might have posed certain operational problems. But I have access to dimensions unavailable to you, and I made room for myself there with the proper interpenetrational configurations. Not that it mattered to the three muggers, because they were dead of shock the moment they saw me towering before them.

I raised my foot and ground them into the pavement like noxious vermin.

Then, in the twinkling of an eye, I was once more a slender, lithe middle-aged American tourist with thinning hair and a kindly smile, and there were three dark spots on the pavement of the alley, and that was that.

It was, I admit, overkill.

But I had had a trying day. In fact, I had had a trying fifty thousand years.

Athens had been so hellish that it put me in mind of the authentic kingdom of Hades, and so that was my next destination, for I thought I might get some answers down there among the dead. It wasn't much of a trip, not for me. I opened a vortex for myself and slipped downward and there right in front of me were the black poplars and willows of the Grove of Persephone, with Hades' Gate just behind it.

"Cerberus?" I called. "Here, doggy doggy doggy! Good Cerberus! Come say hello to Daddy!"

Where was he, my lovely dog, my own sweet child? For I myself was the progenitor of the three-headed guardian of the gate of Hell, by virtue of my mating with my sister, Tartarus and Gaea's scaly-tailed daughter Echidna. We made the Harpies too, did Echidna and I, and the Chimera, and Scylla, and also the Hydra, a whole gaudy gorgeous brood of monsters. But of all my children I was always most fond of Cerberus, for his loyalty. How I loved to see him come running toward me when I called! What pleasure I took in his serpent-bristled body, his voice like clanging bronze, his slavering jaws that dripped black venom!

This day, though, I wandered dogless through the Underworld. There was no sign of Cerberus anywhere, no trace even of his glittering turds. Hell's Gate stood open and the place was deserted. I saw nothing of Charon the boatman of the Styx, nor Hades and Queen Persephone, nor any members of their court, nor the spirits of the dead who should have been in residence here. An abandoned warehouse, dusty and empty. Quickly I fled toward the sunshine.

The island of Delos was where I went next, looking for Apollo. Delos is, or was, his special island, and Apollo had always struck me as the coolest, most level-headed member of the Zeus bunch. Perhaps he had survived whatever astounding debacle it was that had swept the Olympian gods away. And, if so, maybe he could give me a clue to Zeus's current location.

Big surprise! I went to Delos, but no Apollo.

It was yet another dismal disillusioning journey through the tumbledown sadness that is Greece. This time I flew; not on handsome black-feathered wings, but on a clever machine, a metal tube called an airplane, full of travelers looking more or less like me in my present form. It rose up out of Athens in a welter of sound and fury and took up a course high above the good old wine-dark sea, speckled with tawny archipelagos, and in very short order came down on a small dry island to the south. This island was called Mykonos, and there I could buy myself passage in one of the boats that made outings several times a day to nearby Delos.

Delos was a dry rubble-field, strewn with fragments of temples, their columns mostly broken off close to the ground. Some marble lions were still intact, lean and vigilant, crouching on their hind legs. They looked hungry. But there wasn't much else to see. The place had the parched gloom of death about it, the bleak aura of extinction.

I returned to Mykonos on the lunchtime boat, and found myself lodgings in a hillside hotel a short distance outside the pretty little narrow-streeted shorefront town. I ordered me some more mortal food and drank mortal drink. My borrowed body needed such things.

It was on Mykonos that I met Aphrodite.

Or, rather, she met me.

I was sitting by myself, minding my own business, in the hotel's outdoor bar, which was situated on a cobblestoned patio bedecked with mosaics and hung with nets and oars and other purported fishing artefacts. I was on my third ouzo of the hour, which possibly was a bit much for the capacities of the body I was using, and I was staring down the hillside pensively at, well, what I have to call the wine-dark sea. (Greece brings out the cliches in anyone. Why should I resist?)

A magnificent long-legged full-bodied blonde woman came over to me and said, in a wonderfully throaty, husky voice, "New in town, sailor?"

I stared at her, astounded.

There was the unmistakable radiance of divinity about her. My Geiger counter of godliness was going clickity-clack, full blast. How could I have failed to pick up her emanations the moment I arrived on Mykonos? But I hadn't, not until she was standing right next to me. She had picked up mine, though.

"Who are you?" I blurted.

"Won't you ask a lady to sit down, even?"

I jumped to my feet like a nervous schoolboy, hauled a deck hair scrapingly across and positioned it next to mine, and bowed her into it. Then I wigwagged for a waiter. "What do you want to drink?" I rasped. My throat was dry. Nervous schoolboy, yes, indeed.

"I'll have what you're having."

"*Parakolo*, ouzo on the rocks," I told the waiter.

She had showers of golden hair tumbling to shoulder length, and catlike yellow eyes, and full ripe lips that broke naturally into the warmest of smiles. The aroma that came from her was one of young wine and green fields at sunrise and swift-coursing streams, but also of lavender and summer heat, of night rain, of surging waves, of midnight winds.

I knew I was consorting with the enemy. I didn't care.

"Which one are you?" I said again.

"Guess."

"Aphrodite would be too obvious. You're probably Ares, or Hephaestus, or Poseidon."

She laughed, a melodic cadenza of merriment that ran right through the scale and into the infra-voluptuous. "You give me too much credit for deviousness. But I like your way of thinking. Ares in drag, really? Poseidon with a close shave? Hephaestus with a blonde wig?" She leaned close. The fragrance of her took on hurricane intensity. "You were right the first time."

"Aphrodite."

"None other. I live in Los Angeles now. Taking a little holiday in the mother country. And you? You're one of the old ones, aren't you?"

"How can you tell?"

"The archaic emanation you give off. Something out of the pre-Olympian past." She clinked the ice-cubes thoughtfully in her glass, took a long pull of the ouzo, stared me straight in the eyes. "Prometheus? Tethys?" I shook my head. "Someone of that clan, though. I thought all of you old ones were done for a long time ago. But there's definitely a Titan vibe about you. Which one, I wonder? Most likely one of the really strange ones. Thaumas? Phorcys?"

"Stranger than those," I said.

She took a few more guesses. Not even close.

"Typhoeus," I told her finally.

We walked into town for dinner. People turned to look at us in the narrow streets. At her, I mean. She was wearing a filmy orange sun-dress with nothing under it and when you were east of her on a westbound street you got quite a show.

"You really don't think that I'm going to find Zeus?" I asked her.

"Let's say you have your work cut out for you."

"Well, so be it. I *have* to find him."

"Why is that?"

"It's my job," I said. "There's nothing personal about it. I'm the designated avenger. It's my sole purpose in existence: to punish Zeus for his war against the children of Gaea. You know that."

"The war's been over a long time, Typhoeus. You might as well let bygones be bygones. Anyway, it's not as though Zeus got to enjoy his victory for long." We were in the middle of the maze of narrow winding streets that is Mykonos Town. She pointed to a cheerful little restaurant called Catherine's. "Let's go in here. I ate here last night and it was pretty good."

We ordered a bottle of white wine. "I like the body you found for yourself," she said. "Not particularly handsome, no, but *pleasing*. The eyes are especially nice. Warm and trustworthy, but also keen, penetrating."

I would not be drawn away from the main theme. "What happened to the Olympians?" I asked.

"Died off, most of them. One by one. Of neglect. Starvation."

"Immortal gods don't die."

"Some do, some don't. You know that. Didn't Argus of the Hundred Eyes kill your very own Echidna? And did she come back to life?"

"But the major gods—"

"Even if they don't die, they can be forgotten, and the effect's pretty much the same. While you were locked up under Etna, new gods came in. There wasn't even a battle. They just moved in, and we had to move along. We disappeared entirely."

"So I've noticed."

"Yes. Totally out of business. You've seen the shape our temples are in? Have you seen anybody putting out burnt offerings to us? No, no, it's all over for us, the worship, the sacrifices. Has been for a long time. We went into exile, the whole kit and kaboodle of us, scattered across the world. I'm sure a lot of us simply died, despite that theoretical immortality of ours. Some hung on, I suppose. But it's a thousand years since the last time I saw any of them."

"Which ones did you see then?"

"Apollo—he was getting gray and paunchy. And I caught sight of Hermes, once—I think it was Hermes—slow and short-winded, and limping like Hephaestus."

"And Zeus?" I asked. "You never ran into him anywhere, after you all left Olympus?"

"No. Never even once."

I pondered that. "So how did *you* manage to stay so healthy?"

"I'm Aphrodite. The life-force. Beauty. Passion. Those things don't go out of fashion for long. I've done all right for myself, over the years."

"Ah. Yes. Obviously you have."

The waitress fluttered around us. I was boiling with questions to ask Aphrodite, but it was time to order, and that was what we did. The usual Greek things, stuffed grape leaves, grilled fish, overcooked vegetables. Another bottle of wine. My head was pulsating. The restaurant was small, crowded, a whirlpool of noise. The nearness of Aphrodite was overwhelming. I felt dizzy. It was a surprisingly pleasant sensation.

I said, after a time, "I'm convinced that Zeus is still around somewhere. I'm going to find him and this time I'm going to whip his ass and put *him* under Mount Etna."

"It's amazing how much like a small boy an immortal being can be. Even one as huge and frightful as you."

My face turned hot. I said nothing.

"Forget Zeus," she urged. "Forget Typhoeus, too. Stay human. Eat, drink, be merry." Her eyes were glistening. I felt as if I were falling forward, tumbling into the sweet chasm between her breasts. "We could take a trip together. I'd teach you how to enjoy yourself. How to enjoy me, too. Tell me: have you ever been in love?"

"Echidna and I—"

"Echidna! Yes! You and she got together and made a bunch of hideous monsters like yourselves, with too many heads and drooling fangs. I don't mean Echidna. This is Earth, here and now. I'm a woman now and you're a man."

"But Zeus—"

"*Zeus*," she said scornfully. She made the name of the Lord of Olympus sound like an obscenity.

We finished eating and I paid the check and we went outside into the mild, breezy Mykonos night, strolling for fifteen or twenty minutes, winding up finally in a dark, deserted part of the town, a warehouse district down by the water, where the street was no more than five feet wide and empty shuttered buildings with whitewashed walls bordered us on both sides.

She turned to me there and pulled me abruptly up against her. Her eyes were bright with mischief. Her lips sought mine. With a little hissing sound she nudged me backward until I was leaning against a wall, and she was pressing me tight, and currents of energy that could have fried a continent were passing between us. I think there could have been no one, not man nor god, who would not have wanted to trade places with me just then.

"Quickly! The hotel!" she whispered.

"The hotel, yes."

We didn't bother to walk. That would have taken too long. In a flash we vanished ourselves from that incomprehensible tangle of maze-like streets and reappeared in her room at our hotel, and from then to dawn she and I generated such a delirium of erotic force that the entire island shook and shivered with the glorious sturm and drang of it. We heaved and thrust and moaned and groaned, and rivers of sweat ran from our bodies and our hearts pounded and thundered and our eyes rolled in our heads from giddy exhaustion, for we allowed ourselves the luxury of mortal limitations for the sake of the mortal joy of transcending those limitations. But because we *weren't* mortal we also had the option of renewing our strength whenever we had depleted it, and we exercised that option many a time before rosy-fingered dawn came tiptoeing up over the high-palisaded eastern walls.

Naked, invisible to prying eyes, Aphrodite and I walked then hand in hand along the morning-shimmering strand of the fish-swarming sea, and she murmured to me of the places we would go, the things we would experience.

"The Taj Mahal," she said. "And the summer palace at Udaipur. Persepolis and Isfahan in springtime. Baalbek. Paris, of course. Carcassonne. Iguazu Falls, and the Blue Mosque, and the Fountains of the Blue Nile. We'll make love in the Villa of Tiberius on Capri—and between the paws of the Sphinx—and in the snow on top of Mount Everest—"

"Yes," I said. "Yes. Yes. Yes. Yes."

And what I was thinking was, *Zeus. Zeus. Zeus. Zeus.*

And so we travel about the world together, Aphrodite and I, seeing the things in it that are beautiful, and there are many of those; and so she distracts me from my true task. For the time being. It is very pleasant, traveling with Aphrodite; and so I permit myself to be distracted this way.

But I have not forgotten my purpose. And this is my warning to the world.

I am a restless being, a mighty thrusting force. I was created that way. My adversary doesn't seem currently to be around. But Zeus is here somewhere. I know he is. He wears a mask. He disguises himself as a mortal, either because it amuses him to do so, or because he has no choice, for there is something in the world of which he is afraid, something from which he must hide himself, some god greater even than Zeus, as Zeus was greater than Cronus and Cronus was greater than Uranus.

But I will find him. And when I do, I will drop this body and take on my own form again. I will stand mountain-high, and you will see my hundred heads, and my fires will flash and range. And Zeus and I will enter into combat once more, and this time I will surely win.

It will happen.

I promise you that, O small ones. I warn you. It will happen.

You will tremble then. I'm sorry for that. The mind that came with this body I wear now has taught me something about compassion; and so I regret the destruction I will inevitably visit upon you, because it cannot be avoided, when Zeus and I enter into our struggle. You have my sincerest apologies, in advance. Protect yourselves as best you can. But for me there can be no turning away from my task.

Zeus? This is Typhoeus the Titan who calls you!

Zeus, where are you?

DOCTOR WEIRD: '*THE SWORD AND THE SPIDER*'

SCRIPT: GEORGE R. R. MARTIN
ART: JIM STARLIN AND HOWARD KELTNER

DR WEIRD CREATED BY HOWARD KELTNER

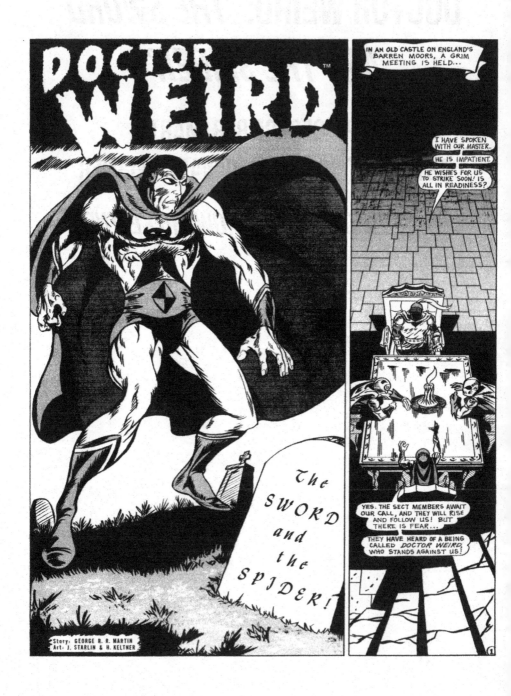

IT IS WELL! HE IS NECESSARY TO THE PLAN. THE CURSE PLACED UPON OUR MASTER DOTH QUELL HIS POWER UNTIL HIS CHAMPION SHALL DESTROY A CHAMPION OF GOOD! ONLY THEN MAY OUR MASTER REGAIN HIS FORMER GLORY SO THAT THE SECT CAN RISE AGAIN, AND DOMINION OVER ALL THE EARTH PASS INTO OUR HANDS!

THIS DOCTOR WEIRD, WHO IS THE PROTECTOR OF THE MORTALS, IS THE CHAMPION OF GOOD WE SEEK. BY DEFEATING HIM, WE SHALL DISPOSE OF OUR CHIEF OPPOSITION AND LIFT THE CURSE AT THE SAME TIME!

OUR MASTER HAS PREPARED TOOLS WITH WHICH TO DO THIS... AND HE HAS SELECTED HIS CHAMPION FROM AMONG US...

I AM THAT CHAMPION!

LATER, WHEN THE OTHERS HAVE GONE...

MASTER, I CALL! YOU HAVE PROMISED TOOLS WITH WHICH TO DEFEAT THE CHAMPION OF GOOD! I WOULD HAVE THEM NOW, FOR THE TIME IS AT HAND THAT I MIGHT LIFT THE CURSE!

FROM BEYOND LIVING FLAMES, A BOOMING VOICE RESPONDS...

I COME, URRATHON, MY SERVANT! MY PROMISE SHALL BE FULFILLED! ON THE MORROW YOU SHALL HAVE THE STEED I PROMISED YOU, A DEMON-BEAST FROM THE LAND OF ETERNAL NIGHT! CHOOSE FOR YOUR BATTLE THE OLD GRAVEYARD ON THE MOOR WHEN THE MOON IS FULL;

BUT, MASTER, HOW MUST I DESTROY THIS DOCTOR WEIRD?

HE IS A SPIRIT; I CANNOT SLAY ONE ALREADY DEAD!

YOU CAN DESTROY HIM, AND END HIS EXISTANCE FOR ALL ETERNITY! THE BITE OF THE DEMON-BEAST WILL DO THAT! BUT THERE IS MORE...

REJOICE, URRATHON, FOR NOW YOU CANNOT BE DEFEATED! BEHOLD-- I GIVE YOU DEMONREAVER, THE BLACK BLADE FORGED IN THE DEEPEST PITS OF THE ABYSS, BY MORTIS, THE DARK LORD! IT WILL SEVER BOTH FLESH AND SOUL...

--THERE AND THEN THE EVIL POWERS SHALL BE STRONGEST!

YOU SHALL HAVE A WEAPON-- A WEAPON SUCH AS EARTH HAS NEVER SEEN!

--AND LEAVE AGONY IN ITS WAKE! NO CHILD OF EARTH NOR DARKNESS CAN STAND BEFORE DEMONREAVER!

2

Panel 1: Undaunted, the Phantom Protector leaps to the attack...
"WHATEVER YOUR NAME, YOU ARE TRULY A FOOL!"
"MORTAL WEAPONS CANNOT HARM A SPIRIT!"

Panel 2: "HA, HA, HA, HA! BUT DEMONREAVER IS NO MORTAL WEAPON!"
"AAARRRGG! MY ARM!"

Panel 3: In pain and shock, the Astral Avenger recoils from the blow...
"MY SHOULDER! BURNING LIKE A MILLION FIRES OF FAKSTUR!"
"BUT I MUST REMAIN ALERT!"

Panel 4: Quickly Urrathon closes for the kill!
"NOW IS THE CURSE REMOVED!"

Panel 5: The shriek of DEMONREAVER cutting the air is like the wailing of lost souls!
"A PLAGUE UNTO YOU, SPIRIT! STAY STILL, THAT I MAY END YOUR MISERABLE LIFE!"

Panel 6: Gripping an immense tombstone, DOCTOR WEIRD strikes back...
"MY ARM IS... ALMOST USELESS!"
"YET I CAN STILL LAUNCH AN ATTACK!"

(5)

133

HOLDING OUT FOR A HERO

A JOE LEDGER/ROGUE TEAM INTERNATIONAL STORY

JONATHAN MABERRY

-1-

Sometimes I feel like that android guy at the end of *Bladerunner*. The dying one who tells the cop that he's seen things people wouldn't believe. Things only someone like him could have witnessed because normal people never have to. As existential statements go, it was a real heartbreaker.

I'm no android, but I get where he was coming from.

I've seen things, too. Things you wouldn't believe. Things you shouldn't have to know about and, thank god, mostly don't. How do I know you haven't? You can sleep at night.

I rarely do.

-2-

Phoenix House
Omfori Island, Greece

This one started fast and ugly and went downhill from there.

I was catching calls, meaning I was the officer of the day reading reports or watching surveillance videos to assess events and possible crimes. Most of it was stuff we turfed over to local law or Interpol. It's hard to put a label on exactly *our* kind of thing. Mostly it's terrorist groups who are using some kind of weird science weapon. Weaponized spongiform encephalitis, directed energy weapons, stealth tech for high-level assassinations. That kind of thing.

We used to be a bunch of science nerds and first-chair shooters for Uncle Sam, working for the Department of Military Sciences, one of those shadowy organizations you can be lucky you never heard of. But politics drove us off my home soil and now we operate as an independent group of nerds and shooters based on a small island in Greece. We are friendly and occasionally cooperative with the U.N., but we don't work for them, either. So far none of my gigs had required me to go back to the good ol' U.S. of A.

Our new group is RTI, or Rogue Team International and I'm a senior case manager. James Bond without the martinis, the cool cars, or the high likelihood of an STD from casual sex. We're a reactive group because we don't know who to spank until someone starts causing trouble on the playground.

Hence me sitting in a leather chair, drinking way too much coffee, eating Greek pastries, and looking for trouble in intelligence reports we, um, borrowed from agencies around the world. I may not have a cigarette lighter that shoots lasers but we do have a spiffy and very functional quantum computer named MindReader Q1 that does some ninja stealth shit to intrude into encrypted databases, poke around, steal a lot of shit, and then sneak out without leaving a single trace that it was ever there. Spiffy as fuck.

There was a lot to go through, so I skimmed sometimes, looking for stuff that was a bit out of the box.

What I found was something that smashed the damn box all to hell. It was a video of three men robbing a liquor store in my old hometown of Baltimore. The email was sent by a woman who used to run with my old DMS team but who was now a consultant for BPD. Her accompanying note read: "Joe...this looks like your kind of thing."

She wasn't wrong.

I watched the video six times, and then I made a lot of calls. An hour later I was on a fast jet to the States.

-3-

In Flight Over the Atlantic

While I flew, I reviewed the video again. It was grainy, no sound. Standard low-end store security camera. There was a dual feed, one of which was a continuous fixed-point monitor and the other a slightly better motion-activated high def camera that used a wide-angle lens and also tracked movement.

At 8:52 at night, local time in West Baltimore, three men walked into a liquor store. They did it right and waited for the last customer to leave. The store closed at nine and this was a Tuesday night, so there wasn't likely to be another customer. The register would be filled with the whole day's takings. I'd seen a hundred videos like this one when I was on the cops. Maybe a thousand. There's a pattern as predictable in its way as any standard business transaction.

One man goes in and picks out something to buy. Gum, maybe, or a can of Red Bull. Generally not liquor, unless it's a single can. He wears a hat with the brim pulled low, or a hoodie. Doesn't matter if this is happening in a black neighborhood, a white or brown one, or on fucking Mars. The pattern is old and it works most of the time.

The customer stalls the cashier, maybe saying something, dropping an item, or otherwise drawing his focus. That's when the other two come in, and as soon as the bell over the door jangles, the first guy has produced a handgun.

Same here. First guy had an Orioles cap *and* a hoodie, which shielded his face from the camera. He stood at an angle so the camera wouldn't catch even a glimpse. He was skinny and short and was probably a teenager trying to make his bones with a local gang. The other two were bigger, clearly older even though they had stocking caps on when they pushed through the door.

It was a no-win for the store owner—a Muslim wearing a kufi with a West African pattern—and he knew it. He didn't try to be John Wayne, either. He raised his hands and even though there was no sound it was obvious he was following verbal orders as he opened the register and put all the cash, including rolls of quarters, into a doubled-up plastic shopping bag. There was a brief altercation as he kept pointing to a small safe and shaking his head. Trying to sell the fiction that it was on a timer. That was bullshit, and everyone there knew it, but it was part of the drama. The man in the kufi finally relented after guns were jabbed toward him threateningly. He turned and began hastily working the safe's dial.

If the world had been more firmly on all four wheels, it might have ended right there. The money would be handed over, the three thugs would leave, cops and insurance companies would be called. The owner would be hurt and outraged, but also philosophical about such things. It's deeply unlikely this was his first robbery. And normally those three bad gangbangers would be snorting coke and getting blow jobs within the hour.

But that's not what happened.

The door opened and another masked man entered the store.

And when I say 'masked' I'm not talking about a ski mask or some Halloween costume thing. No. This guy wore a mask like the Lone goddamn Ranger.

He also wore a very tight sweatshirt and what looked like satin gym shorts over sweatpants. He wore fingerless black gloves and Doc Martens. And he wore a cape.

Yeah.

A fucking cape.

The cashier and the three thugs all turned to look at him and there was a beat where none of them did anything except stare. The newcomer had a big red circle on his chest in the middle of which was a stylized letter H.

I had two of my guys with me on the jet: Bradley Sims, known as Top, and Harvey Rabbit—yes, that's his real name—known as Bunny. They hunched over my right and left shoulders.

"Whoa," said Bunny in his Orange County meets Keanu Reeves accent, "am I seeing this shit right or did I just have a cerebral accident? Is that clown dressed up like some kind of superhero?"

"That's what I'm seeing, Farm Boy," said Top. Even though Bunny comes from Southern California he looks like a kid from one of those big midwestern farms. "Guy thinks he's Batman."

"Yeah," said Bunny, "and he's about to get his Bat-ass handed to him."

"Keep watching," I suggested.

The guy in the costume was making big, choppy gestures.

"Looks like he's telling them to drop their weapons," said Top.

"Dude must be out of his gourd," Bunny observed.

"Well, hell, Farm Boy, he's wearing a Batman suit."

"It's not actually a Batman suit. It's—"

What happened next cut his words off as surely as a hatchet. The tallest of the three robbers raised his pistol, aimed dead center of the newcomer, and shot him four times in the chest. Distance was maybe six feet. The gun was a Glock G19, firing 9mm rounds. All four shots hit center mass, driving the guy in the costume back.

Maybe three full inches.

And that was all.

"What the fuck...?" breathed Bunny.

Top said, "Even if he's wearing body armor how the hell is he still standing?"

"Keep watching," I said again.

The man in the mask stepped forward with blinding speed. He rushed the man who'd shot him and swung a big righthand punch. The shooter was street-savvy and brought his arm up, elbow bent, fist pressed against his head, hunching to let his skeleton absorb the force of that huge blow.

Except that's not how it played out.

The punch hit the bunched muscles of the shooter's upper arm and then the thief was flying through the air, his arm looking mashed, flattened. His body crashed into a row of gin and exploded it, sending glass, broken bottles, alcohol, and blood flying everywhere. The other two thieves dove for cover as their friend collapsed to the floor. He lay there and it took a moment to process the amount of damage he'd suffered. Top and Bunny bent close to the screen, gasping, making small sounds of denial. The shooter's fist had been braced against his skull, but now that side of the skull was a spongy mass of shattered bone, and the fist was buried three inches into it. It looked like every bone in his arm was broken and from the angle of the shooter's head it was obvious the blow had broken his neck. Above where he lay the heavy metal shelves were twisted out of shape.

From one blow of the human hand.

After taking four shots to the chest.

The tableau froze for maybe four full seconds.

And then there were flashes as both remaining pistols opened up. Spent brass bounced off the walls and the glass divider behind which the clerk stood and screamed. There was no sound, but you could see it—mouth wide, eyes bugging with absolute shock.

The masked man spun toward the other two shooters and we could catch a flash image of his face. He was either snarling or smiling. Hard to tell. It was not a sane look in either case.

He rushed the two shooters and began wailing on them. Big, heavy punches. Sickeningly fast. Impossibly hard. One blow caught the teenager on the hinge of his screaming jaw and literally tore it from the boy's face. It was a huge, rending, awful thing to see. For a horrified moment the boy stood there, his entire lower jaw nine feet down an aisle, his tongue lolling obscenely, blood pouring down his chest. The eyes were the worst, though, because in that moment he was totally aware of what had just happened. Maybe he thought he was tough or working on being tough; maybe doing crimes was his vision for getting out of the ghetto and into a life that mattered. But in that moment he was aware of everything in his past that had led to this moment, and could look past it to a future where—at best—he would be a broken and disfigured freak. A ruined person.

Then the guy in the costume hit him again, this time right on the bridge of the nose. Even in a silent movie you could almost hear the facial bones crack apart and the vertebrae cut through the spinal cord.

The other man, the last shooter, stood wide-legged, hands clutched to his stomach. To what was left of it after the attacker punched him hard enough to flatten every internal organ against the back wall of his spine. He vomited a quart of blood and debris and dropped to his knees. Then he fell sideways and lay still.

It was over. The punches weren't any kind of fancy martial arts moves. They were ordinary hooks. The speed, though.

The *power*.

The killer stood over the three corpses, chest heaving. We

could see sweat gleaming on his cheeks and his eyes were completely wild. He backed away from the carnage and looked down at his hands. Opening his fists, flexing his fingers, staring as if trying to understand what they were. Then he whirled and fled, hitting the door hard enough to rip the heavy-grade steel security door from reinforced hinges. The impact tore the hinges from the wood and ripped away half the frame.

The video feed changed to that of an exterior security camera on a 7-11 a block down the street. The man was running badly. Staggering and stumbling, as he tore the mask from his face. I froze one image and we could see that his eyes were wide with shock and wet with tears.

-4-

In Flight Over American Airspace

When he could speak, Bunny pointed to the screen and said, very slowly and deliberately, "What. The fuck. Was that?"

"If I saw this anywhere else," muttered Top, "I'd think it was a scene from a movie. One of those flicks that deconstruct the whole comic super-hero scene. *Watchmen* or some shit."

I nodded. "Doesn't sell the 'hero' part."

"He saved the cashier's life," said Bunny, but Top shook his head.

"No, he didn't," said Top. "Cashier was cooperating. Everyone there was handling it like a transaction. Another ten seconds and those boys'd be in the wind and nobody heading to the morgue."

"Agreed," I said.

"So, again I say," said Bunny, "what the fuck was that? What are we into here, boss?"

"This is the fifth such event," I said. "The first four were not picked up on cameras, and there were no fatalities. In the first, a carful of drug dealers was attacked. And by that, I mean someone—presumably our guy here—attacked the actual car on the street. Smashed the windows, mashed the hood, tore off two doors, and beat the crap out of five Vietnamese gang members. All of them wound up in the hospital, but only one in serious condition."

"So, this isn't race," said Top. "Those cats were Vietnamese and the ones on the video were black. What about the others?"

"Oh, our boy is an equal opportunity ass-kicker," I said. "Second time was up in Philly. He tore apart a group of guys, but the details on that are sketchy. Four men, three white and one black, were brought into Episcopal Hospital in Philadelphia with traumatic injuries. They were not, however, gang members. Not as such. They were private security for a biotech firm. The labs at the firm were trashed and the computer systems literally smashed to pieces. He also stole a lot of records—and in some cases whole steel file cabinets—as well as an SUV. Here's the odd part, though—none of the injured guards claim to remember who attacked them."

Bunny snorted. "Which sounds like bullshit."

"It is, and I'll get to that later," I said. "Next attack was another biotech firm, this time in Delaware, and that's where we get our first fatalities. Our boy apparently used information taken from the hit in Philly to get into a lab that was doing some stuff on a Department of Defense contract."

"Uh oh," said Bunny.

"Eight security personal on duty. And before you say anything, yes, that's a lot for a small lab. There was an altercation resulting in the lab burning to the ground. Three of the eight guards died in the fire, though autopsies suggest that they were already badly injured and dying when the place burned. The other five guards were admitted to local hospitals and all of them are in critical condition. None of them will talk to anyone except through the company lawyer, and he claims they were ambushed and don't recall specific details."

"Suspicious as fuck."

"More than you think," I said. "And the last one is more like the one we saw on the video. Our guy kicks in the door of a so-called social club—meaning Mafia counting house—and does a lot of damage to a whole slew of wiseguys. Leaves forty kilos of smack on the floor and a whole table piled high with bundles of cash, but sent another three guys to the morgue. Everyone associated with the social club has lawyered up and won't say a word. And, of course, a place like that had no internal cameras. And that brings us to that liquor store." I sat back. "I'm open to theories."

"One motherfucker's doing all this damage? How?" asked Top. "Is this some kind of special gear? Some kind of impact-absorbing mesh under that stupid outfit? They've been doing a lot with graphene composite nodules to absorb foot-pounds. And maybe ceramic plating."

"Yeah," said Bunny, "and maybe he's wearing one of those flexible-circuit undergarments that enhance performance."

"You really think some kind of mesh exoskeleton would give a man that much speed and strength?" I asked.

"Well, sure…though the fact that it's so thin doesn't sell that, come to think on it," admitted Bunny, shifting uncomfortably. He was six-and-a-half feet tall and carried more toned muscle than is necessary on any human being. "But something gave him some extra oomph."

"And those fingerless gloves," mused Top, "could be steel reinforced. Wouldn't explain all of what he did, but it could explain some of the damage."

He, like Bunny, sounded doubtful. I certainly was.

"I had Doc Holliday and her team go over the video very carefully," I said. Doc was the head of the RTI integrated sciences division. "And she doesn't think that the man was wearing any known kind of exoskeleton. He was wearing a very tight sweatshirt and you can see his own muscle definition. There aren't any bulges, particularly at wrist, elbow, or shoulder where servos would ordinarily be. And no visible bulges for power packs."

"Then what's her theory?" asked Top. "She's our resident super genius."

"Her considered opinion—and I quote—'It beats the shit out of me'."

The pilot *binged* to let us know we were beginning our descent into Baltimore.

"Okay," I said, "local law picked up a clean set of prints from the door handle and window glass of the liquor store. They ran them and got a hit, but that hit comes with complications."

"There are *always* complications," complained Bunny.

"Welcome to the real world," said Top.

"Here's what we know," I said and tapped a key on my laptop. It brought up photo of a young man of mixed race—Latino and black, with some Caucasian. A good-looking though ordinary face. You see a million guys like that all across the USA. Some pitted skin from old acne, a small scar through his left eyebrow, a chipped tooth. Hair was shaved high and tight in military fashion. "Meet Hector Brock. This was his induction photo when he enlisted in the army. He was nineteen then and is thirty-one now."

I showed them another photo of Brock. A bit older and dressed for desert combat. Carrying the full sixty-plus pounds of battle rattle—the equipment a soldier in Iraq, Afghanistan and similar areas had to hump over the sand wherever he went. Brock's face was more stern and confident here, and he had staff sergeant's stripes on his shoulder.

Next picture was a radical change from the last. It was of Brock, but only just. The man in the photo looked only barely human. He was half-cooked meat tangled in the burning wreck of what had been an army Humvee. Half his face was gone and there were deep lacerations in his skin. Most of his clothing and gear had been ripped away by the force of the IED that killed four of his friends and nearly killed Brock. One arm was a disjointed wreck of broken bones. The other hand was gone, along with most of his forearm.

Top and Bunny studied the image and then turned to me with identical frowns.

"Can't be the same guy," said Bunny. "Looks like Staff Sergeant Brock got himself blown to dog meat. I mean…did he even survive?"

"He did," I said.

"How?" asked Top, then his frown deepened. "Is this going to be some kind of *Six Million Dollar Man* bullshit up in here? I know they're doing all kinds of hinky cybernetic implant stuff at DARPA."

The Defense Advanced Research Projects Agency was a group

within the Department of Defense that was, in essence, mad scientists playing with government-level R&D budgets. They were the cats who invented the Internet as well as some stuff that was far more secret and far more dangerous.

"Here's where the math on that gets screwy," I said. "The prints the CSU folks lifted were from Brock's left hand."

They looked at the picture again and their frowns grew deeper still.

"Can't be," said Bunny. "That's the one he lost. With that much tissue damage there's no way they were able to reattach it. Half his forearm was blown off."

"Yes," I said, "but the prints match."

"Identical twin?" suggested Top.

"No. Only child. Not adopted, either."

"So, what have we got here?"

"No one knows," I said. "The cops have been looking for the guy, and my guess is those biotech firms are looking. And a bunch of gangbangers of different stripes are looking."

Top said, "Are we sure it's Brock who hit those two biotech places? Because otherwise it looks like he's trying be a hero here. Tried to protect a civilian from three shooters, busting up gangs and drug runners. I mean, sure, he wore a costume—"

"—A superhero costume—," cut in Bunny.

"—so his head's messed up. But what's our play, boss?"

I shook my head. "We'll determine that on the ground. There's a lot of this story we don't know, and that includes the one bit of information I didn't share with you guys. I had Bug and his team tear apart Brock's life all the way back to potty training. And that includes his service record and the files from Brock's treatment at the field hospital where he was taken after the IED went off."

"I'm not going to like this, am I?" asked Bunny.

"No," I admitted. "None of us are. Staff Sergeant Hector Block was medevacked out to a triage center where he would have been flown to the military hospital in Balad, and would probably have been transferred from there to the Landstuhl Regional Medical Center in Germany. Except Brock was pronounced DOA in Balad. Attempts were made to revive him, but he was unresponsive and they bagged him for a flight back to the states. He was buried in Western Cemetery on Edmondson Street in West Baltimore."

They stared at me.

"I got nothing," said Bunny.

"Whoa," said Top, "was he CIA? Did they cover things up? Maybe he was taken to Germany after all. Maybe they fixed him up. Enhanced him."

I nodded. "Brock's platoon was tied to a few CIA ops. But I don't think the Agency is our villain here. I had Bug dig really deep, starting with the CIA black ops records. You know that most alterations to computer records leave a mark, right? A scar. Mostly it's tiny fragments of code, or stuff deleted without taking the extra steps to totally clean the drives. Anyway, he went back to the incident report filed after Brock's squad ran over the IED and then followed it through the chain of command. He found the point where the case was closed as KIA, but that's where the trail got interesting. The matter was closed but the body itself didn't go through the normal channels to be sent back home. Turns out Brock actually *was* sent to Landstuhl in Germany. There's a file they tried to delete that mentions a badly wounded soldier that could not be identified due to extensive trauma and loss of ID. Which is bullshit. That looks good on a report read by someone in Washington, but the army knows how to ID a dead soldier. Fingerprints, dental records, DNA."

"What happened to him in Landstuhl?" asked Bunny.

"That's when Hector Brock officially disappeared. There are no records of anyone of that name ever arriving, being treated, or anything. He was sent there and then vanished. However, there's a guy listed as *Sechzehnter Freiwilliger*. Volunteer Sixteen. And he's on record as a volunteer for a heavily funded program of experimental therapies known as *Nächster Mensch*, which means 'Next Human.' It's multinational, based in Germany."

"Next human," mused Top, "sounds like some kind of enhancement program."

"That's what I think it is," I agreed. "*Nächster Mensch's* injuries are a perfect match for Brock, so that was easy. Anyway, he was admitted into a special program. Not DARPA, by the way. It's funded by several private corporations that have interests in current and postwar Iraq, mostly minerals and oil. But here's the fun part—one of the corporations tied to this group is Blue Diamond Security. Remember those cats?"

Top growled and Bunny snarled. We all remembered Blue Diamond. They provided private military contractors to sketchy organizations around the globe, though their clients list included the United States. They're so shifty they make Blackwater look like Carmelite Nuns. Me and my guys ran into them a bunch of times when we worked for Uncle Sam and no one came away from those events with the warm fuzzies.

"What Bug was able to find," I continued, "is that the program was ticking along very nicely and quietly, with resources and 'volunteers' flooding in and no info at all getting out. A lot of cybersecurity, which means nothing to my guys; but there must have been a lot of verbal-only orders because too much is missing from computer records. That's tech companies getting crafty in the age of computer hacking by going truly analog—paper records or spoken words. Anyway, from what Bug found is that the program was cancelled very abruptly two years ago."

"Why and by whom?" Top asked.

"Well, the lab where the actual volunteers were sent after triage and treatment at Landstuhl was a place in Austria. One of those old castles up in the mountains. There was some kind of accident and the whole place burned down. Total loss of life. It was reported as a generator malfunctioning during a thunderstorm. And maybe that's true, but I don't buy it."

"Yeah...too close to what happened to those biotech labs," said Bunny, then he brightened and snapped his fingers. "Shit, boss, the guards at those labs...are you going to tell us they were also Blue Diamond?"

"Yup," I said. "Every last one of them."

Top got up, fetched fresh coffee, and sat back down. "Then this starts to make sense," he said slowly. "I think they went full-tilt Frankenstein on this boy. And maybe they put Brock and other 'volunteers' in the field. Had 'em do some evil shit because that's what PMCs like those Blue Diamond cocksuckers do—and then for some reason they decided to shut down the program and delete their assets. Brock was officially dead, so he would have to know his life wasn't worth a used rubber. They'd want to tidy things up. That pissed off Brock and he decided to do some damage on the way down."

"Maybe," said Bunny. "Or maybe they couldn't control Brock anymore. I mean…what he did in the liquor store isn't rational. He might have decided to sneak back home somehow, saw that his neighborhood turned to shit and wanted to play Masked Avenger, but he's over the edge. He's killing people."

"If they enhanced him some other way than cybernetics," I said, "say genetic manipulation, chemical treatments, whatever…then that can't really be an exact science. They sure as hell couldn't have done years of documented clinical trials. If they Frankensteined our boy up, then the process they started might be accelerating. And I tend to think it has. They turned Brock into a monster and now he wants to punish them for it."

"Breaks my heart, though," said Bunny softly. "I mean, he enlisted at nineteen. Served several tours. Has to be a patriot. But when he got hurt in the service of the country, they made him into a monster. He's not just trying to tear down the people who did this to him…he's also trying to do some good and be a hero. A real god damned *super* hero."

We flew a bunch of miles before anyone spoke.

Top looked at me. "So where are we going? Baltimore's a big town."

"True," I admitted, "but there's only one biotech lab left in that region with Blue Diamond security. Maybe Brock wants to take them all out, or maybe he's looking for something specific. Either way, I want to be there when he kicks the door."

-5-

Albrecht Airstrip-Md48
Glen Arm, Maryland

We landed at a private airport where an SUV was waiting for us. Since RTI is international and carrying guns through customs means red tape, we tapped a local asset to provide the ride and lots of goodies. Guns, body armor, coms units. The works.

Then we drove through the late afternoon gloom to Consolidated Research Labs, which is as generic a name as you can get. Might as well post a sign like: Nondescript Lab for Making Hinky Shit.

The place was way the hell out of town and not all that easy to find, even with GPS. Deep in the woods and all by itself on a few acres of parking lot in the middle of no-damn-where. Top was driving and pulled to the side of the road two miles out; Bunny launched a couple of crow drones. The birds rose into the air and flew above the trees. From anything more than ten feet away they look totally real. We sat idling and watching their camera feeds on wrist-mounted tactical computers.

"Coming up on it, boss," said Bunny. Then he cried, "Holy shit."

'Holy shit' was right. Top threw the car into gear and slammed back onto the road.

Consolidated Research Labs was burning.

-6-

Consolidated Research Labs
Near Loch Raven Reservoir Park

There was a big fence with a sturdy steel gate, but the gate was laying twenty feet inside the fence perimeter. The hinges were twisted like pasta and the whole frame was warped out of shape. A guardhouse lay on its side, the splintered wood splattered with bright blood. There were dozens of spent shell casings on the asphalt near a red lump of a thing that was probably human once, but no longer looked it.

"Fuck me," said Bunny. He had a big Atchisson assault shotgun with a thirty-two round drum magazine.

"What's the play here, boss?" asked Top as he drove in an arc around the body and the gate.

"I'd like to take Brock in," I said. "If we can. Maybe Doc Holliday and her team can help him. Maybe reverse what was done to him."

"And if he won't let us take him?"

"Nobody's invincible," I said quietly.

"These guys might not agree," said Bunny.

"These guys aren't us," I said.

The entry road curved and opened into a broad lot in which there were about thirty cars. There were bodies in the parking lot. A couple of the cars were little more than crushed lumps of glass and metal. One lay on its side, the tires burning, and blood splashes on the inside of the windshield.

Beyond all of that was the building. It was three stories tall, gray stone, and built like a stumpy octopus with three wings jutting out. Two of those wings were burning—one partly and the other completely engulfed. We could hear screams and gunshots coming from the one wing that was still undamaged, and I could read the scene. The attack on the fence tripped alarms and some of the Blue Diamond thugs had come out of the building to ambush Brock. That, clearly, was a bad fucking idea. He'd slaughtered them and then entered one wing, presumably the one burning furiously. We couldn't tell if any of the lab staff were here or if this place was packed with Blue Diamond PMCs. The fight had spilled over into the second wing and was now in the third.

We parked and got out.

"They were ready for this boy," said Top, looking around at the bodies. "But not ready enough."

"If he's able to do this kind of stuff," said Bunny, "how exactly do you *get* ready?"

We were wearing top-of-the-line body armor that was supposed to stop anything short of a sniper bullet. But we were not enhanced, we wore no combat exoskeletons, and we were not armed with Star Trek phasers. We turned on our coms units, checked our weapons, and then went into the building.

It was like stepping into hell.

Even in the third wing there were already some fires burning. Brock seemed to have thrown a lot of papers onto the floor or on desks and lit them. Against one wall was a row of file cabinets and fingers of fire wriggled up from each open drawer. I could smell gasoline, and we passed one empty red container. In the first few rooms we found destruction, arson, blood, and three mangled bodies.

"What about the PMCs, boss?" asked Bunny. "We've tussled with them before but that was then. What's their current designation?"

"To be determined," I said, "but our cover is that we're feds. They should respond to us as friendlies. Or, at least not hostiles."

"Hope they know that."

There were footprints through splashes of red. Some showed the tread of a kind of rubber-soled work shoe favored by PMCs working domestic gigs. Similar to what we were wearing. But one set of prints was clearly from large Doc Martens. I crouched down and looked at a place where that set of prints paused. I signaled to the others to look and they saw the same thing— pools of blood around those shoes.

"He's bleeding," said Top. "That's a lot of blood. Might be bleeding out."

"Would simplify things," said Bunny. "Though I'd rather walk him out of here than bury him."

A voice cried, "Hey!"

We whirled to see a group of Blue Diamond guards come running toward us. They wore blue windbreakers unzipped to allow access to shoulder holsters. They each had a Kevlar chest protector. Two of them held long guns at port arms.

I held up a badge folder. The credentials were phony, but they didn't know that. I even called out a warning, "Federal agents, we're here responding to a—"

And they opened fire.

No questions, no discussion. Their guns rose and we scattered, chased by heavy caliber rounds. Top dove behind a heavy metal desk and I faded sideways to crouch behind one of the burning file cabinets.

Bunny, though, held his ground and opened up with the Atchison. He was loaded with modified FRAG-12 high-explosive rounds and had his weapon set to full-auto, which gave him a fire rate of three hundred rounds per minute. He burned through the full magazine in seconds, his huge frame braced for the continuous recoil. Each round was a fin-stabilized 19mm warhead that, once fired, armed itself as soon as it traveled three meters from the muzzle and detonated on impact. I saw bodies leap into the air and fly apart, the pieces trailing blood and debris.

Bunny dropped the magazine and swapped in another.

"So much for being friendlies," he said.

Top scowled. "They didn't even pause. They'd have cut us down if we'd been real feds and the Farm Boy here wasn't carrying a fucking howitzer. Seems to me they're acting like people with something to hide."

"Color me surprised," I said, and we moved off.

We didn't need schematics of the building to find our quarry. All we had to do was follow the mayhem. The sounds were muted, though, and it soon became apparent that it was coming from downstairs. We found the stairwell and walked down through smoke, careful not to slip on blood. There were parts of a man littered on those stairs. Parts.

We reached the bottom and followed a corridor into a section of interconnected rooms. Most were dedicated to computer workstations, but soon those gave way to labs, biohazard hot rooms, surgical suites, and then a big room with rows of hospital beds. More than half the beds were empty, but at the far end of it we saw about a dozen that were occupied. Men and women. Scarred from injuries and surgeries, hooked up to machines and IVs, their wrists, ankles, and waists secured by leather-wrapped chains.

There were nurses and doctors huddled into a corner, hiding behind the last dozen of the Blue Diamond contractors. Between where we stood and that group were at least a dozen corpses and more spent brass than I could count.

And there, standing like something out of a twisted fantasy, was Hector Brock. He wore his superhero outfit—boots, fingerless gloves, sweats, shorts, and cape. He wore his Lone Ranger mask. His hands were smeared with bright blood all the way to the elbows. His clothes were soaked with red. He faced the PMCs and the medical staff, his chest heaving, hands opening and closing.

"Brock!" I roared. *"Stop!"*

But the moment I spoke the Blue Diamond guards opened up again. I saw Brock stagger as all those rounds hit him. But he did not fall. He held a forearm across his eyes and moved forward, step by impossible step.

That was insane. Surreal.

It was one thing to see something like that on a silent video feed because it looks like TV special effects. It was an entirely different thing to see it for real. The PMCs were armed with handguns and AR-15s. In the space of a few seconds they hit him with at least two hundred rounds. Brock's costume was little more than rags, and as pieces flew away, we could see his skin. It no longer looked human. It was pale, like a mushroom, but there was a weird and unpleasant metallic sheen to it. And everywhere were long lines of purple scar tissue. These scientists hadn't just enhanced him, they'd stripped way his humanity.

This guy had joined the military because he believed in something. He had literally given his life for his country. But greedy hearts did not beat for any kind of patriotism. To them he was a commodity. A trained soldier who had no shot at survival, so they took the very last thing he had left to give—the thing that made him human. They'd twisted him into something else. He was a golem; a construct of flesh and steel and god knew what else.

Had to be some kind of super soldier program. There were dozens of those around the world, some government sanctioned and others, like this, created by corrupt corporations who wanted their own private armies.

Beyond where Brock stood, the patients in the other beds were screaming. The sounds were appalling. Louder than human voices should have been able to scream. Awful cries, filled with pain and horror. Their bodies thrashed in the beds, fighting against the chains.

We rushed forward, swerving to one side to stay out of the line of fire and wanting to come up to where Brock could see us, and could also see that our guns were not pointed at him.

But then several of the Blue Diamond guards spotted us and opened fire.

"What the fuck," growled Top as once more we took cover, this time behind empty beds.

"Target the PMCs," I yelled. "Try not to hit the medical staff. We need someone with a pulse to explain what the hell's going on down here."

"Good luck with that," said Bunny as he fired.

The next few minutes were beyond sane. Brock tried to bull his way through the hail of bullets, but it was pretty clear that even his freakish skin was not totally impervious. Blood poured down his frame and left a trail behind him like some giant crimson snail. He was staggering, slowing.

Dying.

He wasn't going to make it.

Despite all the killing this man had done, seeing him failing now, broke my heart. I understood his mission. Sure, under other circumstances he would have to answer for his crimes. For the death of those teenagers at the liquor store. For the other murders. There were still laws.

But what he'd done here? And to the other biotech labs? That felt like a real mission for a superhero. Stopping super villains from doing something horrible.

Brock staggered and went down to one knee. Emboldened, the PMCs came at him, slapping in new magazines. They were even grinning.

We could have waited until they'd cut Brock down. We probably should have. Those guards had a legal right to defend themselves and their employers. All we had to do was wait until Brock was down and try the badges again. Try a calm, sane approach again.

But I said, "No."

Just the one word. Barely loud audible. It was enough. Top and Bunny understood. They knew me. Same way I could.

We rose up, firing at the contractors, not trying to wound. Every shot was aimed center mass and we fucking killed them all.

The doctors and nurses cringed back, screaming, begging for mercy.

We damn near killed them, too.

God, I wanted to. We all wanted to. The moral outrage for what they'd done shrieked in our minds. They had taken soldiers, wounded soldiers, and turned them into science projects. Into tools. Into monsters. Every single one of them deserved to die.

But they were unarmed.

We slaughtered the guards, though. Without mercy. Without hesitation.

Top and Bunny moved past me to take charge of the lab staff. They were not nice about it. Not nice at all.

I went over to Brock and knelt in front of him. He was on his knees, tilted forward, his fists braced against the floor.

"Staff sergeant Brock," I said. "Hector. It's okay. The battle's over. You won."

He raised his head. Tears streamed down his cheeks, turning pink and then red as they mingled with blood. His mask was still there, though. It no longer looked ridiculous. Now it really did look like a hero's mask.

"I'm not one of them," I said. I showed him my gun and placed it on the floor well within his reach. Then I sat crossed legged in front of him and showed him my empty palms.

"Who...are...you...?"

He had to fight to get each word out, and tiny droplets of blood flecked his lips. There was a knowing glaze in his eyes that I've seen in other soldiers who are fully aware that they are nearly gone. Had he had that look when they peeled what was left of him from that Humvee?

"My name is Colonel Joe Ledger," I said. "I used to be a regular soldier like you. I think I understand what these sons of bitches did to you."

Brock looked at the other victims. They still fought against their restraints, but the screams had died down. Most of them were now watching me and Brock.

"Listen to me, Brock," I said, "and hear me. I really get why you did this. I respect it. And I can't even begin to imagine what you've been through. No one but you and those poor bastards in those beds can."

Brock nodded but when he tried to speak, he began coughing. Blood ran freely from both corners of his mouth.

"I'll do everything I can for the others. I swear it to you."

He just looked at me. Tears running.

"But you have to know you're done."

Brock nodded again and he sagged a bit, as if admitting it took most of the strength he had left.

"We have the medical staff, and we have whatever records you didn't destroy. My people will rip their worlds apart with it. Everyone here is going to jail, and some may ride the needle. But it won't stop there. My group is international. We're going to go hunting for these fuckers and we will take them down. All the way and very damn hard."

He managed a word. "Why?"

"Because there are actual good guys in the world, corny as that sounds," I said. "My men are stand up. Wish you could have met them. No politics, just a warriors' desire to stand between the innocent and pricks like these. I know you understand that. Even after everything they did to you, you fought back *as* a hero. The costume…I get it. I do. You wanted anyone who knew about you to understand that you're not some vet with PTSD going off the rails. Hell, Brock, you're an actual goddamned superhero. And you saved the damn day."

I made my little speech, but then I realized I was talking to myself. Brock's eyes were still open, but the glaze had turned into a stare. He looked at me and through me and through the world. When he began to topple over, I caught him and lowered him to the floor as gently as I could.

I held him for a while. Feeling the last of the muscular tension ebb out of him. Feeling a little faintness of a stir in the air. His spirit leaving the ruined house of his life.

In death he did not look like a monster at all. He looked like a fallen soldier. A hero.

I adjusted the mask so that it fit properly, and I closed his eyes. Then I stood.

I wanted to do something to mark the moment. A salute. Something. But I was surrounded by death and there was work to do. I looked at the medical staff, cowering as Bunny and top zip-cuffed them.

Then I walked over to the people in the beds.

Brock had been transformed into a monster, but these people were much worse. Metallic skin. Reptilian skin. Thousands of stitches. Infusion ports for exotic chemicals. Wires inserted into their brains. Enormous muscles, distorted features. Each of them had heavy cables attached to their chests and I followed the lines to a panel on the wall in which a heavy breaker switch was mounted. If Brock had destroyed this building, too, the power would have gone out and maybe killed all of them.

Was that his plan? Kill the real monsters and set the creatures like him free?

It was tragic and horrible, and it stabbed me through the heart.

"I'll get medical teams here," I promised them. "You'll be okay."

It was a lie. Not even a good one. They stared at me with human eyes in inhuman faces. One of them, the closest one, looked at me and then over to the breaker, and back.

"No," I said. "We'll get the best medical…"

My words trailed off. All of them were looking at me. There was so much terror and awareness in their eyes. So much fear.

So much need.

And hope.

The patient looked over to Brock and then back to me. His mouth was an almost amphibian lipless horror. Even so he formed a single word.

"Please."

I closed my eyes and felt my own tears burning in my eyes.

Please.

God, it was too much to ask of anyone. I shook my head.

Please.

I walked over to the breaker and gripped it with a trembling hand. A sob broke in my chest.

"Yes," I said.

THE LADY AND/OR THE TIGER

NEIL GAIMAN AND ROZ KAVENEY

The Library of the Conspiracy is currently to be found in a small university town in West Virginia, in the southern United States. The town has no litter in the streets, and its buildings are painted white; a shopping mall was proposed at the county seat ten miles away, but nothing came of it. Once the Library was in Rome, in catacombs adjacent to those where the Sibylline books were held; some say it still contains copies of those books of prophecy which the Sibyl affected to have burned when King Tarquin the Proud refused her asking price, though the Librarians denied this to the Prefect Sejanus when he came calling with his clients, informers and hired bravoes. Later the Library was in Alexandria, then for many years in Venice, and later still in London, moving to its current location in the late 1930s. It is privately funded and little-known, save in certain circles.

In the broad wooden shelves of the Library there are sections on all manner of subjects: Lee Harvey Oswald has almost half a wall, as has John Wilkes Booth, and Joshua Norton, the self-proclaimed Emperor of the United States. There are shelves devoted to the Illuminati, and to the Suicide Royale, and the 1929 World's Fair; the secret patterns on the scarves of the Thugs are documented here, as are the names of the Quechua's bird of hope and the True Name of the Chinese adventurer who called himself the Younger Brother of Jesus Christ. These are on open shelves, and are freely available to legitimate researchers, although they may not be taken from the building.

Researchers need a letter guaranteeing good character and

serious intentions; moreover, the usual authorities are not always accepted as a reference here: the Vatican Librarian is good for a reference, as is the small public library of the town of Elgin, Illinois. But the Librarian of the Athenaeum Club quarrelled with the four Head Librarians of the Conspiracy over certain documentation that could, it was felt, have persuaded the requisite full twenty-four Bishops of the Anglican Church to assemble for the opening of the sealed box Joanna Southcott left at her death; this was in 1851, and courtesies have not been resumed.

There are open shelves. There are sealed stacks. And there are also the cellars.

One of the four Head Librarians must approve any requests for inspection of materials to be found in the sealed stacks, and these must be read at the high desk in his or her office. Where certain of the manuscripts are concerned, a Librarian will turn the pages for the reader. The Librarians of the Conspiracy have no uniform, but each of them wears white silk gloves; to turn some pages they add a second pair of gloves, and these are black.

The young man with the lank black pony-tail sat at the high desk, taking copious notes. He turned to the Head Librarian. "Thank you," he said. "I think I'm finished with this."

The Head Librarian took the manuscript, a twelfth century illuminated chronicle, and placed it carefully on his desk.

"Is there anything else you'll be needing today, Mr Lamb?" he asked.

The young man shook his head. "Not today," he said. "I'm still trying to make sense of what I've already found." He paused. "This is a very remarkable place."

"Yes, sir."

"So." Lamb hesitated, then, "How long have you been working here?"

The Head Librarian stroked his grey moustache with his white silk gloves. "Sir, it is time to close the Library. And private discussion with our readers is frowned upon, on Library premises."

"Oh. I see. I'm sorry. I just wondered…"

The Head Librarian looked at him, quizzically. "Yes, sir?"

"Well, did you answer an advertisement in *The New York Times* to work here? Or what?"

The Head Librarian blew a tiny scrap of dust from the tip of his white silk finger. "The Library does not advertise, sir."

Lamb looked away from the Head Librarian, embarrassed, and shuffled his notes into a portfolio. They went out into the corridor. The Head Librarian turned off the lights behind them, leaving his office to the darkness of the December evening.

"I–I'm sorry," said Lamb. "I didn't mean anything. I mean, I wouldn't want to get you into trouble. Talking." He shrugged. "Sorry."

The Head Librarian nodded, gravely. "I fully understand, sir. And I regret that our conversation, such as it is, in this building must be limited. However, were you to be on the corner of Main Street and Elm in say, half an hour, there is a small establishment in which drinks may be purchased..."

The young man smiled suddenly, widely. "I'd like that," he said. "I'll be there."

Lamb sipped his beer and waited. The juke-box was playing a country song, something about a woman who had finally discovered, after twenty years of marriage, that she never really knew her man.

"Hallo."

He started. "I didn't see you come in. Something to drink?"

"A soft drink. Ginger ale will suit me perfectly."

"Are you sure I can't buy you a beer? I'm on expenses..."

The older man looked down briefly. "Thank you, but no. I had," he paused, then began again, "...some slight problems with alcohol, many years ago. I no longer drink."

"My mom was an alcoholic," volunteered the younger man.

"Then you know that one never ceases to be an alcoholic. One simply does not drink alcohol, a day at a time. My name is Chepstow. Roland Chepstow."

"Harry Lamb."

"I know." They shook hands. Chepstow no longer wore his

white silk gloves; his hands were clean and perfectly manicured. The juke-box sang.

And these days you come home and I don't know you any more,
Seems you never really get to know your man.

A waitress came, took their order, returned almost instantly with the drinks.

"The Library. It's a wonderful place."

Chepstow nodded. "It is indeed remarkable. I get, alas, little time for reading. But I enjoy watching our readers. We attract a particular type of person. Did you notice the gentleman at seat 15H? The Asian gentleman with the muffler?"

"The big purple scarf. Sure. He seemed to be asleep."

"Exactly. He has been coming here for two years now. He is gathering evidence to prove that Indira Gandhi was murdered not by her Sikh bodyguards, but by agents acting on behalf of the hereditary chairman of the East India Company, in collusion with the British House of Lords. He arrives here first thing in the morning, he orders his books and goes to sleep, waking when the Library is closing to return the books."

Harry Lamb grinned. "For two years? It's an expensive place to nap. Doesn't he ever read?"

"When once I ventured to tax him upon the subject, he told me that the precise page of the precise book he was seeking would eventually be revealed to him in a dream. For now, he sleeps."

Lamb sipped his beer. The Virginia heat was getting to him, even in his T-shirt and jeans. He eyed the Librarian in his sober suit. "You must hear some strange theories in this place."

"Indeed, sir."

"Harry. Call me Harry."

Chepstow shook his head. "I'd rather not, sir." He signalled to the waitress. "Another beer for my colleague and another ginger ale for me."

"A...," Lamb paused, "A...woman I used to know...once told me that all conspiracies are parts of the same conspiracy, that they are all cells of an ultimate Beast. Like the story of the blind men and the elephant."

Chepstow nodded. "People have come to us seeking proof of

such ideas, and stayed for years in the attempt to prove it."

"I don't think that can be true, though. It's like the physicist said, Heisenberg–you know what he said…"

"I had the honour," Chepstow said quietly, "of meeting Herr Heisenberg once, in the company of Mr William Donovan."

"He said," Lamb said, "that the act of looking disturbs what is looked at. So if you are a particular sort of person the conspiracy you find, when you look, will mirror what you think, what you are."

"I would agree with that. There are certain features that some of the Library's readers have in common. For example, it is my experience that those who lay the planet's difficulties at the feet of the Illuminati tend towards slightly bulging eyes and to be less careful about personal hygiene than those who, for example, seek to prove the existence of the cartel of international bankers. The banker-theorists are by far the best groomed.

"And it has also been my experience that certain types of people orbit certain conspiracies. The last thing Ripperologists want to know is the identity of poor Jack. That's there for the asking; but no one ever cares enough to ask. They are seeking themselves on the cobbles of Mitre Street and in the mists of Whitechapel."

"So what am I?"

"I beg your pardon?"

"C'mon. If you can recognise types, what type am I?"

Chepstow looked intently at his drinking companion.

"That would not be fair, sir. I processed your application, after all. You are a journalist. And journalists, in my experience, can be on the trail of…" a small shrug, "…anything."

"Well, yeah. But–"

"The books, manuscripts and newspapers you have been examining are without any thread that is apparent to me. Today, for example, you examined a cryptographer's report on the dimensions of the Red Fort at Agra, a transcript of the tapes taken on Mr Hoover's orders of the last telephone conversations of Miss Jayne Mansfield, and Herr Weisshaupt's suppressed commentary on the libretto of *The Magic Flute*. I think we could describe your interests, Mr Lamb, as either wilfully eclectic or globally paranoid."

Lamb looked around the room. There was no one near them, and the juke-box was playing loudly enough to mask their conversation from casual listeners. He grinned and said it.

"I'm hunting werewolves."

If Chepstow was in any way surprised by this statement he failed to show it. He flicked an invisible morsel of lint from the sleeve of his dark grey suit. "Werewolves. Ah. Do you know, I believe you're the first werewolf man we've had here in a good decade."

"Really? What happened to the last guy?"

The Librarian shrugged. "I have no idea. You people come here, you read, you leave. Sometimes you write your own books and we file them on our shelves."

"You do? Well, you'll be filing mine in a year or so."

"If I might make so bold as to inquire—what will it be called?"

Harry Lamb scratched the side of his cheek with his beer glass. "I don't know. I'll probably call it something like: *Notes Toward a Theory of Co-Evolution: Emulative Mimicry Amongst the Higher Orders.* And if anyone publishes it they'll probably call it *Werewolves Among Us!* and put a photo of Lon Chaney Jr. on the cover, with his face all hairy and a wet black nose."

"How unfortunate."

"Yeah."

A tall woman entered the bar. She walked over to a man in the corner. They spoke in low voices urgently, angrily; then the woman walked out and the man followed her. Lamb shook his head slowly. "I wonder what the story is behind that, then?"

"I doubt we will ever know."

"You married?"

"The Librarians of the Conspiracy are…well, I suppose you could call us a celibate order. And you?"

"I came close once. She's dead."

"I'm sorry."

There was a pause in the conversation. The record on the juke-box ended and suddenly, for a few seconds, the bar was silent.

The young man checked his watch. "Twenty of eight. You ever notice that? A room full of people talking falls quiet, it's always twenty-past or twenty-to?"

"I can't say that I have. Would you like another beer?"

"Yeah. No. What the hell, sure. It's not a long drive back. I got rooms. You live local?"

"The Library provides living quarters for us nearby, Mr Lamb. So…what set you on the trail of werewolves, then?"

"They aren't werewolves."

"I thought you said…"

"People think they're werewolves. But they aren't. Not really."

"Ah. Psychosis. People imagining themselves as…"

Lamb shook his head. "No, no. Not mad people. Not people. They look like people, but they can look like any large animals. Mimics. Imitating us, living among us."

"So what do they really look like?"

Caroline…

On the juke-box a man sang emotionally about his woman and his bottle and his gun. Steel guitars wailed in the background. Lamb was silent.

"Did I…Did I say something wrong, Mr Lamb? I'm sorry. I must say your theory sounds eminently more practical than that of the previous werewolf gentleman. As I recall, he maintained that all politicians had eyebrows that met in the middle, and hunted on all fours when the moon was full."

"They…they wouldn't be politicians. I don't think so. That would be too conspicuous. They…they want to blend in." Lamb thought of Caroline; her smile, her voice, her face. And the way her face had danced and changed when the bullets hit her.

If she comes home tonight
Then I'll be waiting in the darkness
For my woman with my bottle and my gun…

The waitress gave them their drinks. Lamb paid the tab and tipped her generously. Intense, he began to talk to the Librarian in short, staccato bursts–astonished to find himself saying out loud the thoughts that had, until this time, been reserved for his notebook, for himself.

"They've been living among us since we were in the caves. They're older than that, though. I don't know how old. Real old. We give them a home. We give them a place to hide. I don't know what they're hiding from; I don't think it's just us, most of the time. If you look carefully you can see their traces in the history books, in legends, in folk songs."

"Ah. And that's what you have, then? History books, folk songs?"

Lamb drained his drink. He smiled the confident smile of the slightly drunk. "Got more than that. They aren't as careful as they think they are. And even they can be unlucky."

Chepstow left the last of his ginger ale untouched. "I'll walk you to your car."

"Yeah. Okay."

The street was dark and deserted.

"Her name was Caroline," said Lamb. "We were covering a story in Naples. She was my photographer, and a damn good one. No, I'm sorry. That sounds so dimenovel, so dumb. And she wasn't just my photographer. We were fucking. Maybe if I'd got my shit together we would have married. I don't know. What does anyone know? They said that the shipment we were tracking was coming through that night and we waited in an alley. She had her cameras. There wasn't any shipment.

"They shot her in the chest. I held her as she died, and I watched her change…Change into something. And I had to know. What had I been sleeping with? What had I loved?"

In the distance Lamb heard something move, then scream: a night animal, a little death. Something was feeding, somewhere in the shadows.

Chepstow looked at him with quiet, intelligent eyes. He nodded. "You were right about the caves. But they go back a long way before that. All the way back through the ice and the comets and the Dark; they were not the first intelligent species to walk the Earth, but they were the second and they are, by far, the oldest."

"But…then…but," said Lamb. "You…?"

"The Library of the Conspiracy has many names and many

purposes," said Chepstow. "And we know things you are unlikely to know. We know of the Fifty Lives, and of the Darkcallers, and of Those Whose Names Are No Longer Sung."

Lamb drew back slightly; curled his hands into fists.

"Don't be ridiculous," said Chepstow. "I am as human as you. But I too have looked at some interesting files in my time. Perhaps you should accompany me back to the Library; there are some things that you should read."

Lamb thought about running. Then he sighed, and side by side with the older man, walked back towards the Library down the clean, dark sidewalks of the pretty little town. Once he stopped, convinced he had heard something behind him: an animal perhaps. He looked around, scanning the shadows, but saw nothing. No one. Chepstow took his arm and led him gently towards the Library. They entered the building by a padlocked door at the back. There was a deep stairwell there, and at its bottom several more locked doors; Lamb had thought Chepstow limped, but perhaps it was the weight of his keys. They passed through another door, and they were in the cellars of the Library of the Conspiracy.

The cellars of the Library of the Conspiracy are airy rooms of various sizes. When the Library was in Venice, certain seekers after knowledge would agree to be immured in the cellars of the Library in return for the knowledge they sought; it was an awkward compromise between the Library's function as a repository of information and its need that certain information be withheld from the world outside. It is said that this no longer happens; and indeed it would not be credible in this day and age.

Chepstow led Lamb through a labyrinth of small rooms and corridors, and finally through a door with many locks into a large room, its walls all lined with cardboard boxes, each filled with files to overflowing.

At the far end of the room was another door.

The room contained a desk and two chairs—one cheap, red plastic that sat by the desk, the other an ancient armchair, in the far corner of the room.

Chepstow locked the door behind them.

On the desk that stood in front of them, lit by a solitary lamp, were various papers–part of a German scientific paper and a photograph of a small, unsmiling woman; a clipping from a Manchester evening newspaper from the year before and a broadsheet printed in Prague in 1618: a sheaf of bar bills, in Spanish, and a stack of Xeroxes of what seemed to be scientific formulae; and other remnants of tales. Each had a commentary attached.

"I think," said Chepstow, "that these are what you are looking for."

Lamb nodded, took his seat at the desk, and began to read.

And, before any of the Fifty Lives is sung:
We moved among them quietly, lest we disturb them
in their meditations.
In the palace of their thought
Our walking was not even an echo:
Their servants, and their lovers, and their pets.
Sharers of hearth and bed and counsel.

They thought of strange things
and strange gods.
They walked in closed chambers of the mind
And bowed to what they found there.
Then the Dark came
and in a season they were gone;
in their folly they were eaten and were gone.

The star fell, and the world was dark.
It fell, the great city.
And we moved quietly, for a thousand thousand lives.

We paced the cage of silence lest the Dark hear us.
We hunted with the beasts;
With the wolf and the hyena we lay down.
We forgot fire;
In the cold of night we remembered loss.
We remembered our song;
And many times cursed the pain of remembrance.

Man came;
Young apes in their nakedness.
We waited in silence;
Quietly we watched what they might do.
They made fire.
In the night there came flame and warmth.
We watched.
And we warmed our hands;
In the light of the fire we watched and were no more cold.

They made cities;
Halls of stone they built.
We were silent.
And we were glad of shelter.
In their palaces we walked silently.
They followed strange gods.
And we killed.

In the moment of their idolatry
We struck them down.
We move among them, quietly,
Their rulers, and their lovers and the beasts at their throat.

The Dark will not come again;
Nor shall the firelight end.
Who does not heed this, their life shall be sung no more
Their name shall be forgotten.

Lamb stopped reading. His head hurt and he had a cramp in the back of his leg. He had read enough. He checked his watch; dawn must be breaking by now. Chepstow was asleep in the armchair in the corner of the room. Lamb stared at him, wondering if he were truly human, if any of us were.

The Librarian's eyes opened.

"So, Mr Lamb." He looked at Lamb inquiringly.

"So what comes next?" Lamb said. "Something bursts through that door behind us, and tears my throat out?"

"Not necessarily," Chepstow said. "It all rather depends on you. Why don't you open the desk drawer?" Lamb pulled it open; inside the drawer were a revolver and, next to it, a pair of white gloves.

"You need not take the gloves," said Chepstow. "And if you take the revolver, you may do with it what you will; we give you one bullet and that is all the help you will get from us."

Lamb hesitated.

"You were a marked man long before you came to the Library," Chepstow said. "You have disturbed what you looked at. They were watching you long ago. You may, if you wish, take the gloves, and stay with the Library; it may not be the life you planned for yourself, but it is life. If not, well, one of the tokens of white gloves is that we have washed our hands…"

"It's not enough," said Lamb. "The knowledge is not enough, and that is all I would ever have. There's more than that."

"Ah," Chepstow said. "The woman."

"Who shot her? Who was it? And what was she? Was she trying to get away from them? Or was it one of these damned factions, wiping out a member of another? Now that I know this much I have to know the rest. I have to find out who killed Caroline."

"And then?"

"I'll kill them." Lamb paused. He stood up, and closed his eyes. "Once her face was done with changing, she looked so calm it was almost as if she was alive. She was still beautiful, you know, when I left her lying there."

"It is," said Chepstow, "at least conceivable that she is beautiful still."

Lamb opened his eyes, and looked at him.

"The Weerde are, after all, rather hard to kill," Chepstow said. "And the person who was following you did appear to be female, not that that means very much."

Lamb paused.

"Thank you," he said, and began to walk the length of the long underground room, one step at a time.

"Take the revolver," Chepstow urged. "You may need it still."

Lamb shook his head. "What's behind the door, Chepstow?" he asked. "Is there…is there anyone there? Really?"

"That question is not one I could presume to answer, sir. I am afraid I must leave the matter with you." The Librarian of the Conspiracy stood up and walked to the other door, and opened it. "If I do not have the opportunity of seeing you again, sir, may I say it has been a pleasure. Goodbye." And he was gone. The lock of the door snapped shut behind him.

Lamb stood alone, and he waited in the silence beneath the earth. He thought about Caroline. He remembered her perfume, remembered it so vividly that he imagined he could smell it now. He looked at the revolver on the table, and the gloves. Then he walked back to the table, and made his choice.

There was a gentle tap on the door. Lamb went to answer it in a joyful decisiveness, although he truly did not know which to expect–the lady, or the tiger.

SUPER-DOC AND THE TEN-DAY CURE FOR THE ZOMBIE APOCALYPSE

HEATHER GRAHAM

Day 1

They say that the only cure for the zombie plague is a bullet to the brain.

I have decided that they're wrong. Because my fellow survivors know I believe I will eventually find the cure, because I still have an office and see patients, they have come to call me Super-Doc.

Therefore I, Super-Doc, intend to keep records, a calendar, a journal. Since the beginning of what I hope will be an end to the deadly manifestation that threatens to end humanity, I have been certain that, with determination and hard work it can come to an end. But then the event occurred that cemented my determination. Perhaps I wasn't yet, but I would become Super-Doc.

I will begin—at the beginning. This is necessary should I fail, and yet, out there somewhere, there are survivors who come upon this record.

I suppose I should explain this, too. At least, knowing that I couldn't just be called Super-Doc, that I must truly become Super-Doc.

I love her. She is my wife, my confidant, the sweet beauty who changed life itself for me, who did the impossible, making me a happy and optimistic man.

Enough. Back to the beginning. Well, the beginning of Super-Doc.

We all know this—they were doing experiments in a remote

island country in the South Pacific. A remote island country, is, of course, a good place to perform medical experimentation.

And yet, as with all things, life—as we know it, and others as well—has a way of surviving.

As with so many things, a mistake caused the beginning of the end. Dr Atherton Fulmore, head of the project, grew exhausted in his efforts to cure the long-known paralyzing disease that had claimed his son; he mixed up the vials he was using.

His son died, as he would have died anyway—his disease had been incurable and progressive.

But his son returned to life that very night. The best anyone was ever able to fathom, his son returned to life with a ravenous hunger, consumed his father, three other scientists, a caretaker/handyman, and, it's believed, a large indigenous lizard.

He then proceeded to the boat dock.

He made his way to Singapore where he managed to infect several people before a policeman realized they were dealing with a different type of criminal and eschewed the concept of warning shots, taking down Avery Atherton with a shot directly into the forehead.

But, too late. There was panic in Singapore; many who had been infected lied in their desperation to return to their homes around the globe. Soon it was in ten countries, then twenty countries...

Communication systems began to fail.

And bit by bit, we were all but wiped out. And, still, of course, there were those of us who hunkered down, who created communities.

I, myself, am lucky. The walls around Sanctuary went up quickly; my office and lab were within those walls. I was already working as a private physician on State Street, with a lovely little courtyard that offered a high brick wall. Jennie and I used the office as our residence as well, and we loved it.

We were planning a family—starting with one child, of course, and the place would have been perfect; offering us our bedroom (which had sliding glass doors out to the courtyard), my lab, my office, a diagnostic room, a guest room—and a room to be prepared for a baby.

She still carries that baby. It is one of the reasons I fight so hard, and one of the reasons I lie to others, and stay here, day after day, certain I am coming up with the right ingredients for a cure.

There must be a cure. And, yes, of course, I understand how it all started; I understand how Dr Atherton caused it. He loved his son.

I love her.

And humanity, of course. They—the military leaders who commanded our walled section of the devastated world—would not understand. So, we stay in. And I don't let on in any way that Jennie was infected when one of the creatures—not yet showing the truth of his death and zombie resurrection—came into the office. She was so gentle, so kind. He complained of illness, and she went to bring him water and a pillow while he awaited me. And when I came in…

He was chewing on her left arm and Jennie was screaming and screaming…

Naturally, I went for a scalpel. But before I slit him to ribbons—not bloody ribbons, he didn't seem to have any blood—he told me the brains were the most important, but Jennie's arm had been absolutely beyond delicious, an appetizer.

He hadn't expected me to come upon them so soon.

If I hadn't known before, I then realized most of what we had told in tales through the years about zombies was true. They could be shot through the head, the head could be bashed in, or one could simply decapitate the creature, slice the head clean from the body.

And a bite causes the infection…

Back to Day 1

Jennie didn't deteriorate immediately. I still knew I should have shot her, right through the head. I'd served in the military, and I still knew how to wield a gun. My revolver held seven-plus-one rounds. Most people had weapons; the zombie apocalypse had meant a fight for self-survival until we'd found our way to hold and keep Sanctuary.

I was always prepared for the day when I might have to shoot

Jennie and then myself.

Now, of course, not so much.

And Jennie...this was different. So different.

I thought there might be hope. I wasn't lying to myself—there was hope!

But then I found her in the kitchen, devouring a rat—or the rat's head. She looked at me in horror, realizing what she was doing.

But, due to the situation, there are plenty of rats. I always rather liked the creatures myself; they are very smart little pests.

And this was a plague that man was carrying—not the rats.

I had read everything I could on Atherton's work, and I used many of his ideas on my own series.

I have injected Jennie. I am hoping to still the tide of her infection.

I will add to this journal every day. I believe within ten days, I, Super-Doc, will have found the cure!

Day 2

Jennie has lost the power of speech. She is now grunting. I try to calm her and reassure her and see to it that she has many rats.

I have upped the intake of the serum. I believe it is working. She began to articulate words again. She sat before her dressing table and brushed her hair.

I talked her into taking a shower.

The smell was getting bad.

Day 3

I have now had to leave the premises to acquire more rats. Serum increased to six ccs.

Day 4

It was inevitable that one of my patients should come by. I should say former patients, since I no longer have a receptionist or a nurse, nor do I care about insurance forms or Medicaid.

But I am a doctor, therefore, I will say patient.

It was always a small community and my patients were our friends. Jennie had taught school when there had been a school in which to teach. Before the infection, she had often spoken about running classes for the children—for there were children in Sanctuary—in whatever building or facility she could find.

Sergeant Bill McCluskey had been a patient and a friend. He was still a patient and a friend. But he was military, and the military—with the support of the remaining populace of Sanctuary—had agreed that any infected person must be eliminated immediately.

I understood.

The infected grew worse; they lost the ability to speak. They began to attack others, then died, and became full-blown monsters, attacking without care or thought of injury or death.

Well, they were already dead. They didn't fear—destruction.

Michael knocked on the door just as I was preparing the day's serum and reading my calculations on dosage and the possibility that stronger doses of antibiotics needed to be added to the concoction.

I flew to the door, hoping to avert whoever might have come.

But it was Michael and he had been friend and patient and he'd pushed his way through the door before I had a chance to invent a reason to keep the door closed.

"I haven't seen you out much, Super-Doc!" he told me. Michael was a decent man. Still young—he'd been just out of the naval academy and in the military when the world had all gone to hell—he was one of the commanders of the ground patrol—those who tested doors and gates and walls and guard posts at Sanctuary night after night, day after day. He was a tall fellow, a good six-four, a handsome kid, the kind you'd want your daughter to marry.

I forced a smile. "Michael! Hey, what can I do for you?"

"My stomach has been bugging me—guess it's the diet," he said dryly. Besides being a guard, Michael was a procurer, heading out of the walls now and then. Luckily, we'd been outside the major city, surrounded by farms and ranches when it had all gone to hell. While the zombies did attack just about anything, what they really needed was brains. That meant that hogs, cattle, chickens and other animals roamed freely and desperately.

So far, procurers brought in the sustenance that was keeping us alive.

"Sure, Michael. I've got some good antacids left; I'll get you something right away."

"How's Jennie?" he asked.

"Fine, fine—resting now," I said. I didn't like the way he asked the question. I realized it wasn't because I thought he was suspicious about her becoming a zombie, but...

It was a little too personal.

Jennie was beautiful. She had long brown hair, soft as silk, seductive gray eyes easily filled with laughter, and a body that didn't quit.

I'd always been amazed that she'd fallen in love with me, a loner doctor-scientist. I don't belong in the ugly school or anything like that, mind you, but I'm tall, a little gangly—and better now that Jennie set me on an exercise routine.

Not because she didn't love me just as I was—but, with the zombie thing happening, the brawn and stamina to move fast might one day be required.

Mainly, I was just quiet. An aging nerd. But with her, I loved music and parties and even dancing, and I learned how to trim my hair and shape a little beard so I was almost handsome.

Of course, I'd be an idiot not to know other men would find her attractive, too.

More than attractive. Beautiful.

"I'll just look through the stash I have left—" I began.

But Jennie chose that moment to leave the office where she was waiting for me to give her an injection and come waltzing out to the front door.

She managed speech.

The serum was working!

"Michael! How are you?" she asked.

"Well, Jennie, well, great to see you!"

He walked over to her, ready to give her a brotherly hug. She hugged him back, of course. Her eyes met mine.

I saw her mouth open.

The sharp edges of her teeth as she prepared to take a massive bite out of his shoulder.

"Jennie!"

I stepped forward, almost wrenching her away from Michael. This, of course, surprised him.

"She's sick," I said.

"She's what?" he demanded suspiciously.

"No, no, Michael," I liked. "Nothing like that. She's got a cold—a common cold. But, hey, you guard us and you get our food! Can't have you coming down with something."

"Ah, Jennie, I'm sorry," Michael said.

He kept staring at her. I could see how he felt about her.

And she smiled at him. With longing.

The poor bastard didn't realize it was with longing for his brains.

"Jennie, come with me, please, help me find the antacid for Michael.

"Coming, love!" she said.

Still, I had to take her arm to get her to come with me.

I chastised her as we hurried to the office. "Jennie, Jennie, please—I'm trying so desperately to get us through this. Jennie, I love you. You can't eat Michael or Michael's brains. Please. I know that it's like fighting an addiction, but I'm trying so hard…"

She answered me. Something guttural that was incomprehensible.

I gave her one shot, and then another, and then I quickly began rifling through the cabinets for the antacid that would help Michael.

Michael thanked me and told me he and his crew had taken down a few big hogs and he'd be bringing me a good supply of meat soon.

I thanked him.

"Got to keep our good doctor going!" he told me.

Then he left.

Jennie stared after him, longingly.

I managed to get her back in our bedroom.

Despite the dark fog that most often seemed to rule her mind, she still enjoyed a good soap opera or novella that I could play for her on the battery-operated DVD system.

I prepared what was left of the chicken meat along with some of our supply of white rice and some canned green beans.

My cooking effort was tasty enough.

I enjoyed my own cooking.

Jennie did not.

I had to shackle her to the bed and head out for a rat hunt. I was able to secure ten of the creatures, apologizing to them even as I did so.

I couldn't just kill them.

Jennie, like a constrictor, liked her food live.

She didn't touch my perfectly seasoned chicken.

She savored every one of the rats.

Day 5

Serum, doubled, works better. I need to keep making more, and I fear I will run out of supplies. But if I cure Jennie and can present my findings, there are many medical supply houses within reach of our teams of military men—now called, officially, the Sanctuary Guard.

We don't have a president or a governor or even a mayor.

Captain Hicks is our supreme leader, but he is a good man, and his guard obey him and they all—at this point—work for the populace, the hundred and fifty or so of us who remain.

No one stopped by today; Jennie was good. She had her speech.

I ate the tiny bit of chicken that was left.

Outside, I couldn't find any rats.

I heard a dog barking. Mrs. Paulson, who lived in an apartment a block down, had a German shepherd.

That would make Jennie happy.

"Hey, there, Fritz!" I called to the dog.

Fritz had always liked me. He came rushing over to be scratched and petted.

I figured I could use my belt for a leash, and I was about to slip the belt around his collar when Mrs Paulson and her ten-year-old boy, Teddy, came running down the street.

Mr Paulson had been infected.

Sadly, he'd been shot in the street, twice, a bullet through each eye. And Teddy had been there.

"There you are, Fritz! Come on now, can't go getting lost these days!" Mrs Paulson said.

She'd been an attractive woman once. Not long ago. Now, her hair was a steely gray color and while her face remained pretty, she was worn, and she was way too thin.

But she smiled at me. "Super-Doc!"

"Morning, Mrs. Paulson."

"How is your work going?" she asked softly. She was a good woman; she still cared.

"I hope I'm a little closer to the cure every day."

"You and Jennie need to get out more. I realize how careful we all have to be these days, but if we can't remember friendship and love and caring and…and humanity, what are we surviving for?" she asked, and that smile of hers kept any sting from her words. "Hey, when Michael and the boys bring us some pork, you two must come over for dinner. We'll have a night together. We can…"

"Play charades!" Teddy offered hopefully. "With Super-Doc! That would be so much fun."

Fritz—big, beautiful, trusting old Fritz—barked, as if he understood and agreed.

"We have to eat!" Mrs Paulson said.

So did Jennie!

I looked at the dog. I smiled. I told her, "Sure. And thanks."

Twenty minutes later, I returned to my house and office with food for Jennie.

No, I didn't kill the dog. I found a stray raccoon rattling through a trash can. I felt guilty about the damned raccoon and wondered how I was justifying the murder of a raccoon against that of a dog. Silly? Such thoughts go through one's head during a zombie apocalypse.

There was a bit of the chicken left.

I enjoyed it.

I realized, watching Jennie eat raccoon brains and slobbering them everywhere, just how much I loved her.

Raccoon brains and blood flying everywhere only to be lapped up and savored wherever they might have fallen is not a pretty event to observe.

Day 6

The raccoon lasted a while. My serum was doing well. Jennie didn't speak much, but she easily took her serum.

I did find a few more rats.

Jennie seemed to wear a secretive smile.

Michael stopped by to thank me for the antacid. He didn't hug Jennie, but he smiled at her and she smiled at him.

I worried that he still didn't understand the true nature of that smile.

Day 7

I awoke in fear; Jennie was not at my side.

I jumped out of bed, terrified, but rushed out of the bedroom, calling her name.

"Jennie!"

"Here, my love!"

Here, my love?

My serum! It was working, truly working.

"I'm not sure I can enjoy it yet, but there was coffee...and I thought you might enjoy some," she told me.

I was amazed. Beyond amazed. She was almost just like my impossibly beautiful wife had been before the infection.

"Coffee would be lovely!" I told her.

We went out back for me to drink the coffee and for her to tell me she was enjoying the aroma. Then she sighed and leaned back and said, "It's not at all like I thought!"

"What isn't?"

She turned to me, laughing. "Oh, darling! Vampires, werewolves, mummies—zombies! I always loved my soap operas and stories, you know. But I never got into the whole zombie thing—when it was all still fiction! I mean zombies! Decaying flesh. I just couldn't even begin to envision a romance." She gave me a teasing look. "You know—I mean how horrible would it be if a decaying part just broke off in the middle of…well, you know!"

I shook my head and told her passionately. "We're on the way to curing you! We will both survive, I swear." I paused. It had been a while; survival had been the key to everything. "And, we'll have the baby!"

She shook her head sadly. "The baby…the baby is gone. I don't know how I know, but I do. Maybe…it's best."

"Because, when you're well, we'll try again!" I promised.

She nodded. She smiled. She touched me, and we just looked at one another.

I thought then that Mrs Paulson had spoken well—what was life without the things that mattered? Caring for one another, caring for others…

I loved Jennie so very much.

I gave her a wicked smile. "Hey. My parts are all just fine— they won't fall off, I promise."

She laughed delightedly, and then shook her head.

"Not yet, my love. I'm still afraid that the urge to bite into your head might cloud my mind if let myself go, and darling… we do let ourselves go!"

I nodded.

Water still came through our pipes.

Cold water.

But that was the kind I needed.

And still…it was a beautiful day.

I tripled her serum, certain that in a day or two, I could present her to others in all triumph. We would have the cure—I would have the cure—to save the zombie population.

Day 8

I awoke to the wonderful aroma of coffee again. And more!
Sizzling bacon.

Michael had been by, she said, bringing us meat from the pigs they had slaughtered.

Of course, we were cooking everything on a little kerosene stove, but it was beyond belief that Jennie had managed to prepare and cook the bacon. I was grateful and amazed, even before the succulent delicacy met my taste buds.

Jennie was watching me, a little smile on her face.

"What?"

"I was just thinking that…well, zombies have to eat brains. They eat other meat, but I guess there is something in the brain that is necessary to life for the…dead. Or infected. And it seems horrible—but not really. Societies have eaten animal brains for years. *Cervelle de Vea—cow brains!* A delicacy in Morocco. They even make brain sandwiches in some places. So, what is the problem with the infected—with zombies—eating cow brains?"

"I think the problem comes with the fact that zombies prefer *human* brains," I reminded her.

She smiled. "Maybe that's your cure; convincing all zombies that human brains will make you fat and cow brains are the keto diet of the future!"

We laughed together. It was a good day.

Jennie took her serum; I didn't have to hunt that night for rats—raccoons, or desperately, a dog.

She had leftover pork brains.

She hummed before she fell asleep.

I watched her, in love with the sweet drape of her body across our bed.

It was coming; I was so close.

Any day, I would have the cure.

Day 9

A few patients came by. I tried to explain that Jennie couldn't come out to see people—she had a cold. Just the common cold.

They all hung on my every word. After all, I was Super-Doc.

And, hey, even in a world filled with zombies, who wanted to be sick and sniffle and cough all over the place?

We still had pork.

I decided to try giving Jennie the serum twice a day, in the morning, and again at night.

She'd been so good lately.

We talked on in the back yard again that afternoon. I marveled at her clarity of speech, at the laughter in her eyes.

In my lab, I checked my supplies. I was low on just about everything.

My gun, a Smith and Wesson, was in a drawer with fine needles for my patients with diabetes. I looked at it, smiling. Maybe the world wouldn't have to be armed soon, maybe we wouldn't live in fear. Maybe we had found a cure.

And maybe, maybe Jennie and I could make love again. The thought made me smile. She was still worried, and I wanted to joke and tease with her. I wasn't the one infected or decaying, and I was the one with the body that just might...

Break off!

Two doses of the serum, a breakfast of bacon and rice for me...

Pig brains for Jennie.

I do hope, in the future, she learns to eat with a little more... finesse.

As beautiful as Jennie is, it's quite unsettling to watch her when she licks the walls and floor.

And it's very unnerving when a slimy bit falls on me, and she licks me, and I see her eyes.

Because it's still there. The desire to bite into my head. She wouldn't want to do it; she'd be horrified if she did, but the instinct was there, and it was...

The cure. It was almost upon us.

By the tenth day...

In the kitchen, cleaning the best one could under the circumstances, I saw Michael in the street. He was looking at my house. Just studying it.

He waved suddenly and smiled.

Except he wasn't looking at me; he was looking past the front windows.

At my bedroom windows.

I sighed. I knew the man was looking at Jennie, that she was either watching one of her programs, or straightening up. The cure, the cure, was almost upon us!

But if she was looking at him with something he discerned as longing, well...

Again, I could only warn him the longing was for his brains.

Michael, Michael. Well, he was a good guy and I could hardly blame him for being enamored of the woman I so adored. She was mine. And soon, so soon, we could start dreaming about life again, life in which I had a real office again, supplies with which to treat patients...

A cure, maybe not for those who had completely changed, but for those who were just infected. In time, we'd change it all back. The healthy living would outnumber the infected and the zombies.

Soon.

Night seemed to come quickly. Jennie was wonderful.

We did three doses of the serum that day. Her speech was clear and beautiful. I even talked to her about the invitation I'd received from our neighbor—I told her how I had almost brought the big, beautiful German shepherd, Fritz, home for her.

"That dog! Oh, I love that dog!" she said, eyes alight with laughter.

She was living; she was human. She was my wife.

I loved her.

Almost as if she had a sixth sense and knew I'd been talking about her, Mrs Paulson arrived at our front door.

Jennie gave her a hug and I froze as I always did at such moments.

But Jennie didn't even show her teeth.

Mrs Paulson asked us to come over for dinner.

Jennie said it was delightful idea.

We arrived just at seven; Teddy, dressed up for company, opened the door along with the dog, Fritz. Jennie pet Fritz, and the dog didn't react with any kind of a negative response—which animals often did with the infected.

"Love Fritz!" she assured Teddy. "In the good old days, I'd have little scraps and beef bones ready for him when he'd sneak out!"

"He's a great dog; I love my dog so much!" Teddy said, hugging the animal.

I thought of how the dog had come so close to being dinner for Jennie and I was heartily glad I'd thought better of the notion.

And that poor raccoon had cemented Fritz's freedom by seeking garbage in a nearby can.

Mrs Paulson prepared a delicious dish; she had grits left and some cheese, and she created a delicious meal with bacon and cheese and the grits. She'd been growing herbs in her house, and she'd added several, and served it all with string beans out of a can.

I watched Jennie. She tired to take a bit; I saw that she was almost sick.

I managed to get most of her food to Fritz.

Well, it made Fritz happy.

And Jennie would eat later.

When we finished the meal, we played charades, just as Teddy wanted. We acted out the motions for books and movies and plays and those creations that were books, movies, and plays. It was Jennie and me against Teddy and his mom, with Fritz barking now and then with excitement for all of us.

It was wonderful.

I was out with my wife. Jennie was a wonder, laughing, petting the dog, making Teddy laugh. It was almost as if...

She was cured.

Tomorrow. I believed by tomorrow it would be proven. She had managed to put a bit of real food to her lips. She had spoken clearly and well all night, she had laughed, she had looked at me with a sparkle in her eyes and I was even imagining...

What could properly be done with body parts!

Time went so quickly. I was stunned to realize it was nearly midnight.

"I should have put Teddy to bed a few hours ago," Mrs Paulson said. "But we've been having such a lovely time and it's so seldom...well, Jennie! We are going to have to see so much more of you. This is so normal and nice!"

"A lovely meal; a lovely night!" Jennie assured her.

At last, we bid them good evening, and made our way up the block or so to our own home.

"It was wonderful," I whispered, and I dared to kiss her lips.

She let me kiss her, but she didn't kiss me back, and I knew she was still afraid.

Trust in herself would come, I was certain.

I unlocked our door, ever careful. Jennie yawned, ready to go to sleep.

I, on the other hand, felt vaguely uneasy. I realized I hadn't left our office/house in a while and that—though I might be paranoid—I needed to check everything out.

"Get some sleep; I'll be right in," I told her.

I could never say why, but walking through the house, I felt something was wrong. That meant I went straight to my office and slipped my revolver into my hands. I was being silly, of course, but I was in the middle of surviving the zombie apocalypse.

I went out back, to the beautiful little courtyard where Jennie and I had chatted and where it had seemed there was so much hope.

Nothing.

I went to bed.

"Fixed you a toddy!" Jennie said. "Found a bit of whiskey left. Thought it might help you sleep!"

I thanked her and kissed the back of her head.

I pretended to drink her toddy, but I was waiting for day ten—just minutes away, really.

I spilled the little bit of liquid, rubbing it into the floor, not wanting her to think that I hadn't appreciated her thoughtfulness.

And I didn't need the toddy; I fell asleep easily, dreaming of day ten.

But I didn't sleep long. I woke because I heard a strange noise. When I turned, Jennie wasn't in bed. In panic, I jumped up and hurried out to the kitchen, and I tore through all the rooms, one by one, stopping in my lab again, seeking the drawer that held my gun.

Then I realized the noise was coming from the back and it was growing louder and louder.

I rushed to the back and looked out and…

The moonlight showed a scene of such horror I couldn't begin to imagine.

They were there together, my Jennie—and Michael.

They had both stripped away their clothing; naked and bathed in the blood and bone and *brains* of *people* Michael had dragged into the enclosure. They were slathering each other with the mess, kissing and licking one another...

Making love in a pool of blood and bone and brains.

Something alerted them to my stunned presence.

They turned. They looked at one another again and they started to laugh as Michael came forward, ripping open the back door.

"Super-Doc! Super idiot! Oh, the cure! The cure—the cure is brains, you damned idiot! Don't you see it—Jennie got better not from your stupid serum, but because I brought her brains, real brains, human brains. And, hey, well, you know...I bet your brains are going to be exceptionally delicious!" he told me. "What say, my darling?" he asked Jennie.

"Well, he is so smart, if that has anything to do with taste," Jennie said, sliding her body against his and licking his torso.

I was stunned. Frozen—but only for seconds.

Hey, I'd been a medic in the military.

I had my revolver; I lifted it, and I showed Michael all about brains—I blew his through the backyard and beyond, point blank.

I hadn't expected what happened with Jennie. I hadn't expected her to move so fast, or with such fury.

She tore at me with such speed the gun was knocked out of my hands. She forced me down and stared at me, and it wasn't hatred that was in her eyes, it was hunger and fury.

She opened her mouth. I could see the jagged, razor-like edge to her teeth.

She leaned closer to me, and I knew it was all over...

Until he came.

Fritz.

I'll never know how the damned dog did it, but he leapt an eight-foot wall.

And he flung his hundred-plus pounds on Jennie, throwing her halfway across the yard.

She sprang back to her feet, gurgling and incensed, ready to slam the dog to death.

But she didn't have time.

Instinct and reflex had kicked in. I had my gun again.

The dog saved me. I save the dog.

Jennie's head exploded; my aim had always been true.

Day 10

And into the Future

They say the only cure for the zombie plague is a bullet to the brain.

I have decided they're right.

I am no longer Super-Doc, rather I have become exceptionally good at what I do now.

I am Sanctuary's commander of the home guard and zombie hunters.

It's funny, in an odd way—not a "ha-ha" kind of way, but rather in a sadly ironic sense.

They call me Super-Shot.

And I am.

I am a survivor, and still, I know that life, the value of life, lies in more.

Maybe I'm a Super-Dreamer.

Maybe, one day, I'll marry again. Mrs Paulson is starting to look better and better.

LOVEMAN'S COMEBACK

RAMSEY CAMPBELL

Surely she was dreaming. She lay in bed, but the blankets felt like damp moss. Her eyes were white and blind. She suffered a muffled twinge of nightmare before she realized that what filled her eyes was moonlight and not cataract. Sitting up hastily, she saw the moon beyond the grubby pane. Against it stood a nearby chimney, a square black horned head.

The light must have awakened her, if she were awake. The moonlit blankets and their shadows retained a faint tousled outline of her. As she gazed at the vague form she felt hardly more present herself. She was standing up, she found, and at some point had dressed herself ready for walking.

Why did she want to go out? Frost glittered on the window, as though the grime were flowering translucently. Still, perhaps even the cold might be preferable to the empty house, which sounded drained of Life, rattling with her echoes. It hadn't sounded so when her parents—No point in dwelling on that subject. Walk, instead.

No need to hurry so. Surely she had time to switch on the light above the stairs. Her compulsion disagreed: moonlight reached across the landing from her open bedroom door and lay like an askew fragment of carpet over the highest stairs; that was illumination enough. Her shadow jerked downstairs jaggedly ahead of her. Her echoes ran about the house like an insubstantial stumbling crowd, to remind her how alone she was. To escape them, she hurried blindly down the unclothed stairs, along the thundering hall, and out.

The street was not reassuring. But then so late at night streets seldom were: they reminded her of wandering. Or was that a dream too? Hadn't she wandered streets at night, the more deserted the better, alongside others—friends, no doubt—sharing fat multicoloured hand-rolled cigarettes, or locked into the depths of themselves by some chemical? Hadn't houses shrunk as though gnomes were staging illusions, hadn't bricks melted and run together like wax? But she couldn't be sure that she was remembering; even her parents resembled a dream. The urge to walk was more real.

Well, she could walk no faster. Underfoot, the roadway felt cracked: on the pavements dead streetlamps held up their broken heads. At one end of the street she'd glimpsed a street soaked in moonlight; it seemed to her like the luminous skeleton of something unimaginable. But her impulse tugged her the other way, between unbroken ranks of houses whose only garden was the pavement. Moonlight covered the slated roofs with overlapping scales of white ice. As she passed, the dim dull windows appeared to ripple.

She was so numb that she felt only the compulsion to walk. It was a nervousness that must be obeyed, a vague nagging like a threat of pain. Was it like the onset of withdrawal symptoms? She couldn't recall—indeed, wasn't sure whether she had experienced them. Had she gone so far with the needle?

Litter scuttled on the chill wind; something broken scraped a lamp's glass fangs. Terraced houses enclosed her like solid walls. In the darkness, their windows looked opaque as brick; surely nobody could live within. Could she not meet just one person, to convince her that the city hadn't died in the night?

The dimness of her memories had begun to dismay her. Her mind seemed dark and empty. But the streets were brightening. Orange light glared between walls, scaring her eyes. A coppery glow hovered overhead, on gathering clouds. When she heard the brisk whirr of a vehicle she knew she was approaching the main road.

Bleak though it was, it heartened her. At least she would be able to see; groping and stumbling along the side streets had reminded her of her worst secret fear. She could walk beside the dual carriageway.

Even the drivers, riding in their tins as though on a conveyor belt, would be company. Perhaps one might give her a ride. Sometimes they had.

But she wasn't allowed to walk there. Before she had time even to narrow her eyes against the glare, her impulse plunged her into the subway, where graffiti were tangled in barbaric patterns. Long thin lights fluttered and buzzed like trapped insects. A car rumbled dully overhead. The middle of the subway was a muddy pool that drowned the clogged drains. Though she had to walk through it she couldn't feel the water. Didn't that prove she was dreaming?

Perhaps. But as she emerged onto the far pavement she grew uneasy. She knew where she was going—but her mind refused to be more explicit. She was compelled forward, between two hefty gateposts without gates, beneath trees.

Memories were stirring. They peered out, but withdrew before she could tell why she was unnerved. Her compulsion hurried her along the private road, as though to outdistance the memories. But there were things she'd seen before: great white houses standing aloof beyond their gardens, squat self-satisfied brick faces cracked by the shadows of branches; families of cars like sleeping beasts among the trees; lamp standards or ships' steering wheels outside front doors; boats beached far from any sea. When had she been here, and why? In her unwilling haste she slipped and fell on wet dead leaves.

Gradually, with increasing unpleasantness, her mind became strained. Opposing impulses struggled there. She wanted to know why this place was familiar, yet dreaded to do so. Part of her yearned to wake, but what if she found she was not asleep? Oblivious of her confusion, her feet trudged rapidly onward.

Suddenly they turned. She had to fight her way out from her thoughts to see where she was going. No, not here! It wasn't only that a faint threatening memory had wakened; she was walking towards someone's home. She'd be arrested! Christ, what was she planning to do? But her feet ignored her, and her body carried her squirming inwardly towards its goal.

Hedges pressed close to her; leafy fists poked at her face. She slithered on the grassy path that led her away from the road; she saved herself from falling, but the hedge snapped and threshed. Someone would hear her and call the police! But that fear was almost comforting—for it distracted her from the realisation that the place towards which she was heading was very much unlike anybody's home.

At a gap in the hedge she halted. Surely she wasn't going— But she forced her way through the creaking gap, into a wider space. Trees stooped over her, chattering their leaves; infrequent shards of moonlight floated on the clouds. She stumbled along what might be a path. After a while she left it and picked her way blindly over mounds, past vertical slabs that scraped her legs; once she knocked over what seemed to be a stone vase, which toppled heavily onto earth.

Dark blocks loomed ahead. One of them was an unlit house; she must be returning towards the road. Was there a window dim as the clouds, and a head peering out at her? This glimpse prevented her from noticing the nearer block until she was almost there. It was a shed that smelled of old damp wood, and her hand was groping for the doorknob.

No. No, she wasn't going in there. Not when the tics of moonlight showed her the unkempt mounds, some of them gaping— But her body was an automaton; she was tiny and helpless within it. Her hand dragged open the scaly door, her feet carried her within. At least please leave the door open, please—But except for trembling, her hand ignored her. It reached behind her and shut her in the dark of the graveyard shed.

It must be a dream. No shed could contain such featureless dark. She couldn't move to explore, even if she had dared; her body was stopped, switched off; waiting. Wasn't that nightmarish enough to be a dream? Couldn't the same be said of the slow footsteps that came stumbling across the violated graveyard, towards the shed?

She must turn; she must see what had opened the door and was standing there silently. But fear or compulsion held her still as a doll. Timid moonlight outlined a low table before her, over which most of the shadow of a head and shoulders was folded, deformed. Then the dark slammed closed around her.

Three paces had taken her into the shed; no more than three would find her. She heard the shuffling feet advance, one pace, two—and fingers clumsy as claws dragged at her hair. They reached for her shoulders. Deep in her a tiny shriek was choking. The hands, which were very cold, lifted her arms. As she stood like a shivering cross in the dark, the hands clutched her breasts.

When they fumbled to unbutton her dress her mind refused to believe; it backed away and hid in a corner muttering: a dream, a dream. Her breasts were naked beneath the dress. The fingers, cold as the soil through which she'd stumbled, rolled her nipples roughly, as though to rub them to dust. Her mind, eager to distract her, was reminded of crumbling cannabis onto tobacco. When at last her nipples came erect they seemed distant, no part of her at all.

The hands pushed her back against the. table. They pulled her own hands down to grip the table's edge, and spread her legs. She might have been a sex doll: she felt she was merely an audience to the antics of her puppet body. When the hands bared her genitals the sensation was less convincing than a dream.

She felt the penis enter her. It seemed unnaturally slippery, and quite large. Her observations were wholly disinterested, even when the fingers teased out her clitoris. The thrusting of the penis meant as little to her as the pounding of a distant drum. The grotesqueness of her situation had allowed her to retreat into a lonely bleak untroubled place in her mind.

She felt the rhythm quicken, and the eventual spurting, without having experienced even the hint of an orgasm; but then, she rarely did. The familiar dissatisfaction was oddly reassuring. Only the nervous gasping of her partner, a gulping as though he'd been robbed of breath, was new.

As soon as he'd finished he withdrew. He shoved her away, discarded. Her hands sprang up to ward off the clammy planks of the walls, but touched nothing. Of course she mightn't, in a dream. She teetered giddily, unprepared to have regained control of her body, and glimpsed the abruptly open doorway, a bow-legged figure stumbling out; its vague face looked fat and hirsute as mouldy food. It snatched the door closed as it went.

Perhaps she was imprisoned. But her mind could accept no more; if she were trapped, there was nothing it could do. She dressed blindly, mechanically; the buttons felt swollen, pebble-thick. The door was not locked. Yes, she was surrounded by a graveyard. Her numbed mind let her walk: no reason why she shouldn't go home. She trudged back to the deserted main road, through the flooded subway. The moon had passed over; the side streets were dark valleys. Perhaps once she reached her bed her dream would merge with blank sleep. When she slumped fully clothed on the blankets, oblivion took her at once.

When she woke she knew at once where she had been. In her dream, of course. Understandably, the dream had troubled her sleep; on waking she found that she'd slept all day, exhausted. She would have preferred her deserted house not to have been so dark. The sky grew pale with indirect moonlight; against it, roofs blackened. In the emptiness, the creak of her bed was feverishly loud. At least she was sure that she had been dreaming, for Loveman was dead.

But why should she dream about him now? She searched among the dim unwieldy thoughts in her dusty mind. Her parents' death must be the reason. Of all her activities that would have shocked and distressed them had they known, they would have hated Loveman most. After their death she'd kept thinking that now she was free to do everything, without the threat of discovery—but that freedom had seemed meaningless. The thought must have lain dormant in her mind and borne the dream.

Remembering her parents hollowed out the house. She'd felt so small and abandoned during her first nights with the emptiness; she hadn't realised how much she'd relied on their presence. For the first time she'd taken drugs other than for pleasure, in a desperate search for sleep. No doubt that explained why she slept so irregularly now.

She hurried out, not bothering to switch on the lights; she

knew the house too well. It wasn't haunted: just dead, cold, a tomb. She fled its dereliction, towards the main road. The light and spaciousness might be welcoming.

Terraces passed, so familiar as to be invisible. Thoughts of Loveman blinded her; she walked automatically. God, if her parents had found out she'd been mixed up in black magic! Not that her involvement had been very profound. She'd heard that he called his women to him, whether or not they were willing, by moulding dolls of them. The women must have been unbalanced and cowed by the power of his undeniably hypnotic eyes. But he hadn't needed to overpower her in order to have her—nobody had. He'd satisfied her no more than any other man. So much for black magic!

Then—so she'd gathered from friends—his black magic had been terminated by a black joke. He had been knocked down on the main road, by a car whose driver was a nurse and a devout Christian, no less. Even for God, that seemed a mysterious way to move. Had that happened before her parents' death or after? Her memories were loose and imprecise. Her jagged sleep must have blurred them.

And the rest of her dream—Just a nightmare, just exaggeration. Yes, he had lived in that private road and yes, there had been a graveyard behind his house. No doubt be was buried there; her dream appeared to think so. Why should she be troubled? But she was, and was recalling the night when she'd gone to Loveman's house only to meet him emerging from the graveyard. As he'd glanced sidelong at her he had looked shamefaced, aggressively self-righteous, secretly ecstatic. She hadn't wanted to know what he had been doing; even less did she want to know now.

Here was the main road. Its lights ought to sear away her dream. But it remained, looming at the back of her mind, a presence she was never quick enough to glimpse. Cars sang by; the curtains of the detached houses shone. There was one way she might rid herself of the dream. She could take a stroll along Loveman's road and oust the dream with reality.

But she could not. She reached the mouth of the subway and found herself unable to move. The tiled entrance gaped, scribbled with several paints, like the doorway of a violated tomb. A compulsion planted too deep in her to be perceived or understood forbade her to advance a step nearer Loveman's road.

Something had power over her. Details of her dream, and memories of Loveman, crowded ominously about her. Suppose the graveyard, which she'd never entered, were precisely as she'd dreamed it? A stray thought of sleepwalking made her flinch away, front the cold tiled passage, the muddy pool which flickered with ghosts of the dying lights.

All of a sudden, with vindictively dramatic timing, the road was bare of cars. The lit windows of the houses served only to exclude her. Abruptly she felt cold, perhaps more emotionally than physically, and shuddered. Across the carriageway, ranks of trees that sprouted from both pavements of the private road swayed together overhead, mocking prayer.

She was afraid to be alone. She could no more have returned to the empty house than she would have climbed into a coffin. Driveways confronted her, blocked by watch dog cars. Beyond the smug houses stood a library. She had been in there only once, to score some acid; books had never held her attention for long. But she fled to the building now, like a believer towards a church.

Indeed, there were churchy elements. Women paced quietly, handling romances as though they were missals, tutting at anyone who made a noise. Still, there were tables strewn with jumbled newspapers, old men covertly filling the crosswords, young girls giggling behind the shelves and sharing a surreptitious cigarette. She could take refuge in here without being noticed, she could grow calm—except that as she entered, a shelf of books was waiting for her. *Black Magic. Grimoire. Truth About Witchcraft.* She flinched awkwardly aside.

People moved away from her, frowning. She was used to that; usually they'd glimpsed needle tracks on her arms. She pulled her sleeves down over her hands. Nobody could stop her sitting down—but there was no space: old men sat at all the tables, doodling, growling at the newspapers and at each other.

No: there was one almost uninhabited table, screened from the librarian's view by bookcases. A scrawny young man sat there, dwarfed by his thick shabby overcoat; a wool cap covered his hair. He was reading a science fiction novel. He fingered the pages, rather as though picking at a dull meal.

When she sat down he glanced up, but with no more interest than he would have shown had someone dumped an old coat on her chair. His limp hands riffled the pages, and she caught sight of the needle tracks on his forearm. So that was why this table was avoided. Perhaps he was holding stuff, but she didn't want any; she felt no craving, only vague depression at being thus reminded of the days when she had been on the needle.

But the marks held her gaze, and he glanced more sharply. "All right?" he said, in a voice so bored that the words slumped into each other, blurring.

"Yes thanks." Perhaps she didn't sound so convincing; her fears hovered just behind her. "Yes, I think so," she said, trying to clarify the truth: his stare lay heavily on her, and she felt questioned, though no doubt he simply couldn't be bothered to look away. " I've just been walking. I wanted to sit down," she said, unable to admit more.

"Right." His fingers obsessively rubbed the comer of a page, which grew tattered and grubby. She must be annoying him. "I'm sorry," she said, feeling rebuffed and lonely. "You want to read."

The librarian came and stood near them, disapproving. Eventually, when he could find nothing of which to accuse them, he stalked away to harangue an old man who was finishing a crossword. "What's this, eh, what's this? You can't do that here, you know."

"I'm not reading," the young man said. He might have been, but was perversely determined now to antagonise the librarian. "Go on. You were walking. Alone, were you?"

Was there muffled concern in his voice? Her sudden loneliness was keener than the dully aching emptiness she had been able to ignore. "Yes," she muttered.

"Don't you live with anyone?"

He was growing interested; he'd begun to enunciate his words. Was he concerned for her, or was his anxiety more selfish? "No," she said warily.

"Whereabouts do you live?"

His self-interest was unconcealed now; impatience had given him an addict's shamelessness. "Where do *you* live?" she countered loudly, triumphantly.

"Oh," he said evasively, "I'm moving." His nervous eyes flickered, for her triumph had brought the librarian bearing down on them; the man's red face hovered over the table. "I must ask you to be quieter," the librarian said.

"All right. Fuck off. We're going." The interruption had shattered his control; words were as jagged as his nerves. "Sorry," he said plaintively at once. "I didn't mean that. We'll be good. We won't disturb you. Let us stay. Please."

She and the librarian stared at him, acutely embarrassed. At last the librarian said "Just behave yourself" and dawdled away, shaking his head. By then she had realised why the young man was anxious not to be ejected: he was waiting to score dope.

"I'll be going in a minute," she whispered. "I'm all right now. I've been having strange dreams, that's all," she added, to explain why she hadn't been all right before. Only dreams, of course that was all, just dreams.

"Yeah," he said, and his tone shared with her what dreams meant to him: he'd seen the marks on her arms. " You don't have to go," he whispered quickly; perhaps she'd reminded him of what he craved, and of the loneliness of his addiction. "You can get a book."

Something about him—the familiar needle tracks, or his concern, however selfish—made her feel less alone. The feeling had already helped her shrug off her dream; it could do her no harm to stay with him for a while. She selected books, though none seemed more attractive than any other.

She flicked rapidly through them, lingering over the sexual scenes, none of which reached her; they were unreal, posturings of type and paper. Opposite her his fingertips poked at the novel, letting the pages turn when they would.

The librarian called "Five minutes, please." The clock's hands clicked into place on the hour. Only when the librarian came frowning to speak to him did the young man stand up reluctantly.

Nobody else had visited the table. He hurried to the shelves and slammed a book home—but she saw that he'd feinted; with a conjuror's skill, he had vanished the science fiction novel beneath his coat.

Outside the library he said "Do you want to go somewhere?'

She supposed he meant to score. The proposal was less tempting than depressing. Besides, she suspected that if she accompanied him, she wouldn't be able to conceal from him where she lived. She didn't want him to know; she'd lost control of situations too often, most recently in the dream. She didn't need him now—she was rid of the dream. "I've got to go home," she said hastily, and fled.

Glancing back, she saw him standing inert on the library steps. His pale young withered face was artificially ruddy beneath the sodium lamps; his thin frame shivered within the long stained overcoat. She was glad she wasn't like that any more. She dodged into the nearest side street, lest he follow. It had begun to rain; drops rattled on metal among the streets. The moon floated as though in muddy water, and was incessantly wreathed by black drifting clouds. Though it soaked her dress, the onrush of rain felt clean on her face; it must be cold, but not sufficiently so to bother her. She was cleansed of the dream.

But she was not, for on the far side of a blankness that must have been sleep she found herself rising from her bed. Outside the window, against the moon, the chimney glittered, acrawl with rain. She had time only for that glimpse, for the impulse compelled her downstairs, blinking in the dark, and into the street.

How could she dream so vividly? Everything seemed piercingly real: the multitude of raindrops pecking at her, the thin waves that the wind cast in her face, the clatter of pelted metal. Her ears must be conveying all this to her sleep—but how could she feel the sloshing of cold pools in the uneven pavement, and see the glimmer of the streaming roadway?

Some of the lights in the subway had died. The deeper pool slopped around her ankles; the chill seized her legs. She hadn't felt that last night. Was her dream accumulating detail, or was her growing terror refusing to allow her to be so unaware?

The private trees dipped. Raindrops, glaring with sodium light, swarmed down trunks and branches. The soft vague hiss of the downpour surrounded her. She could be hearing that in bed—but why should her dream bother to provide a car outside Loveman's house? There was a sign in the window of the car. Before she could make it out she was compelled aside, between the hedges.

All the leaves glistened, and wept chill on her. Her sodden hair slumped down her neck. When she pushed, or was pushed, through the gap, the hedge drenched her loudly. She was too excessively wet for the sensation to be real, this was a dream of drenching—But she was staggering through the dark, among the stones, the unseen holes which tried to gulp her. What had there been in that opened earth? Please let it be a dream. But the cold doorknob, its scales of rust loosened by the rain and adhering to her hands, was no dream.

Though she struggled to prevent it, her hand twitched the door shut behind her. She stumbled forward until her thighs collided with the edge of the table. It must be the rain that filled the darkness with a cloying smell of earth, but the explanation lulled her terror not at all. Worse still, the clouds had left the moon alone. A faint glow diluted the dark of the shed. She would be able to see.

The first sound of footsteps was heavy and squelching; the feet had to be dragged out of the earth. She writhed deep in her doll of a body, silently shrieking. The footsteps plodded unevenly to the door, which creaked, slow and gloating. Hands fumbled the door wide. Perhaps their owner was blind—incomplete, she thought, appalled.

Moonlight was dashed over her. She saw her shadow, which was unable even to tremble, hurled into the depths of the shed, The darkness slammed; the footsteps advanced, dripping mud. Wet claws, that felt gnarled and soaked as the hedges, seized her shoulders. They meant to turn her to face her tormentor.

With an effort that momentarily blinded her, she battled not to turn. At least let her body stay paralysed, please let her not see, please! In a moment the claws ceased to drag at her. Then, with a shock that startled a cry almost to her lips—the incongruity and degradation—she was shoved face down over the table and beaten. He bared her, and went on. Suddenly she knew that he could have compelled her to turn, had he wanted; he was beating her for pleasure. She felt little pain, but intense humiliation, which was perhaps what had been intended.

All at once he forced her legs urgently wide and entered her from behind. He slithered in, bulging her. She became aware only of her genitals, which felt chilled. The dark grew less absolute: weren't there vague distorted shadows ahead of her, miming copulation? She was not dreaming. Only a sense that she was not entirely awake permitted her to cling to that hope. A dream, a dream, she repeated, borrowing the rhythm of the penis to pound her mind into stupidity. When his orgasm flooded her it felt icy as the rain.

He levered himself away from her, and her sodden dress fell like a wash of ointment over her stinging buttocks. The shed lit up before the slam. The squelching footsteps merged with the hiss of mud and rain. When she buttoned herself up, her dress clung to her like a shroud.

The compulsion urged her home. She stumbled over the gaping earth. Stone angels drooled. She was sobbing, but had to make do with rain for tears. In a pitiful attempt to preserve her hope, she tried to touch as few objects as possible, for everything felt dreadfully real. But the pool in the subway drowned her shoes while she waited shivering, unable to move until a car had passed.

Rain trickled from her on to the blankets, which felt like a marsh. She lay shuddering uncontrollably, trying to calm herself: it was over now, over for tonight. She needed to sleep, in order to be ready—for she had a plan. As she'd trudged sobbing home it had grown like an ember in her mind, faint but definite. Tomorrow she would move in with one of her friends, any one. She must never be alone again. She was still trying to subdue herself to rest when sleep collapsed over her, black as earth.

She was a doll in a box. Around her other dolls lay, blind and immobile and mindless, in their containers. Her outrage burned through her—like a tonic, or like poison? She wasn't a doll, for she had a mind. She must escape her box, before someone came and bought her. She thrust at the lid that blinded her. Slowly, steadily. Yes, it was moving. It slid away, and the enormous fall of earth suffocated her.

She woke coughing and struggling to scream. The earth was only darkness; she was lying on her back on top of her bed. *Only darkness?* Despite her resolve she had overslept. All right, never mind, she hushed her panic. Some of her friends would surely be at home. She lay massaging pliability into her stiff chill limbs. Whom would she try first, who was kindest, who had room for her? Her limbs were shaking; the damp bed sounded like a sponge. Just one friend would do, just one good friend—But her whole body was shuddering with panic which she struggled not to put into words. She could remember not a single name or address of a friend.

No longer could she pretend she was dreaming. She had been robbed of every memory that could help her. Perhaps the thing which had power over her made her sleep during the day; perhaps his power was greater at night. Her empty house was a box in which she was kept until she was wanted.

Then she must not stay there. That was the one clear thought her panic allowed her. She ran from the house, hunted by her echoes. The moon skulked behind the roofs. The houses faced her blindly; not a window was lit. Even if there had been—even if she battered at the doors and woke the streets with the scream that threatened to cut her open, like a knife of fear—nobody would believe her. How could they?

She fled along the streets. Deprived of the moon, the sky was so dark that she might have been stumbling along an enclosed passage. Far ahead, the main road blazed with unnatural fire; the sullen clouds glowed orange. Suppose he weren't in the library, the young man? Indeed, suppose he were? He couldn't be much help—in his addiction, he was as helpless as she. She didn't even know his name. But he might be the only living person in the world whom she could recognise.

She struggled with the double doors, which seemed determined to shoulder her out. People turned to stare as she flung the doors wide with a crash and ran into the library. The librarian frowned, and made to stalk her. For a terrified moment she thought he meant to tell her to leave. She outdistanced him, and ran to the concealed table. Nothing would rob her of the vague reassurance of the bright lights. They'd never get her to leave. She'd fight, she'd scream.

The young man was toying with a different book. He glanced up, but she wasn't the visitor he'd hoped for; his gaze slumped to the pages. "Back again," be said apathetically.

The librarian pretended to arrange books on a nearby shelf. Neither he, nor the young man's indifference, could deter her. She sat down and stared at a scattered newspaper. An item caught her eye, something about violated graves—but an old man hurried to snatch the newspaper, grumbling.

She could only gaze at the young man. He looked less tense; smiles flickered over his lips—he must have obtained something to take him up. Could the same thing help her fight her compulsions? If she were honest, she knew it could not. But she was prepared to do anything in order to stay with him and whatever friends he had. "Are you going somewhere later?" she whispered.

He didn't look up. "Yeah, maybe." He wasn't interested in the book: just less interested in her.

She mustn't risk making him impatient. Read. She went to the shelf next to the spying librarian. He needn't think she was scared of him; she was scared of—Panic welled up like abrupt nausea. She grabbed the nearest book and sat down.

Perhaps she'd outfaced the librarian, for he retreated to his desk. She heard him noisily tidying. She smirked; he had to make a noise to work off his frustration. But at once she knew that was not the point, for he shouted "Five minutes, please."

Oh Christ, how could it be so late? In five minutes the young man would go, she'd be alone! He was preparing to leave, for he'd slipped the book into hiding. When she followed him towards the exit he ignored her. The librarian glared suspiciously at him. Oh God, he would be arrested, taken from her. But though she was streaming and shivering with panic, they escaped unmolested.

She clung gasping to a stone pillar at the foot of the steps. The young man didn't wait for her; he trudged away. God, no! "Are you going somewhere, then?" she called in as friendly a voice as she could manage, trying not to let it shatter into panic.

"Dunno." He halted, but evidently the question annoyed him.

She stumbled after him, and glimpsed herself in the dark mirror of the library window: pale and thin as a bone, a wild scarecrow- the nightmares in the shed must have done that to her. Her hair had used to shine. How could she expect to appeal to him? But she said "I was only thinking that maybe I could come with you."

"Yeah, well. I'm moving," he muttered, gazing away from her.

She mustn't plead; having lost almost all her self-respect in the shed, she must cling to the scraps that remained. "I could help you," she said.

"Yeah. Maybe moving isn't quite the word." She could tell that he bitterly resented having to explain. "I haven't got anywhere to live at the moment. I was staying with some people. They threw me out."

Nor must she allow her pride to trick her. The sodium glow filled the road with fire, but it was very cold. "You can come home with me if you like," she blurted.

He stared at her. After a pause he said indifferently "Yeah, okay."

She mustn't expect too much of him. All that mattered was that she mustn't be alone. She took his clammy hand and led him towards her street. Without warning he said "I never met anyone like you." It sounded less like a compliment than a statement of confusion.

They groped along the dark streets, their eyes blinded by lingering orange. "Is this where you live?" he said, almost contemptuously. Where did he expect? The dreadful private road? The thought convulsed her, made her grip his lank hand.

Thin carpets of moonlight lay over the crossroads, but her road brimmed with darkness. It didn't matter, for she could feel him beside her; she wouldn't let go. "You're so cold," he remarked, speaking a stray thought.

Since she had no drugs, there was only one method by which she might bind him to her. "In some ways I'm not cold at all," she dared to say. If he understood, he didn't respond. He held her hand as though it were something fragile that had been thrust upon him, that he had no idea how to handle.

Though he didn't comment when they reached her house, she sensed his feelings: disappointment, depression. All right, she knew it was a bit dismal: the scaly front door, the windows fattened with dusty grime, the ghosts of dust that rose up as she opened the door. She'd had no enthusiasm for keeping the place clean, nor indeed for anything else, since her parents had died. Now she'd enticed him so far, her fear was lightening slightly; she was able to think that he ought to be grateful, she was giving him a place to stay although she didn't even know his name.

She led him straight to her bedroom. Since her parents' death she had been unable to face the other deserted rooms. Moonlight leaked down the stairs from her door. As she climbed the vague treads she could feel him holding back. Suppose he decided not to stay, suppose he fled! "Nearly there now," she blurted, and became nervously still until she heard him clambering.

She pushed the door wide. Moonlight soaked the bed; a trace of her shape lay on the luminous sheets, a spectre of virginity. Dust came to meet her. "Here we are," she said, treading on the board which always creaked—now she wasn't alone, she could enjoy such familiar aspects of the room.

He hesitated, a dark scrawny bulk in the doorway. It disturbed her not to be able to see his face. "Isn't there a light?" he muttered.

"Yes, of course." She was surprised both that he should ask and that it hadn't occurred to her to turn it on. But the switch clicked lifelessly; there was no bulb. When had it been removed? "Anyway, it's quite light in here," she said uneasily. "We can see."

He didn't advance, but demanded "What for?"

He wanted to know why she'd brought him here; he expected her to offer him dope. She must persuade him not to leave, but could she? A worse fear invaded her. Even if he stayed, might not the power of the thing in the graveyard drag her away from him?

"No, we don't need to see." She was talking rapidly, to make sure of him before her trembling shook her words to pieces. "I only offered you somewhere to stay." No time for self-respect now; her panic jerked out her words. "Come to bed with me."

Oh Christ, she'd scared him off! But no, he hadn't shifted; only his hands squirmed like embarrassed children. "Please," she said. "I'm lonely."

If only he knew how alone! She felt the great raw gap where her memory had been. She could go to nobody except the thing in the graveyard shed. Her panic made her say "If you don't, you can't stay."

At last he moved. He was heading for the stairs. Her gasp of horror filled her mouth with dust. All at once she saw what his trouble might be. Heroin might have rendered him impotent. "Please," she wailed, clutching his arm. "I'll help you. You'll be all right with me."

Eventually he let her lead him to the bed. But he stared at it, then leaned one hand on the blankets. Disgusted, he flinched back from the squelching. She hadn't realised it was still so damp. "We'll spread your coat on top," she promised. "You haven't got anywhere better to go, have you?"

She unbuttoned his coat. His jeans were the colours of various stains; his drab sweater was spotted with flesh-tinted holes. She undressed him swiftly—naked, he couldn't escape. In the moonlight his penis dangled like the limp tail of a pale animal.

She managed to smile at him, though his ribs ridged his chest with shadows and his limbs were spindly. She didn't need a dream lover, only a companion. But he was stooping to his shoes, perhaps to cover up the inadequacy of his penis. She hoped he might open her dress. She stood awaiting him. At least she could see his reaction, unlike the face in the shed. But there was no reaction to see. Undressing him had been like stripping a dummy, and it might have been a dummy that confronted her, its face slumped, its hands and penis dangling.

She removed her dress. It was dry; she spread it over his coat.

She slid off her panties and dropped them on the small heap of clothes, all friends together. Both of them were shivering, she more from panic than with chill. They must be quick. If the thing reached out of the dark for her she would have to go—but sex with the young man might anchor her here. It would. It must.

She persuaded him on to the bed, though he shuddered as his leg brushed the damp blankets. He lay on his coat and her dress, like a victim of concussion. Then irritability seemed to enliven him. He pushed her back and knelt over her, kissing her nipples, trying to find her clitoris with both hands. She felt her nipples harden, but no pleasure. He fell back abruptly, defeated by his lack of desire. His limp penis struck his thigh as though he were whipping himself.

God, he mustn't fail her! The creaking of the bed was thin and lonely in the deserted house. She was surrounded by empty rooms, dark streets, and—far too close—the shed. What would the thing's call be like? Would she feel her body carrying her away towards the shed before she knew it? She gazed trembling at the young man. "Please try," she pleaded. He glared at her with something like hatred. She'd succeeded only in reminding him of his failure. She must help him. Her mouth moved down hls body, which was very cold. Her head burrowed between his thighs, like a frightened animal; his penis flopped between her lips. She tried every method she could summon to raise it, but it was unresponsive as a corpse.

Please, oh please! The call from the dark was about to seize her, she could feel it lurking near, it would drag her helpless to the shed—The nodding of her head became more frenzied; in panic, her teeth closed on his penis. Then she faltered, for she thought his penis had stirred.

The dark blotch of his face jerked up gasping. It *had* stirred, and he was as surprised as she. She redoubled her efforts, nipping his penis lightly. Come on, oh please! At last—though not before she felt swarming with icy sweat—she had erected him. Terrified lest he dwindle, she mounted his body at once and worked herself around him.

In the moonlight his face lay beneath her, white and gasping as a dead fish. Despite her sense of imminent terror she was almost angry. She'd liven him, she'd make him respond to her. She moved slowly at first, drawing his penis deeper, awakening it gradually. When the room was loud with his quickened breathing she drove faster. Make him grateful to her, make him stay! His penis jerked within her, lively now. She encouraged its throbbing, until all at once the throbbing cascaded. His gasp was nearly a scream; he clung to her with all his limbs. Though she experienced no pleasure, she was gratified that he had achieved his orgasm. Of this situation at least she was in control.

She lay on him. His cold cheek nuzzled hers. "I didn't think I could," he muttered, amazed and shyly boastful. She stroked his face tenderly, to make sure that he would stay with her. She had embraced his shoulders, hoping that she could sleep in his arms, when the summons came.

She couldn't tell which sense perceived it. Perhaps its appeal was deeper than any sense. She had no time to know what was happening, for her body had risen on all fours, like an instinctively obedient pet. Her consciousness was merely an observer, and could not even voice its scream.

No, it could do more. For the first time she was awake when summoned. Her panic blazed, jagged as lightning, through her nerves. It convulsed her, and made her nails clutch her partner's shoulders. He gasped, then his limbs seized her. He thought she was eager for sex again.

All at once her body sagged. Incredibly, seemed free. The summons had withdrawn, balked. She slumped on the young man, who embraced her more closely. She'd won! But she was nervous with a thought, urgent yet blurred: the summons might not be the only power with which her tormentor could seize her. She glared wildly about. The horned black head of the chimney loomed against the moon. She was still trying to imagine what might come to her when she felt it: disgust, that spread through her like poison.

At once the young man was intolerable. His gasping fish-like lips, his flesh cold and pale as something long drowned, his limbs clutching at her, bony and spider-like, his dull eyes white with moonlight, his moist flabby penis—She tried to struggle free, but he clung to her, unwilling to let her go.

Then she was flooded by another sort of power. It had seized her once before: a slow and steady physical strength, enormous and ruthless. Appalled, she thought of her dream of the boxes. She tore herself free of the young man—but the strength made her go on, though she tried to close her eyes, to shut out the sight of what she was doing. Somewhere she'd read of people being torn limb from limb, but she had thought that was just a turn of phrase. She had never been able to visualise how it could be done—nor that it could be so deafening and messy.

By the time she had finished, her consciousness had almost managed to hide. But she felt the summons marching her downstairs. Rooms resounded with her helplessly regular footsteps. As she heard the emptiness, she remembered how utterly lonely she had felt after her parents' death. One night she had emptied a bottle of sleeping tablets into her hand.

The call dragged her from the house. Moonlight spilled into the street, and she saw that all the houses were derelict, windowed with corrugated tin. She was allowed that glimpse, then she was marching: but not towards the main road—towards the church.

Her mind knew why, and dreaded remembering. But she must prepare herself for whatever was to come. She struggled in her trudging body. The only memory she could grasp seemed at first irrelevant. The words that she'd glimpsed in the window of the car outside Loveman's house had been DISTRICT NURSE.

Loveman wasn't dead. At once she knew that. The rumour of his death had been nothing more. Perhaps he had spread the rumour himself, for his own purposes. He must have married the Christian nurse; no doubt she had nursed him back to health. But married or not, he would have been unable to forgo his surreptitious visits to the graveyard. He still preferred the dead to the living.

She knew what that meant. Oh Christ, she knew! She didn't need to be shown! But the power forced her past the massive bland church and into the graveyard. She was rushed forward, stumbling and sobbing inwardly, past funereal dildos of stone. If she could move her hand just a little, to grab one, to hold herself back—But she'd staggered to a halt, and was forced to gaze down at a fallen headstone surrounded by an upheaval of earth.

Still he must have felt that she was insufficiently convinced. She was forced to burrow deep into her grave, and to lie there blindly. It was a long time before he allowed her to scramble her way out and to trudge, convulsively shaking herself clean of earth, towards the shed.

THE MEDICI STILETTO

JANEEN WEBB

In the sleaziest sector of the orbital colony, down near the space-port, Brunelli's day was beginning peacefully enough. She powered up the hologram that hid the entry to her bar, deciding that today her establishment would masquerade as a café on the Piazza San Marco. As the scene coalesced, the square's famous stone lions watched impassively while she unlocked the heavy steel shutters and opened her doors. Some of her regulars were already waiting in the shadowy laneway: they began at once to slip inside for their first illegal coffees of the day.

The unmistakable aroma of freshly ground Arabica was soon percolating through the bar's stale, recycled air, and the anxious habitués began to relax—shift workers in overalls rubbing shoulders with young scions of society still in evening dress. Brunelli's Bar relocated on a regular basis, but everyone in the colony knew how to find it. The authorities turned a blind eye: up here on the orbital, Brunelli's bootleg coffee was a most necessary vice.

On the other side of the city, safe within the tightly guarded security of the opulent de Glorian mansion, Tomaso Trevenna was in trouble. His hand shook as he pulled the library door closed. He took a deep breath, squared his shoulders, and walked purposefully down the marble hallway that led to the morning room. He knocked softly, reluctant to disturb the family at such an early hour.

"Come in."

Duke Frederico de Glorian glanced up sharply from the white-linen draped table where he was taking breakfast with his wife. Both were formally dressed: Frederico in a dark business suit, Francesca in a tight, lace-edged black bodice and a long skirt that draped elegantly to the black-and-white tiled floor. The room was warm with the morning smells of toast and bacon. A fine Venetian glass bowl of peaches nestled beside crystal dishes of butter and raspberry conserves; fragile porcelain plates were set with gleaming silverware: the couple looked for all the world as if they were sitting for a painting by one of the old masters whose many works graced their crowded walls.

De Glorian was icily polite. His tight smile did not reach his eyes. "Mr Trevenna," he said. "Do come in." His tone could not have been less welcoming.

Trevenna faltered. He stopped short beside a Donatello sculpture, feeling underdressed in casual jeans, Gucci loafers, and a white shirt that he wore open at his throat to reveal the heavy links of a gold chain. He wished he had thought to put on a jacket.

"My profound apologies for the intrusion, sir," he said at last.

Francesca heard the anxiety in his voice, and saw that he was struggling to speak. "Tomaso," she said, "has something untoward happened? Is Jo Jo all right?"

"Your daughter is fine, Duchess," Trevenna replied. "But there is a small…ah…difficulty. I thought it unwise to call the maid."

"I'll come at once," Francesca said. She folded her starched white napkin and reached across the table to pat her husband's hand. "No need for you to trouble yourself with this, Freddy," she said. "You were just about to leave for your board meeting. I'll deal with the domestic issues. I always do."

She rose gracefully, shook out the folds of her trailing velvet skirt and crossed the room to take Trevenna's arm. "Now, Tomaso," she said firmly, "show me the source of your concern."

Brunelli's clients were just settling in for the morning when an urgent message flashed across her implanted lenses. The text was coded, sent on the private, secure link dedicated to the service of her long-standing aristocratic patron.

"I'm on my way," Brunelli replied, sub-vocalising the text. "Don't touch anything."

She knew the last instruction was superfluous: the Duchess would have the situation completely under control. She always did.

Brunelli turned back to her customers. "Sorry, folks," she said. "I have an emergency. I'm closing up here for a while."

One or two of her clients grumbled, but no-one argued with Brunelli. No-one dared. It was rumoured that the beautiful Brunelli—dark haired, dark eyed, and dangerously fit—was a woman who relished a fight. It was common knowledge that she was an ex-Imperial guard. It was also whispered that she carried far more personal weaponry than was strictly legal, expensive state-of-the-art body augmentation that was considered extreme even down here in the dangerous port district.

Brunelli unrolled the sleeve of her tight, white T-shirt and retrieved the holo-scene's tiny remote control from its usual place, tucked just above her bulging bicep. She dimmed the bar's already low lights.

"Come along, folks," she said. "Finish your drinks. I have to go."

The last customer put down his cup and stood, hunching his skinny shoulders inside his grubby, scuffed denim jacket. "What's up?" he asked. "Anything I can use?"

"Nothing of interest to you, Raffi, or to that scurrilous network you stickybeak for," Brunelli said. "Out!"

Raphael Antony Totaro, generally known around the local clubs and bars as The Rat, pushed back his unruly mop of corkscrew-tight blonde curls from his forehead and pretended that Brunelli had hurt his feelings. There was nothing remotely innocent about his wide, blue-eyed gaze. "Don't be like that," he said. "It's a perfectly legitimate news feed."

"Sure it is. Now go, before I ban you from my bar!"

"I'm going." The Rat made a show of swaggering back towards the entry, his hands in his pockets. "Maybe I'll see you later, then," he said. "Maybe not."

Brunelli knew her customers. She just nodded, irritated by the whining note that had crept into his voice. He'd been whining a lot, lately. She knew he'd be back: he always came back. Where else could he get his fix of black market coffee? She watched the scrawny Rat slouch his way along the bare metal laneway before she powered down the holograph. The stone lions faded, the cobbled entry became a blank metal wall, and Brunelli's bar was invisible once again—just the way she liked it. She finished locking up, swung her old red leather jacket over her broad shoulders and strode away, soundless in her supple leather boots. She knew he would try to follow her, but she wasn't worried. The Rat would never get past security. Brunelli was heading for the palatial de Glorian mansion, right at the gated heart of the colony.

It was Josephina Jocetta, only child and heir to the de Glorian family fortune, who opened the door. She was impeccably dressed, as always—the perfect picture of a celebrity heiress: today she wore a cropped black leather jacket over a vintage Valentino short dress of layered red tulle and skin-tight sharkskin pants.

Brunelli smiled. "Good morning, Princess," she said. "Where's your mother?"

"In the library," the girl replied. "She's been in there since Tomaso noticed there was a problem. She's sent the servants away. She asked me to wait for you."

"Quite right, Princess," Brunelli said. 'Thank you." Her eyes narrowed. "And what exactly was Tomaso Trevenna doing in your father's library, so early in the day?" she asked.

Josephina Jocetta—Jo Jo to her family and friends—had the grace to blush. But a note of defiance crept into her voice. "Tomaso spent the night with me," she said.

"Was that wise, Jo Jo?"

"I don't care."

"You do know that the families won't change their position, don't you? You know they'll never allow the match."

Josephina Jocetta shrugged. "We don't have to marry," she said. "We're fine as we are."

"True enough," said Brunelli. "Neither family will care if you share your bed with him—it's the corporate implications of a legal relationship that concern them. And you haven't answered my question. What *was* Tomaso doing in the library?"

"Maybe he was looking for a book."

"This isn't a game, Jo Jo," Brunelli said. Her manner was mild, but there was steel in her voice. "I'll go talk to your mother."

Josephina Jocetta pouted. "I'll come with you."

"No need. I know the way. Why don't you go find Tomaso? I *will* need to speak to him."

"Okay, if that's what you want." Josephina Jocetta turned abruptly, teetering on her bright red patent leather high heels as she flounced away. Her perfect blonde curls bounced on her shoulders, but her perfectly lipsticked red mouth was set in a petulant line.

She sulked her way upstairs, looking for Tomaso.

Brunelli switched her lenses to *Record*—a necessary precaution—as she walked silently between the priceless Renaissance bronze statuettes that lined the hallway to the de Glorian library. She pulled open an intricately carved door and stepped into the living past.

Frederico de Glorian's library was magnificent. Tall mahogany bookcases housed the Duke's famous collection of illuminated manuscripts and leather-bound first editions gleaned from the best libraries on Earth. The books were interspersed with paintings by Botticelli and Caravaggio and Tintoretto, Bernini's *Apollo and Daphne* stood just inside the entry, and the perfectly proportioned room was dotted with smaller marble sculptures. The de Glorian mansion was full of such things: the Duke employed agents to collect them whenever the few remaining law enforcement agencies on Earth could be persuaded, by whatever means, to look the other way. Neither money nor ethics concerned Frederico in his pursuit of the objects of his desire: he described himself as a true patron of the arts, insisting that he was rescuing Earth's treasures and protecting them from destruction.

The governors of Earth's galleries had a different view, but de Glorian was safely beyond their reach—as indeed were all the wealthy colonists who had re-located to the sanctuary of their neo-feudal corporate empire up here on the orbital station, well away from the pestilence and famine of the failing mother planet.

"Ah, Brunelli!" Francesca de Glorian rose gracefully from the tapestried wing chair that had hidden her from the doorway. "Thank you for coming so promptly."

"My pleasure." Brunelli advanced cautiously, careful not to disturb the scene.

Francesca pointed. "This is the problem."

"Nasty," said Brunelli.

The body that lay upon the sumptuous silk Bokhara rug seemed almost an appropriate addition to the library's furnishings, an elegant effigy of its former self. The man was perfectly composed in his starched white shirt, his traditionally tailored grey cashmere suit, and his patent leather shoes. His manicured hands were crossed neatly upon his breast, and a heavy gold signet ring gleamed on his right index finger. His eyes were closed, and his patrician nose pointed up at the coffered ceiling, as if he disdained to notice the stiletto that protruded from between his ribs, or the blood that had flowered into a dark stain above his heart.

Brunelli peered more closely, realising that the murder weapon was itself a work of art. The stiletto was exquisitely carved, inlaid with gold, crusted with rubies. The man had died as he had lived—at the hand of luxury.

"Do you know him?" Brunelli asked.

"He called himself Veneziano," Francesca said. "The Venetian. He is—*was*—an art dealer. He came here two days ago—rather unexpectedly, I might add—to offer us a particular painting by Titian that my husband has coveted for some time."

"*Freshly stolen.*" Brunelli did not voice her thought. In the de

Glorian mansion it was impolite to enquire too closely about the exact provenance of the Duke's acquisitions.

"Veneziano was staying in the guest wing while my husband had the painting authenticated," Francesca said.

"And staying out of sight,' Brunelli thought. "Do you have any more information about the man?" she asked.

"Alas not," said Francesca. "He was a minor business acquaintance of my husband, nothing more."

"And the Duke?"

"Has been obliged to attend a most important board meeting this morning," Francesca said smoothly. "I have already assured him that you and I will deal with this situation."

"Of course." Brunelli gazed at the dead man, considering her options for his disposal. "I'll take care of the details."

"Much appreciated," Francesca said. "You really are a most necessary woman."

Brunelli inclined her head, accepting the compliment. "I assume you want me to identify the killer?"

"I'd like to know who breached our security."

"But?"

"But the family is to be protected, at all costs."

"That goes without saying. And Tomaso?"

Francesca shook her head. "Tomaso isn't family," she replied.

Brunelli didn't even blink. She had her instructions.

Francesca turned her attention back to the body. "Frederico will be terribly upset if that stiletto has been damaged," she said. "It's a pretty thing, and its price is far beyond its rubies—it's the pride of his Medici collection. He's a direct descendant of the Medicis, you know."

Brunelli raised an eyebrow.

"The de Glorian family is ancient nobility," Francesca said, "and their history records a Medici marriage. But Frederico is a fastidious man: his DNA has been checked against authenticated Medici remains. It's a match. There's no question of his pedigree."

"I understand," Brunelli said, mentally counting the cost of such a procedure. "The Duke is reclaiming his ancestral inheritance."

"Precisely," said Francesca. "He regards himself as a latter day

Cosimo Medici. He's building his private museum up here on the orbital." She gestured towards a display case, where items of be-jewelled wearable weaponry—long stilettos, razor-sharp hair pins, hinged rings and brooches that concealed poisons, even a crossbow tiny enough to slip inside a sleeve—were carefully arranged on a black velvet cloth. A pair of superbly chased silver duelling swords hung suspended by scarlet silk cords above the case. "I must say I'm relieved that the killer didn't choose one of those," Francesca added. "Imagine the mess!"

Brunelli almost smiled.

Francesca eased a linen handkerchief from the stiff lace folds of her bodice and moved a little closer to the corpse. She stooped swiftly and pulled the stiletto from the Venetian's breast. As she straightened up, wiping the blade, the ruby-set hilt caught the light, glowing a dark red that seemed almost to reflect the blood on the victim's suit.

"A handkerchief will hardly remove all the blood," Brunelli said drily.

"No matter," said Francesca. "All of these objects have tasted blood before today. Frederico says it's part of their charm."

"And you?"

"I just like to keep things running smoothly. And I prefer not to see Frederico distressed. So I'll put this back where it belongs," Francesca said. She deliberately re-positioned the priceless stiletto back at the centre of the display, careful to match its indentation on the thick velvet cloth. "There," she said. "That's better." She paused, musing on the collection. "These are all designed to kill at close quarters," she said softly.

"Well," said Brunelli, "the Venetian was certainly dispatched by a single, perfectly placed knife thrust. And one would need to be very close indeed to kill so neatly, so unexpectedly."

"Indeed," said Francesca. "I am reminded that Niccolo Machiavelli once admonished a Medici prince to keep his friends close and his enemies closer. Perhaps this is what he meant: to keep one's enemies close enough to be stabbed through the heart, should the occasion arise."

"Perhaps," Brunelli conceded. "There are no defence wounds.

There was no struggle. The Venetian must have died in the embrace of his killer."

"So it would seem."

Brunelli looked around the room. "And there is no damage at all to the library," she added. "No evidence of a fight."

"I wonder if he was killed here at all," Francesca said. "I have been thinking about that while I waited for you. The body has been so very carefully laid out. Do you see how he lies exactly at the centre of the rug, preserving the symmetry of the design?"

"It's perfectly clear that the scene has been stage managed," Brunelli replied. "The murderer wanted this body to be found, and found exactly here."

"It's hardly a secret that this is my husband's private place," Francesca said. She gestured towards an alcove where an exquisite medieval Book of Hours stood open on a gold lectern fashioned in the form of an Imperial eagle with outstretched wings. "The library is his passion."

Brunelli nodded, remembering the first time she had seen Frederico de Glorian standing at his lectern, white-gloved, fastidiously viewing a single page, turning a gold-crusted vellum leaf with exaggerated care. "Could the Venetian have been followed here?"

"That's certainly possible," Francesca said. "But why kill him when he was no longer in possession of the painting?"

"The murderer may not have known that."

"True," Francesca conceded. "But the murderer would certainly have known that Veneziano's visit was not, shall we say, official."

"Sure," said Brunelli. "What will become of the Titian painting?"

"I have no doubt that my husband will take good care of it, always supposing it proves to be genuine."

"A windfall for the Duke, then."

"If you like." Francesca hesitated. "It's useful that this one" — she poked the body with the toe of her shiny patent-leather shoe—"is most unlikely to be missed."

"In that case," said Brunelli, "I'll go ahead and arrange a removalist. I've seen enough here." She turned away, sub-vocalising the necessary instructions to her most reliable operative.

Francesca sighed. "I'm relieved that's done," she said. "Thank you. Would you care for tea? I'll have it served in the drawing room."

"Thank you, yes." Brunelli waited while Francesca locked the library, feeling suddenly glad to be out of the silent company of the dead stranger, glad to be out of the claustrophobic atmosphere of the room that Duke Frederico de Glorian had so lovingly stuffed full of deadly relics.

Half an hour later, Francesca and Brunelli were sitting companionably in comfortable armchairs, sipping orange pekoe tea from dainty porcelain cups, talking of the Michelangelo marble that dominated the room. On the wall above them hung another Titian painting, the *Venus d'Urbino*, one of the Duke's earlier acquisitions from the beleaguered Uffizi Gallery.

Brunelli put down her teacup when Josephina Jocetta flung open the door and entered the room, leading Tomaso by the hand.

"Hello again, Princess," Brunelli said. "And thank you for joining us, Mr Trevenna."

Tomaso was wearing his jacket now. He stepped forward, offering his hand.

"Brunelli. Good morning. Nice to see you again," he said, attempting to conceal his palpable uneasiness beneath a show of confident charm.

Brunelli could not help but admire Tomaso's olive skin, curling black hair, dark eyes and aquiline nose: the features that gave him a rugged, masculine appearance which offered a striking contrast with Jo Jo's pale, sculptured beauty. Together, they were, indeed, a very handsome couple—both had had the best genetic engineering that money could buy.

Francesca frowned. "Do sit down, both of you," she said. "Shall I pour tea?"

Josephina Jocetta did not try to hide her impatience. "We don't want tea, Mother," she said. "We just want to get this whole horrible thing over with."

"As you wish," said Francesca.

Brunelli got straight down to business. "How did you come to find the body in the library, Tomaso?" she asked.

"I had a message," Tomaso said. "I thought it was from the Venetian."

"You knew him?"

"Not at all. We'd never met."

"You weren't introduced at dinner?"

Josephina Jocetta interrupted. "We didn't dine with the family last night," she said. "We were out for the evening, and after that we were upstairs. I can vouch for Tomaso."

"All night, Princess?" Brunelli said mildly. "You didn't sleep at all? That must have been some session."

Josephina Jocetta looked down at her designer shoes. "I might have dozed off," she admitted.

"Then you can't be sure Mr Trevenna was with you the whole time."

"I'd have noticed if he wasn't," Jospehina Jocetta said stubbornly.

Brunelli turned her attention back to Tomaso. "So why did you agree to meet a man you didn't know?"

"Jo Jo had told me he was here in the house. She said he was an art dealer, here to do business. I assumed he was legitimate. I went to the library because the message claimed he had rare antique jewellery to sell. I thought I might surprise Jo Jo with something pretty."

"I see," Brunelli said. "Can you confirm this, Jo Jo?"

"I did tell Tomaso about the dealer. But I didn't know about the message." Josephina Jocetta smiled radiantly at Tomaso. "It wouldn't have been a surprise if he'd told me, would it?"

"I guess not." Brunelli stared hard at Tomaso. "Do you want to save us all a lot of time and tell me why you killed him?" she said abruptly. "Did you fall out over the jewels?"

"What?" Tomaso paled, looking suddenly less confident. "I've never killed anyone. Ever."

Josephina Jocetta was outraged. "You can't seriously imagine Tomaso is the killer!"

"Why not? He found the body. His story sounds pretty flimsy to me."

"And I've heard that the person who finds the body is often the guilty party," Francesca added.

Tomaso glowered at her. "You're trying to set me up for this, aren't you?" he said.

Francesca was unmoved. "Why would I do that?"

"Because you want me out of Jo Jo's life. I love your daughter, and you can't stand the idea that she might be happy with me."

"Nonsense," said Francesca.

"Is it, Mother?" Jo Jo snapped.

Brunelli shook her head. "This really isn't helping," she said. "Jo Jo, please take Tomaso back upstairs. Don't either of you leave the house."

"What happens next?" Tomaso asked.

"No need for you to concern yourself with that," Brunelli said firmly.

Francesca held up her hand. "Don't ask, Tomaso," she said. "I shall undertake to believe in your innocence in return for your absolute discretion. Do I make myself clear?"

"Transparently," Tomaso said.

Josephina Jocetta tugged at his arm. "Let's go, Tomaso," she said. "Brunelli knows you didn't do it. This is just Mother's way of reminding us she's in control."

Francesca's smile was brittle as broken glass. "I'll expect you both at dinner," she said. "Drinks at seven."

When Brunelli had concluded the initial, necessary business at the de Glorian mansion, she decided not to miss her regular workout at her gym. She needed to clear her head. She needed exercise. She changed clothes in the locker room and swung gratefully into her usual routine—treadmill, rowing machine, squats, and then weights. She was lying on her back, bench-pressing a serious weight load when she felt someone walk up behind her. And then that someone loomed into view, standing over her.

"Do you mind?" Brunelli said. "This is a private room. I don't like an audience when I'm training."

"Too bad. I have a message for you." The voice was rough, guttural.

"I'm listening." Brunelli made to return the weights to the stand so that she could sit up.

The burly man blocked her, forcing the heavy bar back down towards her exposed throat.

Brunelli's muscles bulged as she took the strain.

"Got you!" The man pushed down harder. "My message is: back off. This morning's little incident does not concern you."

"Is that so?" Brunelli met force with force. She took a deep breath, and then waited a beat while the adrenalin kicked in, activating her enhanced body technology. She surged upward, twisting the bar out of shape. She threw it, and her assailant, clean across the room. The weights clattered to the floor and rolled away.

The man scrambled to his feet. He pulled an ordinary steel stiletto.

Brunelli flexed her shoulders, triggering her surgically augmented reflexes. She adopted a fighter's stance and slid her blades from beneath her fingernails—ten short, wafer thin, deadly sharp knife tips. Her grin was murderous. "Come on, then," she said. "Let's see what you've got."

The attacker grunted. He circled warily, and then took a step towards Brunelli.

It was enough.

Brunelli executed a sequence of blindingly fast movements. And then she was holding her disarmed assailant from behind. His right arm dangled uselessly from his dislocated shoulder, and blood was seeping from five neat puncture wounds in his chest where Brunelli's splayed fingers now rested. Her other hand was around his throat. "Who sent you to kill the Venetian?" she asked.

The man struggled to breathe. "The Uffizi," he rasped.

Brunelli scowled. "Tell the Uffizi that de Glorian is protected." She flexed her fingertips for emphasis. Blood trickled down the man's neck. "Got it?"

He moved his head the merest fraction, afraid to nod.

"Good."

The gym manager dashed into the room. He stopped short when he saw Brunelli, his glance registering her weaponry, her captive, and the knife on the floor. "What's going on here?" he said. "I heard a crash."

Brunelli ignored him. She retracted her finger blades, released her grip on her assailant's throat, and took hold of his injured arm.

The man winced.

"Hold still," Brunelli said. "I'll fix your shoulder."

"Don't," he said. "I'll…

Brunelli rotated his arm, and pulled.

The assassin fainted.

The manager stared. "What should I do with him?" he said at last. "Should I call Security?"

"Just put him out with the rest of the trash," Brunelli said. "I need to clean up."

Brunelli stood under the shower for a long time, letting the hot water sluice away her frustrations, letting her heightened adrenalin levels drop. She felt better by the time she was ready to go, her black hair framing her face in damp curls.

The manager met her in the lobby. "I'm sorry to trouble you again, Ms Brunelli," he said. He swallowed hard, trying to control the nervous tremor in his voice. "There's a man waiting for you at reception. He claims his business is urgent."

"It had better be," Brunelli muttered under her breath.

Brunelli glanced through the glass door, recognising the scuffed denim jacket and the mop of mouse-blonde curls that belonged to the skinny youth who was busily chatting up the gym's receptionist.

"I really don't have time for this," Brunelli said. "I'm out of here."

The Rat turned around at the sound of her voice and hurried towards her. "Please, Brunelli," he said. "I have something for you. At least let me walk with you."

Brunelli sighed. "Come on, then." She turned on her heel and strode out into the street.

The Rat had to scurry to catch up. When he finally matched her stride, he lowered his voice conspiratorially. "I've heard a whisper that might interest you," he said.

"So?"

"So what's in it for me?"

Brunelli stopped. She turned to face him. "Listen, Raffi," she said. "I am having a difficult day. How about you spit out whatever it is you want to tell me, and in return I won't ban you from my bar. Deal?"

The Rat gulped. "I guess so. I don't have to tell you."

"I don't have to make your coffee. Come on, out with it."

The Rat sighed theatrically. "I have a name for you," he said. "Let me guess: *Uffizi*."

"How did you…?"

"I have my sources."

"So you know about the jewel robbery too?"

"Say that again?"

"There's a rumour that some incredibly valuable jewellery was stolen this morning."

"Of course!" Brunelli kissed the Rat on the cheek. "It was staring me in the face!" she said. "Raffi, I owe you a drink. I'll see you later!"

Brunelli set off at a run, leaving the astonished Rat to wonder why his inconsequential scrap of news had caused such a reaction. He smirked: whatever it was, he was back in Brunelli's good graces. His coffee fix was assured, and that was all that mattered.

By the time Brunelli arrived back at the de Glorian mansion it was cocktail hour. She was shown into the drawing room where Francesca and Frederico now sat, together again, surrounded by their priceless artworks. They were calmly sipping very dry martinis.

The Duke rose. "Do come in, Brunelli," he said. "I understand we owe you a debt of gratitude for your exemplary efforts today. Would you care for a drink?"

"Thank you, yes," Brunelli said. "But I fear we still have a little bit of today's business to conclude."

Francesca cut across the pleasantries. "I got your message, Brunelli," she said. "I've checked the safe. There's nothing missing."

"And Jo Jo?"

"Her jewellery is accounted for as well." Francesca shrugged. "It's always possible your informant was mistaken."

"I doubt it. There was an attempt on my life this afternoon."

"Goodness!" Francesca put her hand to her throat. "Are you all right?"

"Perfectly." Brunelli brushed Francesca's concern aside. She turned her attention back to Frederico. "Have you verified your Medici collection, your Grace?" she asked.

"You saw for yourself that all the pieces are there," Francesca said.

"Yes, but are you sure they are the right pieces?"

Frederico did not hesitate. He abandoned his glass on a side table and strode from the room.

Francesca put her hand on Brunelli's arm. "Give him a moment," she said softly. "His collection is the one true love of his life." She reached for the silver cocktail shaker. "Let me pour you a martini."

When the women arrived in the library, cocktails in hand, the Duke was standing beside the open display case. His face was dark with fury. His hand trembled as he held up the ruby stiletto that Francesca had pulled from the dead man's chest.

"This," he said, "is a preposterous fake!"

"How...?" Francesca began.

"I knew there was something not quite right about that murder," Brunelli said. "I knew it couldn't have been just about the painting." She shook her head. "I'm sorry, Francesca. I should have seen the truth of it sooner."

"Seen what?" Francesca asked.

"Seen that the body was a distraction, a side-show to keep us from looking too closely at the stiletto."

"And Tomaso?"

"Just another diversion," Brunelli said. "Tomaso isn't family. The assassin knew you'd suspect him. Tomaso was tricked."

"No need to tell *him* that," Francesca said sharply. "I'd prefer he didn't feel too comfortable. His liaison with my daughter must be stopped."

Brunelli thought for a moment. "No problem," she said. "My contact at the newsfeed, Raphael Totaro, just lives for gossip. I owe him a favour. I'll whisper a word in his ear."

Francesca's smile was complicity itself. "Much obliged," she said.

Frederico tapped his foot impatiently. "Can we get back to the point, Brunelli?" he said. "Do you know who *is* responsible for this outrage?"

"I was given a name, your Grace: *Uffizi*."

Francesca put the pieces together. "The Gallery governors must have hired a professional," she said. "There's no other explanation."

"I might have known!" said Frederico. "Those miserable men have failed in their duty. The Uffizi collection is no longer safe. The Medici artefacts are my inheritance, not theirs." His voice shook with anger. "They have no right to interfere!"

Francesca touched his hand. "Don't upset yourself, Freddy," she said softly. "Brunelli is here. Everything will be all right."

"If you'll forgive the expression, your Grace," Brunelli said, "the perpetrator appears to have killed two birds with the one stone—or stiletto, in this case. The Venetian was killed for his part in the removal of the Titian painting. The Uffizi officials have never been squeamish when it comes to acquisitions. They knew that the painting would never be returned, so they directed their operative to steal the famous Medici stiletto as recompense—tit for tat, if you like."

"Can you get it back, Brunelli?" the Duke asked.

"I have no doubt that your stiletto was on the first shuttle back to Earth this morning," Brunelli said. She shrugged. "But I'm overdue a visit. And I like Florence. So yes, your Grace: if you wish, I'll retrieve your property for you."

"Is there anything you need?" Francesca asked.

Brunelli shook her head. "Nothing," she said. "It won't be hard to locate the stiletto. I've identified the man who attacked me: I'm already following the money trail." She paused, concentrating on the highly classified data now streaming across her implanted lenses. "Got it!" she said. "The Uffizi officials have the stiletto. It's heavily guarded." She smiled. "But then," she added, "I always like a challenge."

"Do whatever it takes, Brunelli," Frederico said coldly. "Unlimited resources. Whatever it takes."

Brunelli's smile broadened to a grin. "Understood, your Grace," she said. She finished her martini in a single gulp. "Thanks for the drink. I'll see myself out. I'll be in touch."

Brunelli strode away, soft footed, lithe and lethal.

Francesca watched her go, and then turned back to her fretting, fidgeting husband. "Stop fussing, Freddy," she said. "Let me get you another drink. There's nothing more you can do for now. You'll have to be patient. But remember this: Brunelli never fails."

DOUBLE SPACE

WILLIAM F. NOLAN

We were standing by the water cooler on break at the shoe store one gloomy Wednesday when Adam Niles said to me: "Freddie, been thinkin' about your problem. I bet I know how you could earn some extra dough."

"Yeah? How?" I was skeptical. We were roomies, so he knew what straits we were in most of the time with rent, food, and utilities always going up, but our paychecks staying the same year-in and year-out. Commission on shoe sales was a tough grind, anyway. Now we had to worry about robots and artificial intelligence crowding us out of retail. So Niles always had crazy ideas about procuring more money. One such scheme that had inspired him a few years back was when a couple friends of his vanished looking for copies of *Action Comics* #1, the first appearance of Superman. He never heard from his buddies again, but he figured they were the anonymous sellers who unloaded one shortly thereafter at auction. Whoever it was made a *fortune!* Ever since he had been on a quest to get rich quick, and was always scouring Craigslist, eBay, and other websites hoping to cash in on…something.

"You know the old brick building downtown—the one at the end of the block next to the bank?"

"Closed down years ago," I said, nodding.

"Right. But it's been converted to some kinda medical joint. They need a subject for a lab experiment. Had an ad online. Bet they'd take you." He patted his gut.

"What kind of experiment?"

"Dunno exactly. Something about 'muscle power.'"

I filled my cup with water, furrowing my brow. "Well, I can't quit this gig for some kind of wacko 'experiment.' I need a steady job. Why don't *you* do it if it's so great?"

"'Cause I hate needles. There might be needles." He shivered. "Anyways, you don't have to quit," he told me. "They just need a subject for a coupla weekends according to the ad. Pay is a flat *thousand bucks*. Easy money, bro!"

Now he had my full attention. *A thousand smackers!* "A grand sounds good! Is it…is it dangerous?"

"Not the way they described it. Piece of cake." Niles rubbed his belly as he talked. "I'll send you the link."

I crushed my paper cup dramatically. "I'll check it out."

And that's how it began.

The following Saturday, having made an appointment, I showed up at the renovated med building. The interior was impressive—a dazzling presentation of chrome and tinted glass, complete with marble flooring. Obviously, big money involved.

I gave my name to a trim-figured redhead in surgical whites who led me down a long, brightly lit hallway, opened a door, and showed me inside.

"Doctor Baden will be in shortly to interview you," she said. "Please remove all of your clothing." She handed me a dressing gown, sizing me up. "Put this on."

After a few minutes, the wizened Dr Hans Baden appeared. He was pale, with grey hair. A long-fingered man in rimless glasses. His shaggy eyebrows and jowled face reminded me of a beagle. He walked over to the table where I was seated, scribbling some notes on his tablet. He cleared his throat before tilting his head back and regarding me underneath his spectacles. "Remove the gown so I may inspect your…*frame*."

His voice had a slight accent. The request felt weird, but I complied.

"*Ahem*…you have on still your…*undertrousers*." His enormous white eyebrows rose at the end of every sentence. It was some sort of nervous tick.

I swallowed hard. "I mean—do I need to be completely *naked* for this? It's not a figure-drawing class or anything. I thought this was about some kind of 'muscle power' test or something."

He scowled. "Yes...yes it *is*, mister...," he looked at his notes. "Mister *Weiss*. A good German name!" He leaned in closer. "But I need to see if the treatments affect...*everything*." Eyebrows.

I thought about it. Then I thought about how useful that money would be. I reluctantly dropped my boxers.

Baden poked at my chest. Measured my biceps. Suddenly bent over to intensely scrutinise...other places, the whole while making detailed notes on his tablet. A strange smile crept over his face. "So far...*sehr good*."

After donning the gown again, I was asked a series of questions. He seemed pleased with my answers. Finally: Would I be available for the next two weekends? I said I would.

"We will need to take blood samples," he told me. "Once the test results are in we may...*proceed*."

I smiled, relieved. "Then I'm accepted?"

Baden clasped his hands together, pursing his lips. "Depends on the lab results," he said. "But you do look...*promising*."

The interview was over. Once the blood samples were taken, I was allowed to dress. Then the pretty redhead led me to the exit. "You'll hear from us within the week."

I walked back to my car under a dark, mottled sky.

The test results proved I was ideal subject material.

I returned to the medical building, anxious to get the test started. The sooner the tests were completed, the sooner I'd be paid!

Baden greeted me in the lobby.

"Mr Weiss! How well for you to see me again! We have one last...*detail*." He motioned at the sexy red-haired receptionist. "Agatha, will you present...*the forms?*"

She smiled at me. "Here you go. Have fun." She then lifted

what looked to be a *ream* of notebook paper onto the table.

"Jesus!" I couldn't help the exclamation. "What-what's all *this?*"

Dr Baden smiled, shook his head and said: "Just ein...*formality*, Herr Weiss. This is just some...*protections*. For you. Us." His eyebrows danced like some insect on a griddle as he explained it.

I riffled the two-inch thick stack of papers. "Holy *moly!* Am I signing my life away here?" I chuckled. Looking up, I could see that Agatha's eyes had widened incredibly; Dr Baden's had narrowed to slits in his scowling face.

"Well, if you have...*issues*, Mr. Weiss—"

The air was staticky, charged. I swallowed. "No, no problem, Dr Baden."

His face relaxed. "I'm glad we have...*understandings*, Herr Weiss." His lips curled at the corners, just slightly.

Two hours later, I finished signing and turned the pages over to Agatha. Then Dr Baden whisked me into the building.

Beyond the corridors holding the exam rooms, the place was vast and imposing, and housed a grouping of odd-shaped, strange-looking devices that made me uneasy. *What have I signed up for?* My hands were shaking.

"No need to worry," declared Baden, noting my nervous state. "Probably nothing will...*happen*." He then strapped me into a large metal chair, securing my arms and legs with heavy steel bands. "Try to relax. I can assure you that the procedure will be totally...*painless*." He waved over a masked assistant. Honestly, the guy seemed a bit strange, all hunched over with one eye larger than the other. He just grunted whenever Baden directed him to do things.

They rolled up my shirt sleeve and a silver needle pierced my arm; after a minute or so, I felt woozy. *Very* woozy. I shut my eyes as the chair began to vibrate: A powerful thrumming, like a million hornets, filled the room.

I fell into darkness.

Slowly I regained consciousness. The vibrations had ceased, and the thrumming died away. A wave of raw power swept through me. I shifted in the chair, easily snapping the steel leg and arm bands. My chest had expanded, and my shoulders bulged and rippled with muscle, splitting the seams of my shirt.

I faced a ring of broadly smiling doctors. "It *worked!*" exclaimed one of them. "Just *look* at him! My God, he's *stunning!* By golly you've *done* it, Hans!" He turned to shake Baden's hand.

"So it...*seems*," said the disheveled medical man. He shook their hands as his masked assistant hopped puckishly around the room.

I stood, pumping my new biceps. I had the neck of a bull, with legs like marble pillars, ridged with muscle that strained the cotton of my denims. My brain, however, was in turmoil. "What-what have you *done* to me?"

"You have been...*transformed*," declared Baden, pointing his finger into the air for emphasis. "From a normal young man into a highly-advanced physical *master*work—"

"I-I feel like a *freak!*"

"Tut-tut! You should be proud of your new body," Baden chided me. "And I have enhanced your psychology, as well. I have heightened some of your senses, which may not be apparent... *at first.*"

"Oh, yeah?" I replied. "Sounds like a weird thing to do—"

"But...*necessary*. We want to create the perfect man. In addition, I have done some...*extraction.*"

I swallowed. "What-what does that mean? You *cut* on me, you quack?" I flexed at the group menacingly. It felt strangely empowering.

"*Nein!*" Baden yelled. "Not with a knife, at least. With an Emotion Divider."

I shook my head, baffled. He continued.

"We can't give you this power without some...*controls*. So we gathered your worst impulses and deposited them into a safe place. We were afraid you might become undefeatable, or use your new powers for evil, otherwise."

The others nodded, muttering in agreement.

"Of course, we don't know the long-term effects of the experiment," stated one of the doctors. "You'll be kept under observation for a period of thirty days."

"*Oh, no!*" I said. "You're guaranteed no more than two weekends of my time."

Baden nodded. "True enough, but I'm afraid we'll have to revise that...*agreement*. It was in the papers you signed. Perhaps read more...*carefully* in the future, no?"

"I've had enough." I told them. "I'm leaving! Try and stop me, pencil necks!"

As I started for the exit door, two of the doctors moved to block me. "We cannot allow you to—"

I picked them both up, holding them aloft, their eyes wide in shock. "Easy now, boys!" I parked them on a lab shelf. "Don't try to mess with me!"

No one else dared.

I felt like a *real* superhero. All I needed was a red cape and tights. *This is insane! I have to be dreaming.* And the testosterone spike! I noticed things had...changed for the better when I stopped to take a leak before I left the complex.

Outside, on the main street. Self-conscious about my ragged appearance, trying to hide my new "endowment," I was *determined* to get home and sort this out. Even my shoes were separating at the soles, loudly flopping against my heels. I was so huge, people crossed the street, pointing at me in disbelief. *Man, this sucks! Those idiot doctors ruined me!*

Luckily, I was soon able to make good use of my new-found superpowers. Half a block ahead, a large yellow bus, packed with school kids, hit a patch of spilled oil. The heavy vehicle skidded out of control, straight toward oncoming traffic. I bounded forward, scooped up the bus, and set it down gently on an empty parking lot.

The driver was goggle-eyed. He was trying to thank me, but the words locked in his throat. The kids were all yelling. I gave them a friendly wave and headed back to my apartment. My face flushed as I sped away, able to walk with giant strides away from the scene.

I felt proud of myself for the first time in years.

Adam was startled when I entered the apartment. "Who the hell are *you*? You're that freak that saved those kids! It's all over the news! You can't come bustin' in here! I'll call the cops!"

"No need for that," I told him. "It's me—your ole buddy—but with a lot of new muscles." I moved to the fridge, flipped the top off a quart of milk, and took it down in a single gulp.

"*Freddie? That's you?!* Holy Toledo! Your clothes…what's goin' on here?!"

Adam slumped down into a chair at the kitchen table, bewildered and shaking his head in disbelief. I stuffed my face with *pounds* of leftovers for about twenty minutes, ravenous. *Must be all these muscles!*

"Okay…" I finally said, "lemme tell you about that experiment."

Afew days later I was minding my own business on lunch break from my crummy job at the shoe store when things got hectic. I had practically gone through my last check buying new clothes (nothing fit my muscle-bound physique anymore) when the headaches started up. I finally understood what was happening after a few pounders kept me awake for two nights: My hearing had become *super* sensitive. I could hear things *blocks* away. Even the faintest little sounds were deafening… caterpillars inching along sounded like jackhammers; car horns were like the blast of a cannon. It was miserable! Sometimes I could even pick up broadcast signals on the airwaves. It was like I had become a human radio antenna or something. All of it was pretty distracting when you're trying to shoehorn some granny's size 11-wide foot into a size six high-heel, but I had bills to pay, so had to bear down with it and hope the hearing thing subsided.

Stuff took a turn when one of the broadcasts blared into my head at lunch that day, though. A commercial jetliner was having landing gear trouble. Looked like a crash-land situation was brewing. I dropped my PB&J sandwich and sprinted the eight miles to the airport in under a minute. Then I vaulted over the airport fence and jumped about 800 feet into the air to grab the plane's tail, pulling the big jet down to a safe landing.

A crowd quickly gathered. News copters buzzed overhead. Reporters surrounded me. It was pure chaos! I was trying to explain who I was when this other guy appeared. Big muscles. Wide-chested. He looked exactly like me, and I mean *exactly*— only his features were twisted, and his eyes blazed like snuffed coals in his sore-pocked face. Dressed all in black. He was sure no superhero—he was a *monster*.

He began picking up members of the crowd and tossing them over the airport fence, laughing as they fell on the tarmac, bruised, bloodied, broken.

"Hey now, *quit* that!" I yelled at him. "You're going to kill somebody!"

"That's the whole idea, idiot!" he growled, leering at me. "I enjoy killing people. It's a real hoot!"

I tried to subdue him, but he was every bit as strong as I was. Had a punch like a steamroller. He knocked me down. I knocked him down. We were well into it when Baden arrived at the scene in a lab truck. He hopped out, brandishing some kind of odd-shaped futuristic gadget.

"Stop!" Baden yelled from the truck. He aimed the weapon at the guy I was grappling with, repeatedly blasting at him with a blue-white beam. We were too busy going at it for Baden to hit him. I punched my opponent double-hard and he slammed into the air traffic control tower, which began to crumble. He came back for more, tossing me at the structure, which I smashed through like a bullet-train out of control. The tower lurched and toppled over in a huge cloud of dust, smashing onto a fleet of planes sitting on the field. There were explosions as fuel ignited in the sparks thrown off from the collapse. I blew the flames out with a titanic breath, just before my doppelgänger attacked me again.

"You can't beat me, moron! *I am you!*"

"He's right, Freddie!" Baden shouted, still trying to blast the guy. "He's your *dark side*...from the Emotion Divider process!

Schwartz Freddie! He was being stored in a clone we created from your blood, but he was deceptive and lied to our intern. He escaped the lab before we could re-integrate you! He's pure distilled evil and aggression!"

My dark half chuckled knowingly as he landed another punch to my ribs. "Say goodbye, creep!"

I blocked his next punch and kneed him in the stomach. Then I smashed down hard on his head, driving him into the Earth like a massive nail. Momentarily confined but still raging, it was the instant Baden needed: He blasted the clone with his weapon. Schwartz Freddie gasped, twitched, expired.

Baden ran over and checked his carotid artery pulse. "Dead," he flatly declared.

I breathed a sigh of relief. The guy had been tough to deal with and I was glad to see him put down. But something weird was happening. I felt a tide of weakness sweep over me. I was rapidly losing my super strength, reverting to the normal-bodied fellow I'd been before the experiment.

I sat down on the tarmac, swamped in my now oversized clothes, trying to make sense of the change. *Why is this happening?*

Baden looked at me, his expression pensive. "Confused, you are?" he asked at last.

I nodded slowly. "Damn right."

The scientist pressed his lips together. "We can re-integrate your psyche back at the lab using my Emotion Divider device; for fusion, we simply reverse the process. We still have access to his emotional storage for several hours yet. It will take another few days for you to fully return to your old...*self.*"

I blinked at him. "So, I'm a hero *and* a horror?"

He nodded. "*Jah.* As we all can be, so that's one way to phrase it. Not unlike the two sides of a coin. We all occupy a kind of... *double space* in the universe. A positive one, and a negative one."

I nodded. "Will I be getting my big muscles back? Will I be able to go on helping humanity?"

"Sadly, not like this. Other ways, perhaps. The experiment was...*a failure.* As your DNA twin died, so did the effect of the bodily change."

"What about my thousand bucks? Do I still get all that or only half now that he's gone?"

"All of it, of course." He extracted ten, crisp one hundred-dollar bills from his wallet, handing them to me. "You certainly earned it. We appreciate your...*cooperation*. And I *do* wish you had been able to retain your incredible strength, but..." He sighed. "We don't always get what we want out of life, Mr Weiss."

"I understand, doc. I was sure super for a while, though," I said.

He nodded, patting my shoulder. "You most *certainly* were."

And we walked back to the lab truck together.

[*Special thanks to Jason V Brock for input on this story.* —WFN]

MYLAKHRION THE IMMORTAL

BRIAN LUMLEY

There was a time when I, Teh Atht, marvelling at certain thaum-
aturgical devices handed down to me from the days of my
wizard ancestor, Mylakhrion of Tharamoon (dead these eleven
hundred years), thought to question him with regard to the
nature of his demise; with that, and with the reason for it. For
Mylakhrion had been, according to all manner of myths and
legends, the greatest wizard in all Theem'hdra, and it concerned
me that he had not been immortal. Like many another wizard
before me I, too, had long sought immortality, but if the great
Mylakhrion himself had been merely mortal...surely my own
chance for self-perpetuity must be slim indeed.

Thus I went up once more into the Mount of the Ancients,
even to the very summit, and there smoked the Zha-weed and
repeated rare words by use of which I might seek Mylakhrion
in dreams. And lo!—he came to me. Hidden in a grey mist so
that only the conical outline of his sorcerer's cap and the slow
billowing of his dimly rune-inscribed gown were visible, he
came, and in his doomful voice demanded to know why I had
called him up from the land of shades, disturbing his centuried
sleep.

"Faceless one, ancestor mine, o mighty and most omniscient
sorcerer," I answered, mindful of Mylakhrion's magnitude. "I
call you up that you may answer for me a question of ultimate
importance. A question, aye, and a riddle."

"There is but one question of ultimate importance to men,"
gloomed Mylakhrion, "and its nature is such that they usually

do not think to ask it until they draw close to the end of their days. For in their youth men cannot foresee the end, and in their middle span they dwell too much upon their lost youth; ah, but in their final days, when there is no future, then they give mind to this great question. And by then it is usually too late: For the question is one of life and death, and the answer is this: yes, Teh Atht, by great and sorcerous endeavour, a man might truly make himself immortal…

"As to your riddle, that is easy. The answer is that *I am indeed immortal*! Even as the great Ones, as the mighty furnace stars, as Time itself, am I immortal—for ever and ever. Here you have called me up to answer your questions and riddles, knowing full well that I am eleven hundred years dead. But do I not take on the aspect of life? Do my lips not speak? And is this not immortality? Dead I am, but I say to you that I can never truly die."

Then Mylakhrion spread his arms wide, saying; "All is answered. Farewell…" And his outline, already misted and dim, began to recede deeper still into Zha-weed distances, departing from me. Then, greatly daring, I called out:

"Wait, Mylakhrion my ancestor, for our business is not yet done."

Slowly he came back, reluctantly, until his silhouette was firm once more; but still, as always, his visage was hidden by the swirling mists and only his dark figure and the gold-glowing runes woven into his robes were visible. Silently he waited, and all was silent as the tomb of the universe at the end of time, until I spoke yet again:

"This immortality of yours is not the sort I seek, Mylakhrion, which I believe you know well enow. Fleshless, bodiless, except for that shape given you by my incantations and the smoke of the Zha-weed, voiceless other than when called up from the land of shades to answer my questions…what is that for immortality? No, ancestor mine, I desire much more from the future than that. I want my body and all of its sensations. I want volition and sensibility, and all normal lusts and passions. In short, I want to be eternal, remaining as I am now but incorruptible, indestructible! That is immortality!"

"There is no such future for you, Teh Atht!" he immediately gloomed, voice deeply sunken and ominous. "You expect too much. Even I, Mylakhrion of Tharamoon, could not—achieve—" And here he faltered and fell silent.

I perceived then a seeming agitation in the mist-wreathed phantom; he appeared to tremble, however slightly, and I sensed any eagerness, however slight, to be gone. Thus I pressed him:

"Oh? And how much *did* you achieve, Mylakhrion? Is there more I should know? What were your experiments and how much did you discover in your great search for immortality? I believe you are hiding something from me, o mighty one, and if I must I'll smoke the Zha-weed again—aye, and yet again— leaving you no rest or peace until you have answered me as I would be answered!"

Hearing me speak thus, Mylakhrion's figure stiffened and swelled momentarily massive, but then his shoulders drooped and he nodded slowly, saying, "Have I come to this? That the most meagre talents have power to command me? A sad day indeed for Mylakhrion of Tharamoon, when his own descendant uses him so sorely. What is it you wish to know this time, Teh Atht of Klühn?" For this was by no means the first occasion of my seeking Mylakhrion out in dreams.

And I answered him thus. "While you were unable to achieve immortality in your lifetime, ancestor mine," I answered him, "mayhap nathless you can assist me in the discovery of the secret in mine. Describe to me the magicks you used and discarded in your search, the runes you unravelled and put aside, the potions imbibed and unctions applied to no avail, and these I shall take note of that no further time be wasted with them. Then advise me of the paths which you might have explored had time and circumstances permitted. For I *will* be immortal, and no power shall stay me from it."

"Ah, youth, it is folly," quoth he, "but if you so command—" "I do so command."

"Then hear me out and I will tell all, and perhaps you will understand when I tell you that you cannot have immortality... not of the sort you so fervently desire."

And so Mylakhrion told me of his search for immortality. He described for me the great journeys he undertook—leaving Tharamoon, his island-mountain aerie, in the care of watchdog familiars—to visit and confer with other sorcerers and wizards; even journeys across the entire length and breadth of Theem'hdra. Alone he went out into the deserts and plains, the hills and icy wastes in pursuit of this most elusive of mysteries. He visited and talked with Black Yoppaloth of Yhemnis, with the ghost of Shildakor in lava-buried Bhur-esh, with Ardatha Ell, a traveller in space and time who lived for a while in the Great Circle Mountains and studied the featureless, vastly cubical houses of the long-gone Ancients, and with Mellatiquel Thom, a cousin-wizard fled to Yaht-Haal when certain magicks turned against him.

And always during these great wanderings he collected runes and cantrips, spells and philtres, powders and potions and other devices necessary to his esoteric experiments—but never a one to set his feet on the road to immortality. Aye, and using vile necromancy he called up the dead from their ashes, even the dead, for his purposes. And this is something I, Teh Atht, have never done, deeming it too loathsome and danger-fraught a deed. For to talk to a dream-phantom is one matter, but to hold intercourse with long-rotted liches…that is a vile, vile thing.

But for all his industry Mylakhrion found only frustration. He conversed with demons and lamias, hunted the legendary phoenix in burning deserts, near-poisoned himself with strange drugs and nameless potions and worried his throat raw with the chanting of oddly cacophonic invocations. And only then did he think to ask himself this question:

If a man desired immortality, what better way than to ask the secret of one *already* immortal? Aye, and there was just such a one…

Then, when Mylakhrion spoke the name of Cthulhu—the tentacled Great One who seeped down from the stars with his spawn in aeons past to build his cities in the steaming fens of a young and inchoate Earth—I shuddered and made a certain sign over my heart. For while I had not yet had to do with this

Cthulhu, his legend was awful and I had heard much of him. And I marvelled that Mylakhrion had dared seek out this Great One, even Mylakhrion, for above all other evils Cthulhu was legended to tower like a menhir above mere gravestones.

And having marvelled I listened most attentively to all that my ancestor had to say of Cthulhu and the other Great Ones, for since their nature was in the main obscure, and being myself a sorcerer with a sorcerer's appetite for mysteries, I was most desirous of learning more of them.

"Aye, Teh Atht," Mylakhrion continued, "Cthulhu and his brethren: they must surely know the answer, for they are—"

"Immortal?"

For answer he shrugged, then said: "Their genesis lies in unthinkable abysses of the past, their end nowhere in sight. Like the cockroach they were here before men, and they will supersede man. Why, they were oozing like vile ichor between the stars before the sun spewed out her molten children, of which this world is one; and they will live on when Sol is the merest cinder. Do not attempt to measure their life-spans in terms of human life, nor even geologically. Measure them rather in the births and deaths of planets, which to them are like the tickings of vast clocks! Immortal? As near immortal as matters not. From them I could either beg, borrow or steal the secret—but how to go about approaching them?"

I waited for the ghost of my dead ancestor to proceed, and when he did not immediately do so cried out: "Say on then, forebear mine! Say on and be done with beguiling me!"

He sighed for reply and answered very low: "As you command...

"At length I sought me out a man rumoured to be well versed in the ways of the Great Ones; a hermit, dwelling in the peaks of the Eastern Range, whose visions and dreams were such as were best dreamed far removed from his fellow men. For he was wont to run amuck in the passion of his nightmares, and was reckoned by many to have bathed in the blood of numerous innocents, 'to the greater glory of loathly Lord Cthulhu!'

"I sought him out and questioned him in his high cave, and

he showed me the herbs I must eat and whispered the words I must howl from the peaks into the storm. And he told me when I must do these things, that I might then sleep and meet with Cthulhu in my dreams. Thus he instructed me...

"But as night drew nigh in this lonely place my host became drowsy and fell into a fitful sleep. Aye, and his ravings soon became such, and his strugglings so wild, that I stayed not but ventured back out into the steep slopes and thus made away from him. Descending those perilous crags only by the silver light of the moon, I spied the madman above me, asleep yet rushing to and fro, howling like a dog and slashing with a great knife in the darkness of the shadows. And I was glad I had not stayed!

"Thus I returned to Tharamoon, taking a winding route and gathering of the herbs whereof the hermit had spoken, until upon my arrival I had with me all the elements required for the invocation, while locked in my mind I carried the Words of Power. And lo!—I called up a great storm and went out onto the balcony of my highest tower; and there I howled into the wind the Words, and I ate of the herbs mixed so and so, and a swoon came upon me so that I fell as though dead into a sleep deeper by far than the arms of Shoosh, Goddess of the Still Slumbers. Ah, but deep though this sleep was, it was by no means still!

"No, that sleep was—*unquiet*! I saw the sepulchre of Cthulhu in the Isle of Arlyeh, and I passed through the massive and oddly-angled walls of that alien stronghold into the presence of the Great One Himself!"

Here the outlines of my ancestor's ghost became strangely agitated, as if its owner trembled uncontrollably, and even the voice of Mylakhrion wavered and lost much of its doomful portent. I waited for a moment before crying: "Yes, go on—what did the awful Lord of Arlyeh tell you?"

"...Many things, Teh Atht. He told me the secrets of space and time; the legends of lost universes out beyond the limits of man's imagination; he outlined the hideous truths behind the N'tang Tapestries, the lore of dimensions other than the familiar four. And at last he told me the secret of immortality!

"But the latter he would not reveal until I had made a pact

with him. And this pact was that I would be his priest ever and ever, even unto his coming. And believing that I might later break free of any strictures Cthulhu could place upon me, I agreed to the pact and swore upon it. In this my fate was sealed, my doom ordained, for no man may escape the curse of Cthulhu once its seal is upon him…

"And lo, when I wakened, I did all as I had been instructed to attain the promised immortality; and on the third night Cthulhu visited me in dreams, for he knew me now and how to find me, and commanded me as his servant and priest to set about certain tasks. Ah, but these were tasks which would assist the Great One and his prisoned brethren in breaking free of the chains placed upon them in aeons past by the wondrous Gods of Eld, and what use to be immortal forevermore in the unholy service of Cthulhu?

"Thus, on the fourth day, instead of doing as bidden, I set about protecting myself as best I could from Cthulhu's wrath, working a veritable frenzy of magicks to keep him from me…to no avail! In the middle of the next night, exhausted by the physical and mental phylacteries of my labours, I slept, and again Cthulhu came to me. And he came in great anger—even *greater* anger!

"For he had broken down all of my sorcerous barriers, destroying all spells and protective runes, discovering me for a traitor to his cause. And as I slept he drew me up from my couch and led me through the labyrinth of my castle, even to the feet of those steps which climbed up to the topmost tower. He placed my feet upon those stone stairs and commanded me to climb, and when I would have fought him he applied monstrous pressures to my mind that numbed me and left me bereft of will. And so I climbed, slowly and like unto one of the risen dead, up to that high tower, where without pause I went out onto the balcony and threw myself down upon the needle rocks a thousand feet below…

"Thus was my body broken, Teh Atht, and thus Mylakhrion died!"

As he finished speaking I stepped closer to the swirling wall of mist where Mylakhrion stood, black-robed and enigmatic in mystery. He did not seem so tall now, no taller than I myself, and for all the power he had wielded in life he no longer awed me. Should I, Teh Atht, fear a ghost? Even the ghost of the world's greatest sorcerer?

"Still you have not told me that which I most desire to know," I accused.

"Ah, you grow impatient," he answered. "Even as the smoke of the Zha-weed loses its potency and the waking world beckons to you, so your impatience grows. Very well, let me now repeat what Cthulhu told me of immortality:

"He told me that the only way a mere man, even the mightiest wizard among wizards, might perpetuate himself down all the ages was by means of reincarnation! But alas, such as my return would be it would not be complete; for I must needs inhabit another's body, another's mind, and unless I desired a weak body and mind I should certainly find resistance in the person of that as yet unborn other. In other words I must *share* that body, that mind! But surely, I reasoned, even partial immortality would be better than none at all. Do you not agree, descendant mine?

"But of course you do. And like me, you would want a body—or part of one—close in appearance to your own, and a mind to suit. Aye, and it must be a keen mind and curious of mysteries great and small...that of a wizard, mayhap? And indeed it were far better if your own blood should flow in the veins of—"

"Wait!" I then cried, searching the mist with suddenly fearful eyes, seeking to penetrate its greyness that I might gaze upon Mylakhrion's unknown face. "For I find...I find your story most...most disturbing, illustrious ancestor mine. And—"

"—And yet you must surely hear it out, Teh Atht," he interrupted, doom once more echoing in his voice. And as he spoke he moved flowingly forward until at last I could see the death-lights in his shadowy eyes. Closer still he came, saying:

"To ensure that this as yet unborn one would be all the things I desired of him, I set a covenant upon my resurrection in him. And this condition was that his curiosity and sorcerous skill must be such that he would first call me up from the Land of Shades ten times, and that only then would I make myself manifest in his person...*And how many times have you now called me up, Teh Atht?*"

"Ten times—fiend!" I choked. And feeling the chill of subterranean pools flowing in my bones, I rushed upon him to seize his shoulders in palsied hands, staring into a face now visible as a reflection in the clear glass of a mirror. A mirror? Aye! For though the face was that of an old, old man—*it was nonetheless my own*!

And without more ado I fled, waking to a cold, cold morn atop the Mount of the Ancients, where my tethered yak watched me with worried eyes and snorted a nervous greeting...

But that was long ago and in my youth, and now I no longer fear Mylakhrion, though I did fear him greatly for many a year. For in the end I was stronger than him, aye, and he got but a small part of me. In return I got all of his magicks, the lore of a lifetime spent in the discovery of dark secrets.

All of this and immortality, too, of a sort; and yet even now Mylakhrion is not beaten. For surely I will carry something of him with me down the ages. Occasionally I smile at the thought and feel laughter rising in me like wind over the desert...but rarely. The laughter hardly sounds like mine at all and its echoes seem to linger o'erlong.

THE STEAM MAN OF THE PRAIRIE
AND THE DARK RIDER GET DOWN

A DIME NOVEL
FOR PHILIP JOSÉ FARMER
JOE LANSDALE

Foreword

Somewhere out in space the damaged shuttle circled, unable to come down. Its occupants were confused and frightened.

Forever to the left of the ship was a rip in the sky. And through the rip they saw all sorts of things. Daylight and dark. Odd events.

And dat ole shuttle jes go'n roun' and roun' and roun'.

(1)
In Search Of

The shiny steam man, forty feet tall and twenty feet wide, not counting his ten-foot-high conical hat, hissed across the prairie, farted up hills, waded and puffed through streams and rivers. He clanked and clattered. He made good time. His silver metal skin was bright with the sun. The steam from his hat was white as frost. Inside of him, where the four men rode in swaying leather chairs, it was very hot, even with the steam fan blowing.

But they pushed on, working the gears, valves, and faucets, forever closing on the Dark Rider. Or so they hoped.

Bill Beadle, captain of the expedition, took off his wool cap and wiped the sweat from his face with an already damp forearm. He tried to do this casually. He did not want the other three to know how near heat exhaustion he was. He took deep breaths, ran a hand through his sweat-soaked hair, and put his cap back on.

The cap was hot, and though there was really nothing official about his uniform or his title of captain, he tried to live by a code that maintained the importance of both.

Hamner and Blake looked at him casually. They were red-faced and sweat-popped. They shifted uncomfortably in their blue woollen uniforms. Through the stained glass eyes of the steam man they could see the hills they had entered, see they were burned brown from the sun.

It was midday, and this gave them several hours to reach the land of the Dark Rider, but by then it would be night, and the Dark Rider and his minions, the apes in trousers, would be out and powerful.

Only John Feather, their Indian guide, looked cool in his breechcloth and headband holding back his long, beaded, black hair. He had removed his moccasins and was therefore barefoot. Unlike the others, he was not interested in a uniform, or to be more precise, he was not interested in being hot when he didn't have to be. He could never figure out the ways of white men, though he often considered on them. But mostly he considered the steam man, and thought: Neat. This cocksucker can go. A little bouncy on the ass, even in these spring-loaded seats, but the ole boy can go. The white men do come up with a good thing now and then.

They clanked through the hills some more, and through the right ear canal of the steam man, also stained glass, they could see the wrecks.

Beadle was always mystified by the wrecks.

Most people called them saucers. They lay in heaps and shatters all over the place. Strange skeletons that weren't quite bone had been found in some of them, and there were even mummified remains of others. Green squid with multiple eyes and fragments of clothing.

There was no longer anyone alive who really knew what had happened, but what had been handed down was there had been a war, and though damn near everybody came, nobody really won. Not the world, not the saucer people. But the weapons they used, they had brought about strange things.

Like rips in the sky, and the Dark Rider.

Or so it was rumoured. No one really knew. Story was, the saucers had ripped open the sky and come to this world through a path alongside the sky. And that after the war, when the saucer men gave it up and went home, the Earth changed and the rips stayed. What was odd about the rips was you could toss things into them, people could enter them, and things could come out. And there were things to see. Great bat-like creatures with monstrous wingspans. Snake-headed critters with flippers and rows of teeth, paddling across the blue-green ether inside the rip. Strange craft jetting across odd landscapes. All manner of things. If you stood near the dark openings, which reached from sky to ground, you could feel them pulling at you, like a vacuum, and if you stepped too close, well then you were gone. Sucked into the beyond. Sometimes the people who were pulled, or went by choice into the rips, came back. Sometimes they didn't. But even those that came back bore no real information. It was even reported by a few that the moment they stepped through the rip, they merely exited where they had entered.

Curious.

As for the Dark Rider, no one knew his origin. A disease caused by something from one of the saucers was the usual guess, but that's all it was. A guess. The Dark Rider sucked blood like a vampire, had prodigious strength and odd powers, but had no aversion to crosses, garlic, or any of the classical defences. Except one. Sunlight. He could not tolerate it. That much had been established.

He also had an army of ape-like critters who traveled with him and did most of the shit work. When the Dark Rider was not able to do it, he sent the apes in britches to do his work. Rape. Murder. Torture. Usually by impalement. His method was to have the victim stripped naked and placed on an upright stake with the point in the anus. The pressure of the victim's weight would push him or her down the length of the shaft until the point came out the upper part of the torso. Usually the neck or mouth, or even at times through the top of the head.

Beadle had seen enough of this to give him nightmares for the rest of his life, and he had determined that if it ever appeared he was about to be captured alive by the Dark Rider or his minions, he would kill himself. He kept a double-barrelled derringer in his boot for just such a circumstance.

The steam man clanked on.

It was near nightfall when they stomped out of the foothills and into the vast forest that grew tall and dark before them and was bordered by a river. It was a good thing, this forest and river. They were out of wood and water, and therefore out of steam.

Though the night brought bad possibilities, it was also preferable to the long, hot days. They grabbed their water bags, pulled their Webb rifles over their shoulders on straps, and disembarked from the steam man via a ladder that they poked out of its ass. Like automated turds, they dropped out of the steam man's butt and into the coolness of the night.

The white men left John Feather to guard the steam man with an automatic pistol and a knife on his hip, a Webb rifle slung over his shoulder on a strap, a bow and a quiver of arrows, and went down to the river for water.

John Feather knew he would be better off inside the steam man, in case the Dark Rider and his bunch showed up, but the night air felt great and sucked at a man's common sense. Behind him the steam man popped and crackled as the nocturnal air cooled it.

John Feather tapped the ammo belt strapped across his chest and back, just to make sure it was there. He took one of the heavy clips from his bandolier and squeezed it with his fingers, a habit he had developed when nervous. After a time, he put the oiled clip back on the bandolier and wiped his greasy fingers on his thigh. He looked for a time in every direction, listened intently. Normally, though he liked them, he didn't miss the white men much, but tonight, he would be glad to have them back. Safety in numbers.

Beadle, Hamner, and Blake inched down the slick riverbank, stopped at the water, and listened to it roar and churn dirt from the bank. There had been a big rain as of late, and the river was wild from it. The reflection of the moon was on the river and it wavered in the water as if it were something bright lying beneath the ripples.

Beadle felt good outside of the metal man. It was wonderful to not have his ass bouncing and his insides shook, to be away from all that hissing and metal clanking.

The roar of the river, the wind through the pines, the moon on the water, the real moon in the sky, bright and gold and nearly full, was soothing.

He eased one of his water bags into the river, listened to it gurgle as it filled.

"We ought to bring Steam down here, Captain," Hamner said. He had removed his cap, which was pretty much the understanding when nightfall came, and fixed it through his belt. The moonlight shone on his red hair and made it appear to be a copper bowl. "We could camp closer to the water."

"I'm afraid Steam's furnaces may be too cold and too low of fuel to walk another inch," Beadle said. "There's just enough left for us to get settled for the night. It would take an hour to heat him up. At least. I'm not sure it's worth it just to have him walk a few hundred feet."

"It is pleasant here, though," Hamner said.

"Not so pleasant we don't need to get this over with and get inside," Beadle said.

This indirect reference to the Dark Rider settled down on them suddenly, and the need for fresh air, wood, and water was eclipsed by a wave of fear. Just a wave. It passed over them and was tucked away. They had grown used to fear. When you hunted the Dark Rider and his boys, you had to learn to put fear on the back burner. You thought about it too much, you'd never breathe night air again. With the Dark Rider, fear and horror were a constant.

Beadle looked at the nearly full moon and wondered if the Dark Rider was looking up at it too. Beadle had sworn to get the

Dark Rider. It's what he was being paid for, he and his team. He had formed Steam Man and Company a year back, and during that time he had killed many of the Dark Rider's ape boys, his minions as Beadle liked to call them, and his employers had been very happy, even giving him the honorary title of Captain. But he hadn't gotten the Dark Rider. There was the real deal. And the big money. The reward for the Dark Rider was phenomenal. And Beadle wanted the bastard, reward or not. He thought of him all the time. He wrote dime novels based on his team's exploits, stretching the truth only slightly. He had made a silent vow to pursue the Dark Rider to the ends of the Earth.

As Beadle looked at the moon, he saw the last of the white steam that was issuing from the steam man's tall, conical hat float across the sky, blurring it, and then the steam dissipated.

"Let's finish," Beadle said.

They made numerous trips with their bags of water, but soon they were famished. Then, leaving John Feather once again to guard Steam, they gathered wood. That accomplished, they took tools from inside the steam man, chopped and sawed the wood and hauled it inside with the water.

As Beadle had expected, the furnaces had cooled. They were lucky they had been able to find water. They might have had to spend a long night in Steam with little to drink until the morning, when it was safe. This way, they could be more comfortable. Even baths could be taken.

"Do you think the Dark Rider is near?" Beadle asked John Feather as they stacked the wood inside the steam man.

"He is always near, and always far away," John Feather said.

This was one of the Indian's odd answers that disturbed Beadle. He knew if he asked John Feather to decipher it, he would merely give him another hard-to-understand remark. It was best to consider the answer given, or just discard it. When John Feather was in this kind of mood, there was no reasoning with him.

Beadle decided to answer his own question, which actually

had been foolish, sprung out of fear and the need for something to say. The truth was obvious: they couldn't be too far away from the Dark Rider. Just the day before, they had passed through the burnt and reeking remains of a village with a hundred or so inhabitants with stakes rammed up their asses. Even cats and dogs and three parakeets had been crucified. It was the Dark Rider's calling card. Therefore, he could not be far away. And he always fled to this part of the world, amongst the thick, dark woods with its bad things, near the place where the sky was most ripped and you could see into it and view all manner of strange and terrifying things not seen elsewhere.

Beadle pulled up Steam's ass flap and locked it for the night with bolt and key. While the wood burned and the water heated, they ate a cold supper of beef jerky and hardtack and washed it down with water, then each retired to his own devices. Beadle had wanted to read, but the kerosene lamps made the place smoky and uncomfortable, even with the steam man's vents. After first usage of the lamps and a miserable night of smoke and kerosene stink, they had decided to withhold from using them. He could, of course, read by candle light, but he found this uncomfortable and only resorted to this when he was absolutely bored out of his mind.

He did, however, light a candle and put it in a candle hat and used the ladder to descend into one of the steam man's legs, past the machinery that made it walk, and into the foot where he found a can of oil.

Steam had been well-oiled the night before, but it never hurt to do it again. There was always a fear of rusty devices, gritty gears, a metal rod gone bad. And considering who they were hunting, it wouldn't do to have Steam play out.

When he finished there, he went throughout the steam man with his candle hat and his can of oil, dripping the liquid into all of its parts. He paid special attention to the backup controls in the trunk of the steam man. If the head controls failed, these, though simpler, cruder, could manage the machine's basic movements.

After a time the water was heated, and they drew straws for who bathed first, as the others would have the same water. Beadle lucked out. He got naked and climbed in the tub at the top of Steam's head. He set the timer. He had fifteen minutes before the next bather had a shot at the suds, and he greatly enjoyed every minute of his time.

Deep in the woods, outside his compound, hanging about for lack of anything else to do, the Dark Rider, alias the Time Traveler, alias many other names, turned his face to the moon as he jerked his dick and thought of blood. At his climax he gave up blood and sperm in thick, waddy ropes that splattered on the leaf mould and the body of the dog. He imagined the dog a woman, but it had been days since he had had a woman, tasted a soft throat and sweet blood. He would have settled for a man or child, an old person, but none had been available. Just the dog, and it had been a gamey wild dog at that. Still, feeding on anything made him horny, which was both a blessing and a curse.

Finished, he made the mistake of haste, caught a hunk of dick in his zipper and cursed. The others, who had been patiently waiting for the Dark Rider to finish, said nothing. You didn't laugh at the Dark Rider, not even if he caught his dick in a zipper. Laugh at him, you might find your face on the other side of your head.

The Dark Rider worked for a while, managed his whang free, put it in his pants and zipped up, looked around for anyone with a smile on their face. Most of his minions, as the dime novels written by his nemesis, Beadle, called them, were looking about, as if expecting someone.

In a way they were. Beadle and his regulators, and that infernal tin man.

When the Dark Rider was certain he was fixed, he nodded to his flunkies, and they waddled forward to take the dog and to lick the blood and sperm on the ground. The toadies began to fight amongst themselves, tearing at the dog, rolling and thrashing about in a hungry fury, ripping at the meat, scattering fur, spewing what blood was left in the critter.

After waiting for a while, the Dark Rider became bored. He took hold of one of the apes and threw him on the ground and pulled his britches down. He took out his dong again and ass fucked the beast. It wasn't very pleasant, and he grew angry at himself for resorting to such entertainment, but he went ahead and did it anyway. Consummated, he snapped the animal's neck and gave him to the others as a gift. Some of the ape men fucked the corpse, but pretty soon they were eating it. The dog just hadn't been enough.

The Dark Rider thought about what he had done. If he kept popping the necks of these little beasts, pretty soon he might have to gather wood for the impalement stakes himself. He'd have to go easier on them. They were not limitless. It was too big a pain to get others.

When they had all bathed and the water was run out of the tub and down the pipes and out what served as Steam's penis—a tube with a flap over it—they settled in for the night, secure in the giant man.

Beadle, in his hammock at the top of Steam's head, dreamed pleasantly at first of a lost love, but then the dream changed, and the Dark Rider came into it. He was dressed, as always, in dark pants and shirt, high black boots, wide black hat, and long black cape. His eyes were flaming sockets, his teeth white as snow, sharp as sin. In the dream, the Dark Rider took Beadle's love, Matilda of the long, blonde hair and sleek, rich body, and carried her away.

Beadle awoke in a sweat. It was a dream too real.

Matilda. Sucked dry of blood, and then, for the sport of it, impaled through the vagina, left for the heat, bugs, and birds. That had been the beginning for Beadle. The beginning of Steam and Company, his hunt for the Dark Rider. His vow to pursue him to the ends of the Earth.

(2)
In The Bad Country

The next morning, early, just as light was tearing back the black curtain, they worked the bellows inside the steam man and made the furnace hotter. The steam man began to chug, cough, sput, and rock with indigestion. They cranked him up and worked the gears and twisted the faucets and checked the valves. When the steam man's belly was volcanic, they climbed into their chairs, at their controls, Beadle in the command seat.

"Let's do it," Beadle said, and he pulled a gear, twisted a faucet, and took hold of the throttle. The steam man began to walk. He went down the riverbank with a clank and into the river with a splash. The water rose up to his waist, and though there was resistance, and Beadle had to give him nearly full throttle, Steam waded the river and stepped up on the bank. The step would have been a climb for a man.

Now the woods were before the steam man. These woods were the known domain of the Dark Rider, and only a few had ever been this far and returned alive. The survivors told of not only the dark woods, but of the wild creatures there, and of the Dark Rider and his white apes, and beyond the forest, a great rip in the sky. Perhaps the biggest rip there was. A rip so big and wide you could see not only creatures inside it, but stars, and at times, a strange sun, blurred and running like a busted egg yolk. Beadle wondered if the Dark Rider would run again. That was his strategy. Hit and run and hide. But would he run from here, his own stronghold? Would he be prepared to stand and fight? Or would he go to ground, hide and wait them out?

The good thing was they had the day on their side, but even during the day, the Dark Rider had his protection.

It was best not to think about it, Beadle decided. It was best to push on, take it as it came, play it as it laid.

Deep down in the cool, damp ground, the Dark Rider lay wrapped in clear plastic hauled from one of many possible futures, plastic used to keep dirt off his clothes.

The grave was deep. Twenty feet. It had been dug by the ape men, or as they were more properly known, the Moorlocks. A sheet of lumber had been placed over the top of the grave to keep out stray strands of daylight.

Nearby, in underground catacombs, the Moorlocks rested. Unlike him they were not destroyed by light, just made uncomfortable. It was their eyes; they were like moles, only not really blind, just light sensitive. He had tried building sunglasses for them from pieces of stained glass and wire framing, but the daylight still affected them. Beneath their white fur, their pink skin was highly sensitive. He had taught them to sew shirts and pants, make shoes from skins, but the sun burned right through their clothes. They had abandoned shoes, shirts, and glasses, but they still wore the pants. Something about the pants appealed to the Moorlocks. Maybe they liked the confinement of trousers better than letting their hammers swing; their snatches grab dust.

As the Dark Rider lay there, hiding from the light, he began to cry. How in God's name…No, fuck God. God had put him here. Surely it was God. Fate. Whatever. But the bottom line was still…Why?

Once upon a time, though which time he was uncertain, he had been an inventor and had traveled the ages via machine. A time machine.

Then there had been the dimensional juncture.

If he could but do that moment over he would not be what he had become. Sometimes, it was almost as if his old self had never been, and there had always been what he was now, the Dark Rider.

And Weena. How he missed her. She had been the most wonderful moment of his life.

Once upon a time, he had lived as an Englishman in the year 1895, wherever that now existed, if it existed. He had been an inventor, and the result of this invention was a machine that traveled through time.

Oh, but he had been noble. Saw himself as a hero. He traveled to the far future where he discovered a world of soft, simple people who lived above ground, were supplied goods by the machinery of the Moorlocks below ground. And they, without wishing to, supplied the Moorlocks with a food source. Themselves.

These simple people were called the Eloi.

While in this future, he met a beautiful and simple Eloi maiden named Weena. He made love to her, and came to love her. She was stolen by the Moorlocks, and after a desperate but futile battle to find and rescue her, he was forced to escape in the time machine. But he had pushed the gear forward, went farther into the future, to a world with a near burned-out sun, populated by crablike creatures and a dull, dead ocean.

He returned then to his own time to tell his tale. But he was not believed when he explained that there were four dimensions, not three. Length, width, depth...and time.

Returning to the era of the Eloi, he discovered Weena had escaped from the Moorlocks, and he decided then and there to become the champion of the Eloi, and within a short time he had taught the mild-mannered people how to do for themselves. He traveled through time and brought to the Eloi animals that no longer existed in their future. He taught them to raise meat and vegetables. He taught them how to fight the Moorlocks.

It was a great time, ten years he judged it.

But then he discovered on one of his exploratory journeys through time that there was a fifth dimension. It existed alongside the others; a place where time took different routes, numerous routes.

Somehow, by his travel he had opened some kind of wormhole in time, and now it had all run together and its very fabric had begun to rip. It was believed in this time that the rips had been caused by squid-like invaders in saucers, but in fact, they were the result of his blunders through the Swiss cheese holes of time.

Returning to the Eloi and Weena, he discovered, through his dimensional traveling, he had not only screwed up time and crosshatched it and connected it in spots and disconnected it in others, but he had also contracted some strange malady.

He craved blood. He was like a vampire. He had to have blood to survive.

Weena stood by him, and he made the Moorlocks his prey. He discovered other side effects of the dimensional plague. He had tremendous strength, speed, and agility, and a constant erection.

But there was a great sourness in him, and soon he began to change. Even when he did not want to change, he changed. Day became repellant, and he found that he enjoyed being amongst the bodies of the dead Moorlocks that he fed on. He liked the smell of death, of rotting meat.

Weena tried to help him, make him whole again. But there was nothing she could do. And in a moment of anger, he struck her and killed her. It was the final straw. Gloom and doom and the desire to hold destruction in his hand overwhelmed him. He fell in love with the horrors.

Only the memory of Weena remained clean. He had her body mummified in the deep sands beyond the garden world of the Eloi, and he had her placed in a coffin made of oak and maple. Then he buried it in one of the great gardens and a tree was planted to mark it.

Time took the tree and the garden, and now there was just the dirt and her mummified remains, and even that, eventually, his former joy, and now his nemesis, time, would take.

He had made an old museum his home. It housed the wares of many centuries. It was unique. It was a ruined palace of green porcelain, fronted by a giant sphinx that had been some sort of monument. Below the museum, beneath the sphinx, and other sites, were the Moorlocks' tunnels and their machines. Machines that had ground out simple goods for the Eloi.

He became their king, and in time, the Eloi became their food again. And his.

The machines roared below ground once more.

The Eloi quivered again.

And then came the rip.

Time lies tight between, within, and behind dimensional curtains, and these curtains are strong and not easy to tear, but somehow, presumed the Dark Rider, his machine had violated the structures of time, and by its presence, its traveling through, it had torn this fabric and other times had slipped into the world of the Eloi and the Moorlocks, slipped in so subtly that a new time was created with a past and a present and a possible future. There was not only a shift in time, but in space, and the Wild West of America collided with a Steam Age where inventors from his own time, who had never made such inventions, were suddenly now building steam ships and flying ships and submarines. Time and space were all a jumble.

The disease in him would not kill him. It just made him live on and on with a burning need to kill, maim, and destroy. Perhaps his disease was merely one that all mankind bore in its genes. A disease buried deep in the minds of every human being, dormant in some, active in others, but in him, not buried at all.

Was he not merely a natural device, a plague, helping to monitor a corner of the universe? Was he not nature's way of saying: I'd like to destroy all this and start over. Just take this Petri dish and wash it off and disinfect it?

The Dark Rider liked to believe he was the ultimate in Darwinism, and that he was merely doing what needed to be done with a world of losers. Instead of combating evil, did it not make more sense to merely be evil so that mankind could go back to what it had originally been?

Nothing.

The sun was scorching again, and inside the steam man it was hotter than the day before. Beadle and his companions sweated profusely, worked the steam man forward with their levers and valves. Steam tore at trees with his great metal hands, uprooting them, tossing them aside, making a path through the forest as they went in search of the Dark Rider's lair, which though not entirely known, was suspected to lie somewhere within, or on the other side of, the great forest.

As the hot day wore on, and more trees were ripped and tossed, a road began to appear through the great forest. Inside the steam man it was hotter yet as Hamner and John Feather tossed logs into the furnace and worked the bellows and stoked the flames that chewed at the wood and boiled the vast tank of water and produced the steam that gave power to the steam man's working parts.

The steam man clanked and hissed on, and finally they broke from the trees, and in the distance they could see a great, white sphinx, and near it another building of green stone. Though run down and vine-climbed, both had a majestic air about them.

Beadle said, "If I were the Dark Rider, that would be my den."

John Feather made a grunting noise. The others nodded. The steam man pushed on.

Then the ground opened up, and the steam man staggered and fell in. His knee struck the rim of the trench and he was knocked backward, then sideways, came to rest in that position, one leg deep in the hole, the other pushed up and behind him and on the surface. His left shoulder and head leaned against one side of the trench.

The fall caused logs and flames to leap from the furnace, and Blake's pants leg caught on fire. He came out of his chair with a scream, lost control of his levers and valves, and the steam man faltered even more, its hands clutching madly at the edge of the trench, tearing out great clods of soil. Wads of steam spurted from Steam's hat and his metal body heaved and screeched at the grinding of machinery.

John Feather leaped forward, shut the furnace, threw the guard latch in place. Beadle, thrown from his chair, standing on the side of the steam man, since the floor was now askance, wobbled to the controls, turned off the steam.

"We seem to have stepped into a trap," Beadle said, slapping cinders off his pants.

"Goddamn it," Blake said, from his position on the floor. "It's my fault. I let go of my controls."

"No," Beadle said. "You had no choice, and besides, Steam was already falling. It's the Dark Rider's fault. Let's not brood. Let's assess the damage."

They went up the winding staircase to the steam man's hat and used the emergency opening over his ear. They threw open the door and lowered the flexible ramp.

Outside, in the midday sun, what they saw upset them. But it was not as bad as they had feared. Steam's left leg lay on the back side of the trench, while his other leg and lower torso were in it. His head and chest poked out of the deep ditch, and he was leaning to port. The leg that was bent behind him looked to be solidly connected, stretched a bit, but serviceable.

"Maybe he can climb out," Blake said.

Beadle shook his head. "Not with his leg like that. He may pull himself out, but I think there's a chance he'll twist his leg off, then where will we be?"

"Where are we now?" Blake said.

"In a hole," Hamner said. "That's where we are."

"The tripod and winch," John Feather said.

"Yes," Beadle said. "The tripod and winch."

Inside the steam man, stored in a number of connecting parts, was a tripod and winch device. It was there for moving large trees when heating materials were needed and small wood was not available. So far, it had never been used, but it was just the ticket.

They unloaded and fastened the device together, set the tripod up over the trench, fastened the cables to the steam man, then set about lifting him.

The sun was past noon and starting to dip.

By late day, they had lifted the steam man three times, and each time his great weight had sagged the crane, and he had fallen back into the pit, straining the leg even more.

Finally, in desperation, they cut some of the smaller trees from the forest behind them, and used them to reinforce their apparatus. This was hard business, and the four of them, even with the smaller trees trimmed and topped, had a hard time moving them, pushing them upright and into place, lodging them tight against the ground.

When they had a tripod of trees to reinforce their tripod and winch, John Feather climbed to the top with Hamner, and they bound the trees tightly to their metal tripod with cable.

All set, they checked and tightened the cables, made sure the steam man was solidly fastened, and set about lifting him once more. Shadows spread across the ground as they worked, filled the trench and cooled the air.

Beadle, dirty and sweaty, an itch in his ass, looked up from the winch lever they were working and saw that the sun was falling down behind the sphinx and the building of green stone. "Gentleman," he said. "I suggest we hasten."

(3)
The Dark Rider Awakes

Beneath the green rock museum, in the darkness of his grave, the Dark Rider stirred, removed the plastic and sat up. Almost at the same moment, the Moorlocks removed the wooden cover.

Effortlessly, the Dark Rider leaped from the pit, landed at its edge, straightened and looked out at the mass of red eyes around him. When he looked, the red eyes blinked.

In a corner of the dark room sat the Time Machine, draped in spiderwebs. All except the saddle, which the Dark Rider used as his throne.

The Dark Rider took his place on the saddle and a Moorlock brought him his black hat. He sat there, and for a moment, astride his old machine, he felt as if he were about to venture again into time and space. A wave of his old self swelled up inside of him and washed him from head to foot. There were warm visions of Weena. But as always, it passed as immediately as it swelled.

His old self was gone, and venturing forth in his machine was impossible. The machine had worn out long ago, and he had never been able to repair it. Certain elements were no longer available. For a while, he searched, but eventually came to the conclusion that what he needed would never be found.

And besides. What was the point? Time and space were collapsing. Not more than a month ago he had come upon men and women from the Stone Age killing and eating a family in a Winnebago.

He and his Moorlocks fought and impaled the prehistorics,

and he only lost ten Moorlocks in the process. Once upon a time the loss of the Moorlocks would not have bothered him at all, but with the death of most of the Moorlock women through sheer chance and his own meanness, there were only a few females left. He kept them in special breeding centres in caverns beneath the ground. But though the Moorlocks loved to fight, they did not dearly love to fuck. Oh, now and then they'd rape some of the women they came across, before they impaled them, but it just wasn't the way it used to be. When they got home they weren't excited like they had been once upon a time; so excited they'd mate with the Moorlock women, impregnating them. Nature was trying desperately to play them out.

Thinking on this, the Dark Rider frowned. It wasn't that he cared all that much for the Moorlocks, it was simply that he liked servants. He supposed he could enslave others, but the Moorlocks were really perfect. Strong, obedient, and not overly bright. Other races had a tendency to revolt, but the Moorlocks actually thrived on stupidity and control, as long as they were allowed their little delights now and then.

But he had more immediate worries tonight. The steam man and the fools inside it. The whole operation might cost him a kit and caboodle of Moorlocks.

Sighing, the Dark Rider concluded that their loss was one of the necessities of business. Which was, simply defined, fear and destruction and a good solid meal.

One of the Moorlocks waddled up to the Dark Rider with his head held down.

"What it is it, Asshole?"

Asshole was the Dark Rider's favourite of the Moorlocks.

Asshole leaped about, slapped his chest, made some noise.

"They are near?" asked the Dark Rider.

"Uh, you betcha," Asshole said.

"Then, I suppose, we should go greet them. Get Sticks."

270

Just about everything that could go wrong, had gone wrong. The tripod had turned over. Blake had fallen and sprained an ankle, but was otherwise all right. They cut him a crutch from an oak tree, and he hobbled about, tugging on ropes and struggling to free Steam.

Eventually everything was in place again, and Steam was lifted just enough to free his leg. Beadle climbed back inside and stoked up the dying embers. John Feather climbed in after him and handed him new wood from the stockpile. Beadle put it in on top of the meagre flames, then they worked the bellows. The flame flared up and the logs got hot, and still they worked the bellows.

When the fire was going good, Beadle went out on the ramp under Steam's ear and called down to Blake and Hamner. "Crank the winch up tight, then stand back."

When Beadle disappeared back inside Steam, Hamner and Blake took hold of the winch crank together and set to work. They managed to lift Steam even more, allowing his trapped leg to slip into the pit with the other. It was hard work, and when they were finished, it was all they could do to keep standing.

Inside, Beadle and John Feather worked the controls, and Steam climbed easily out of the pit. When he stood on solid ground again, Hamner and Blake cheered, and inside Steam, Beadle and John Feather did the same.

But it was a short-lived celebration. John Feather pointed at one of Steam's eyes, said, "Bad shit coming."

"My God," Beadle said. "Lower the ladder, let them in."

(4)
Sticks A'Steppin'

The Dark Rider's contraption was a man made of sticks, and it stood at least twenty feet higher than Steam. The sticks had been interlaced with strips of rawhide, woven and strapped, tied to form the shape of a man. There were gaps in the shape, and through the gaps you could see the apes in trousers, as well as flashes of metal. It made cranking and clanking sounds. And the damn thing walked.

John Feather lowered the ladder in Steam's butt, and Hamner scrambled up, followed by the not so scrambling Blake and his crude crutch.

Once inside they took their seats and ran their hands over their controls.

"Steam is bound to be stronger than a man of sticks," Hamner said.

"Don't underestimate the Dark Rider," Beadle said. "We have before, and each time we've regretted it."

Hamner nodded. He remembered when their team had consisted of several others. Mistakes and miscalculations had whittled them down to this.

"What's the game plan then?" Blake asked.

"We approach him cautiously, feel him out."

"I don't think we'll have to worry about approaching him," Hamner said. "He seems to be coming at a right smart clip."

And indeed, he was.

Sticks and Steam approached one another. From the rooftop of the museum, the Dark Rider watched. He hoped a kill could be made soon. He was very hungry. And he dearly wanted Beadle. The bastard had been chasing him forever. He would impale the others, but Beadle he would have some fun with first. To humiliate him, he would fuck him. Maybe fuck a wound he would tear in his body with his hands, then he'd torture him some, and drink his blood of course, and call him bad names and pull out his hair, and maybe fuck another wound, then he'd have him impaled after boiling his feet raw, coating them with salt and having a goat lick the soles until the skin stripped off.

Well, he might have to lose that part with the goat. He'd already killed and sucked dry every damn goat in these parts, not to mention sheep, a lot of dogs, a good mess of cats, deer, and of course there wasn't a human outside of Beadle and his bunch within a hundred miles. Not a living one anyway. That was the problem with having his kind of urges. You soon ran out of victims. Rats were plentiful, of course, but even for him they were hard to catch.

Then a thought occurred to him. He could get Asshole to do the foot-licking part. He could be the goat. Asshole, like all the Moorlocks, had a rough tongue, and dearly loved salt any way he could get it. With this in mind, the Dark Rider began to feel content and confident again.

Up close, Beadle and his boys could hear machinery inside of Sticks, and they could see into the huge, open eyes, and there they saw the apes in trousers, howling, barking, running about, the moonlight illuminating their little, red peepers.

Inside Sticks, the Moorlocks worked furiously. Most of their equipment ran on sprockets and cables and bicycle gears, and in the centre of the stick man, and at the back of his head, were bicycle seats and pedals, and on the seats, pedalling wildly, were the Moorlocks. The pedalling engaged gears and sprockets, and allowed the head Moorlock, Asshole, who sat in a swinging wicker basket, to work levers and guide gears.

As the steam man and the stick man came in range of one another, Asshole pulled levers and yelled and barked at his humanoid engines, and Sticks reached out and grabbed Steam by the head, brought a stick and wicker knee up into his tight, tin stomach.

The clang of the knee attack inside of Steam resounded so loudly, Beadle, without thinking, jerked both hands over his ears, and for a moment, Steam wobbled slightly.

Embarrassed, Beadle grabbed at his gears and went to work. He made Steam throw a left, and Sticks took it in the eye, scattering a handful of Moorlocks, but others rushed to take their place.

Blake, who worked the right arm, tried to follow with a right cross, but he was late. Sticks brought up his left arm and wrapped it around Steam's right, and they were into a tussle.

Beadle realized quickly that from a striking standpoint Steam was more powerful, but in close, Sticks, with his basket woven parts, was more flexible.

Blake tried to work Steam's right arm free, but it was no go. Sticks brought his right leg around and put it behind Steam's right, kicked back, and threw Steam to the ground, climbed on top of him and tried to pummel him with both tightly woven fists.

Great dents jumped into Steam's metal and poked out in humps on the inside. Sticks used a three-finger poke (he only had four fingers on each hand) to knock out one of Steam's stained glass eyes. The fingers probed inside the gap as if trying to find an eyeball, touched Beadle slightly, and disappeared.

Lying on his back as he was, Steam rocked right and left, and inside of him his parasites worked their gears and valves and cussed. Finally it came to Beadle to have Steam's right leg lift up and latch around Sticks's left leg. Then he did the same with the other side, brought both knees together so Steam could crush Sticks's ribwork and the Moorlocks inside.

But the ribwork proved stronger and more flexible than Beadle had imagined. It moved but did not give. He decided it was Steam's turn to grab Sticks's eye sockets. He called out orders, and soon Steam's hands rose and he grabbed at the corners of Sticks's eye sockets with metal thumbs, shook Sticks's head so savagely Moorlocks flew out of the eyeholes.

Moorlocks began to bail through the eyeholes onto Steam's chest, poured in through the busted left eye of Steam.

John Feather leaped out of his harness seat, drew his knife and went at them. Blood flew amidst screams of pain. John Feather slashed and stabbed, killed while he sang his death song. The Moorlocks leaped on top of him. Hamner started to free himself to help John Feather, but Beadle called, "Work the controls."

Sticks' head began to tear and twist off, came loose in a burst of basket work and sticks that flipped and scattered Moorlocks like water drops shaken from a wet dog's back.

Bicycle parts went hither and yon, crashed to the ground. One Moorlock lay with a bicycle chain wrapped around his head, another had a fragment of a pedal in his ass.

Inside Steam, John Feather still fought while Beadle and his crew worked the gears and made Steam roll on his right side.

In the process, John Feather crashed about, along with the Moorlocks.

Then Steam stood up. John Feather and the Moorlocks fell back, past the seats and the controls and down the long drop of the left leg to the bottom of Steam's left foot. Beadle heard the horrid crash and winced. It was unlikely there were any survivors, Moorlocks or John Feather.

Beadle steeled himself to his present task, began to walk Steam, stomping fleeing Moorlocks with the machine, spurting them in all directions like overstuffed jelly rolls.

From his position atop the museum, the Dark Rider watched and grew angry. Damn dumb Moorlocks. Never give an ape a vampire's job.

The Dark Rider rushed downstairs with a swirl of his cape. He went so fast, the front of his hat blew back.

Near the anterior of the museum stood the Dark Rider's clockwork horse. It was ten hands high and made of woven wooden struts and thin metal straps, and at its centre, like a heart, was a clockwork mechanism that made it run.

The Dark Rider took a key from his belt, reached inside the horse, inserted the key, turned it, wound the clock. As he wound, the horse lifted its head and made a metal noise. Lights came on behind its wide, red eyes.

The Dark Rider pulled himself on top of his horse, whom he had named Clockwork, sat in the bicycle seat there, put his feet on the pedals, and began to pump. Effortless, the bicycle horse moved forward at a rapid gait, its steel hooves pounding the worn floor of the museum, knocking up tile chips.

Two Moorlocks who stood guard at the front of the museum jumped to it and opened the door. With a burst of wind that knocked the Moorlocks down, the Dark Rider blew past them and out into the night.

(5)
Things Get Pissy

"The Dark Rider," said Hamner.

Beadle and Blake looked. Sure enough, there he was, bright in the moonlight, astride his well-known mechanical horse. Its hooves threw up chunks of dirt and its head bobbed up and down as the Dark Rider pedalled so furiously his legs were nothing more than the blurs of his black pants.

"He looks pissed off," said Blake.

"He's always pissed off," said Beadle.

Beadle set the course for Steam, and just as the old metal boy made strides in the Dark Rider's direction, a Moorlock, bloodied and angry, came hissing out of the stairway in the left leg of Steam and leaped at Beadle.

Beadle lost control of his business, and Steam suddenly stopped, his left arm dropping to his side and his head lilting. This nearly caused Steam to tip over, and it was all Blake could do to shut down his side of the machine.

The Moorlock opened its mouth wide and bit into Beadle's shoulder. Beadle grabbed it by the scruff of the neck and pulled, but the Moorlock wouldn't come loose. Hamner came out of his seat and jumped at the Moorlock, sticking his thumbs in its eyes, but even though Hamner pushed at the beast's head, causing its eyes to burst into bleeding lumps, still it clung to Beadle.

Beadle beat dramatically at the Moorlock's side, but still it held. Both men hammered at the beast, but still, no go. The old boy was latched in and meant business.

Then John Feather, bloodied and as crazed as the Moorlock, appeared. He had a knife in his teeth. He put it in his hand and said, "Step back, Hamner."

Hamner did, and John Feather cut the Moorlock's throat. With a spew of blood and a gurgle, the Moorlock died, but still its dead head bit tight into Beadle's shoulder.

John Feather sheathed the knife. He and Hamner tried to free the head, but it wouldn't let go. Its teeth were latched deep.

"Cut the head off," Beadle said.

John Feather went to work. As he cut, Beadle said, "I thought you were dead."

"Not hardly," John Feather said. "I got some bumps and my

ass hurts, but the Moorlocks cushioned my fall, and I cushioned this guy's."

"Shit," said Blake, who, with his injured leg had not left his chair, "he's on us."

The Dark Rider, moving at an amazing clip, was riding lickety-split around Steam, and he was whirling above his head a hook on a long-ass rope. He let go of the rope with one hand and the hook went out and buried itself in the right tin leg of Steam and held.

The Dark Rider continued to ride furiously around Steam, binding its legs with the rope, pulling them tighter and tighter with the power of the mechanical horse.

Beadle, the head of the Moorlock hanging from his shoulder, struggled at the controls, tried to work the legs to break the rope. But it was too late.

Steam began to topple.

(6)
Steam All Messed Up

Steam fell with a terrific crash, fell so hard his head, containing Beadle and his crew, came off and rolled over the Dark Rider and his horse, knocking Clockwork for more than a few flips, causing it to shit horse turds of clockwork innards. Steam's head rolled right over the Dark Rider, driving him partially into the ground, but it had no effect.

Inside Steam's torso Beadle unfastened his seat belt, fell out of his seat, got up and wobbled, trying to adjust to the Moorlock's head affixed to his shoulder.

One glance revealed that Hamner was dead. His seat had come unfastened from the floor and had thrown him into Steam's right eye, shattering it, poking glass through him. Blake was loose from his seat and on his crutch. He reached and took a Webb rifle off the wall.

John Feather reached his bow and arrows from the wall, unfastened the top of his quiver and threw it back, slipped the quiver over his shoulder and took his bow and drew an arrow.

Beadle took a Webb rifle off the wall. Beadle looked at John Feather, said: "Today is a good day to die."

"It's night," John Feather said, "and I don't intend to die. I'm gonna kill me some assholes."

Actually, it was Asshole himself who was approaching the beheaded Steam, and with him was a pack of Moorlocks previously scattered from the remains of Stick.

Beadle and his crew went out the hole under Steam's ear. "I'm gonna die," Beadle said, "I'd rather do it out in the open."

Nearby lay Steam's body, leaking from its neck the remains of the exploded furnace: embers, fiery logs, lots of smoke and steam.

The Moorlocks came in a bounding, yelling, growling rush. Strategy was not their strong point. All they really knew was what the Dark Rider told them, and good, old-fashioned, direct ass whipping. The Webb rifles cracked. Arrows flew. Moorlocks went down. But still they closed, and soon the fighting was hand to hand. The Moorlocks were strong and would have won, had not their leader, Asshole, leaping up and down and shouting orders, received one of John Feather's arrows in the mouth.

Asshole, still talking in his barking manner, bit down on the shaft, shattering teeth, then, appearing more than a bit startled, turned himself completely around and fell on his face, driving the shaft deeper, poking it out of the back of his neck.

In this instant, the Moorlocks lost courage and bolted.

The Dark Rider came then, called: "Get the fuck back here, or I'll impale you all myself."

These seemed like words of wisdom to the Moorlocks. They turned and began to stalk forward. Beadle picked out the Dark Rider and shot at him, hit him full in the chest. The bullet went through him with a jerk of flesh, an explosion of cloth and dust.

The Dark Rider, though knocked down and dazed, was unharmed.

Slowly, the Dark Rider stood up.

"That's not good," said Beadle.

"No," John Feather said. "It's not. I guess tonight is a good night to die. And while we're at it, if we're gonna go, I must tell you something, Beadle."

"What?"

"I've always wanted to fuck you."

"Huh," said Beadle, and John Feather let out with a laugh and loosed an arrow that took a Moorlock full in the chest, added: "Not!"

Amidst laughter, Beadle began to fire, and the Moorlocks began to drop.

But the ole Dark Rider, he just keep on comin' on.

The Dark Rider was on them in a rush. He tossed John Feather hard against Steam's head, grabbed at Beadle, missed, grabbed at Blake who was hitting him with his crutch.

When Beadle regained his feet, the Dark Rider had Blake down and was poking at his ass so hard with the crutch, he had ripped a hole in his pants.

Before the Dark Rider could impale him, Beadle shot the Dark Rider in the back of the head. It was a good shot. No blood came out, just some skull tissue, and the Dark Rider flipped forward and over and came up on his feet, hatless.

He reached down and picked up his hat, dusted it on his knee, and put it on. He looked mad as hell.

John Feather had recovered. He let loose an arrow and it struck the Dark Rider in the chest with a thump, stayed there. The Dark Rider sighed, snapped the arrow off close to his chest.

The Moorlocks surrounded them.

The Dark Rider said, "And now it ends."

Then the Moorlocks swarmed them. Shots were fired, an arrow flew. But there were too many Moorlocks. In a matter of seconds, it was all over.

(7)
Getting the Shaft

They were carried away to a place outside of the museum, stripped nude, tied with their hands behind their backs, then surrounded by Moorlocks.

Though Hamner was dead, he was the first to be impaled. His body was partially feasted on by the Dark Rider and the Moorlocks, then he was raised into the moonlight with a freshly cut wooden shaft in his ass. The end of it was dropped into a prearranged hole. His dead weight traveled down the length of the stake and the point of it gouged out of his right eye. He continued to slide down it until his bloody buttocks touched the ground.

Second, the Dark Rider, out of some perverse desire for revenge, had Steam impaled. A large, sharpened tree was run through the trap door in the steam man's ass, poked through his neck, then the battered, steeple-topped head was placed on top of the stake.

With arms tied behind their backs, Beadle and his Moorlock head, John Feather, and Blake, who could not stand because of his leg, awaited their turn. The Moorlocks were salivating at the thought of their blood and flesh, and Beadle was reminded of a pack of hunting hounds at feeding time. He regretted that he had not gotten to his derringer in time, but the derringer was no longer an issue; like his clothes, it had been taken from him.

The Dark Rider, his hat removed, his face red with Hamner's blood, strands of Hamner's flesh hanging from his teeth, said, "I'm going to save you, Mr. Beadle, until last, and just before you the Indian. And you, what is your name?"

"Blake. Mr. James Blake to you."

"Ah, Blakey. Defiance to the last.

"Moorlocks ..." the Dark Rider said.

The Moorlocks all leaned forward, as if listening at a keyhole.

"Gnaw his balls off."

They rushed Blake, and there was an awful commotion. Beadle and John Feather struggled valiantly to loose themselves from their bonds and help their friend, but the best they could manage were some lame, ignored kicks.

Blake was lifted up screaming, and while his legs were held

apart by Moorlocks, the others, their heads popping forward like snapping turtles, tore at Blake's testicles, and when they were nothing more than ragged flesh (they got the penis too), a stake was rammed in his ass and he was dropped down on it. He screamed so loud Beadle felt as if the noise was rocking his very bones.

The Moorlocks carried Blake to a prearranged hole, dropped him in, pushed in dirt, and left him there. Courageously, Blake yelled, threw his legs up as high as he could. The movement dropped his weight, and the sharpened stick went through him and out of his throat, killing him quickly.

"That will be the way to do it," John Feather said. "It's how we should do it."

Beadle nodded.

The Dark Rider, who sat in a large, wooden chair that had been brought outside from the museum, said, "My, but he was brave. Quite brave."

"Unlike you," Beadle said.

"Ah," the Dark Rider said, "I suppose this is where you are going to challenge me, and with my ego at stake, and your ass at stake, so to speak, I'm going to take you on, one on one, and the winner survives. If I win, you die. If I lose, well, you all go to the house."

"Are you too much of a coward to do that?" Beadle said.

The Dark Rider removed a handkerchief from inside his vest and wiped Hamner's blood from his face and put on his hat. He tossed the handkerchief aside. A Moorlock grabbed it and began to suck at the blood on the cloth. A fight broke out over the handkerchief, and in the struggle one of the Moorlocks was killed.

When this moment had passed, the Dark Rider turned his attention back to Beadle.

"I don't much care how I'm thought of, Mr. Beadle. Since very little causes me damage, and I have the strength of ten men, it's sort of hard to be concerned about such a threat. And besides, in the rare case you did win, my Moorlocks would eat you anyway. In fact, if I should die, they would eat me. Right, boys?"

A murmur of agreement went up from the Moorlocks. Except for those eating the corpse of the loser of the handkerchief battle. They were preoccupied.

"No, I'm not going to do that," the Dark Rider said. "That would be too quick for you. And it would give you some sense of dignity. I'm against that. In fact, I actually have other plans for you. You will get the stake, but not before we've had a bit of torture. As for the red man, well, I can see now that the stake, if you're courageous like your friend, can be beat. I could tie your legs, Indian man, of course, stop that nonsense. But no. I'm going to crucify you. Upside down. And keep the boys off of you for a while so you'll suffer. As I remember, a saint was crucified upside down. Perhaps, Mr. Red Man, you will be made a saint. But I doubt it."

A cross was made and John Feather was put on it and his hands were nailed and his feet, after being overlapped, were also nailed. John Feather made not a sound while the Moorlocks worked, driving the nails into his flesh. The cross was put in the ground upside down, John Feather's head three feet from the dirt, his long hair dangling.

Beadle was taken away to the museum. The Moorlocks were given Blake's body to eat, all except the left arm which was wrapped in cloth and given directly to the Dark Rider for later.

Beadle was placed on a long table and tied to it. The Dark Rider disappeared for a time, about some other mission, and while Beadle waited for the horrors to come, the lone Moorlock left to watch him played with Beadle's dick.

"Lif id ub, pud id down," he said as he played. "Lif id ub, pud id down."

"Would you stop that, for heaven's sake?" Beadle said.

The Moorlock frowned, popped Beadle's balls with the back of his hand, and went back to his game. "Lif id ub, pud id down..."

(8)
A View From Doom

John Feather, in pain so intense he could no longer really feel it, could see the horizon, upside down, and he could see the ground and a bunch of ants. He had been taught that the ants, like all things in nature, were one, his kin. But he didn't like them. He knew what they wanted. Pretty soon they'd be on the cross, then the blood on his hands and feet. Then would come the flies. With kinfolks like ants and flies, who needed enemies? He could kind of get into accepting rocks and trees as his kinfolk, though he was, in fact, crucified on one of his kin, but ants and flies. Uh-uh.

He heard a squawk, lifted his head and looked up. At the top of the cross, waiting patiently, a buzzard had alighted.

John Feather remembered he had never had any use for buzzards, either. Come to think of it, he didn't like coyotes that much, and the way his luck was running, pretty soon they'd show up.

They didn't, but he did hear flies buzzing, and soon felt them alight on his bloody hands and feet.

When the Dark Rider showed, the first thing he did was light a kerosene lamp, and the first thing he said was, "I suppose we shall remove the Moorlock head. This will give us a wound to work with."

The Dark Rider took hold of the Moorlock's jaws, pried them apart, tossed the head, sent it bouncing across the floor. The assisting Moorlock watched it bounce. He looked longingly at the Dark Rider.

"Do your job here," the Dark Rider said, "and you can have it all to yourself."

The Moorlock looked pleased.

The Dark Rider, who had brought a roll of leather, placed it just above Beadle's head and uncoiled it. It was full of shiny instruments. The first one he pulled out was a long metal probe, sharpened on one end.

He held it up so Beadle could see it. It caught the lamplight and sparkled.

Beadle told himself he would not scream.

The Dark Rider poked the probe into the bite wound on his shoulder, and Beadle, in spite of himself, screamed. In fact, to his embarrassment, he thought he screamed like a girl, but with less restraint.

Inside the great time and space cosmic rip, the metal ship hurtled by again, and inside the ship, or as they called it, the shuttle, peering out one of its portholes, was an astronaut named McCormic. He was frightened. He was confused. And he was hungry. He and his partners, a Russian cosmonaut and a French astronaut, had recently finished their last tube of food and the water didn't look good. Another forty-eight hours they'd be out of it, another three or four days they'd be crazy and drinking their urine, maybe starting to think of each other as hot lunches.

Through a series of misfortunes they had lost most of their fuel and could not return to Earth. They were the Flying Dutchman, circling the globe. They had lost contact with home base. The radio waves were silent. It was as if the world beneath them had died. To add tension to all this, their air supply was draining. It would in fact play out at about the same time as the water supply, so maybe they would never get to drink their urine or dine on one another.

To top it off, McCormic was having trouble with his haemorrhoids, which was their way, to appear only at the least opportune time.

And then, there was the rip.

No matter where they were while circling the Earth, the rip was always to their left. They watched it constantly, saw inside it strange things. The rip made no sense. It fit nothing they knew or thought they knew. McCormic felt certain it was widening, even as they watched.

McCormic turned to his partners. The Russian was sitting on the floor. His name was Kruschev. Like his companions, he had removed his helmet some time ago. He was reading from the Frenchman's copy of *Huckleberry Finn,* in French. He didn't understand the jokes.

The Frenchman, Gisbone, said, "I know what you are thinking, my friend McCormic. I am thinking of the same."

McCormic glanced at the Russian. The Russian nodded. "It is closer than our Earth, comrade."

McCormic said, "It would be easy to use the thrusters. Turn into it. I say we do it."

John Feather thought perhaps the best thing he could do was pull with all his might and tear his hands free. The flesh there was not that strong, and if he could pull them through the nails, and was able to free his hands, then…Well, then he could hang upside down by his feet and die slowly of what he was already dying of, only with his hands free. Loss of blood.

But hell, it was something. He balled his hands into fists around the nails and pulled with everything he had.

Boy did it hurt.

Boy did it hurt a lot.

He pulled the flesh of his palms forward until the nails touched his clenched fingers. He jerked forward, and with a scream and burst of blood, John Feather's hands were free.

At about that time the shuttle, blasting on the last of its fuel, came hurtling through the crack in the sky, whizzed right by him so hard it caused the impaled steam man to rattle and the cross on which John Feather was crucified to lean dramatically.

The shuttle's wheels came down, but it hit at such an angle they crumpled and the great craft slid along on its belly.

John Feather, from his unique vantage point, watched as the ship tore up dirt, smashed through what was left of the smouldering stick man, turned sideways, spun in several circles and stopped. There was a popping sound from the craft, as if metal were cooling.

After a long moment, the door of the craft opened. John Feather waited for a squid in harness and overalls to appear. But something else came out. Something white and puffy, shaped like a man, but with a bright face that made it look like some kind of insect.

At this moment, John Feather's cross finally came loose in the ground and toppled to the earth with him on top of it. He let out a howl of pain.

Fuck that stoic red man shit.

McCormic was first. He wore his helmet, had his oxygen tank turned on. After a moment, he turned off the oxygen and removed the helmet. He came down the flexible staircase breathing deeply of the air.

"Very fresh," he said.

The Frenchman and the Russian came after him, removing their helmets.

"I believe it ees our Earth," said the Frenchman. "Only fugged up."

From where he lay, John Feather tried to yell, but found that he had lost his voice. That scream had taken it out of him. He was hoarse and weak. But if he could get their attention, whoever, whatever they were, they might help him. They might eat him too, but considering his condition, he was willing to take the chance.

He tried to yell, but the voice just wasn't there. He tried several times.

The men with parts of their heads in their hands, turned away from the ship, walked around it, and headed away from him, in the direction from which he and his friends and the steam man had come.

When they were dots in the distance, John Feather's voice returned to him in a squeak. But it didn't matter now. They were out of earshot.

All he could manage was a weak "Shit."

The Dark Rider had a lot of fun poking Beadle's wound, but he eventually became bored of that, left, came back with a salt shaker. He shook salt in the wound. Beadle groaned. The Moorlock hopped up and down. He hadn't had this much fun since he'd helped eat his first-born young. The Dark Rider smiled, tried not to think of Weena.

After lying there for a while, John Feather sat up and looked at his crucified feet. They hurt like a bitch. It took balls, but he reached down and grabbed both feet with his hands, and jerked with all his might.

The nail groaned, came loose, but not completely. The pain that shot through John Feather was so intense he lay back down. He prayed to the Great Spirit, then to the white man's god Jesus. He threw in a couple words for Buddha as well, even though he couldn't remember if Buddha actually did anything or not. Wasn't he just kind of an inspiration or something? He tried to remember the name of the Arabic god he had heard mentioned, but it wouldn't come to him.

Great Spirit, Jesus, Buddha, all seemed on vacation. The men carrying their heads didn't show up either.

John Feather sat up, took hold of his feet again, wrenched with all his might.

This time the nail came free, and John Feather passed out.

With pliers, one by one, the Dark Rider removed, with a slow wrench, Beadle's toenails.

John Feather found he could stand, but it was painful. He preferred to go forward on knuckles and knees, but that wasn't doing his hands any good.

Finally, using a combination of stand and crawl, he made it to the steam man, looked up at the spike in its ass, saw there was room to enter inside between shaft and passageway. Painfully, he took hold of the shaft and attempted to climb it. It was very difficult. His hands and feet hurt beyond anything he could imagine and the wounds from them slicked the stake with blood.

He fell twice and hit the ground hard before finally rubbing dirt in his wounds and trying a third time. It was slow and deliberate. But this time he made it.

"**A**nd this little piggy cried wee-wee-wee, all the way...HOME!" With that, the Dark Rider jerked out the last toenail on Beadle's left foot.

Beadle groaned so loud, for a moment, even the Moorlock was startled.

"Now," the Dark Rider said, "let's go for the other one. What do you say?"

Beadle was too much in pain to say anything. And besides, what would it matter? He was going to save his breath for groaning and screaming.

Inside Steam, John Feather found water and washed the dirt from his wounds and used herbs and roots from his medicine and utility bag, applied them in a quick poultice, then bound them with ripped sheets from one of the locked cabinets. He made a breech cloth from some of the sheet, found his extra pair of soft moccasins and slid inside of them. His feet had swollen, but the leather was soft and stretched. He was able to put them on without too much trouble, and he found the cleansing and dressing had relieved the pain in his feet enough so that he could stand. It wasn't by any means comfortable to do so, but he felt he had to.

He tied his medicine bag around his waist, got a Webb rifle from its rack, his extra bow and quiver of forty-five thin arrows with long, steel points.

Then he paused.

He put the rifle, the bow and quiver of arrows aside. He looked out of Steam's ass at the shaft that ran through it and out the neck, looked at the head balanced on top.

John Feather climbed down inside the right leg and took a canister off the wall. He carried it to the gap in Steam's ass and opened it, even though the action caused his hands to bleed. Inside was kerosene. He poured the kerosene down the shaft. He took flint and steel from his medicine pouch and struck up a spark that hit the soaked shaft and caused it to burst into flame. Fire ran down the length of the shaft and it began to burn.

John Feather took wood from the sealed hoppers, built a fire in Steam's belly.

"**J**ust two more to go on this foot," the Dark Rider said, "then we start on the fingernails. Then we're going to see if you've been circumcised. And if not, we're going to do that. And if so, we're going to do it really close, if you know what I mean."

"Can I have 'em? Can I have 'em?" the Moorlock asked.

"You can have them, but as it looks to me, you should start on and finish your head."

The Moorlock grabbed the head of his brethren and began chewing on it.

Between bites he said, "Thank you, Master. Thank you."

"Let's do the right thumb first," the Dark Rider said. "What do you say?"

It was a rhetorical question. Beadle knew it was useless to ask for mercy from his enemy. He kept wishing he'd just pass out, but so far, no such luck. This hurt like hell, but was survivable, and therefore stretched out the possibilities. None of them good. It was made all the worse by the fact that the Dark Rider took his time. A little tug here, a little tug there, almost a tug, then a tug, easing the nails out one slow nail at a time.

Not to mention that the Dark Rider liked to pause with his pliers to squeeze the joints themselves, or to pause and poke at the wound in his shoulder.

The Dark Rider seemed to be having the time of his life.

Beadle wished he could say the same.

John Feather worked the bellows. The fire was going nicely. It wasn't normally a wise thing to do, but John Feather doused the interior of the furnace with kerosene, and as a result, a rush of fire burst out of it and singed his eyebrows, but the wood blazed.

John Feather checked the shaft in Steam's ass.

Burning nicely.

He went back to the bellows, worked there vigorously, stoking up the flame. The water in the chambers began to heat, and John Feather continued to work the bellows. Smoke came up through Steam's ass as the shaft blazed and caught solid.

"Now we have the pinky on the right hand...And, there, isn't that better just having it done with?"

Beadle couldn't understand what the Dark Rider was saying. He couldn't understand because he couldn't quit screaming.

The Dark Rider said, "And now let's do that lefty."

Vapour from the pipes pumped up and out of Steam's headless neck. Steam toppled forward and struck the ground hard, throwing John Feather against the side of the furnace, and in that instant, John Feather realized the shaft had burned through. Slightly burned from the furnace, John Feather recovered his feet, closed the furnace door, crawled along the side of Steam and began to work the emergency controls in the mid-body of the machine. They were serviceable at best.

Working these controls, he was able to make Steam put his hands beneath him and right himself.

John Feather clung to a cabinet until Steam was standing straight, then he took his stance on the platform in front of the seats and moved from one position to the other, working levers, observing dials.

It was erratic, but John Feather managed to have Steam lurch forward, find his head, and set it in place. Or almost in place. It set slightly tilted to the left.

John Feather climbed into the head and refastened the steam cables that had come unsnapped when the head came loose. He had to replace one from the backup stock. He tried the main controls. The fall Steam had taken had affected them; they were a little rough, but they worked.

John Feather started Steam toward the museum.

Condensation not only came out of the hole in the steam man's hat, but it hissed out of his eye holes and neck as well. He walked as if drunk.

(9)
Ruckus

The wall came apart and Steam tore off part of the roof too. He grabbed a rip in the roof and shook it. A big block of granite fell from the ceiling, just missed Beadle on the table, passed to the left elbow of the Dark Rider, and got his Moorlock companion square, just as he was sucking an eyeball from the head he had been eating.

Steam ducked his head and entered the remains of the museum.

"I swore what I'd do to you Beadle," the Dark Rider said. "And I'll do it."

With that, the Dark Rider ducked under the table Beadle was strapped to, lifted it on his back, his arms outstretched, his hands turned backward to clasp the table's sides, and with little visible effort, darted for the staircase.

Steam, head ducked, tried to pursue him, but as he went up the stairs the ceiling was too low. John Feather made Steam push at the ceiling with his head and shoulders like Atlas bearing the weight of the world, and Steam lifted.

The ceiling began to fall all around and on Steam.

The Dark Rider was up the stairs now, heading for the opening to the roof. When he came to the opening, he flung the table backward so that Beadle landed on his face, breaking his nose, bamming his knee caps, and in the process, not doing his already maligned toes any good.

The Dark Rider grabbed the table and tore it apart, causing

the straps that bound Beadle to be released. He grabbed Beadle by the head, like a kid not knowing how to carry a puppy, and started up a ladder to the roof.

When the Dark Rider reached the summit of the ladder, he used his free hand to throw open the trap, then, still holding the struggling Beadle by the head, pulled him onto the moonlit roof.

To the Dark Rider's right, he saw that the rip in the sky had grown, and that a rip within the rip had opened up a gap of darkness in which strange, unidentifiable shapes moved.

Below his feet the roof shook, then exploded. Steam's crooked head poked through. And then rose. It was obvious the steam man was coming up the stairs, and he was tearing the roof apart.

The Dark Rider picked Beadle up by shoulder and thigh, raised him over his head. The Dark Rider thought the easy thing would be to toss Beadle from the roof.

Game over.

But that was the easy thing. He wanted this bastard to suffer.

And then he knew. He'd take his chances inside the rip. If he and Beadle survived it, he'd continue to make Beadle suffer slowly. Nothing else beyond that mattered. He realised suddenly that Beadle had been all that mattered for some time now, and when Beadle was dead, he would have only the memory of Weena again. Nothing else to preoccupy his thoughts. No more Beadle, no more steam man or regulators.

With Beadle raised over his head, the Dark Rider growled and started to run toward the rip.

John Feather saw through the shattered eye of Steam what the Dark Rider planned. Painfully, he grabbed at the quiver he had discarded, picked up his bow, took a coil of thin rope from the wall, tied it to the arrow with one quick loop, and watched as the Dark Rider completed the edge of the museum's roof, which was where the rip in the sky joined it.

The Dark Rider leaped.

John Feather let the arrow fly, dropped the bow, grabbed at the loose end of the rope and listened to the rest of it feed out.

The shot was a good one. It was right on the money. It went through Beadle's left thigh, right on through, and into his inner right thigh.

John Feather heard Beadle yell just as he jerked the rope with all his might. Beadle came loose from the Dark Rider's grasp in midair and was pulled back and slammed onto the museum roof, but the Dark Rider leapt into the dark rip with a curse that reverberated back into this world, then was nothing more than a fading echo.

The Dark Rider's leap had carried him into a place of complete cold darkness. His element. Or so it seemed.

He passed between shapes. Giant bats. They snapped smelly teeth at him and missed.

In time, he thought it would have been better had they not missed.

Because he was falling.

Falling…falling.

His leap had carried him into an abyss. Seemingly bottomless, because he fell and fell and fell, and if he had been able to keep time, he would have realised that days passed, and still he fell. And had he needed oxygen like normal men he would have long been dead, but he did not need it, and therefore he did not die.

He just continued to fall.

He thought of Weena. He wondered if there really was a plane on which her soul survived, wondered if he could join her there, if she would want him now that he was what he was.

And he fell and he fell…and he is falling still…

But, back to John Feather and Beadle.

John Feather found a knife, dropped the ladder out from under Steam's ear, hobbled down it and out to Beadle. John Feather, while Beadle protested, cut the arrowhead out of Beadle's thigh, hacked the arrow off at the shaft, and using one injured, bleeding foot against the outside of Beadle's leg, jerked it free.

"We're going to have to help one another," John Feather said. "I'm not feeling too strong. My hands are seizing up."

"Did you have to shoot me with an arrow?"

"It was that, or follow him. And if he had gone into that rip, I would not have followed. I'm not that much of a friend."

The two of them, supporting one another, hobbled back to Steam.

Inside, Beadle found spare pants and shirt and boots and put them on. John Feather doctored his wounds again. Then, in their control chairs, they worked Steam and brought him out of the remains of the museum. They saw a few Moorlocks through Steam's eyes, but they were scattering. The sun was coming up.

"We should try and kill them all," Beadle said.

"I'm not up to killing much of anything," John Feather said.

"Yeah," Beadle said. "Me either."

"Without their leader, they aren't much."

"I think we're making a mistake."

John Feather sighed. "You may be right. But..."

"Yeah. Let's take Steam home."

John Feather, in considerable pain, looked through one of Steam's eyes at the landscape bathed in the orange-red light of the rising sun. There were more rips out there than before, and he saw things spilling out of some of them.

"If we still have a home," said John Feather.

Epilogue

The astronauts, who had shed their heavy pressure suits and were wearing orange jumps, stopped walking as a green Dodge Caravan driven by a blonde woman with two kids in it, a boy and a girl, stopped beside them.

She lowered an electric window.

"You look lost," she said.

"Very," said McCormic.

"I suggest you get in." She nodded to the rear.

The astronauts glanced in that direction. A herd of small but very aggressive looking dinosaurs were thundering in their direction.

"We'll take you up on that suggestion," McCormic said.

They hustled inside. The boy and girl looked terrified. The astronauts smiled at them.

The blonde woman put her foot to the gas and they tore off.

Behind them the dinosaurs continued to pursue. The woman soon had the Caravan up to eighty and the dinosaurs were no longer visible.

"How much gas do you have?" asked McCormic.

"Over half a tank," she said. "Where are we?"

McCormic looked at the others. They shrugged. He said, "We haven't a clue. But I think we're home, and yet, we aren't."

"I guess," said the blonde woman, "that's as good an answer as I'm going to find."

The Caravan drove on.

All about, earth and sky resounded with the sounds of time and space coming apart.

BIOGRAPHIES
(IN ORDER OF APPEARANCE)

J SCHERPENHUIZEN aka J. (Johannes AKA Jan) Scherpenhuizen is an academic, writer of fiction, artist, editor and publisher. His comics, illustrations and prose pieces have appeared in Australia and the United States. As well as collaborating with other talents, he has also acted as sole writer and illustrator, notably on the gritty horror graphic novel *The Time of the Wolves*. As an editor and manuscript appraiser he discovered a number of professional authors who have credited him with playing a significant role in helping to establish their careers. Jan's recent work includes contributing illustrations and a short story to the well-received *Sherlock Holmes: The Australian Casebook*, and art for the hit graphic novel *SuperAustralians*. His short story 'The Island in the Swamp' was published in *Cthulhu Deep Down Under Volume 2*. Discover more about Jan's activities as a manuscript assessor and writing mentor, etc. at www.janscreative.com. His illustrations can be viewed at www.jscherpenhuizenillustrator.com

STEVE PROPOSCH is publisher and editor of *Trouble* magazine (www.troublemag.com). Previously he has edited the seminal street press magazine *Large* and has had fiction, poetry and non-fiction published in various books, magazines and literary journals. His short fiction has appeared in various places including the story 'The Knowing Stone' in the *Goldfields* (Accidental Publishing, 2019) anthology, released as part of the Bendigo Writers Festival. In collaboration with co-editors Bryce Steven and Christopher Sequeira he has edited the three volume *Cthulhu Deep Down Under* anthology series and *Cthulhu Land of the Long White Cloud* (IFWG), as well as *War of the Worlds Battleground Australia* (Clan Destine Press).

BRYCE STEVENS Once upon a time Bryce Stevens helped edit and illustrate horror magazines *Bloodsongs, Terror Australis* and *Severed Head*. He published *The Fear Codex: Australian Encyclopaedia of Dark Fantasy & Horror* CD. Several collections of his horror tales have been published including *Stalking the Demon* and *Skin Tight*. In 2013, with Christopher Sequeira and Steve Proposch, Bryce set up Horror Australis, an editing combine designed to create projects of quality for antipodean spec fiction genre writers to contribute to. For several years until recently Bryce worked for an Australian wildlife agency as a reptile handler. In 2021 IFWG Publishing released *Bedding the Lamia: Tropical*

Horrors by David Kuraria; a work which could not have been completed without Stevens.

CHRISTOPHER SEQUEIRA is a writer and editor who has written scripts for flagship comic-book brands such as *Justice League Adventures* for DC Entertainment, and *Iron Man* and *X-Men* stories for Marvel Entertainment. He conceived of, edited and contributed to *Sherlock Holmes and Doctor Was Not* (IFWG Publishing), *Sherlock Holmes: The Australian Casebook* (Echo-Bonnier), *The SuperAustralians* graphic novel (Black House-IFWG Publishing) and, in collaboration with co-editors Steve Proposch and Bryce Stevens, edited the three volume *Cthulhu Deep Down Under* anthology series and *Cthulhu Land of the Long White Cloud* (IFWG), as well as *War of the Worlds: Battleground Australia* (Clan Destine Press). *Dracula Unfanged;* and *Nosferatu: A Centenary Horror Collection* will be his next two anthologies for IFWG Publishing.

MARK WAID is an award-winning comics author and historian with nearly two thousand stories to his credit. In between bouts of typing, he's also served comics as an editor, a publisher, an artist, a colorist, a letterer, a production designer, a PR flack, and more, having held every job in comics there is to hold aside from the guy who staples the pages. He lives in Santa Monica, California with no dogs, no cats, a Phantom Zone Projector, a working Infinity Gauntlet, and enough batarangs to defend his home from most intruders.

JACK DANN is the multi-award-winning author of the international bestseller about Leonardo Da Vinci, *The Memory Cathedral*. His latest novel is *Shadows in the Stone*. Kim Stanley Robinson called it "such a complete world that Italian history no longer seems comprehensible without his cosmic battle of spiritual entities behind and within every historical actor and event." Forthcoming is a Centipede Press *Masters of Science Fiction* volume.

BARRY N. MALZBERG is a playwright, critic, and a prolific author whose iconic metafictional work has been both wildly praised by critics and attacked by proponents of 'hard science fiction'. His novel *Beyond Apollo* won the first John W. Campbell Award for Best Science Fiction Novel. He is also the recipient of a Schubert Foundation Playwriting Fellowship and the Cornelia Ward Creative Writing Fellowship. His novels include the Sigmund Freud fiction series, *Oracle of the Thousand Hands, Screen, The Falling Astronauts, Overlay, In the Enclosure, Herovit's World, The Men Inside, Guernica Night, Galaxies, Chorale, The Running of Beasts* (with Bill Pronzini), and *Cross of Fire*. He is also the author of the nonfiction titles *Engines of the Night: Science Fiction in the Eighties, Breakfast in the Ruins: Science Fiction in the Last Millennium,* and *The Bend at the End of the Road*.

COLLEEN DORAN is a *New York Times* bestselling cartoonist. Her published works number in the hundreds with clients such as The Walt Disney Company, Marvel Entertainment, DC Comics, Image Comics, Lucasfilm, Dark Horse Comics, Harper Collins, Houghton Mifflin, Sony, and Scholastic. Her credits include *Amazing Spiderman, Guardians of the Galaxy, Sandman, Captain America,*

Wonder Woman, The Legion of Superheroes, The Teen Titans, Walt Disney's Beauty and the Beast, Anne Rice's The Master of Rampling Gate, Clive Barker's Hellraiser, Clive Barker's Nightbreed, A Distant Soil, The Silver Surfer, Lucifer, and many others. Recent works by Colleen include art for Stan Lee's autobiography, AMAZING FANTASTIC INCREDIBLE STAN LEE, the multi-award-winning SNOW GLASS AND APPLES with Neil Gaiman, and again with Gaiman, TROLL BRIDGE, a NYTimes best-seller. She also did art for Wonder Woman 750, the first issue of Wonder Woman to top the comic industry sales charts in the book's history.

JIM KRUEGER is one of the top-rated writers currently working in American comics. Significant successes include the prestigious Earth-X Trilogy from Marvel Comics, and Justice (a New York Times Bestseller, and winner of an Eisner Award) from DC Comics, with colleagues Alex Ross and Doug Braithwaite. In addition, he has had notable projects with Avengers, X-Men, Star Wars, The Matrix Comics, Micronauts, and Batman. With Ross again, and others, he did Avengers/Invaders, and Project Superpowers for Dynamite Entertainment. He has been a creative director at Marvel Comics, and is also a freelance comic book writer/property creator whose original works include The Foot Soldiers, Alphabet Supes, The Clock Maker, The High Cost of Happily Ever After and The Last Straw Man.

ROBERT BLOCH (April 5, 1917 – September 23, 1994) was a prolific American writer, primarily of crime, horror and science fiction. He is best known as the writer of Psycho, the basis for the film of the same name by Alfred Hitchcock. He many times remarked that he had "the heart of a little boy", quipping "I keep it in a jar on my desk." He wrote hundreds of short stories and over 20 novels and was also a prolific screenwriter and a major contributor to science fiction fanzines and fandom in general. He won the Hugo Award (for his story "That Hell-Bound Train"), the Bram Stoker Award, and the World Fantasy Award. He served a term as president of the Mystery Writers of America (1970) and was a member of that organisation and of Science Fiction Writers of America, the Writers' Guild, the Academy of Motion Picture Arts and Sciences and the Count Dracula Society. In 2008, The Library of America selected Bloch's story "The Shambles of Ed Gein" for inclusion in its two-century retrospective of American true crime.

KAREN HABER is the author of nine novels including Star Trek Voyager: Bless the Beasts and received a Hugo Award nomination for editing Meditations on Middle Earth, an essay collection celebrating J.R.R. Tolkien. Her recent work includes the short story collection The Sweet Taste of Regret. Among her long-form publications are The Mutant Season series, the Woman Without a Shadow series, Masters of Science Fiction and Fantasy Art, and a YA novel, Crossing Infinity. She has edited several movie tie-in anthologies including Exploring the Matrix, and Science of the X-Men. Her short fiction has appeared in Asimov's Science Fiction Magazine, The Magazine of Fantasy and Science Fiction, and many anthologies including The Time Travellers' Almanac, This Way to the End Times, and *Worst Contact*. She also reviews art books for *Locus Magazine*. She lives in Oakland, California with her spouse, Robert Silverberg, and two cats. WEBSITE: http://karenhaber.com/

ROBERT SILVERBERG has been a professional writer since 1955, the year before he graduated from Columbia University, and has published more than a hundred books and close to a thousand short stories. His books and stories have been translated into forty languages. Among his best-known novels are *Lord Valentine's Castle, Dying Inside, The Book of Skulls, Nightwings, The World Inside,* and *Downward to the Earth.* He is a many-time winner of the Hugo and Nebula awards, was Guest of Honor at the World Science Fiction Convention in Heidelberg, Germany in 1970, was named to the Science Fiction Hall of Fame in 1999, and in 2004 was named a Grand Master by the Science Fiction Writers of America, of which he is a past president. Silverberg has also been the editor of dozens of science fiction and fantasy anthologies including THE SCIENCE FICTION HALL OF FAME. In addition, he has written archaeological, historical, and scientific nonfiction. He is currently a columnist for *Asimov's Science Fiction Magazine.* Silverberg was born in New York City, but he and his wife Karen have lived for many years in the San Francisco Bay Area. They and an assortment of cats share a sprawling house of unusual architectural style, surrounded by exotic plants.

HOWARD KELTNER, as part of the Texas Trio, was one of the editors and publishers of the early fanzine *Star-Studded Comics* where he created the character Doctor Weird, among others. A pioneer of comic book fandom, he began his *Index to Golden Age Comics* in 1953. Published in 1976, it influenced other later indexes. In the later years of his life, he took up oil painting, specializing in landscapes. Widely known as a gentle man and a gentleman, he left this world in 1998.

GEORGE R. R. MARTIN is a celebrated American novelist, screenwriter, television producer and short story writer. He is the author of the series of epic fantasy novels *A Song of Ice and Fire*, which were adapted into the Emmy Award-winning HBO series *Game of Thrones* (2011–2019), has been called "the American Tolkien", and in 2011 was included on the annual *Time* 100 list of the most influential people in the world. He has won many awards, including the Locus Award, Nebula Award, Inkpot Award, Bram Stoker Award, Premio Ignotus, Goodreads Choice Award, Primetime Emmy Award, Northwestern University Medill Hall of Achievement Award, New Jersey Hall of Fame induction, An Post International Recognition Award; and he holds an Honorary Doctorate, from Northwestern University.

JIM STARLIN James P. "Jim" Starlin is an Eisner Award Hall of Fame winning American comic book writer and artist. With a career dating back to the early 1970s, and holding numerous nominations and award wins he is perhaps best known for "cosmic" tales and space opera; for revamping the Marvel Comics characters Captain Marvel and Adam Warlock; and for creating or co-creating Marvel characters that have become increasingly popular via the

Marvel movie iterations, such as Thanos, Drax the Destroyer, Gamora, Eros, Pip the Troll, and Shang-Chi, Master of Kung Fu. Original characters/series that he has created include *Dreadstar*.

JONATHAN MABERRY is a *New York Times* best-seller, five-time Bram Stoker Award-winner, anthology editor, comic book writer, executive producer, magazine feature writer, playwright, and writing teacher/lecturer. He is the editor of *Weird Tales Magazine* and president of the International Association of Media Tie-in Writers. He is the recipient of the Inkpot Award, three Scribe Awards, and was named one of the Today's Top Ten Horror Writers. His books have been sold to more than thirty countries. He writes in several genres including thriller, horror, science fiction, epic fantasy, and mystery; and he writes for adults, middle grade, and young adult.

NEIL GAIMAN is the *New York Times* bestselling author and creator of books, graphic novels, short stories, film and television for all ages, including *Norse Mythology, Neverwhere, Coraline, The Graveyard Book, The Ocean at the End of the Lane, The View from the Cheap Seats*, and the *Sandman* comic series. His fiction has received Newbery, Carnegie, Hugo, Nebula, World Fantasy, and Will Eisner Awards. *American Gods*, based on the 2001 novel, is now a critically acclaimed, Emmy-nominated TV series, and he was the writer and showrunner for the mini-series adaptation of *Good Omens*, based on the book he co-authored with Sir Terry Pratchett. In 2017, he became a Goodwill Ambassador for UNHCR, the UN Refugee Agency. Originally from England, he lives in the United States, where he is a Professor in the Arts at Bard College.

ROZ KAVENEY is a poet (*Dialectic of the Flesh*), novelist (the *Rhapsody of Blood* series) and critic (*Teen Dreams*) living and working in London.

HEATHER GRAHAM is the *New York Times* and *USA Today* bestselling author of more than two hundred novels and novellas. She has been honored with awards from booksellers and writers' organizations for excellence in her work, and she is also proud to be a recipient of the Silver Bullet from Thriller Writers and was also awarded the prestigious Thriller Master in 2016. She is also a recipient of the Lifetime Achievement Award from RWA. Heather has had books selected for the Doubleday Book Club and the Literary Guild, and has been quoted, interviewed, or featured in such publications as *The Nation, Redbook, Mystery Book Club, People* and *USA Today* and appeared on many newscasts including Today, Entertainment Tonight and local television.

RAMSEY CAMPBELL was born in Liverpool in 1946 and now lives in Wallasey. The *Oxford Companion to English Literature* describes him as "Britain's most respected living horror writer". He has received the Grand Master Award of the World Horror Convention, the Lifetime Achievement Award of the Horror Writers Association, the Living Legend Award of the International Horror Guild and the World Fantasy Lifetime Achievement Award. In 2015 he was made an Honorary Fellow of Liverpool John Moores University for outstanding services to literature. PS Publishing have brought out two volumes of *Phantasmagorical Stories*, a sixty-year retrospective of his short fiction, and a companion collection, *The Village Killings and Other Novellas*. His latest novel is *Somebody's Voice* from Flame Tree Press, who have also recently published his Brichester Mythos trilogy.

JANEEN WEBB is a multiple award-winning author, editor, and critic who has written or edited a dozen books and over a hundred essays and stories. She is a recipient of the World Fantasy Award, the Peter MacNamara SF Achievement Award, the Aurealis Award and the Ditmar Award. Her most recent book is *The Gold-Jade Dragon* (PS Publishing, UK, 2021). She is currently co-writing an alternate history series, *The City of the Sun*, with Andrew Enstice: the first book, *The Five Star Republic*, was released by IFWG Publications late in 2021. Janeen has taught at various universities, is internationally recognised for her critical work in speculative fiction, and has contributed to most of the standard reference texts in the field. She holds a PhD in literature from the University of Newcastle. She currently divides her time between Melbourne and a small farm overlooking the sea near Wilson's Promontory.

WILLIAM F. NOLAN wrote mostly in the science fiction, fantasy, and horror genres. Though best known for co-authoring the classic dystopian science fiction novel *Logan's Run* with George Clayton Johnson, Nolan was the author of more than 2000 pieces (fiction, nonfiction, articles, and books). An artist, Nolan was born in Kansas City, MO, and was an integral part of the writing ensemble known as "The Group," which included Ray Bradbury, Charles Beaumont, John Tomerlin, Richard Matheson, Johnson and others, many of whom wrote for Rod Serling's 'The Twilight Zone'. Of his numerous awards, there were a few of which he was most proud: being voted a Living Legend in Dark Fantasy by the International Horror Guild in 2002; the honorary title of Author Emeritus from the Science Fiction and Fantasy Writers of America, Inc.; the Lifetime Achievement Award from the Horror Writers Association in 2010; and as recipient of the 2013 World Fantasy Convention Award along with Brian W. Aldiss. He was also named a Grand Master by the World Horror Society in 2015. A vegetarian, Nolan resided in Vancouver, WA until his death in July 2021 at age 93.

BRIAN LUMLEY was born on the north-east coast of England on 2nd December 1937. He began writing, as a career soldier, in 1967 in Berlin. He produced his early work under the influence of the Weird Tales authors, H.P. Lovecraft and Robert E. Howard, and his first tales were published by the then "dean of macabre publishers," August W. Derleth at now legendary Arkham House, in Wisconsin. He left the army as a Sergeant Major, began writing full-time in 1980, and five years later completed his breakthrough novel, *Necroscope®*, now grown to 18 volumes and published world-wide in millions of copies. The list covers the US and Europe; along with the Czech Republic and Russia. *Necroscope®* is a Lumley trademark™, where a role-playing game, graphic novels, figurines and many E- and Audio-books have been created from the much-loved series. Moreover, the original story has long been optioned for movies, a project that is alive and kicking, with a ready-made audience holding its breath! Along with the *Necroscope®* series, Lumley is the author of more than thirty-five additional books and is the winner of many awards.

JOE R. LANSDALE is the multi-Award nominated and award-winning author of forty-five novels and four hundred stories, essays, reviews, film and TV scripts, introductions and magazine articles. His popular HAP AND LEONARD novel series was made into a television series (which he also scripted for). Among his awards are THE EDGAR, for his crime novel THE BOTTOMS, THE SPUR, for his historical western PARADISE SKY, as well as ten BRAM STOKERS for his horror works. He has also received THE GRANDMASTER AWARD and the LIFETIME ACHIEVEMENT AWARD from THE HORROR WRITERS ASSOCIATION. He has been inducted into the INTERNATIONAL MARTIAL ARTS HALL OF FAME, as well as the UNITED STATES MARTIAL ARTS HALL OF FAME and is the founder of the Shen Chuan martial arts system. He lives in Nacogdoches, Texas with his wife, Karen, pit bull, and a cranky cat.